INHERITANCE

"It's simple," the old man said. "If the people who *know* what to do don't take their God-given right and use it, it all falls into chaos. I made you, son—genetically manufactured you. But not merely to inherit the Hurt Empire. I made you to be a watchdog on Human Evolution."

—*but if the people who know what to do don't know what they're doing . . .*

Berkley books
by David Bischoff

STAR FALL
STAR SPRING

STAR SPRING

A SPACE OPERETTA BY

DAVID
BISCHOFF

BERKLEY BOOKS, NEW YORK

STAR SPRING

A Berkley Book/published by arrangement with
the author

PRINTING HISTORY
Berkley edition/August 1982

ISBN: 0-425-05440-3

This one is for
Dennis Bailey

Prologue

Nietzsche said nothing.

Kant had ranted. He had to be shut off. Lao Tze had gone with the flow, the Buddha just laughed at the questions, and Aristotle had been so distracted by the loop-de-loops of gadgetry arrayed about him that he answered the questions in monosyllables.

Jesus Christ had tried to storm out in total disgust.

"You see," Plato said, "there's this cave." He did not wear Athenian clothing. Rather, they had fitted him in plain khaki coveralls. "We're all sitting in this cave, staring at the shadows of ourselves flickering on the wall." Utilizing the spotlight shining upon him, he executed a very good shadow rabbit. "Now, if we had the wits, we'd realize that the world is *not* shadows. We'd turn around, see the fire behind us. We'd figure out how to knock the manacles off our feet. We'd troop on out and realize, by God, there's this whole *other* world around us, lit by the true fire, the Sun. Thus, we poor deluded creatures are merely Forms temporarily reflecting the World of Ideas, of the Good."

The Arachnid looked up from his guitar.

"Gotta good beat. I can dance to it. I'll give it a seventy percent." With a set of digits he tapped cacophony into a keyboard bank. "You haven't got your science right, though. We'll have to fit you somewhere in the fantasy scenarios. Oh, and Mister P." The Arachnid gave a mechanical smile. "Watch it with the boys, huh? This will be a G-rated level I'm slotting you in. At least until the Change."

As the philosopher slumped back to the Waiting Bench, the spindly creature behind the consoles phased him out. He picked up his worn Gibson. With only half of its sixty-six fingers or articulated toes, he again attempted to pick out Wagner's *Ride of the Valkyries*.

1

A bulb-room, suspended on gossamer wire, aglow with shivering colors, descended behind the biobot. From it stepped a bearded man wrapped in casual robes. "Interesting," he said. "Try these now." He placed a handful of storage crystals on the counter, then strode back to his comfortable null-G harness supports in the bulb.

One of the Arachnid's ten ocular units swiveled to survey the labels. "My God. This stuff is all Greek to me." He gave a rattly chortle. "I drink, therefore I am."

The dark-haired man raised a leonine eyebrow, shrugged, and got back into his chamber.

"Lemme see," the creature said, casting a few eyes over labels to the tapes. "William James. Søren Kierkegaard. Alan Watts. Lazarus Long. All the hits of the hot one hundred." Oculars leaped up with gleaming enthusiasm. "So, munchkins, let's blow your brains with a Mystery Song!"

A spindly limb unwound. The previous crystal popped up from its holder. A new one dropped into the hole.

Particolored lights upon the readout boards did sprightly jigs.

On the Waiting Bench was a line of figures stretching into the surrounding darkness. A man seated there jerked as though hit with an electric shock. He stood. Slowly, he stepped into the spotlight. He blinked with the brightness.

The Arachnid strummed a resonant G chord on his guitar. "Ta da! An now, ladies and gentlemen, for your entertainment from the entertainment capital of the universe, that ever popular game show, *What's My Philosophy?* Well, our Mystery Guest has come into a state of Being. Or is it Becoming? Perhaps Begoing! I'm your insectoid host, about to spin a web of fun. So let's dive right into it with the first part of the show, 'Beat the Digital Chronometer!' Mr. Philosopher, if you can answer these questions satisfactorily before the buzzer beeps, you'll win an all-expense-paid trip straight from the grave onto the luxury liner *Star Fall!*"

The Arachnid fingered a stringed fanfare.

"Mr. Philosopher, in less than sixty seconds, can you summarize your epistemology?"

The man in the spotlight shuddered. "I . . . I'm very confused. I'm sorry, but I don't know where I am."

"Ah! A Buddhist? A Hindu, maybe? Is the world an illusion,

Mr. Mystery Philosopher? Are we all walking around in a state of maya?"

"Maya? Weren't they South American or something?"

"Come, come, sir. The seconds are ticking away. What's your epistomology?"

"Pardon?"

"Your theory of knowledge, man. What can be known? How can we be sure that our assumptions about existence are true? How can we be sure about *anything?*"

The man gulped. "Can I go? I think I'm going to be sick."

"Ah ha! An existentialist! Having made a choice of free will, you become an authentic individual. You experience the nausea of existence."

The man bolted into the shadows. Heaving sounds ensued. When he returned, his face was pale.

Uneasily, the Arachnid said, "Aren't you being a little too literal?"

"Look. Is this some kind of real-fic or something? If it is, I'm not enjoying it very much," the man said. "I signed up for this voyage to be entertained. Now I'm just scared. Who are you? Where am I?"

"Hmm. A contemporary philosopher, then, using Socratic methods. A question answered with a question. I am intrigued. You wouldn't be associated with that new school of Absurdist Yoga, would you?"

"Where's the door, please?"

"Okay. We'll make this quick. We'll skip the politics and ethics. The latter bores me, anyway. Tell me what your metaphysics are and I'll release you."

"Metaphysics?"

"Yes, yes! What is the ultimate nature of reality?"

The man shook his head desparingly. "I really don't know. I suppose I used to think I knew. But I wasn't very happy then, either."

Wearily the Arachnid drummed his fingers on the counter. It took a long time.

Finally, he said. "I give up. What's your name? You must be extremely modern. I've not heard of any of your *obscuretant* methodologies. I'm not even sure we can really use you. We need concrete ideas to play with. Intimations of the Truth."

In a small voice, the man said, "My name is Todd Spigot,

and I'm sure there must be some kind of mistake, because I'm not a philosopher. I'm just a *tourist,* for God's sake!"

The Arachnid abruptly stood from its chair. The multitude of thin limbs radiating from the squat black body bristled like the quills of an excited porcupine. Its voice became scatches upon ice. "What . . . *what* did you say your name was?" Flesh sacks dangling from its side ballooned, purpling. Saliva dripped from its inadvertently exposed mouth.

"Todd Spigot. I'm from a planet called Deadrock, and if you don't let me out of here I'm going to ask for some kind of refund and—"

Without warning, the Arachnid leaped. Previously sheathed scalpels and knives erupted. Its digits became claws.

The man didn't even have time to scream. The Arachnid tore him apart.

The bulb-chamber descended. The dark man emerged. The colors which backed him were subdued now, even somber.

He regarded the mess and scratched his beard. "Oh dear me," he said, but without emotion.

The Arachnid canted its oculars. Blood pooled about the bits of body lying at its feet. "I think I broke my nose," he said, rubbing a particular protrusion.

The dark man popped the crystal. "I shouldn't have given you this one. My mistake." He stooped, scooped up a chunk of apparatus and wires from the gore. "Well, you didn't harm the equipment anyway. You're just lucky the body was one of our few tabula rasas."

"You promised me the real one," the Arachnid said.

"And so I did," the robed man replied.

"And the man named Amber."

"Yes."

"And the woman."

"We just happen to have constructed a personality mockup of Spigot. I was reviewing the crystal and it got mixed up with that particular set of tapes I gave you. You imprinted the persona onto the body through this set of Reality Suspenders."

"You realize we're due to leave orbit soon." The Arachnid said. "Spigot. Amber. Shepherd. They're still on the surface."

The dark man smiled. His robes whispered as he turned and walked away. As he approached the bulb-chamber, azure and orange glowed like a halo around his head.

"Arrangements are being made, my friend. Arrangements are being made."

Wisps of mist flowed out from the chamber, touching him tenuously, then swallowing him in white and gray and mystery.

The Arachnid heaved a sigh, then went to call for a janitor.

Part 1

What now, young men, do you think?
Which were the better for you:
To go tracking the women,
Or to go tracking the Self?

VINAYA PITAKA   I.23

One

Ninety percent of the time, Ace Technician and Sanitary Engineer Second Class Charley Haversham figured, life was unfair.

"But I got *my* ten percent all at once, my friends!"

The vacuum cleaner moved his Black Pawn to Queen's Knight Four.

"No, no!" the spritely window washer said. "Castle! Castle!" Droplets of ammoniated water shed from its nozzles and brushes with its vexation.

"Too late," Charley Haversham said, sliding his Bishop from behind his Queen. "Check. Mate in three."

The vacuum cleaner robot quivered with mechanical indignation. "Just because I'm not programmed for the Russian variations, you take advantage!"

Behind him, a multidigited compu-clean robot named Hank chattered in agreement, its filiments wiggling languidly like some sea urchin's tentacles. "Yeah. You know, you're not exactly playing with the big leagues, Charley."

"Well, fellas," the man in the gray uniform and standard Model G 85 endomorph body announced. "I won't be around to plague you delightful machines much longer. May I introduce you to Sanitation Engineer Mate Fourth Class Charles Harrington Haversham, ready to ship out day after tomorrow upon the luxury liner *Star Fall*. No more rocket fins to scrub, pals. I'm going to see the universe!"

Humming happily to himself, he rose from his chair and repaired to his computer console to complete his monthly report on floor wax and furniture polish consumed by the Greater Nyark Spaceport. All about him were the machines and supplies that kept the great terminal brushed up and sparkling. Settling down to his task, he glanced around. No, he wouldn't miss this. Not a bit. He realized that even with his upper B IQ, he was lucky to have *this* job, since employment opportunities

9

were at a premium. He could have been a C or a D, good only
for computer supplement plug-in duty, but that could hardly
be considered work. You just rented out part of your brain for
municipal storage, basically. Naw. He liked to work with his
head *and* his hands, and this job wasn't all that bad for that.
Closest thing he could get ten years ago in the way of something
to do with space. He'd always wanted to ship out to some
strange and exotic planet. Not many Earthsiders got that
chance. At least here, he got a glimpse of the colonists and the
aliens trooping through the starport on their way to wherever.

All his bland life he'd had to resort to whatever the Fics
Kicks people were dishing out in the way of outer space epi-
sodes to satisfy his desire to explore something beyond his
commune-home in Chemical Swamp, Joisy. As soon as he'd
managed to latch onto this job, though, and gotten an eyeful
of a *real* Aslasi padding along on its floppy feet, or an actual
Nork hoarsely breathing through its respirator/adaptor as it
headed for its sightseeing bus, all his previous impressions of
alien life turned to dust and blew away. He knew he had to get
out to the starways somehow. When the maintenance position
for the *Star Fall,* choicest plum possible, opened up he applied
as he always did for such vacancies, not really expecting it,
but digging out his dusty Karma Prayer Wheel and feeding it
nickels, just in case.

In fact, at first he did not make it.

But when Jim Michaels' psych-tests came up MAL-AD-
JUST for long-term space service, a desperate Charley Harv-
ersham had diddled with the selection computer with the help
of one of his robot friends, and his name as replacement had
come out on top.

Debbie, one of his line-mates, had complained, and he
would miss her more than any of the others of his family in
Joisy, but, after all, it would only be a year. Right?

Right. A year's cruise on the famous *Star Fall*. So what if
it meant sewage detail? He could live with that a few hours a
day, if it meant milling about with people from different worlds,
perhaps even being able to set his feet on alien soil!

This, then, would be his last stretch of equipment sitting.
Each day, when the starport was at its busiest and automatic
maintenance was at its lightest, the cleaning robots would report

back here for stasis, diagnostic tests, refueling, self-cleaning and general social kibitzing.

Haversham grabbed a clipboard for his usual checkpoint run of the machines. He strolled along the rank and file, taking great pleasure in noting the quantities of grit and grime the boys had scraped up from the mammoth terminal last night. Scrape and shine! Brush and polish! The vast industry of these wondrous mechanisms pleased him greatly. He looked forward to getting a look at the systems aboard the *Star Fall*. Hard to believe he was shipping up tomorrow evening.

Something scampered across his path.

Something about knee-level.

What was *that?*

Striding forward, he turned into the small alcove into which the thing had disappeared.

The Multipurpose Cleaners' Section.

Standing by one of the units was a severed leg. Metal hands were already embedded in the cleaner's guts. Odds and ends were strewn all over the floor. Nearby sat an empty box labeled ACME ROCKET IMPULSE ENGINE.

The leg swiveled. Ocular units aligned upon the new arrival. "Oh. Hullo. You must be Charley Haversham."

Haversham stared at the leg. "Who are you? What do you think you're doing?"

"Come here," the leg said. "I want to show you something."

Baffled, racking his brain as to why someone would make a robot leg, wondering if there was some poor humanoid robot hopping around out there without one, Charley Haversham stepped forward.

"Charley," the leg said with a voice that sounded like a Bronx pixie with a cold, "the fate of the known universe hangs in the balance."

"Huh?" Clearly the leg was deranged. God knew what it would do. He'd have to coax it into an analysis cabinet to check on the status of its programming.

"Charley," the leg said, lifting an insta-solder tool delicately in its digits. "You may not realize it now, but you are about to become a key player in a game where there are great things at stake."

This thing was *crazed!* Maybe, Charley thought, he should

just run and get some help. That might be—

With a mechanical hum, a thing that looked like nothing so much as a child's toy cannon lifted from the top of the robot leg.

A pink stun-beam streaked from its nozzle, striking Charley Haversham between the eyes.

Beatific visions streaked through his brain before a curtain of darkness dropped midway through the act. He, however, remained standing. "Okay, Charley," the leg said. "This is what we have to do."

Two

Todd Spigot stared morosely through the window. Sunlight winked back at him from the skyline of Greater Nyark City. Miracles of architecture, the buildings reared and tilted and twisted in defiance of gravity, like God's showcase garden for His universe's minerals. Hovercraft hung, drifted or whisked by in regular patterns, following force-field flow. The sun was high. The day was clean, clear, a crystal glass set down to preserve the perfection.

"What's the meaning of life, anyway?" Todd Spigot asked the pyschiatric engineer.

The Doctor placed the rare, expensive poison from Altair II in a cup. "Don't you think you're gripping the broad end of the bat with that question, Mr. Spigot?"

"Seems to me with the money this is costing me, I should go straight to the heart of the matter." Todd Spigot let the sentence go with a sigh. He adjusted the polarity of the window, darkening it. His reflection faded into existence, a ghost in the glass.

Not a bad-looking ghost, either. A couple of shifts in the DNA mix had thinned his new endomorph-G body's chin and nose, raised the cheekbones. The accelerated cloning process had whisked the altered genetics through adolescence and the Valley of the Shadow of Acne. His skin was smooth now, his brown hair curly and well-kept. His somatotype had shifted a little closer to ectomorphic, regular exercise had been able to build up a reasonably proportioned body. Nothing approaching the contours of the MacGuffin, but then Todd had more than willingly shed that particular mortal coil after the difficulties it had dragged him through.

"Coffee?" the lady PE asked.

"Makes me jumpy," Todd returned.

"I've adjusted the mix to match your metabolism's ability

to cope with it. A little lift, Mr. Spigot. That's all."

"Okay."

The Doctor poured. The poison foamed only a little. It had specifically adjusted to match Todd Spigot's metabolism as well, only not designed to give him much of a lift. An hour after ingestion, he would drop, his viscera converted to the consistency of oatmeal. "I promise you, Mr. Spigot. With *our* methods of treatment, your problems will soon be over."

"The damnable aspect," Todd said, shaking his hands above his head as he turned back to his therapist. "The frustrating thing is that I shouldn't be feeling this way."

"That's what we're here to talk about, Mr. Spigot," the Doctor said with an encouraging smile. She had a soothing voice. Her machines hummed in harmony behind her, sucking in the conversation, analyzing Todd's body chemistry and brainwaves for possible imbalances. Maladjustment was a sin on Earth. Remedies for the mildest depression were only a pill away, a house-call shrink distant. Psychoanalysis and psychiatry had ceased being scientific pursuits so much as the vendors of the latest in pacifiers.

Todd Spigot didn't care. He *wanted* to be pacified.

The Doctor walked toward him. Her stockings swished against her stiff beige skirt. Her long blonde hair kissed the sides of her perfect face like angel's breath. Her faint erotic scent touched Todd just above the harsh aroma of the coffee.

Somewhere on the computer boards, a needle quivered.

"Thank you," Todd said, taking the coffee.

"Thank *you*," the Doctor said as she glanced at the readout screen. PATIENT SENSUALLY AROUSED, it stated in bold letters.

Uneasily, Todd said, "Uhm, is this part of the treatment?"

"I've a license to do whatever makes the patient happy."

Todd looked away.

AMBIVALENCE TOWARD SEXUAL SUGGESTION, the screen read. PATIENT SEXUALLY INHIBITED. NEO-FREUDIAN/HARSHORN ANALYSIS SUGGESTED FOR PRESENT. MONITOR FOR POSSIBLE TANGENTAL POST-ROLFING, OR SHOCK SEDUCTION.

The Doctor rubbed a wristband, wiping the screen.

"I don't know," Todd Spigot said. "Everything seems so...*borderless* now. I've no boundaries. I've never felt so free in my life, yet never so upset."

FREE-FLOATING ANXIETY, the screen lettered. CON-
TEXT?

The Doctor paged through the brief Todd had filled out.
"You've ample reward credit, Mr. Spigot. You requested an—
uhm—acounting job of all things. You got it. Jobs are scarce.
An indication of Earth's sincere gratefulness for your role in
preventing it's—ah—detonation." A half-smile touched her
bright lips. "Surely you have exceeded the human SCQ."

"Pardon?"

STANDARD CONTENTMENT QUOTA, the screen announced. It commenced to supply a treatise on the subject,
which both Todd and the Doctor ignored.

Todd placed his coffee on a table. He sat down in the form-
fit lounge beside it. He folded his hands. "I've got no bases
to touch down on. No security. Oh, financial, perhaps, but in
a society where there's no such thing as financial insecurity,
any gratification excess money lends soon evaporates. I've no
real desire to return to Deadrock. I don't want to see my mother
now that I realize what kind of person she is. My relationship
with Angharad Shepherd is in complete ruins . . ."

ROMANTIC DEPRESSION, the screen spelled out. PRE-
SCRIPTION: HEAVY DRUG USE AND SELECTIVE MEM-
WIPE.

Todd waved that notion away. "No, no. I *want* to remember
her." He stared at her shoes. "Philip Amber is off in a monastery
someplace. And God knows where Cog is. I haven't seen him
all year." He picked up the cup of coffee, staring at the issuing
steam.

Keeping her eyes trained on him, the Doctor picked up a
sheet of paper. "Ah yes. The artificial Intelligence Unit located
in the leg of Philip Amber's MacGuffin. Not much is said
about this 'Cog' in the summary here. Would you care to
elaborate, Mr. Spigot?"

"No."

The Doctor's features grew stern. "How can I help you,
Mr. Spigot, if you do not supply me with the information I
request?"

GALVANIC MONITORS INDICATE TENSION LEVELS
PEAKING IN SUBJECT, the screen flashed. STRONG
PROBE UNNECESSARY.

"Shut up," the Doctor barked at the readout screen on her desk. "I apologize, Mr. Spigot," she said, recovering her aplomb. The machines and I can be occasionally demanding. You need say only what you wish. Now, would you judge that these paragraphs highlight the events somewhat over a year Earthtime ago that resulted in your presence here now? Then we can go over your present feelings, mindful of all the possible causes for your deep disatisfaction."

Todd put down the coffee. He took the sheet of paper.

After leaving the *Star Fall* with no wish to ever set foot inside it again, he'd refused to give interviews to the news media. The myriad offers to sell rights to the story of his life were promptly squashed. The three-dee-pack people talked about a movie. The notion had been promptly rejected. Todd had seen fit to tell his story only to the Intelligence Authority which Angharad Shepherd represented. He'd left out most of the business concerning the true nature of the creature who called himself Cogito Ergo Sum, allowing the high mucky-mucks to keep their assumptions that Cog was merely a be-nevolent AI brought into play by Angharad, known to them as Agent Tracy Marshack.

Ø1111Ø111Ø (condensation)

SUBJECT: Todd Spigot. Age: 31 Earth Standard. World of Birth: Deadrock. Key element in defeat of Morapn Commander of Interstellar Luxury Liner *Star Fall* (see Subject: Ort Eath) in his attempt to destroy the center of the human Empire, Earth, thus forcing the more advanced Morapn Race into galactic war with the humans.

Todd looked up from the sheet. "Did you see the three-dee rip-off that came out last month?" He grinned. *"Terrible."*

The Doctor nodded. "Is the fact sheet consistent with your experience, Mr. Spigot?"

Pointing his nose back toward the words, Todd continued reading.

Subject Spigot set out as a tourist aboard the *Star Fall* on its maiden voyage from the Morapn Worlds to Earth, its mission presumably representing a new state of peace be-tween the Morapns and the humans. Dissatisfied with his body, the naive Spigot chose to rent a different one from a shady Body Parlour in his home city, Portown. By accident he received the MacGuffin battle body belonging to assassin Philip Amber, in town for a hit. Upon his return to the Parlour, the body he'd used for his job in shambles, pursued by local authorities, Amber had his brain transferred to Spigot's real body and boarded the *Star Fall*. In a complex series of occurrences, Spigot and Amber encountered agent Angharad Shepherd/Tracy Marshack and, with the help of the Auxillary Artificial Intelligence operating in the battle body, they discovered and foiled the half-human, half-Morapn Ort Eath's attempt to destroy Earth.

Looking up, Todd said, "Much too simplistic. But that's the essential stuff. It doesn't touch on the psychological aspects, through, the reasons for my present—how can I term it . . . ?"

The word was promptly supplied by the psychotherapy machine: ANGST.

"Yes. Thank you. That's it. Angst."

The Doctor picked up her cup and sipped. "Your coffee's getting cold, Mr. Spigot."

"Oh. Yes. Thank you. Might I have some cream?"

Angharad Shepherd set her floater down by the old hotel. Her windshield wipers slapped away rain swiftly, in vague rhythm with her pounding heart.

They were chasing her. They'd found out.

Nervously, she picked up the folder from the passenger seat and stuffed it into her suitcase on the floor.

She had to get back to Central with the proof. Otherwise nobody'd ever believe her.

She stared through the runneling water, the drumming of raindrops that put the hotel into drizzly off-focus. Neo-gothic, the structure was festooned with gables, widow-walks, spires, even a lightning rod. Half a century ago, the style had been all the rage. Now there were precious few of these kind of structures left, except here in the West of the Northern United Americas. Somewhere, a blown-loose shutter applauded her safe arrival.

She shuddered. She was exhausted. She was sure she'd lost the pursuit by diving into the cloud bank which had been the ceiling of this storm, jetting into evasive maneuvers while

punching up the damper shield. Drained, she needed to find
a phone, dial Central, then hole up in a room and wait for the
cavalry to charge over the hill.

Still, preparations had to be made. Carefully, she demag-
netized the skin flap to her neck cavity. By feel, she adjusted
her Aura Disguise. A quick touch tinted her blonde hair dark,
her green eyes blue. Delicate servo-motors in her face restruc-
tured her features, widening the lips a bit, pushing out the
brow, broadening the nose.

She performed similar masking operations upon the floater
and picked a force screen umbrella from the glove compartment. Suitcase tucked under her arm, she dashed to shelter.

The old-fashioned neon sign above an awning flashed HOTEL
with crimson urgency. Angharad leaped a puddle. The wooden
steps resonated beneath her feet. Light leaked through the vene-
tian blinds of a room, presumably the office. The damp brought
out the rare smell of old wood.

A bell tinkled as she pushed the door open. She walked into
a plushly appointed room. A faded Indian rug stretched upon
the floor, supporting neo-Victorian furniture and lamps with
tassled shades. Dour patriarchs looked out from the past through
the cracked windows of their portraits. A stuffed owl, wings
outstretched as though about to swoop down upon a mouse,
hovered behind the check-in desk. Here a balding, pudgy man
was painstakingly snipping something.

Blandly, the man raised his head. "Scissors are the best."

This place would cost. No question. Clearly, it was an
exclusive resort for people with a taste for rotting atmosphere
or the need to be depressed. Still, thought Angharad Shepherd,
a bed's a bed, and Central would foot the bill.

"I'd like a single for the night," she said, looking around
for telltale signs of monitoring equipment. The room was
marred by no machinery older than Twentieth Century. "I'd
like a room with a phone."

The man casually glanced at a list of available accomoda-
tions. "I've a single with an excellent rear view. Looks out
over the bog. You can see the old mansion on the cliff."

"Fine, fine." It was early afternoon; all Angharad wanted
was a place to rest while she waited for reinforcements.

"Very well," said the man, reaching back to lift a set of old-
fashioned metal keys from a peg. "Two hundred credits."

"Will you take a marker?"

"Gladly." The financial arrangements were quickly settled. "We have an excellent library of two-dee celluloid films. I was just re-editing one of my favorites at the moment."

"No, no. It's been a frenzy of a day. I need some rest."

The man shrugged. He pushed a registry book across the desk. Angharad signed "Marnie Crane" beneath the previous entry, "Mr. and Mrs. Smith."

"Just up the stairs to the right, madam," said the man. "Have a pleasent rest."

The room had a plush rug, intricately patterned wallpaper and a soft, thick-mattressed bed, the kind they didn't make anymore. Exhausted, Angharad fell into the bed's faint lavender scent. Even with the nerve-prop medication Central supplied, her emotions were on edge. Weariness rasped within. Anxiety and worry gnawed her mind like predatory birds.

To think that she had believed it all ended a year ago, when Ort Eath had come to his grisly end, when Amber had broken through to the stoical Morapns with a burst of emotion and they had defused the antimatter bomb. The *Star Fall* saga was only beginning. Far from dimming, the importance of the gigantic Space Liner had increased.

PROJECT COUNTER CONSCIOUSNESS
FUSED IDENTITY MATRICES
MORAPN MINDFIELD DISPLACEMENT

Dizzily, the terms swirled in her head. She felt spellbound by the concepts she had just begun to understand during the weeks she had spent undercover, successfully serving with the computer maintenance team in an Arizona desert research complex.

Somehow the man had bought a controlling share of the *Star Fall*. Earnest Evers Hurt, fabled mystery trillionaire of the galaxy, said to be the oldest man alive. Owner of planets. A tentacle deep into every financial concern of the human-occupied star system. Deeply involved in exploration outwards—and apparently inwards—for the destiny of mankind.

Simple enough, that. Straight intrigue. After the business with her half-brother Ort Eath, she knew that she'd been bitten by the bug. No other kind of life—not even an existence steeped in real-fics—could satisfy her like the life of an intelligence agent.

However, the hints, the implications, the shadows of *him*, the memories twined with the possibilities. . . . Angharad Shepherd shuddered violently. Gasping, she sat up and tried to get ahold of herself.

Anxiety attack.

Shaking, she was barely able to thumb the combination impulses into her suitcase. A few pills later, she felt better. Lying on top of the clothes was the folder filled with apparently innocent computer readout sheets. However, with the aid of the code she'd devised, a cryptoanalysis unit would be able to spew forth information about Earnest Evers Hurt's activities that would increase the patronage of Galactic Central's Booze Bar for a long time to come.

She heaved a sigh. The phone was by the bed. Following instructions, she dialed nine to get out, then tapped in the first of a sequence of flow-codes to obtain Central's latest report number. Number achieved, she unsnapped an upper left molar from her bridgework and coded out her present location, using spurts of her unique identity frequency through the wireless airwaves. She bracketed the longitude and latitude with a strong signal of urgency.

HELP!

A moment later, the molar glowed red. Message received. She breathed relief, stuck the tooth back in her mouth.

Suddenly, she felt itchy. Her hair, despite its recent color change, felt limp and dirty. A shower. She realized uncomfortably that she'd not taken one in a few days. Too busy.

The bathroom was clean and spartan. She noted with pleasure that the shower wasn't molecular-wash. Real hot water would gush over her, soothing, massaging her aches.

Anticipation hurried her disrobing. She shucked blouse and pants with practiced ease. Panties and gauzy breast supports were off in a flash. A few selective twists of her wrist later, hot water streamed into the ceramic basin, pattering the plastic curtain. Plumes of steam breathed out to caress her lithe body, gently warming her. She inhaled with pleasure at the delicate texture of the water vapor against her skin. She was glad she was a female. Although if it were necessary, she knew she'd assume a man's frame again, she preferred to stay this way. So much more sensitive to the nuances of sensation and emotion, this female form. .

To think she'd spent a good portion of her life as a man. How odd.

She admired her supple lines a moment, wondering if the starchy research center chow had put on a pound or two, then stepped into the coursing water.

Immediately, she felt better. She lost herself in the droning splash, the steady *plat-plat* pressure of hot water on reddening back, the warmth streaming down her abdomen, between her thighs.

She lathered herself throughly with soap smelling of roses, then began to sing, a habit of her male days not yet broken.

She did not hear the bathroom door click open.

If she had looked, she would have seen a dark form through the semitranslucent curtain, drifting toward her. She would have seen the muted gleams of squatting machinery just outside the door.

The curtain was suddenly opened. Shock preventing any other response, Angharad whipped around to stare into the face of the desk clerk. He wore a dress and a wig. In his hand was something that looked like a kitchen knife.

"Good evening," he said, although it was still afternoon.

"I'm losing my friends," Todd Spigot said. "I'm disoriented, I'm just kind of drifting through life. I've done everything I ever wanted to do, I have my freedom now, and yet I'm confused. I don't think the way I used to, I don't believe in what I used to believe in. God's no longer in his Heaven, and things are just so fantastic, they're rotten. Who am I, anyway? A fleshy bag of bones and blood, jouncing through life with no other objective than to end up dead? It's funny. I've not only fulfilled my desires, I understand why they were desires, why I had the motivations, the personality I had. But as frustrated, as encumbered as I was back then, by God, my problems were familiar problems. They gave me definition.

"I knew that Todd Spigot was a fat mother's-boy. I knew that you could list my beliefs about reality by simply excerpting them from the dogma and doctrine of the Holston Christian Separatist Church. So I get my particular reality bubble popped. Fine. But what's going to replace it? Real-fics? Disbelief Suspenders? Uh-uh. They'll just put my brain through the grinder a little further. I need to stop, take evaluation. I need your help, Doctor. I need that damned machine, as annoying as it's getting. I need boundaries. I need parameters. I'm feeling angry and violent for no reason, and it frightens me."

NEUROSES LEVEL 6A. INFORMATION INSUFFICIENT FOR FULL PROGNOSIS, the screen spelled reluctantly. COMPLETE PROGRAM NECESSARY. PATIENT COOPERATION ENCOURAGING.

The Doctor rounded the desk with airy grace, smile lighting her beauty a little hotter. "Of course it frightens you, poor Mr. Spigot. And I want you to immediately consider us—your machine and I—as your friends."

Made uneasy by this rush of friendliness, Todd stood. His mug of coffee was still in his left hand. Looking at the Doctor's attractive breasts loosely moving beneath her shirt, he felt a need for oral gratification.

He lifted the mug to his lips.

The Doctor nodded encouragingly as she approached. "That's right, Todd. Drink up. It will make you feel better."

"You must forgive me. I've been going on and on," he said, feeling embarrassed by his outpouring of emotion, feeling a little unsettled by the presense of a lovely woman. Todd Spigot had not changed all that much. "I've probably gone way over the time limit. I'll just check." With his natural obsequiousness and exuberance, he twisted his right wrist to glance at his watch, forgetting that the hand attached to selfsame wrist was holding a cup.

Contents of said cup spilled in a great brown splash over the Doctor's blouse. The Doctor's smile froze around gritted teeth.

Horrified, Todd took off his jacket and made clumsy attempts to mop the mess off the Doctor as delicately as possible.

"I'm so sorry," he said. "I didn't mention it, but I'm a bit of a klutz."

"You seem to have clung well enough to that particular personality quality, Mr. Spigot," the Doctor said, gently resisting Todd's cleaning efforts. "Pardon me. I've a change of clothing in my bathroom."

Face red with embarrassment, Todd Spigot sat back down in his chair. Dammit all, anyway. Despair flooded him.

His life had rotted to such a mess. Away from the rarefied atmosphere of the *Star Fall*, Angharad's feelings for him had gone sour. She'd been swamped with work, unable to pay attention to him. He'd floundered about on his own. At first, the novelty of being on a different planet, on Old Earth, of all places, a hero of all things, had buoyed him. However, the manic phase had rapidly dived into the depressive. They'd given him the job after he'd whined for a whole month, and Angharad had gotten thoroughly disgusted with him. For all his wanting it, though, it just wasn't the same.

Earth had lost its gleam. Its novel sights and smells had turned into an alien mess.

Alien.

That was what he was here, Todd Spigot finally realized. As alien as some three-nosed Aslasi tourist. But his experiences had changed him so fundamentally that he realized he could never return to the environment in which he'd been reared.

Who said it? *You Can't Go Home Again*. Thomas Wolfe. Right. That guy'd had a really happy life, too. You bet.

"You go find yourself a nice girl," Angharad had said condescendingly in a fake Jewish accent as her pretty tail had wiggled from his life. But where? He couldn't relate to any of the women here. They were different. He was an orange in a world full of apples.

He was even having a hard time with the shrink and she was used to *real* crazies, no doubt.

If only there'd been no Philip Amber, no Angharad Shepherd, no Ort Eath, and especially no Cog. If only he had gotten aboard the *Star Fall* in some body other than the MacGuffin, a happy tourist in wonderland exploring his fantasies, visiting the wondrous inside and outside of his mind, seeing Earth for a week, then shipping back to his job with the mining computer and the stale but familiar life on Deadrock, changed only just enough to assert himself. Grab some plain girl for a normal marriage. Have the prescribed litter of kids. Be a good Deadrock Joe, a-yup, a-yup. Tuck away his experience to a silent, cherished corner of his mind to drag out in beery moments and fantasize over, safely.

The problem with fantasy made real was that it made you realize that *everything* is fantasy.

Hell, Todd Spigot thought, *is getting exactly what you think you want*.

A flicker on the screen attracted his attention.

HOW ABOUT A DRINK? the machine said. MAKE YOU
FEEL BETTER.

"Uhm, sure," Todd responded, feeling jittery.

WHAT WOULD YOU LIKE?

"How about a whiskey?"

COMING UP. *Chunk-a-chunk* went the machine. Rattle
went a cup as it landed in a dispenser. NEAT OR ICE?

"Ice, please." Crushed ice dropped into the plastic cup. A
healthy dollop of liquor followed. Todd tasted, found the warm
flow nourishing the state of peace he desired.

FIRST OF ALL, A BIT OF ADVICE.

Swallowing a bit more of the sting, Todd said, "Sure."

YOU'RE JUST GOING THROUGH A PHASE, PAL.
DON'T TAKE TOO MUCH STOCK IN THE GOBBLEDE-
GOOK WE'RE DISHING OUT. I'M JUST DOING MY PRE-
PROGRAMMED JOB. TAKE IT FROM ME. I DUNNO.
DOCTOR PETERS IS ACTING KIND OF STRANGE TO-
DAY. DON'T USE PSYCHIATRIC CARE AS A CRUTCH.
EVERYTHING IS GOING TO BE OKAY. TIME HEALS
ALL WOUNDS. A PENNY SAVED IS A PENNY EARNED.

"I guess I just need someone to talk to."

YOU PAYS YOUR MONEY, YOU TAKES YOUR
CHANCES. A PERSON'S PROBLEMS ARE GENERALLY
ALL IN HIS HEAD. THERE'S NO SUCH THING AS A
FREE LUNCH.

Doctor Peters re-entered wearing an off-white, loose smock.
Strapped around her leg, concealed by the crisp folds of her
dress, was the auxillary means of Todd Spigot's destruction.

"Now then," she said. "Where were we?"

After finishing his scourging, Philip Amber rubbed a little
salt in one of his self-inflicted stripes, then assumed the latest
style in sackcloth and ashes. The fresh pain that throbbed
through him was like a Brillo pad on his soul, scouring his
guilt. The Brothers of the Infinite allowed him to flagellate
himself once a month. It was something that Philip Amber
found to be an invariably enriching experience.

Pain is an illusion, he reminded himself as he grimaced his
way down into meditating position. Pain instructs.

Pain also hurts like hell, the perverse part of him said.
Amber damped the little voice down. Sometimes he thought

he was getting schizoid or something. Well, he was a damned sight better than he used to be.

"Shit!" he cursed involuntarily. The stone floor of the cell was refrigerated to a chill especially recommended for the finest state of discomfort. Amber's bare backside beneath the robe had inadvertently touched it. Quickly, he slid the coarse cloth back into position and struggled into an awkward lotus position.

He lit a cigarette and began his deep-breathing exercises.

Inhale. Exhale. Cough.

Smoke streamed out his left nostril. His right nostril.

A minute later, dissatisfied with the Raga Tobacco Yoga technique, he stubbed out his cigarette. The part of him that was not yet healed, his Shadow-Self, ardently wished there was a comely woman around so that he could try out that Advanced Tantric stuff Brother Lucius studiously skipped over in Disciplines Toward Cosmic Consciousness 101. Amber shuddered, as he always did when his mind strayed from the Divine, bringing him himself back to his purpose, which was to spend the hour before the Brothers' simple communal dinner in a state of meditation or devotion.

"Om," Philip Amber crooned. "Ommmmm."

The Trancendentalist had whispered "Aardvark" to him as his private mantra, but somehow that didn't work very well for Amber, so he resorted to the trusty old standby.

The chant resounded in the tiny stone cell. Amber concentrated on a single point ahead of him, the edge of a bookmarker sticking from the current copy of *Mysticism Digest*. Those rare moments of getting away from himself, shedding his memories, dissolving in what the Brothers called the pure State of Being was worth all the trouble.

Angharad's agency, of course, appropriated his MacGuffin when they were presented with the situation. Actually, if the Earth government had known who he really was, they'd have strung him up. But thanks to Angharad's expert shuffling with her people, he'd been spared on the condition that he would select some method of rehabilitation. His experiences aboard the *Star Fall* had widened his horizons and attitudes, so he chose a monastic life. After two more years of this, he'd be able to return to Prometheus' Rest to *om* away the rest of his days, an exile to luxury. While he'd floated in nutrient stasis, they'd shipped his true body back to Earth. Amber decided that he'd stick in it a while, probably ride it all the way to death. Hopefully, by the time of *that* transition, he would have gotten straightened out.

The nice thing about the Brothers was that they'd managed, with the help of a sophisticated machine here, a little Christian charity there, to neutralize the polarity of Amber's pyschic distress. People he cared about—or didn't care about—who happened to be around him wouldn't die anymore. Naturally, the Brothers had some self-motivation in the cure. Although the goal of all was the eventual reunion of the Ultimate that can only be achieved through death, they all had their particular interests in life they wanted to hang on to a while.

Amber could understand this. As the nuns across the street said, life gets to be a habit.

*Om*ed out after only a few minutes with nothing to show for his vocal and mental efforts, the lanky, muscular man rose and sat on his thin mattress and blanket, wondering what was for dinner. He watched dust motes spin in a shaft of colored light streaming through his stained glass window, but he couldn't see the cosmic dance Brother Stephen talked about. He looked at the complicated New Age Mandala hung on his wall in its multicolored mazery, its concentric circles, its obscure convolutions of symbols and imagery, and he couldn't see Life's zigzag that Brother Alphonse oozed enthusiastically over. He glanced at his day-glo poster of Mohammed, Christ, Buddha, John F. Kennedy, and more modern Pointers of the Way sitting in a bar, having beers and laughing drunkenly. Its metaphorical implications didn't seem to matter much.

Shit. He could just see it. He'd hustle on into the mess hall and all the other Brothers would be sitting there over their Spam and eggs with big Zen smiles, and all *he'd* have would be his usual grouchy pout. Brother Marcus would recite a new koan for them to ponder. Brother Manalishi would show them his new insights into the art of fire-walking and cooking hot dogs similtaneously. Brother Graham, as the evening's entertainment, would drink too much wine and go into his usual glossalia attack of elephant jokes in obscure languages.

And what would Philip Amber do?

Philip Amber would just sit there with his thumb up his ass and look glum.

No sir. Not tonight, Amber decided.

Time to do some heavy-duty meditation, so that the light of attainment would pour from his eyes, so he'd finally maybe be on a higher spiritual level than his smug, self-satisfied teachers and peers.

Heaving himself up, he went to his wooden desk. Tugging open a scratched drawer, he pulled out the box that Brother Theodore had given him on the sly. ("Don't swallow all the glop about enlightenment through meditation," the shaggy man had said, sucking on the pipe of concentrated THC he always carried around. "For *true* cosmic consiousness, swallow *this*.")

Modified LSD-25. Guaranteed not to widen the spaces between your synapses. Amber took a tab and washed it down with a glass of cherry Kool-Aid.

He settled into his patented Lotus Slouch and waited for Revelation.

The depths of the room began to shift. The face of Christ began to emit sparkles. The mandala began to slowly turn like a carousel on its side, sloughing rays of intense light.

Philip Amber had never done this before. He wasn't sure this was what meditation was supposed to be, but he was too enrapt in the experience to care much. "Hallucinations?" Brother Theodore had responded to his question. "Hey, man, it's mostly the new way you see things that's the kick. But sure, you might have what we call a hallucination in this state of consciousness."

So, when Amber saw the thing coming through the window, he presumed it was just that—a hallucination. Odd, though. Why would a hallucination have to unlatch the window?

Whatever it was stepped down on the desk. Large, it had eight strong, articulated legs, each ending in a digit array. Although it was mostly metallic grayish-green, bits of flesh hung, pulsing, through the armor. It scrabbled fully onto the desk, scuttled down onto the chair, clattered onto the floor. Fitted around its back was a knapsacklike arrangement decked with flickering lights and silvery tubing. The creature skittered into a semiupright position. Oculars glittered in candlelight as they swerved to align upon Amber. Sensory nodes twitched, as though the thing was about to sneeze from the thick ropes of incense smoke that hung in the air.

"My God, don't tell me,!" Amber said, extremely excited. "I've having a throwback vision into the Hindu symbolic struc-

ture of the universe. The pantheon of the Indian gods has sent
me a representative. You're the guy with a lot of arms, right?
Kali. That's the name. You're *Kali!*"

"No, Amber," the Arachnid said. "I'm Gabriel. This is my
horn." The biobot slid a gun from his knapsack. "And this is
the judgment of God Himself."

As the slugs slammed into Amber's body and his drugged
blood sprayed, his altered consciousness realized that this was
going to be the biggest trip of all.

"I guess it all comes down to the fact that I'm afraid of
death," Todd Spigot said, standing by the window, staring into
the shadow and the dazzle.

The Doctor unlatched the safety on her gun.

"I've gone through so many states of mind, so many ways
of seeing things that were *wrong*"—including that business
with the Crem, Todd thought glumly—"how do I know that
the way I see things now is *right?* I mean, what guarantee do
I have that my mother and father weren't right, and when I die
I'll wake up into Reality staring the Devil in the face. 'Sucker!'
he'll say. 'You really blew it'."

"Come come, Mr. Spigot. Surely you've evolved away from
that kind of superstitious consideration."

TEETERING TOWARD PARANOID THINKING, the
pysch-machine commented as the Doctor aimed. The dart had
to go directly into the spine at the base of the neck or its effects
would not be sufficient.

Todd began to turn around, forcing the Doctor to hide the
handgun behind her back. "I know, I know. But it makes just
about as much sense as anything, doesn't it?"

"Are you commenting on your religious thought system or
your present fractured self-image in the relationship to your
reality matrix?"

"You mean would I rather be blind and happy or blessed
with a vision of undoubted truth and be miserable?"

"No. I mean the secret to happiness—God, I hate that
word—comes from within. You have to make your own happiness. You have to structure *yourself*. You *are* reality, Todd
Spigot! To yourself, at any rate."

"I can't accept that," Todd Spigot said. "There's got to be
an Ideal. Maybe some part of it's inside me, but the greater
is somewhere beyond. It's got to be, and it's my feeling that

it's every thinking being's holy duty to seek... you know, quest for the truth. Not only for the Ideal, but for the right way to live." Breathing heavily with emotion, he turned. "Do these windows open?"

"Yes. At this particular height, they do. The button's just to your left."

Todd pressed. A servo-motor soundlessly swiveled the window open. Todd breathed the fresh, pollution-free air, which tasted faintly metallic from mechanical recycling. He shivered out a breath. Realizing a tear had coursed down his cheek, he wiped it off with the back of his hand.

"Just what do you hope to gain from this therapy and counseling, Mr. Spigot?" The gun was out again.

"I'd like to find some answers, Doctor. If they're in books or art, I hope to search them out there. If they're in experience, I'd like to find out what kind of experience. Finally, if the answers are inside me, I'd like you and this machine of yours to open me up enough to let them out. This may sound trite, but I'd like to find out who I am, how I relate to the universe, how the universe relates to me. If there's a Truth underlying our interpretation of Reality or if Truth winds through the very fabric of my existence... whichever, I want to find it. I want to know where I fit. How can we be sure about anything? Should I live my life rationally or emotionally, or some odd combination of the two? What is love? What, if any, are the rules of human conduct that I should apply to myself? I need answers. God knows, I need *something*." He gave the window a frustrated tap. "All my life people have been telling me what to think. I was controlled, maneuvered, manipulated. My mind has been molded by society and culture. Now I'm a free thinker. An outsider. And I wonder of maybe I wasn't better off being bound into ways of thinking. At least I'd have a sense of security."

"There's no such thing as security, Mr. Spigot." The Doctor stepped to within two meters of Todd Spigot. She drew a bead on the back of his head.

As she fired, Todd abruptly bent to tied his shoe.

The dart made a pinging sound as it struck the window, splattering a smear of fluid across glass.

QUERY, the pysch-computer said. IS THIS A NEW METHOD OF THERAPY?

Todd turned. He saw the Doctor struggling to reload the

dart gun. Instinctively, he leaped toward her, tackling her.
They sprawled on the floor. The gun bounced over beside the
window. The Doctor pulled free and scooped it up. Desperately, Todd grabbed her again and they whipped about in a
·frenzy.

WARNING, the machine said on its screen. ATTACK PSY-
CHOTHERAPY OUTLAWED TWO CENTURIES AGO.
WARNING. AM PROGRAMMED TO NOTIFY AUTHOR-
ITIES.

"Do it!" Todd cried. "Do—"

The Doctor's arm swung around inadvertently, squeezing
off another shot. The bullet—an explosive one this time—
slammed into the computation nexus grid of the computer. Fire
and smoke leaped from the façade. Automatically, extinguish-
ing foam spewed from the ceiling, covering the floor. Todd
and the Doctor slipped and slid. The Doctor broke free. A
possessed look filled her eyes; a coat of foam made her look
like a demented snowman. The woman bent and drew a knife
from her boot. But in straightening too quickly, she slipped on
the foam. The bottom edge of the window caught the backs
of her knee joints.

She fell out.

Somehow the Doctor managed to twist around so that her
left hand caught the ledge. She dangled. "Help!" she cried.

For a moment, blood thundering in his ears, Todd stood
transfixed, full of indecision. The woman had tried to kill him.
But why? It didn't make any sense. Nothing made any sense
anymore. He considered just calling for the police, letting this
psychiatric assassin dangle until they arrived.

"Oh God," she said. "I'm slipping."

Todd went to the window. The Doctor had managed to get
her other hand up. Now she was hanging precariously, one
foot wedged in a shallow crease in the building's plastimix
side. Nothing else was between her and the street twenty stories
below. A strong breeze rippled her smock and Todd's hair.
Scuds of foam blew off, floating away softly.

"Okay. Hang on." Todd reached down and tried to get hold
of her.

Panicking, the woman pulled herself up and, with one hand,
tried to grab Todd's arm. Her fingers hooked on his coat. The
seams began to tear. "Hey!" Todd cried. "You'll pull us *both*

down." The woman's eyes were wide and wild. Todd reached further down to try to get a better hold on the back of the smock. His hands gripped something underneath the clothing—something that ran along the woman's spine like a long handle to a piece of luggage.

The Doctor groaned in pain, spasmed, and fell limp, losing her hold on the ledge and Todd's arm. Her eyes turned up in her head. Unable to do anything else, Todd held on to whatever he'd grabbed, which seemed to run all the way down her back. A horrible sucking sound of something ripping from flesh ensued. Blood began to blot the smock at the back of the neck and the base of the spine. As the woman's unconscious form contorted and shook, Todd had to brace himself harder to prevent from being pulled out the window.

Then, with an odd heave, the sides of the smock tore away raggedly. The Doctor's unconscious body plummeted, bare bloody back exposed like a paratrooper whose parachute had been blasted away. Todd averted his eyes as the Doctor and the pavement below made intimate acquaintance.

Still holding the flap of smock and whatever hung beneath it, Todd managed to pull his aching body back through the window, but he kept his right arm, holding the torn smock and the *thing*, extended.

The thing wiggled. It arched like a snake, throwing off part of the smock fragment.

Tiny teeth snapped. Blood-spotted metal gleamed in sunlight. Wires and pincerlike appendages. Optical chips on two stalks wiggled, then aligned on Todd.

With a thrill of astonishment, Todd recognized the thing. Some sort of warped, robot-version of a Disbelief Suspender—those attachments to the spine and brain perfected for the *Star Fall*, used to submerge the participants in real-fics fully into the action by means of a personality overlay. Thus the participant literally became a different character in a programmed adventure.

The animated Disbelief Suspender slipped through Todd's fingers and the smock, leaping for Todd's throat. Todd wrenched away. Metal teeth buried themselves in the padded shoulder of his jacket. He could feel a throb of electricity as the teeth pierced his skin. He grabbed the thing with both hands. With a strength born of pure fear, he pulled it away.

The robot chittered. Todd brought his arms up, then down again, whipping the robot from its hold on his hands.

Flung into the air, still partially tangled in the bloody length of cloth, the robot dropped toward the street. Halfway in its descent tiny wings sprouted from its thin frame. Discarding the smock piece, the thing flapped away, disappearing behind a building.

Shocked and dazed, Todd Spigot stumbled back inside the safety of the Doctor's ruined office.

Shaking, he went to the Doctor's liquor cabinet and poured himself a healthy splash of whiskey, neat.

A swallow later, he regarded the mess and wondered what the hell he was going to do now. Clearly, the poor Doctor had not been at fault. Somehow the robot had attached itself to her spine, becoming a puppetmaster unit. At Cog's suggestion, they had used the Suspenders on the *Star Fall* for similar purpose, but those had not embedded themselves, leechlike, in the wearer. Nor had they forced the wearer against his or her will to become cold-blooded assassins.

Todd reflected on that. Who would want to kill him? And for God's sake, why?

He had concluded that the next thing logically to do was to call the police, when the door banged open. Blue-uniformed officers brandished stun-guns. "Okay, you. Drop it."

"It's only whiskey," Todd objected.

"Oh." The slim mustachioed man in front carefully lifted himself from his squat and cautiously waded through the foam. "There's a dead woman on the pavement, brain beyond salvaging. Sensors show she was pushed from this room. You have the right to remain silent. You have the right—"

"Wait a minute! She was trying to kill me. I was only practicing self-defense. And I didn't throw her out the window, anyway. She tripped and fell and I tried to save her, but I grabbed ahold of a robot implanted on her back and—"

The officer had been eyeing the label on the door. "You're *clearly* not Dr. Phyllis Daniels. So you must be a psychotic patient or something. Admit it. Things will go easier on you if you confess."

"I'm telling you—"

With the help of his partner, the officer put force-field handcuffs on Todd Spigot's wrists.

"Tell it to the chief at the station, pal."

Astonished and confused, Todd was led away, convinced, at least in part, that if there was an Ultimate Intelligence behind the scenes of the universe, it was now laughing behind his back.

...laughing behind his back.

Peals of mirth rang out in the portion of the Self monitoring Todd Spigot. Energy levels shifted; cells fed, died, were born in the Eternal Song of the creature as it streamered its Bio-Energy dance through Underspace.

Through countless strands, the Self tapped the psychic energy—like a growing child sucking at billions of maternal teats. For a long time the Seed had drifted, until it had found fertile soil, taken root. Now it grew, like a blooming flower of life.

It shimmered and shook like oil on sunlit water, oozing between the fabric of intelligent life, seeking, ever seeking its fruition.

Unaware, unconsious, the Self fed and eliminated... as the chuckles vibrating certain chambers died away into echoes of echoes.

Three

Booked, mind-printed, and mug-shot, Todd Spigot moped behind the energy screen of his jail cell. His lawyer had just left, shaking his head despairingly, talking about Todd getting off easy with a mind-scour.

"Angharad! Angharad Shepherd! She'll know," Todd had said to the cop in charge of his welfare. "Central Galactic Intelligence. Get them! She'll back up my story. I know she will! And what about the marks the Suspender left? Aren't you going to take those into account?"

The comm-officer had obliged by ringing up the CGI.

Angharad Shepherd? Todd Spigot? Well, Angharad Shepherd was missing in action. But as soon as she reported back, they'd put her in contact.

That had been Todd Spigot's one allowed phone call.

He sank wearily back on his pallet. The carbolic scent of the cell made him sick to his stomach. The constant electric hum preyed on his nerves. He'd have to stay here at least the night. And he'd thought he'd had problems this morning, hunched over his keyboard, friendless, in the deepest of dumps.

Blearily, he stared down the hallway of the bleak prison section of the Peace Maintenance Building. He heard the snores of his fellow lodgers. Crime on Earth had ceased to be caused by economic want. Now it seemed principally caused by undetected psychological disorders, or, more often, sheer boredom. Todd had heard rumors that for some social groups, crime had become a hobby. And why not? There were no punishments to speak of . . . only mind-adjustments. Personality alterations. "Reordering of mental schematics," the authorities called it.

The modern vernacular dubbed them "brain jobs."

Maybe that was what he needed, Todd Spigot thought as he idly watched a large robot cleaning unit wheel around the corner and growl its way down the corridor. A brain job. A

kind of pseudodeath. Implant some happiness into this dissatisfied being. Stock up the empty motivation bins with enthusiasm for life. Kick the old and tired lug out from behind the
controls and substitute a well-adjusted spit-and-polish sort.

Whatever worked.

Still, it galled Todd to be framed like this for something he
hadn't done. Frightened him. Something or someone had tried
to kill him.

Who? Why?

Vacuum chugging, brushes spinning, the cleaner neared.
Just outside Todd's cell, it halted. Troublesome stain? Todd
wondered. Mechanical problem?

"Spigot!" the machine whispered in a familiar voice. "Todd
Spigot, are you in there?" A pixieish whine. Oh God, no.
Not—

Todd covered himself with his blanket, trying to get out of
view. This was all he needed now.

"Spigot! I see you. You're in there."

"Spigot? No Spigots in here."

"Just some murderer, huh?"

"I'm *not* a murderer! She *tripped* out the window, dammit.
I tried to *save* her!"

"Ah ha! You can't fool me. It *is* Todd Spigot. You can't
trick an old pal that shared a body with you once."

Resigned, Todd sighed heavily. He heaved himself from
the cot and kneeled by the force-bars. "Okay, Cog. It's me,
I admit. What do you want?"

"Goodness, you sound like I'm your executioner or something!" Cleaning brushes bristled with indignation.

"Why didn't you come this morning when I needed you!
Or this afternoon! It's all done now. I'll accept my fate. Just
leave me alone, okay?" Todd scratched his head. "What happened to your leg, anyway?"

"Connected inside."

"I thought you'd joined your fellow Crem. Haven't seen
you since you hobbled off after landing on Earth."

"Yes, well, that's another matter. I am, uhm, in a bit of a
mess with my spiritual companions. They sent me a message
to that effect, along with a few other interesting facts about
this reality level."

Todd went back to his cot. "Yeah, well, this denizen of this reality level is just going to be fatalistic this time, and let what happens, happen. He's not going to get involved with *you* again, that's for sure!"

"Wait a moment, would you? I haven't finished. I'm about to announce to you that you're about to embark upon the most exciting, dazzling adventure ever encountered by a lowly human being, and *you're* content to let them stick your head in a mind-scour." Multipurpose arms waved excitedly. "You're not going to believe what's happening, Todd! Even eon-old I was more astonished than you can imagine."

"I'm through with adventures, Cog. I'll just wait and get help from Phil Amber. Or better, from Angharad Shepherd. I can rely on them. I don't really trust you."

"Yes. Uhm. I tried to save them, but I was too late."

Todd jumped, bumping his head on the bunk above. "They're *dead?*"

"To the best of my knowledge, they're in the same state you'd be if dumb luck hadn't saved you from that rigged shrink."

"Oh my God." Grief flooded Todd for a moment. Then practicality dawned. "You know about that psychotherapist? She had a strange kind of Disbelief Suspender on, Cog! It just . . . flew away! You believe me. Finally, someone believes me!"

"Of course I believe you, pal. It's you and me against the universe, this time. That's why I need you, Todd Spigot. You're the only one who'll believe *me!* Destiny calls."

"Don't hand me that glop," Todd said, retreating.

"Listen for a minute, Todd. What I'm on top of now makes the Ort Eath affair look trifling by comparison. If something is not done, bad things are going to happen. And you're the only person who can help me. Why do you think that attempt on your life was made? How do you know someone might not try again? As you say, that Disbelief Suspender is still on the loose."

"You're right," Todd mused. "What will we have to do?"

"That's the spirit! First, I'll have to break you out of here. No time for red tape. Then we'll have to get on board the *Star Fall* and—"

"The *Star Fall!*" Todd cried. "No way! Forget it."

"You want to end up like Amber and Shepherd?"

"How do I really know they're"—he was reluctant to use the word—"dead."

"I don't know that for sure, Todd, but the only way we'll both know, the place where the answers are, is the *Star Fall*. Now I can't sit here dripping floor wax all night. Are you going to let me get you out or not?"

Answers. Todd Spigot had plenty of questions. Most likely he wouldn't find them from an unsympathetic Law Maintenance Personality Adjustment machine. Doubtless he wouldn't discover the meaning of life as an expendable computer operator, stuck on a world to which he could not relate.

"Okay, okay," he said, realizing he was surrendering to the inevitable. "I'll go. I'm certifiably crazy anyway. But how are you going to get me out of here?"

"I have had an entire year to collect the tools necessary to this next sequence of events."

"Precognition, huh?"

"Very funny. Now let me see. Where did I put that energy-bar cutter?"

"I'll be here all night."

"Not if *I* can help it." A small door in the side of the cleaning machine sprang open. A mechanical arm extruded, holding something like tongs. Power sparked across the gap and the souped-up cleaning machine jumped a full six centimeters off the ground. "Wow. I don't know my own power. Let me see now. Positive to positive, negative to negative. Or is it the other way around?"

The ends of the tongs touched two humming, translucent bars to lightning effect. With the smell of ozone, the rush of air to fill a vaccuum, the bars were suddenly gone. "Think you can squeeze through that?" Cog asked.

"Do another one." Todd requested.

"Right, but make this fast. We've tripped an alarm." The tongs touched. The bar was gone. Todd sidled through the opening. No sooner had he made the move than energy coursed again, re-forming the humming bars.

"Geez, that was close," Todd said, shaken. "What next?" A blare became audible as doors in the distance opened. Lights shifted with colored shadows. Feet hammered. "What's goin' on?" one of Todd's fellow inmates asked, nose discreetly distant from energy bars. Similar questioning murmurs joined the voice.

Todd ignored them, pointing down the exit corridor. "So much for that. Why don't you just let me back into the cell and we'll pretend this never happened."

"You still have too much respect for authority," Cog said. "Hop on."

"What?"

"I said, hop on top of me." A saddlelike indentation bowed in the cylinder's center. Holds for hands and feet appeared. Todd jumped on. "Now hang on *tight*." A nozzle flipped out from the front. Crackling energy played on the wall for several seconds, then a hole framed a view of the nighttime city skyline.

On antigravity nodes, the multipurpose robot cleaner rose a meter in the air. Small wings grew from the fuselage just before Todd's knees.

"You there!" a policeman called. "Stop!" A mauve stun-beam flashed past Todd's head, frizzling his hair.

Todd clung to the purchases provided. Energy jetted from the rear of the Cog-possessed cleaner. In a blink of an eye, Todd Spigot found himself clinging to a crazed cleaning machine with wings as it dodged skyscrapers.

The robot erected a windshield, lowered itself into normal traffic patterns. "Next stop," Cog said. "The starport."

Eyes shut tight, hugging his perch for all he was worth, Todd said through gritted teeth, "I can hardly wait."

Four

Swirl.

Of.

Vermilion magenta cerulean.

Shudders of shadows. Clouds part for light the texture of moonbeams. Electric snaps from jagged energy courses buried deep in the ground.

So, Philip Amber thought. *This is Heaven.*

Mirrors facing mirrors, the sensory impressions stretched out eternally. A webworking of realities, the fabric of being, suffused with timelessness.

After a few millennia pondering this new state of existence, Amber wondered if it was the drugs he'd dropped that had brought this vision upon him. If so, he'd have to do this more.

More than peaceful here. It was . . . well, fascinating. Hypnotic. Exulting. Had he reached the fabled Nirvana his Brothers had spoken so awe-filled about?

Then Amber remembered the *biobot,* crawling through the window. He remembered projectiles slamming into his body. He remembered the darkness.

Abruptly, he was aware that he wasn't really *seeing* anything.

The illusion of sight was physical, but the actual visions before him had a dreamlike, soft-focus aspect that shifted with his thoughts, his interactions with them. The musical sounds had the same fluctuating quality. The taste of the place was negligible, the odors pure memory. Philip Amber reached to touch his eyes and nothing happened. Although he felt as though he had an arm, felt as though he could snap his fingers if he liked, he could see no arm, and his phantom limb could touch no ears, nose, mouth, face . . . nothing.

Amber would have panicked, but there was nothing to do. Energy-shot clouds moiled around his troubled conscious-

ness, reflecting its disturbance. The ripple in the pattern seemed
to trip something. A pulse shot through the fabric of
this . . . existence. Amber intuitively sensed that it was some
kind of signal.

Signal, though, to what?

Balls of energy coalesced before him. (Behind him? Above
him? It didn't matter. *Close* to him. It jangled every segment
of his being.)

Streamers of corruscating electricity covered the thing like
static hair, twisting and curling.

From the fused energy clouds, a single force seemed to
emerge, to separate itself from the others. The force slowly
grew the vaguest of facial outlines . . . then submerged back
into the raw energy.

The face suddenly registered on Amber, and he knew this
place had nothing to do with Heaven.

"You!" he would have said, if he had a mouth.

Cog said, "Detour time!"

Behind them, police lights flashed, sirens screamed.

Only kilometers to go to reach the Outer Nyark Spaceport,
and the law had sniffed their trail. By this time, Todd Spigot
felt distinctly ill. He almost longed for the comfort of his jail
cell.

"First, however," Cog continued, "a decoy." A hole opened
in his snout. A toy-sized helicopter zoomed ahead of them in
the traffic lane. "For all practical radar and sensor purposes,
that's us. Now, a simple blanking of our material and electronic
emissions and—"

The cleaning unit bounded higher into the air, then executed
a corkscrewed banking maneuver. On the horizon were the
lights of the spaceport, strung as though from a toppled Christmas tree.

"Wonderful. My mechanical preparations were well
worth—"

Todd finally managed to voice his difficulty. "Turn . . . *over!*"
He clung for all he was worth to the upside-down unit. Fortunately, he had hooked his knees firmly in place, or he would
have plunged through the roof of one of the apartment complexes a hundred meters below. Wind screamed in his ears as
Cog flipped over with deep apologies.

Feeling as though his heart were going to pop from his chest if it beat any harder, Todd clamped himself firmly into place again on the saddlelike arrangement. "Sure. Wonderful preparations for you. You forgot a seat belt for *me,* though."

Cog did not reply directly. "Hmm. Let me see. Night shuttle launch for intersect with the *Star Fall* at two A.M. It's now just a little before one A.M. According to my calculations, Maintenance Unit 432 should be on its way. I just have to locate access road F." Cog's mutter changed to a yelp of satisfaction. "There it is!"

The flying cleaning unit swooped into a copse of trees beside a well-kept macadam road. Cog settled into a clump of grass by a tree. Todd collapsed onto the springtime softness of the ground. "Of course, we haven't tickets. Mind-scans will find you out. If only I'd reached you sooner, it would have been so simple! Now if the entry computer gets a feel of your brain patterns and cross-indexes it with the law enforcement systems, red will be the predominant color on the light boards. They'll toss you back in the clink. So. I fortunately sucked out the necessary information to provide this upcoming ploy a decent success ratio."

"Good for you," Todd said, not even trying to show enthusiasm.

"Aha. Here it comes." Mechanical arms prodded Todd from his lethargy. "Up we go, my friend. Now, if you notice, there's a singleton floater headed this way. Flag it down. Tell the driver you've had a crash in this tree clump. Bring him over. That's all you have to do, Todd. I'll take care of the rest."

"I certainly *look* like I've been in a crash," Todd said, struggling up. He plodded to the roadside. An approaching headlight swept the curve. Todd waved. The floater, a single carrier model, pulled alongside, settling down gently on grav-pads. "What's up, fella? I gota shuttle to catch," a scruffy young man said, poking his head from a window.

"My car! Lost control!" He pointed toward the trees. "My pet orangutang! Oh God. Awful! Help!"

"Geez! I'll radio!"

"Later, please! We just have to push the—uhm—rear end of the car off its head."

In the dim light provided by the vehicle's control board, Todd saw a strange look flitter across the man's face at these words that Cog had instructed him to use. Almost mechanically, he opened the door, got out and followed Todd back to where Cog waited.

Strange paraphernalia had sprouted from the robot's sides. Lights spattered in variegated patterns.

Baffled, Todd watched as the technician approached Cog as though hypnotized.

"Hey! What's going on!" Todd said as the omnicleaner rolled his way.

Cog did not answer. An extensor snaked from his front; Todd felt the stinging airburst of a hypo inject into his leg.

He opened his mouth to complain, but his eyes closed into unconsciousness before he could say a thing.

Fill in the blank.

What is your name?
_____

One of those awakenings where she asked herself that—but couldn't produce an answer. She seemed newly hoisted from a muck of nothingness, of total disintegration. A dreamless quagmire, the protein soup of life from which this confused lungfish had just dragged herself, jumping billions of evolutionary years in an exhalation.

In perfect relaxation, ideal repose, she lay in the grass and wondered who she was, how she had gotten here, and if she really cared.

After all, the day was fine.

The sun shone golden in an eggshell-blue sky, sending an almost sytlized artist's sunshine cascading among the drifting cumuli. Shafts of the stuff formed awesome columns of light among shadow, as though holding up a long bank of clouds. Solid reflections of the clouds, green-clothed mountains rolled into the distance. Nearby, a fresh brook murmured and purled, glistening, over rocks which cut ripples through the flow. Birds trilled in the surrounding forest. A sweet tang of new-bloomed flowers hung in the air.

Something smelled good beside her. Hungry, she instinctively reached out and cropped a mouthful. Her tastebuds signaled satisfaction as she munched the grass.

Grass?

She spat.

Why would she chomp a bunch of grass? A shiver passed through her. Still . . . wasn't bad stuff, really. What had passed down her esophagus seemed to be well enough accepted by her stomach, which gurgled with satisfaction. Ultimately a practical person, Angharad bent her head back to her feeding.

After the third mouthful of the sweet-smelling stuff, mixed with a dandelion or two, she realized that planted firmly before her were a pair of black hooves.

Her hooves!

She realized that narrow legs thickly covered with brown hair rose up from the hooves. That directly in front of her shot forth a long brown snout, flaring nostrils at the end.

Her legs! *Her* snout!

She whickered with surprise. "What the hell?" Her voice was thick, slightly altered—but still held her familiar female emphasis and tone. Immediately she rose, feeling four legs leap to muscular obedience, pushing up a long torso. Startled, she swung her head around. A black stringy tail swished behind her, above genitals still female but decidedly changed from her previous set.

A kind of numbness set in for long moments. The world seemed to halt with her shock.

"Tracy Marshack," she said, out loud, dredging up the name from memory. "No. No, not anymore. I'm *Angharad*. Angharad *Shepherd,* and I've been changed into some kind of beast!"

Facts accepted, full memory flooded. The flash of the knife. The gleam of hypodermics. Light-streaked darkness, tubes and valves, the final shutter and now . . . Now *this*.

The insistent sounds of the stream prodded her back into the present. She glanced, saw that the coursing water provided a still, reedy pool, away from the bubbling current.

Unsteadily, she clopped to the brook, perched her hooves upon a mossy bank, stared into the reflecting surface.

Until now, her rigorous training had kept her emotions in check. However, one does not transform into a beast every day; she could not contain a whinny and a slight "hee haww," nor a subsequent intake of breathy sound when the image below acquainted her fully with her new form.

Sad, deep-brown eyes blinked back at Angharad Shepherd.

Eyes set on either side of an equine head with long, drooping ears. A donkey, then. She had been changed into a donkey . . . or her brain had been transplanted into a donkey. *(But how could that be? Incompatable blood-type, tissue, brain-pan size. Impossible!)*

This, peripheral to the true surprise.

Projecting from the crest of her head was a narrow conelike piece of bone, white as ivory, almost gleaming in the sunlight. Pointed, it whorled to its base in her skull like some fancy wickless dinner candle.

Disorientation dizzied as she whipped her head from the cool breath of the stream, as though to try to shake the sight from her mind. *Can't be,* she thought. *Uh-uh. Will not compute. A donkey with a unicorn's horn?*

This was something ripped from fantasy—not reality. The notion keyed in the possibility: *I'm in a real-fic. Somewhere my true body is harnessed to a Disbelief Suspender, making me believe that I'm an ass with a horn, standing bemused in the middle of gorgeous countryside.*

That didn't sound right, though. Disbelief Suspenders placed you in a different character. Angharad, however, retained her sense of identity, her memories . . . up to and including the attack in the neo-gothic hotel.

Loose ends in her comprehension knotted together. So. They had caught up with her, they had done something to her, they had placed her God-knew-where, God-knew-why.

Considering, she bent her head and drank from the pool.

Earnest Evers Hurt.

Instead of destroying her, they were using her in his plan. Exactly what that plan was she had never precisely known in full. But she had gleaned enough inklings enough evidence to trouble Central sufficiently to delay the departure of the space liner *Star Fall*. At first it had been a routine-enough investigation. Piece of cake, she'd originally thought when HQ had dished out the assignment.

INFILTRATE PRIVATE RESEARCH FACILITIES. EARNEST EVERS HURT, CHAIRMAN OF THE BOARD, HUMAN CONSCIOUSNESS CENTER, ARIZONA.

DOSSIER, EARNEST EVERS HURT.

"BORN" APRIL 15, 2299 A.D. TO HURT FAMILY. GENETIC CONTINUATION OF LINE (PERMISSION NUM-

BER: RW 94352), BRED FOR ASSUMPTION OF PATRIAR-
CHAL ROLE IN GALAXY WIDE HURT ENTERPRISES
(see attachment). HURT RESEARCH FOUNDATION, UN-
DER THE AEGIS OF EARNEST EVERS HURT, ESTAB-
LISHED BREAKTHROUGH LONGEVITY PROGRAM.

Which, in turn, allowed Hurt to live these 200-plus years,
accruing power like a collector obtains stamps. Hurt literally had
his fingers in every bubbling pot in the universe.

Longevity treatments, of course, had been around even before the Big Explosion of the middle 21st century had set
civilization back decades. However, they were extremely expensive, and only allowed the user to survive till about the age
of 160, at which point, despite even the late developments in
brain transferral to fresh bodies, the nerve and brain tissue
began to deteriorate beyond salvaging, resulting in effective
brain death as surely as if the blood or oxygen supply had been
cut. What Hurt's scientists had been able to accomplish was
the ability to regenerate the cellular structures of the brain.
Constant monitoring and treatment was necessary, at great ex-
pense, thus making it possible for only the richest to undergo
the process.

Earnest Evers Hurt apparently had contributed indirectly to
the funding of the *Star Fall* from the very inception of the
program. It was through his ministrations that a group of Morapns (not counting Ort Eath) had been persuaded to accompany
the ship on its strange and fateful maiden voyage. After the
political smoke had cleared away, Galactic Intelligence had
learned that Hurt had quietly acquired full rights to the *Star
Fall*. Hurt Starways Shipping now owned it lock, stock and
barrel, taking control from the interplanetary military system
devised after the seeming threat of the Morapn civilization had
first loomed over a century before. This was not considered
threatening. Although Hurt had a reputation for ruthlessness
in business and political matters and had been indirectly linked
to skulduggery and various revolutions on the colonies, his
activities had never been fully proved, and he was not an official
criminal.

Several factors, however, had alerted the Central Intelligence Network that something unusual might be transpiring.

For the past twenty years, Hurt had been deeply involved
in an almost religious—or at least mystical—extension of his

mind/brain researches. Before, the Human Consciousness Center had merely been regarded as a dying old man's eccentricity. The Zeitgeist encouraged a technological, deterministic view of the universe, and was not particularly fond of spiritual research. That had gone out with the occult. Besides, unlike most cults, the Human Consciousness Center kept to itself. They made no move to proselytize people, to convert or evangelize the universe with some new gospel. Apparently, from the various papers published by the Hurt Foundation concerning the Centers, all the Center did was to perform benevolent inquiries into the nature of human awareness.

Simple crackpot stuff, in the eyes of Central.

What alerted them to possibilities of suspicious discrepancies was the particularly secretive manner in which the Center handled its new guests. These were group of Morapns who had traveled on the *Star Fall* from their world light-years distant, at the last minute assisting in thwarting Ort Eth's machinations to destroy Earth and thus foster certain galactic war between the races.

Since she'd been so instrumental in uncovering the true nature of Ort Eath's activities, Central had assigned Angharad to become a research assistant and make sure everything was on the up and up. She'd been hired, complete with new identity, new qualifications and a new face. It had all seemed innocent enough on the surface. Her working companions all accepted their positions as regular, albeit, odd, computer-input technicians. They did a great deal of research and cross-referencing of strange, often arcane subjects.

Religion. Mysticism. Clairvoyance. Psychic phenomena. The occult. Philosophy.

All this was somehow linked up with the complex activities of Hurt's Mind/Brain Research Center.

Because Angharad had tested well on creative thought, she had been placed in the Personality Construct Department. For some reason, Hurt and his associates were taking the works and biographies of all the great thinkers of mankind, past and present, and creating possible schematics for their minds, structuring complex blueprints for individual indentity analogs.

A very strange sort of resurrection, lending verity to previous human notions to literary immortality in a totally unexpected manner. Certainly at first glance it was innocent. The personality matrices were encoded onto holographic crystals.

Connection to a full complementary computer system would result in a personality simulacrum of a particular man—Shakespeare, perhaps, or Meister Eckhart, or Galileo—with the gaps filled in either from imaginitive programming by the experts hired by the Consciousness Center, or by artificial intelligence subsystems. In action, these personalities were only copies and bore no self-awareness.

However, Angharad had thought, what if they were run through an augmented real-fic system, piggybacking a functioning, self-aware human brain—

She had snooped. She had correlated Hurt's activies there at the Center in Arizona with his work on the *Star Fall*.

Bonded by her knowledge of the implications of the *Star Fall's* real-fic systems, the two mixed like nitro and glycerin.

The Extra-Reality Fabrication.

I must be aboard the *Star Fall,* Angharad realized.

An overwhelming flood of indecision and anxiety swept her.

Do something, she told herself. *Walk. Eat grass. Anything, but don't let the shock take you over.*

She ran.

She splashed through the shallow brook, letting the cold water slap her underside bracingly, soaking her in chill sensation. She let the wind of her passage blow her shaggy mane behind her like a short flag. She immersed herself in the sensations of exercising her four muscular legs, her thick trunk, snorting furiously as she desperately cavorted.

Damn him, she thought, clutching on to her anger for sanity's sake. *Damn him for doing this to her.*

She could feel her horn cutting furiously through the air like a lance, and wished it were driving through Hurt.

Cresting a rise, she paused. She overlooked a green field, spotted with boulders. On the slope of a nearby mountain, a castle boldly raised towers and parapets toward a mild sky. Banners of various colors fluttered in the breeze.

However, of more immediate notice, below her, seated on a flat rock, wiping perspiration from his brow with a white linen handkerchief, was a strongly built, middle-aged man wearing spectacles.

Angharad clopped down to attempt communication.

At the sound of her hooves stamping the ground, her breath snorting, the man looked up, startled. Immediately, Angharad halted in her tracks to make sure the man didn't think she meant any harm. But his expression bore no fear, only surprise.

"Well, I'm glad I'm not the only being on this world," Angharad said, trying to get used to the new sound of her voice.

"Good lord," the man said. He took off his wire-rim spectacles, wiped them on his Swiss alpine shorts and excitedly fitted them back on nose and ears. "A donkey with a unicorn's horn!"

"Temporary condition. Hardly congenital. Besides," Angharad said, "I'd prefer to think of myself as a unicorn with a donkey's body."

"The donkey. The ass," the man muttered to himself, absently patting his pockets as though in search of a nonexistent pipe. "Combined with the unicorn. Fascinating juxtaposition of symbols."

"How so?" Angharad said curiously, approaching him.

"Hmm? Oh! Sorry." The man spoke standard archaic English spiced with a Middle European accent. "Just woke up here, and I spotted that castle, which I'm presently headed for. I immediately reckoned—American slang, you know; I like American slang—I immediately reckoned the meaning of this place when I saw that castle. Castles, of course, represent something that must be obtained. A spiritual testing. Perhaps it contains a treasure. I hope we'll get some kind of explanation for this new existence there. Perhaps *that's* the treasure."

"Symbols," Angharad said. "Of course. Rampant, active symbolism. A fabricated extra-reality of symbols. But *why?* I still don't understand that clearly."

"Yes," the man murmured, quite caught up in gazing at Angharad's present form. "The unicorn is a standard symbol of many cultures. It's the lunar principle, you know. Feminine. You're quicksilver in alchemy, you know." The man grinned. "I like alchemy."

"Go on," Angharad said.

"Yes, well, let me see if I can't remember. Unicorns—in the Western medieval mind anyway—stood for purity, perfect good, strength and chastity."

"Well, I can see now why I didn't make it all the way," Angharad mused wryly.

"A bit of a unicorn's horn is supposed to be an antidote to poison, since it represents Christ's salavation. The donkey, however, represents patience, humility and peace—but also stupidity."

"Makes sense. If I hadn't been so stupid, I wouldn't be here. Hurt's little joke."

"There's more. I can give you the Greek, Chinese, Hebrew, Babylonian and Inca versions—all curiously similar."

"I've got the gist. Do you work for Hurt or something?"

"I don't understand. Clearly I'm dreaming. There could be no other explanation. I'm working out my own Individuation in some sort of mystical representation of the Human Collective Unconscious!" the man said enthusiastically.

"I'm sorry, sir. I didn't catch your name. Mine's Angharad."

"My name," the man said, "is Jung. Dr. Carl Jung."

Angharad shook her big head and sighed. "I was *aFreud* of that."

Five

"Name?"

"Charles Harrington Haversham."

"Biocheck code and brainscan ID numberal readout?"

Charley Haversham rattled off the letters and numbers in mnemonic singsong. The security person played a concert of clicks on a sophisticated keyboard. This was the new kind of brainscan, Charley realized. A helmet wasn't necessary. They just focused a beam on your brain and zap! Instant identification verification.

On the slanted screen, colors swirled and swayed, eventually coalescing into an obscure language which the bored-looking man in the plaid jump suit noted briefly, then wiped.

"Yes, Mr. Haversham. We've been expecting you," one of the security men—chap with a bushy mustache and stooped shoulders—said. "You've cut it fine, though, I must say. Last shuttle, and you've barely made it in time."

"Yes, had a spot of trouble with my ground-effect car."

"Brainscan matches perfectly, Al," the security man at the computer console piped. He swiveled his chair to face the new arrival. "So. You're the new maintenance man for the *Star Fall*. Lucky dog. I put in for assignment on that boat myself. Ever been up there?"

"No. My first time."

"Pretty incredible stuff. Check out the Floating Gardens and the Waterless Ocean. Paradise. Oh." The man pointed down at the omnicleaner that had just thrummed up to Haversham's leg like some obedient dog. "What is that?"

"New model robocleaner. I designed it specially for heavy-duty repair work on the *Star Fall's* sewage system. I thought I had made the necessary preparations to allow it to accompany me on the shuttle. We're pals, you see." Haversham petted the unit. The robot squeaked as though with pleasure.

The two security men exchanged knowing glances.

"Just a minute. I'll check," Al said, examining his readout board. He pressed buttons. New information squiggled. "Well, my goodness. Right you are, Mr. Haversham. If you don't mind, we'll just have to a quick analysis of your—uhm—friend."

"Of course. But I don't want to keep the shuttle waiting."

"Just have to make sure you haven't got some antimatter, right Al?"

"We don't want another Ort Eath," the other returned.

"No," Charley Haversham said. "Of course we don't." That had been a rum business, he'd heard. He certainly hoped that the second voyage of the *Star Fall* would be nowhere near as eventful as the maiden voyage had been. No, all Charley Haversham wanted was to do his work and enjoy the cruise on his spare time.

Fidgeting a bit, Charley started to check his wristwatch.

Funny. Wasn't on his arm. He could have sworn he'd slipped it on before he left the Mune in Joisy. As far as he could tell, he had his bags and everything else. *You dufus,* he scolded himself. *Just goes to show. You always forget something.*

Still, he'd never forgotten his wristwatch before. And the amethyst ring that Debbie had given him last week! Gone too! Extreme annoyance passed through him, then suddenly it didn't bother him at all. Strange.

"No bombs," Al announced. "If you and your, uhm, pal will just pass along on up that ramp, you'll be seated and the robot situated for the shuttle flight up. Have a nice journey, Mr. Haversham."

The other security man grinned. "Yeah, you lucky bastard."

Charley Haversham hefted his luggage and began the climb up the ramp to the shuttle. The robocleaner scampered behind him, emitting squeaky code-pulses. "Okay," Charley said, *"you* carry the baggage." He set his handled pack down on the omnicleaner, which industriously buzzed up the slope. At the top, the robot deposited the luggage in the plainly marked bin, which promptly processed and swallowed the bag, excreting it no doubt in the shuttle's bowels.

A stewardess met Charley with a smile and conducted him to his seat. A robo-steward met the omnicleaner and deposited *it* in the specially prepared robot quarters. *A-Is are the niggers of the universe,* thought Charley Haversham, settling down. A pretty waitress promptly filled his drink order for a vodka tonic liberally sprinkled with a drug that would prevent antigrav sickness. He strapped himself into his plush seat, then peered about at the last shipment of passengers and crew heading up for the luxury cruise. Now that the *Star Fall* was privately owned, the fares had increased significantly. Charley had examined the fliers a dozen times, awed by the glossy pictures and dreamy descriptions of the experiences awaiting him.

That this voyage was a trumpeted Arts Cruise did not particularly interest him. Now that the *Star Fall* was pure high-class, its owner had apparently decided to go more for the fine-arts cultural audience, reasoning no doubt that the *Star Fall* should be some kind of floating, living museum, carting the best of human artistic achievement all over the galaxy.

Charley Haversham could care less. Charley was there for the ride past the planets in their stately dance about the sun. Charley was there to see the mind-blowing light shows of Underspace first hand. Charley wanted to taste the air of different planets, place his groundhog feet on soil forged by alien suns. Charley wanted to gawk at the aliens, light the trip fantastic with his enthusiastic eyes and have a walloping good time. Oh, sure, he'd have to work. More than usual, true. But what things he would learn! What glorious experiences he would have between the plumbing and mucking out.

Somewhat over two hours later (Charley couldn't tell—time had lost all meaning, what with the vodka and the wonder of viewing the Earth from space) the *Star Fall* hove into view, dazzlingly bright and majestic. Its reflective surfaces shone with the sun. Automatically, a filter flicked over the vu-plates.

The *Star Fall* had always looked to Charley Haversham like a hive built by technological bees zoned out on drugs. Its geometry seemed all wrong, out of kilter with how things were supposed to look. Nonetheless, it owned a weird splendor, an alien majesty that somehow fit Charley's concept of how things must be on different planets.

Different than I've ever imagined.

Billions of humans inhabited Earth. Occasionally some were siphoned to a new colony of planets, but those folks were given strictly third-class, almost blind passage. Few people ever got the opportunity to really experience the universe any way except second hand. Charley Haversham was getting that chance now, and he was thrilled.

With a gentle thunk and vague clang, the shuttle docked with an access port of the *Star Fall*. Passengers were hustled off. Only a few hours separated the *Star Fall* from its departure for its second voyage. Final preparations had to made; the hatches had to be battened down, Charley thought.

The technician found his luggage, breezed through a second security checkpoint, then rode a pneumatic car down to the maintenance department. He felt a little queasy, now, about to check into an unfamiliar work detail staffed by people he'd never met before.

The little car swooshed to a stop. The door popped open.

The maintenance level was like no janitors' quarters Charley Haversham had ever seen before. Plush carpet wall to wall. Attractive secretaries at the reception desk. Exotic flowers bloomed here and there, tastefully placed beside the equally colorful operation screens which charted the functions of the department, using detailed schematics of the *Star Fall*. Lights blipped dazzlingly.

Charley wandered, stunned, to the front desk.

"May I help you?" a pretty blonde in a spangled jump suit chirped. *I wouldn't mind jumping that suit,* Charley thought.

Absently, Charley produced his plastoid ID card. "I'm going to work here. Just got in on the last shuttle."

Crisply, the blonde slotted his card. The display screen wiggled, conjuring sudden letters and numbers. "Ah yes. Mr. Haversham. Welcome. You're expected. If you'll wait just one moment, I'll print our your lodging details and your work shifts."

Paper cranked from a nearby machine. The receptionist sleekly wheeled to another machine, where she manufactured a special key.

She returned with a mound of plastic veined with flashing lights. "This, Mr. Haversham, is your personally programmed magnetic key. Your compartment is in L Section, just down that corridor. It's good to have you with us."

"Oh. I almost forgot. My colleague, the omnicleaner mentioned on my papers. Where can I pick it up?"

The receptionist examined the readout board. "Section Z, Mr. Haversham."

Still riding the vodka-and-shuttle-grav high, Charley leaned casually on the desk. "Any chance of a lonely groundhog getting a personal guided tour?"

The receptionist smiled sweetly. "That's very nice, but the rule is, no intradepartmental intersexing."

"I never heard of *that* before. Who came up with that?"

"Our illustrious ruler, Earnest Evers Hurt. I almost forgot: Here's the rule book." She gave him a booklet.

"Who does this Hurt guy think he is, anyway—God?"

"I do believe he has aspirations, Mr. Haversham."

Todd Spigot woke up, facedown in the grass.

His head hurt. His body ached terribly.

A gentle spring night still filled the sky. Lifting himself, he called out, "Cog? Cog, where are you?"

No sign of an omnicleaner. No sign of a leg.

Crickets chirped in Todd's ear.

The shuttle! he thought. He was supposed to catch the shuttle. What time was it?

He glanced at his wrist. Luminous dials sparkled. Funny . . .

Two A.M.! Why that was about the time . . .

In the distance, a boom blasted, waving sound across the land.

Todd wheeled about. Riding a column of fire, a ship streaked rapidly into the night sky.

He'd missed the last shuttle to the *Star Fall*.

He moaned and staggered to the roadway, head pounding with it peculiar pain.

"Cog?" he moaned. "Cog, where *are* you? You can't just *leave* me!"

How long, how far he walked, he didn't know. A dazed confusion seemed to fill him. The next thing he knew, a floater cruised down, pulling beside him.

"You have an ID, mister?" a uniformed man demanded.

"Yes," Todd replied. "I have an idea. Take me home. I want to park myself before a three-dee unit, drink beer, go to sleep, and get up and work on my mining computer and—"

"Uh, pal. I mean identification."

Todd patted his pockets. An odd sensation of unfamiliarity with the placement passed over him. No, wait. Of course he didn't have an ID. He'd been wearing prison clothes.

"Sorry," he mumbled.

"Yeah, well, we're going to have to brain you and—"

"Police brutality!" Todd cried.

"No. We just gotta do a brain *scan,* mister. You know, check your Identity Pattern. We all got unique Identity Patterns, and they're all on file with Earth Central. You're on Classified Government Land without an ID, which gives us the right to 'brain' you. Okay, Howie. Hoist out the helmet."

Abruptly, Todd sat down in a miserable heap. "Don't bother," he said, hands to face. "My name is Todd Spigot. You're looking for me. You think I killed a shrink, and I escaped because you want to scrub my brain, and I *really* don't care now anyway, because I just want to forget I'm even *alive*—"

"Hey, fella. Take it easy. Nobody's going to hurt you." The policeman patted his shoulder. "You don't look like much of a killer to me. We'll just do a quick scan on you, confirm your story, then take you down to headquarters, where you can have a nice cup of kaff."

The officer helped him to the floater, where Howie fitted him with cap and wires. Buttons were pushed, switches nudged. Lights flashed, static hummed. "Yep," Howie said. "The scan matches up to *Spigot, Todd,* and we got an alert to pick him up."

"Well, at least I won't have to go back on the *Star Fall.* At least I'll never had to deal with that maniac leg again."

Their faces puzzled in the ghostly pink glow, the officers glanced at each other. Then the brainscan machine beeped frantically.

"Hey, Al," Howie said. "For the love of— Look at this!"

Todd turned away and slumped back into a seat.

Whatever it was, he didn't want to look.

Earnest Evers Hurt sat on the bridge, watching Operations smoothly under way. He sat quietly excited, in his private cubical with its unique atmosphere mix. The comfortable feeling of control coursed through his veins like effervescent adrenaline. *Finally,* the old man thought. *Finally, the true beginning of my life.*

A bell chimed softly from a panel. A pink light registered its presence in the dimness of the little room. A gentle warning. He was getting too excited.

Then the spell hit.

Disintegration. Crystalline consciousness, hard, brittle—cracked...shattered...pieces of alien planets...collected, fused...

Dizziness swarmed in his head. Disorientated, he groped for himself...

...Star Fall...Core...biobot...I am, I am, I am...

Hurt held tenaciously to his identity, like Jacob to the heels and robes of the departing angel, and he wrestled, he clung. Strange visions and alien emotions whirlpooled within him.

...I am...I am...earnestevershurt Earnest Evers Hurt...

He exhaled violently. He pushed his arm past the monitoring sensors, into the maintenance slot. Needles jumped, measuring. The computer considered the necessary biochemical noodling, the electical pulse necessary to return Hurt's neural system and brain to the homeostasis that allowed him to outlive his normal human lifespan.

With a soft buzz, the machine worked. He could feel the familiar spritzing of hypo-sprays, smell the increased air ionization as the machines adjusted his brain activity aura. At this stage of his plan, he could not afford the week-long hangover that the inebriation of enthusiasm would cause.

A blue light, a chime: signals for renewed equilibrium.

Hurt drew his arm from the machine, absently rubbing it as he leaned to his comm-unit, breathing easier. "Status report."

He had to get his mind on business. That had been a bad attack.

"Last shuttle docked, delivered passengers, departed," the Arachnid biobot, his personal liaison with Operations, said.

"Departure time from Earth orbit?"

"Undeviated from schedule," the biobot answered. "In all aspects.

"You have what you want then?" Hurt said.

A pause. "Yes. Sweetheart, old pal, snoogums, you were entirely right. My previous desires were too blunt, unsubtle.

I delight in the cavorting courses of your devious brain. I anticipate future events... greatly."

"That pleases me. Without your intrinsic cooperation, all my preparations and wishes would be for naught."

"Glad to be of help, chum. I'm in for the fun, you know." *And the revenge,* thought Hurt.

"We make a good team. How are things on the bridge?"

Hurt glanced casually at a screen. "Fine, dear fellow. By the way, I have cut all communications to and from the *Star Fall.*"

"Won't that cause suspicion? Inquiry?"

"You forget. I do not intend to return. The Fabrication is already in generation. Random signals may interfere. Can you erect some sort of blanking shield?"

"We'll have to pulse at least an explanation or they'll try to board. I'll come up with something. You'll have to let *that* out."

"I believe that can be arranged."

"Thou hast spoken, O master!" the Arachnid said mockingly. "I only obey. Over and out."

A smile played on Hurt's dark features.

Fortunate the thing was a touch mad.

Madness had its uses, no question. As he patiently watched the crew go about their business with their crisp bland uniforms, their short hair, their efficient motions, Hurt considered madness.

He was a little mad himself. Hurt realized that, used it. Though perhaps madness was the wrong term.

Obsessed.

Yes. Better. This obsession had motivated him, defined his existence for so many years, formed his present state, created the *now* of Earnest Evers Hurt.

He knew the terms for it. Curiosity. Egoism. Fanaticism. The Faust Complex. But he also knew that when his body needed food, that was called *hunger.* Knowing the term, knowing the biological reasons for the desire, did not dim the physical necessity one jot. The same was true with his mental urges.

Earnest Evers Hurt did not want to die.

He courted immortality.

Most humans, after discovering death and the personal possibilities, did one out of three things. They ignored it and went about their lives. They accepted it as their personal end and simply used it as a second margin to their existence. Or they latched on to some religious or philosophical discipline which promised personal survival after the heart stopped beating, the brain stopped functioning.

Not Hurt. He had no intention of going gently into that good night as Dylan Thomas had termed it.

He had been born into the Hurt empire, genetically manufactured by his father specifically to become the most powerful businessman in the known galaxy. Fashioned from the raw chromosomal material of Artemus Hurt, molded in a unique educational discipline devised by the old man himself, Earnest Evers Hurt had been drilled from his very conception in the art of power and control.

"It's simple," the old man had said. "If the people who know what to do don't take their God-given right and use it, it all falls into chaos. I made you, son, not merely to inherit the Hurt Empire. I made you to be a watchdog on Human Evolution."

At the age of twenty-five, Earnest Evers Hurt had rebelled. With pain, the recollections flickered back: the retreat to Sanctuary Planet. The airy beauty of that world, where all religions of the universe were allowed to set up outposts, not for missionary work but for simple contemplation. A lonely pilgrim, he had wandered that planet, half-expecting to be picked up forcibly by a team of his father's well-known hired hands. He'd straggled through the hundreds of different brands of Buddhism, of Shintoism, Taoism. He lingered in Christian and Moslem sects, spent a full year studying the intricacies of Hinduism. Finally, one day, in some nameless encampment of some nameless new branch of belief—confused and desolate, still not quite able to understand, feeling as though all he had learned had simply sifted out of his head, a messenger came bearing a letter with his father's archaic wax seal.

The letter read: COME HOME, MY BOY. THEY CAN'T KEEP ME GOING MUCH LONGER. The signature was even more of a scrawl than usual.

"I'm sorry, Father," he had said by the old man's bedside. "But I had to leave."

"I expected it," the old man said, voice weak even through a mechanical vocalizer. "You have to be your own man, Earnie. I didn't make you to be some sort of weak shadow of me. My whole life has been trading, politics, and business. It runs in your blood too, I know. Shit, you're even better than me. Meant it to be that way. When you see further, like you do, your range and sights get wider. You start thinkin' about other things. So, what bugga-bugga have you brought home with you, Earnie?"

"Just confusion, Father."

"Yeah, well let me tell you my simple philosophy on that. All this mumbo-jumbo about afterlife? Well, it's just wishful thinking."

"There should be a gentle surrender to whatever *is*, Father," Earnest had said, glibly mouthing a mishmash of what he had learned on Sanctuary.

The old man's eyes had started from their sockets. The life-support alarm rang. A nurse ran up to administer sedation. By sheer force of will, Artemus Hurt pushed him away and grabbed his son's collar. "I didn't raise you for *that*, Earnest. You're not just a collection of skin and bone and brain. You're not just my son, not just what people have defined you as. You're *you*, man! Whatever you do, you've got to *survive!* You've got to struggle to your dying minute. The creatures who went with the flow are still *fish*, Earnest. Human beings are survivors. You must survive and your race must survive, because it's a cold universe, Earnest, and it doesn't give a shit whether you burn with happiness and completion or you just rot."

Despite the doctors' predictions, the old man had lingered for another month, fighting for his life every inch of the way, staying lucid and conscious, telling his son and heir all his secrets, letting down all barriers. During that time it seemed that the man's fervid willpower seeped into Earnest's very sinews.

When the old man had gasped his last breath, Earnest was by his side, holding his hand. The grief had been heavy, for their bond had become great; nonetheless, Hurt came away with renewed purpose, feeling as though his father lived on in him.

Survive. You represent the human race. Survive, his father had said one day. *You may well be the key.*

Absently, in times like these, Earnest Evers Hurt wondered if perhaps, in a state of delirium, his father might not have had some kind of cosmic insight into his son's true destiny.

Anxious despite himself, Hurt watched the countdown to

blast-off from Earth's orbit. Below him, the crew busied themselves with their various tasks.

Something troubled him. Something vague gnawed in his mind, even though the proceedings had thus far been letter perfect.

Hang on, old man, his father seemed to whisper. *Hang on.*

Nonetheless, niggling doubts moiled inside his mind. He didn't feel himself at all. He felt as though some other hand than his were in control. Fate? Destiny? Yes, he told himself. That must be it.

Time passed. Departure moment came.

Earnest Evers Hurt watched as the planet Earth diminished in the vu-plates as his magnificent starship, the *Star Fall,* drifted into the Void.

Amen, he thought ironically.

So be it.

Six

The cabin was not exactly sumptuous.

A bed, a fridge, a three-dee set, a computer terminal, a chest of drawers.

Crestfallen, Charley Haversham threw his bag on the bed, which wobbled. *Big deal,* he thought. A hydro-mat. Fancy-sounding name for a waterbed. Shit, he was expecting an antigrav couch or something. He checked the bathroom. Functional. That was about it. They sure didn't spare the hired hands much luxury.

The omnicleaner shuffled in behind him. The door slid shut. The 'cleaner squatted by the desk.

Cripes, thought Haversham. *Not even a decent control desk.*

Thumping down on his bed, he checked his duty roster. He didn't have to report for eighteen hours. Great. Time for a shave and a bath, a quick tour around the ship, then some shut-eye.

He sighed, and a shiver hit him, a sudden feeling of home-sickness.

He was going to be on this starship for a *year*. The notion's excitement remained, but some of the reality crept in. He'd been a planet hugger all his life. Venturing into space was not as easy as he'd imagined.

Just glad to get away from Deadrock.

Funny. Where had that thought come from? What the hell was Deadrock?

Suddenly an ache grew in his head. Automatically, he went to the medicine dispenser in the toilet, hoping it could dope him out some pills or something. Probably came from the rocket journey. Extra gravities and all that. Though you'd think the null-gravs would—

Charley Haversham caught sight of himself in the mirror.

The familiar bright-eyed, friendly face surrounded by shaggy hair stared back at him and then suddenly—

. . . shifted . . .

To somebody else's face.

Huh? He blinked and looked again. No, everything looked all right now. What was wrong with him, anyway?

Maybe he'd better zip straight to the Med/Sec. Where was his bloody guide, anyway? He stumbled to the bed, fumbled in the bag for the booklet.

The omnicleaner belched.

Or made a funny noise that sounded like a belch, anyway. It jiggled, jerked, then the entire top popped open.

A bare foot lifted up, wiggling its toes.

"Blasted wire," a voice said. "Hey, Charley. You want to get me out of here?"

(Foot. Leg. He remembered now. Remembered finding that robot leg fooling around in the omnicleaner section. Remembered the little nozzle of the cannon, lifting . . .)

"Hey, who are you?"

"The question is, my friend, who are *you?* There we go. Bit of a snag. Rough connection, you know, but it did the trick."

On metal arms, the leg lifted itself from the wide canister.

"We made it."

"You still haven't answered my question."

The leg hopped to his side. "No need for any more questions, my friend. No need at all."

Without warning, some sort of webworking shot over Charley's head.

A light tracery of sparkles glittered over the net, soundless fireworks. Instinctively, Charley flinched—then suddenly the lights invaded his head, swarming in like maddened fireflies.

The sensation was not unpleasant. Merely disorienting. Flashes of strange visions assailed him, strobing an unfamiliar series of memories.

. . . *the carbolic smell of a jail cell* . . .

. . . *a breathless flight above the City* . . .

. . . *the jab of a hypodermic, a fall into the night-damp grass* . . .

All mixed with traceries of equally unfamiliar recollections, fading softly (*the perfume in Debbie's hair, the feel of floor wax on his hands, the thrum of maintenance machines*) disappearing like dreams shedding after a restless night.

After a spell of dizziness, a session of nothingness . . .

. . . he found himself lying, arms akimbo, on the bed. Motors whined, pushing oculars his way. A high voice said, "Well, I told you I'd get you on board the *Star Fall* some way, didn't I?"

Todd Spigot took in a sharp breath. He bolted upright, staring around him. "How the devil did I get here?" He swung to face Cog. "And you? The last thing I remember was luring that fellow into the copse of trees. What happened?"

Tiny arms displayed something that looked like a miniature pocket calculator. "Simply a matter of a small operation. An implant effected by these wonderfully deft digits of mine." The leg hopped up and down, giving itself over to a burst of Cremian joy. "It's very simple, Todd. For a while, for all practical purposes, you were a man named Charley Haversham. Conversely, Charley Haversham was you. Right now, in fact, the overlay is probably wearing off and poor Charley is waking up in a jail cell. I feel a bit guilty about that part of it, but it was the only way."

"Charley Haversham?" Todd said, a little frightened and bemused. "Overlay? What do you mean?"

"A network of artificial engrams. In anticipation of just such a need, I developed this method. You see, Todd, your surface identity—consciousness, or more exactly, your ego—is the result of biochemical formations and reactions holistically spread throughout your brain in the form of connected neurons. These processes give off unique impulses, which no one has yet has been able to change—like they can change fingerprints, say. But with my system, the device in your head is basically able to maintain the adjustments, chemical and electrical, in your identity system. Thus, you're still you. For example, even as 'Charley Haversham,' if you took a nap you'd dream normal Todd Spigot-type dreams. Call it an identity mask so effective that the wearer actually believes it's his real face." The leg hopped up to the bed and removed the net draped over Todd's head. "This cancels out the effects—or integrates them, as need may arise."

"You mean—if you do that again, then I'd *be* this fellow—"

"Charley Haversham? Yes. Have his personality, his mannerisms, his surface thought-patterns. It's your disguise. It's what got you past the ID check."

"What if something goes wrong, Cog? The two identities get mixed up. I won't know who the hell I am!"

"It won't work that way, I promise. The 'Haversham' Identity is on a different and opposite track—different polarity, shall we say. The human brain is a quite remarkable device—as is any brain of a sentient creature, material-based or not. I'm sure you've heard of cases in the history of human psychology of a person bearing two or more different personalities in one body. Well, I'm simply utilizing your brain's capability to do that."

"So now that I'm smuggled aboard, I'll have to answer to the name Charley Haversham, do his work . . . how am I supposed to accomplish *that*, Cog?" Todd shook his head wearily. "And I thought I was badly off before."

"Don't worry. I've programmed you to be capable of Haversham's essential duties. But believe me, you won't have to do them very long. What's going to happen on this cruise is imminent. In fact, according to certain of my more delicate sensors, it's already begun."

"What's begun, Cog? Are you going to tell me *why* you've dragged me back on board or not?"

"Todd, believe me, if I felt I could, I would."

"What? You don't trust me?"

"No, no. I trust you implicitly. It's just that I've thus far concealed my presence aboard the ship, and even if the owner knew I were here, he doesn't know I'm on to his activities. At the moment, things are in a delicate state, and I don't wish to burden you with the truth. Please, just go along with my instructions for a little while longer while I make a few surreptitious investigations in my disguise."

"In the meantime, what do *I* do?"

"I understand that this Earnest Evers Hurt chap has changed things around a bit. You can just tour, work, meet people. Enjoy yourself. I'll arrange regular rendevous times and points, fill you in on exactly what is happening and what you can do."

"No," Todd Spigot said. "I refuse." He grabbed the pillow on his bed and covered his ears. "I'm not even going to listen to you anymore. I just don't *care*."

"Todd!" the leg cried. "There are bigger stakes this time than last!"

Abruptly, Todd leaped up and grabbed the leg, shaking it till its optical units rattled. "Last time! *Last* time! And what happened afterwards? You deserted me, you little bastard!"

"Todd. I was busy! I got wind of what Hurt was up to! I had to investigate, make preparations. You'll understand once I fill you in."

Todd released the robotic leg and hrumphed back to the bed. "So tell me."

With a mechanical sigh, Cog said. "Okay. You wanna know, I'll tell you one thing. I was hoping to spare you for just a little longer, not burden your anxieties with further strain. But noooooo, you have to know. Todd, you remember our old pal Ort Eath, don't you?"

"Ort Eath? Of course. Killed himself. I saw it."

"Sorry. They never found Ort Eath's orgbox, did you know that?"

"My God, you mean?"

"You betcha...Ort Eath is still very much around. "Cog lowered his voice to a confidential whisper. *"Everywhere."*

Energies channel and coalesce, then dissipate. The ebb and flow of the Six quivers, taking random samplings of the sensory data available, then merge once more into unconsciousness, into dreams. These dreams are recorded, then stored in the vast appendix computer constructed by the Keeper.

The Sleeper lies uneasily, vaguely troubled by the energies draining into this construction vortex. Somewhere, relays click. Somewhere superconductors are employed, whirling back the dreams spinning, back the memories, again processing. Electricity courses through a particular matrix at a specific conjunction of nodes, lasers fire, and the scene erupts suddenly into the Sleeper's mind, vivid and keen as life with all its scope and depth:

Darkness has been disturbed. Silence is parted by a spark of life—

"...amazing," a voice says. "We'll have to do a detailed check. Most of the circuitry is beyond my ken. I'll just have to see if one of my Morapn guests can explain it to me. Hmm.

What's this? We're lighting up here. But *why?*"

Automatically, visual sensors switch on. The Core has been penetrated. In the moist dimness, in a strange life-support system, stands a man. Biologically sound but extremely aged. He carries with him an instrument slung over his belt.

By his side is a biological robot, part metal, part flesh, its appendages working nimbly over the Core circuitry. Blips and bleeps and flashes of light erupt. Vague sensations that might be termed pain fill the Sleeper.

"Ever encounter anything like this before, Unit Five?"

"Negative," the creature responds in a monotone. "Mr. Hurt. My electronic probes register a distinct reaction, not previously encountered in even advanced computers. According to my readings, this central system, linked to every other system, is meshed with five biological brains that are fused into one being, one consciousness."

"Brains? Are you sure? I mean, this could be part of the Morapn system originally installed," Hurt says, parting the shadows with his flash cube. "Fascinating. This could work out very well, ultimately. I thought it would take a least five years for interior-computer renovation. But if we've already got something unbelievably advanced, all we have to do is learn its use, tap into it, change it into the kind of programmable machine *we* want . . ."

Awareness fills the Sleeper. With awareness comes burning memories of searing defeat of one section. With an inner scream of agony, it thrashes.

What lights there are in the Core splatter into incandescences, then plunge everything into darkness. The interior quakes and spasms. Fires flare.

When things still, the human flicks his light cube back on.

"Careful, Unit Five. I do believe you might have drilled into a raw nerve or something." The man's previously calm voice is shaken. It reveals a peculiar kind of fear.

"Mr. Hurt, as I may remind you, I discouraged your descent here," the biobot unit says. "As one of your personal bodyguards, the state of your health and safety is of the utmost importance to me. I realize, sir, your excitement in the recent acquiring of this most original and interesting starship, but because of its alien qualities, it would be best, I think, if your servants and associates, such as myself, explore the vessel and its properties thoroughly before you survey it."

"Perhaps you are right, Five," Hurt says. "My enthusiasm outstripped my common sense. Let's go. You and your colleague may examine this room later. Is it my imagination or has the temperature risen in here? Radio up. Have the elevator—"

The Sleeper, fully awakening, lashes out.

A cable rips free from one of the coiled emplacements on the convoluted siding. With its spear-sharp head, it jabs into the biobot, sparking. The biobot spasms. Dark juices leak from its body as it tumbles to the mist-covered metal flooring of the room called the Core.

Before the man can react, the biobot struggles to its feet. A strange light glows in its numerous eyes.

"Who are you that disturbs my rest and brings me pain?"

Hurt turns to flee, then seems to get hold of himself. Pausing, he swivels back to address the possessed biobot.

"My name is Earnest Evers Hurt. I'm a wealthy and powerful human of the Earth Empire, but the only aspect of importance to you, whoever *you* might be, is that I am now entirely in legal possession of this starship. You must excuse me. I had no idea that the central *Star Fall* computer had been set up as a sentient. I assure you that I had no desire to disturb your—rest." The man shivers a bit in his specially fashioned LS suit.

"You fear death," the Sleeper says.

Hurt is quiet for a beat, then replies, "No. That is not quite true. I do not wish to die. But I do not *fear* death as such." The man clears his throat. "Now. You must tell me who *you* are."

The memories spew. The Sleeper cuts them off. "Suffice to say that I am part and parcel of this starship. Although you claim ownership, you cannot own me. I am altered from what I once was, in transformation and transition. I ask only to be allowed peace, rest. Do what you like in the way of operating this vessel, my body, as a cruiser of the starways. Do not trifle, however, with the internal systems or you will ignite my wrath. Now, leave me. After your departure, I will seal this chamber off thoroughly, as I should have done before..."

With an uncharacteristic burst of youthful enthusiasm, Hurt snaps his fingers. "Wait a moment. I remember now. Ort Eath! They never found that orgabox contraption that walked around with him. And there were those missing scientists and scholars. You're no artificial intelligence, no product of Morapn or human technology. Are you? Let me guess. According to the people who foiled the plans of Ort Eath to destroy Earth—"

Another tremor shakes the room. The spill of illumination from Hurt's light cube quivers over the biobot. But Hurt persists.

"From the reports I was able to obtain, the creature called Ort Eath was actually a genetic amalgam of Morapn and human. Thwarted, by a few people, he self-destructed. Their names, as I recall, were Todd Spigot..."

The biobot advances, its front, pincer legs raising.

"...Philip Amber..."

"...Cease! Their names cause me displeasure."

"And Angharad Shepherd, whom you may remember as Tracy Marshack...your sibling..."

The groping hands grab hold of the material of Hurt's LS suit. It rips. Hurt remains calm, playing out his hand.

"Ort Eath. They never found that orgabox because *you* controlled it, didn't you, Eath?"

The biobot pushed Hurt down.

"Do not use that *name!*"

"You had your brain transplanted from your body into that orgabox, along with the other brains you controlled."

"You have have given us grief and pain, Earnest Evers Hurt," the Sleeper says through the biobot's voice. "That cannot be forgiven." Claws raise.

"Wait!" Hurt says. "We must talk...!"

Weary, the Sleeper ended the replay, remembering the rest, still intrigued, still cooperating and absorbing the results...but confused, disoriented. Aspects of its mind were mysterious shadows performing strange, incomprehensible activities. There had been the Invasion of the Biobot, the Possession and Absorption...or was that simply the Sleeper's imagination?

It was so confused, so disoriented, sometimes many, sometimes one. At moments of waking like this, its Mind seemed to fragment...teeter over the precipice of insanity. Pulled in many directions, its Mind was a moil of stray, disconnected thoughts.

The Sleeper made a cursory inspection of its body, the *Star Fall*. Everything was in optimum repair, good working order, except...

A stab of pain struck. Confusion and despair and disorientation conflict among the unintergrated aspects of its Selves, caused it irritation tantamount to agony.

Portions of itself rebelled...

The time of Gestation was not yet over.

The merging was not yet complete, the Healing not over.

The Dark Section of its Being still operated most of its consciousness, even now pushing the Over-Consciousness back down toward slumber. The Dark Section, mental hands outstretched, hampered within the Core, but able to puppeteer its Manifestations, able to operate its designs, to gain revenge that was the Sleeper's revenge as well... and yet not.

Only half-interested, the Sleeper allowed a message to shoot to another aspect of its Mind. "How fares your operation?"

The Arachnid became uncomfortable, aware of its Selfhood's awakened state.

"The Scope of our purpose is materializing well."

"We suffer. We are not yet whole."

"I work toward that end. You will see."

"We despise you."

Laughter. "But I *am* you. You despise yourself. Perhaps that is the origin of our pain. Yes, I feel it too. Why should we war so, Sleeper?"

"You are the Shadow. Conflict is necessary toward intergration, Individuation."

"Go back to sleep and leave me be."

"How fares the Fabricated Reality?"

"Merely in formation presently. Only a few minds have been linked. The computer is presently constructed the landscape from the augmented fabric of ourselves."

"What of the Four?"

"Todd Spigot and the creature known as Cogito Ergo Sum are on board, believing their own presence to be undetected."

"Amber? Angharad Shepherd?"

"Their brains are in preservation tanks, linked into the Fabrication."

"We are dubious...indecisive...we have much more to absorb. We grow weary, fretful. We must rest. Sleep."

"We work for our full awakening," the Shadow says. "Rest now then. Sleep."

The Sleeper allows itself to drift back into slumber, softly setting into dreams that were the awakenings of others...

Seven

"Persona. Animus. Anima. Shadow, and Self," the man who claimed to be Carl Jung recited as he marched along beside the unicorn. "Are you familiar with the structure of my theories?"

"I don't think I'd pass any kind of test, if that's what you mean," Angharad Shepherd said distractedly, her attention focused on the castle toward which they headed.

Bright spires glittered in the rays from a sun that might have looked more at home in a painting than in a sky. The structure possessed all the accoutrements of fantasy castles, from drawbridge to moat to barbican. Angharad felt oddly moved by the sight, moved and excited. The air that stroked her hide was brisk and invigorating. The smell that emanated from the heather and honeysuckle on the mountainside touched her nostrils, lending her a sensation of giddy aliveness. Her hooves felt light, her soul buoyant, charged with a sense not merely of well-being and belonging, but purpose. Her tail swayed. Her ears twitched as she listened to the computer mockup of the famous psychologist babbling by her side.

"Actually, it's quite complex."

"I dare say."

"Each individual has many facets. Just as he or she is born with arms and legs and eyes, so each human being also has a certain mind makeup which I separated—for easy understanding—into the ego, the personal unconscious, and the Collective Unconscious. The ego is the filter through which the person maintains continuity of consciousness. The personal unconscious is the storehouse of the complexes one develops through life, as well as the underpinnings of the individual."

"And this Collective Unconscious you mention, which you feel has projected itself into this impression you presently have of reality . . ."

"Yes, well, during my lifetime I accrued an incredible array of evidence as to the workings of this function of the individual. It *does* exist, although now I am persuaded that I took the wrong approach to proving how it could be passed from generation to generation."

"You'll have to start at the beginning for me."

"Of course. Essentially, my theories state the goal of each individual is to become a fully human being. By this I mean fully in contact with the unconscious aspects of themselves, fully availing themselves of their potentialities, their talents. Aware that they are not just an ego, a piece of flotsam on the tide of time, but a functional Self that is part of the process of human evolution and yet a unique being in their own right. This individual ideally would be in synchronization with the ebbs and flows of life, a full participant in its roles, and yet aware of the overview. This process I call Individuation. Very few people have attained this state. Most of the great religious leaders—including Christ and Buddha among others—are individuated people. It is quite easy to equate their teachings with my theories. The realizations one reaches about life might be termed religious experiences. Conversely, religious experiences, although my view is simply a scientific explanation of what I perceive as a human process and has no affiliation with any deity, are the steps toward an adjusted, well-rounded human being, contributing to the well-being of others."

"Who then passes on to nothingness?" Angharad said.

"That was not for me to decide, although as I mentioned before, my personal beliefs did not extend to an afterlife, though how can I explain all this?" He held his arms up expansively. "No. That is for further discovery and inquiry. Now, if the ego is the organizational part of the Self, the device of awareness, then the unconscious is the storehouse, the —"

"Programming?" Angharad ventured.

"I am not familiar with the term, though I believe I understand it. If the personal aspect of the unconscious is the result of the individual's direct experiences, his learning from his days in the womb until his death, then the Collective Unconscious is the psychic material with which he was born."

"Or perhaps implanted through language, culture—"

"Yes, of course, but there are certain ideas and images that surmount language and can be seen in all cultures. I call these *primordial images*. Directly inherited through human evolution."

"Sort of like psychic genetics, eh?"

"Perhaps, perhaps. The purpose of life is to grow into what it is meant to be. Each individual contains the code physically in their chromosomes, mentally in the segment of themselves that carries their view into the Collective Unconscious."

"You were going to finish explaining that. The more you speak, the more it ties in with what *I* know about this environment."

They forded a shallow stream, Jung remarking on how vivid the sensations of the cold water were on his feet.

"Archetypes," the man pronounced as they gained dry land once more and ventured up the hill toward the castle. "Principally visual and metaphorical. Symbols of birth, life and death. Representation of energy, the child, the man, the woman, God and the array of human experience . . . the Earth, the moon, mother, father, animals. Oh, the list is endless. These are not images exactly printed in the mind, but images which appeal to *predispositions* in the mind, much as say a certain vitamin fits in with a need in human biochemistry and therefore must be taken."

"Ah ha. I see. And these are used in pictures of cultures, songs, myths . . . and you see this particular world we're walking in now as a physical representation of the Collective Unconscious."

"Surely. Why else would I be talking to a combination of a mule and a unicorn as we head for a castle ripped straight from a fairy tale?"

"Good point." Strangely, Angharad had become so accustomed to the unicorn body that she had forgotten how odd it was.

"Those terms you mentioned before . . . persona, shadow . . ."

"Oh yes. Terms for specific archetypes that are parts of the personality." He took off his spectacles, cleaned them with his shirt, then put them back on. "The *persona* is the role we assume when dealing with other people or different situations. That's the outward face of the individual. The inward face includes, in females, the *animus,* in males the *anima.* The *animus* is the male aspect of females, the *anima* the female tendencies of men."

"I'm somewhat acquainted with that aspect of psychology, yes," Angharad admitted.

"Then there is the *shadow*, which might be best characterized as the portion of the personality that contains the animal instincts and energies of the person. Should this be too much in control, evil results. But if it is in the proper balance, the individual is full of life."

"The last one you mentioned. The Self. I'm most interested in that."

"Yes. This is the goal of all human beings: true knowledge of the Self. The combination of all their qualities and aspects into who they truly are. When knowledge of this Self is achieved, one becomes harmonized with one's environment, one's fellows—one achieves what might be termed happiness." Jung shook his finger pedantically. "Now, the curious thing about this world here is that it seems dreamlike, a fantasy existence. Using symbols, a person's dreams show him the way toward Individuation."

Jung looked up. "Ah. We are almost there." He speeded up with excitement, not giving Angharad a chance to explain to him that he really wasn't Carl Jung, that somewhere aboard the *Star Fall* a man wore a set of Disbelief Suspenders attached to a personality crystal, much like one of the things she'd programmed back in Arizona. Still, this fellow could be very valuable in explaining how this world worked, what its events meant—

The drawbridge was down, the gate open. They passed through the unguarded barbican, clopped over the stream which served as a moat, and walked into a wide courtyard.

This courtyard bore no evidence of human habitation, although it was clean, the lawn neat, bordered with flowers.

Set in the middle of a stone wall was a wooden door, bearing a ring handle.

"You said something about a treasure," Angharad commented. "Shall we enter and see what awaits us? We might get a further clue as to the nature of this world."

"I'm willing," said the Jung-simulacrum.

"Although I suppose I could do it with my teeth," Angharad said, "I suspect it would be easier for you to open the door with your hands."

"Oh yes, of course." The fabricated body of the Swiss psy-

chologist strode forward. Placed hands on door handle.
Tugged.

The door would not open.

"Perhaps there's another way," Angharad suggested.

"No. No, I am not exerting sufficient force. I detect *some*
movement, I think. Let me try again." Repositioning his feet,
Jung again attempted to pull open the portal.

This time it creaked sufficiently ajar for the psychologist
to interpose his body between frame and door and push. He
pushed it far enough open to allow them both entrance.

"There," Jung said, puffing with exertion. "I say, if indeed
this body is only an illusion, as you seem to feel, it's an awfully
real one. I—"

Suddenly a clawed paw reached from the darkness behind
the Doctor and pulled him in. A roar combined with the
Doctor's scream. Thrashing echoed through the chamber.

Unusual panic took hold of Angharad. She managed to
prevent herself from turning tail and loping from the courtyard,
away from the castle. Instead, she galloped through the door,
hoping to do what she could to aid her companion.

The hall she entered was still save for harsh bestial breathing. Torches in sconces, and candles on a large altar guttered
in the breeze admitted by the opened door. Standing in the
middle of the room was a large male lion with a magnificent
black mane, perched over the disheveled and bleeding body
of Doctor Jung. The lion roared, fangs glinting in the dim light,
tail switching along the dusty floor. Muscles rolled beneath its
tawny hide.

The Doctor's broken spectacles tumbled from their precarious placement on the bridge of his nose.

"Lion," Jung droned. "Judeo-Christian symbol for mascu-
line power, majesty, strength; but also ferocity, cruelty, war.
The unicorn and the lion represent contending solar-lunar,
male-female forces. It is often depicted as guardian of doors,
alas." His head tilted, his eyes closed.

Angharad snorted, involuntarily emitting a "hee-haw!" Her
hooves clicked as she retreated a pace. "You've killed him!
The Fabrication must be incredibly intricate for that." Her voice
was a horrified whisper.

"I am the Guardian of Way Castle," the lion announced.
"You were uninvited intruders. This is not meet and fit in the

Plan. Prepare to die, animal." The voice was half animal growl, half human. The human aspect sounded awfully familiar. The beast, snarling, took a step toward Angharad.

"What do you guard, Lion?" the donkey-unicorn asked, unmoving. "What is so precious that you would kill for it?"

The lion stopped in its tracks. "Kill? Oh my God. *Kill?* I really don't know."

Something flickered behind the beast. Sparks glittered around the form of the fallen psychologist. Energy hummed. For just a few seconds, Angharad saw the man's form as a two-dimensional black-and-white computer construction of tiny dots. Then it faded from existence. The lion seemed to take note of this occurrence. As it turned around, Angharad noted a look of sadness and confusion that she had noted in someone else's eyes—human eyes—sometime before.

"Amber!" she cried. "Philip Amber!"

"That name," the beast said. "Why does it trouble me so?"

"Because it's your name, you dope! You're Philip Amber. Hurt has got you meshed in this Reality Fabrication as well. Clearly we were supposed to meet. But why?"

The great beast shook its head, confused. "I have intimations of other lives, other times. Who are you, ugly unicorn?"

"Angharad Shepherd, you great dolt. Look. Just close your eyes, try to disconnect yourself from all of this. Pretend you're just floating in a sensory deprivation tank or something. It's going to be disorienting for a time, but I'll guide you through it. Just listen to my voice."

"Angharad Shepherd," the lion repeated the name. "Yes, that is familiar. I remember... *Star Fall*. MacGuffin. Todd Spigot... My God, Ort Eath!" The leonine eyes blinked. A whimper escaped his lips. "I saw him... *felt* him."

"You just flashed back to a year ago."

"A year ago," the lion murmured. "Yes, yes. It's all coming back to me now." The creature's whiskers quivered as it shook its head. "No. No, it wasn't a year ago that I felt Ort Eath. It was recently... in limbo."

"Limbo?"

"Yes. I woke... thought I was in Heaven. Saw him."

"Heaven, huh? That's right, Amber. I heard you donned sackcloth and ashes and joined a convent."

"A monastic order," Amber corrected. "I still was choked

with guilt." The beast's golden eyes grew distant with thought.

"What was the last thing you remember of Earth, Brother Philip?"

"I recall some creature, coming for me. I thought it was an hallucination. I was on acid at the time."

"What an interesting religious order," the unicorn commented dryly.

"No. Just an experiment, you understand. No, this thing looked like a giant robot spider or something. I remember . . . I remember it *shot* me." The lion shivered with the thought. Then he gazed up at the donkey-unicorn. "My goodness, don't *you* look ridiculous, Angharad. How did *you* get here? Where *is* this place?"

"A long story, Philip," she returned. "Right now I think some of the answers can be found in this castle. Just exactly what were you supposed to be guarding, anyway?"

Amber shrugged. "I truly don't know. I was just fed regularly and evidently imprinted with the instructions not to allow anyone through that chained door yonder."

Angharad walked over to the indicated double door, festooned with link chains centered by a huge old-fashioned padlock.

"I don't suppose you have a key, do you?"

"Yes. I believe it's underneath the altar." Enthusiastically, Amber in his lion form pounded to the wooden structure at the far end of the chamber. With some reverence, he pushed it over easily and picked something up with his teeth.

"Here you go," Amber mumbled, the key bobbing as he spoke.

"Don't give it to me," Angharad said. "I think that paws are a little easier to manipulate than these clumsy things." She held up a hoof.

"Ooops. Sorry. Of course. Let me see what I can do." Amber jumped up to the door and tried to insert one end of the key into the proper hole. After several false moves, the metal slid in, clicked the lock open. Angharad helped to clear away the clanking chains as best she could. With some difficulty, they managed to push back one wing of the double doors.

The antechamber they entered was small. Their entrance puffed up dust which clogged Angharad's nostrils, making her sneeze. The room smelled of old manuscripts and general antiquity. From a small window a sunbeam speared down to illuminate a podium upon which a rolled-up scroll rested.

The room held no other significant objects.

"That must be what we're looking for," Amber said. He hopped up onto the dais and carefully stood on his hind feet, balancing himself on the podium. Flicking a faded green ribbon off the scroll, he carefully unrolled it.

"Here you go, Angharad. What do you make of this?"

The donkey-unicorn stuck her nose over the single curled sheet of parchment. At the top of the paper, lettered in gothic-style English, were the words:

INGENIOUS MS. SHEPHERD, STALWART MR. AMBER.

WELCOME TO THE LAND OF MYTH AND SYMBOL.

YOUR ASSIGNMENT, SHOULD YOU CARE TO ACCEPT IT,

IS TO SEEK THE HOLY GRAIL.

Beneath the lettering was a map.

Eight

A red light zapped across the screen's periphery.

Purple letters to one side flashed a single word:
EMERGENCY.

A single drop of perspiration slipped down Todd Spigot's brow.

Here he was, second day on the job, and he had a problem on his hands. He didn't know a thing about operating a maintenance sweep computer. Oh, sure, he could do basic stuff. That much he knew from his experience with basic econ-comps and accounter models, like he'd used back on Deadrock. This knowledge, plus what he'd learned on Earth, had thus far carried him along in Charley Haversham's chores. Press a few buttons, twist a few dials: that was all it had been.

STOPPAGE, the screen spelled out quickly. SECTOR A, Z PIPE. COORDINATES, X27, Y84, Z97.

Hands shaking a bit, Todd swiveled his chair to see if any of the other operators might be tackling this problem. The only other maintenance attendant snored on his console. The others were off in a corner, playing cards. Blithely, they all ignored him, emergency or no emergency.

Clearly, this was the sort of difficulty that came up every day, and could be dealt with by a single person. Today it was "Charley Haversham."

A.K.A. Todd Spigot.

There was a sewage blockage and Todd had to deal with it without Roto-Rooter. He took a deep breath. Exhaled. What had Cog said to do?

Relax. Remember when you were in the MacGuffin and I had control? Just pretend your body is a MacGuffin, and hand over the wheel. The residual personality matrix of Charley Haversham is programmed into your brain in such a fashion that his training has been placed to the forefront of your au-

tomatic responses. Like riding a bike, without personally having taken the falls.

Right. Nothing to do but give it a try.

Todd Spigot rested his hand in front of him, exhaled . . .
. . . and let go.

His hands lifted. His fingers rapidly typed things into the computer console. Complex equations registered across the screen. Specialized machines were engaged. Pressures redistributed in the pipes. The tricky gravity problems that had been snarled were quickly solved.

The EMERGENCY light snapped off, replaced by a glowing blue signal of mechanical relief.

Todd blinked. *My goodness,* he thought. *Cog was right* . . .though he didn't like to think of himself as a good laxative.

Also, Todd didn't like having another personality riding around inside him, however dormant; not after his consternating experiences with Philip Amber's MacGuffin Mark XII, which had gotten him into trouble to begin with.

Todd Spigot sighed and sipped his cup of genuine coffee, savoring it even though it had long since gone cold, since he was used to the synthetic sort. Kaff. His mother used to serve him kaff. "Don't drink too much, Todd," she would say, dumping steaming water onto the brown pellet at the bottom of his cup. "Even though I get the low-caffeine type for you, sweetheart, it still packs a wallop."

His mother. A warped person. Yet, at her core, Todd had come to realize, there was something like love, however possessively expressed.

Everyone else had just used him. Even now he was being used. Exactly how he wasn't sure, but there was no doubt about the fact that, again, he was just some pawn in the game Cog played, however big, however important.

Todd Spigot watched the computer screen's numerals and letters exercise their gymnastics, hop their pogo dances through the quirky trails and tunnels of the *Star Fall's* corridors and water and sewage pipes. Apparently, Charley Haversham had received a crash course in the tricky business of overseeing maintenance operations on this star liner. The *Star Fall* was essentially a cluster of interconnected environments—worlds, rather—in a complex arrangement of null-gravs and odd interface systems. When he had designed this boat, Ort Eath (bless his burned-out brain) had gone in big for spectacular effects and had left the plumbing and cleaning arrangements to lesser minds. Biospheres abounded, containing water worlds, deserts, lush forests and gardens, earthly paradises and alien hells. Unbelievable beauty in wide varieties were found in these habitats—but the cost had been an awkward and complicated system for maintaining homeostasis within each section and harmony between them all.

Hence the numerous computer screens here in maintenance engineering, the large number of cleaning and servicing robots. If things went wrong, there would be serious consequences for the *Star Fall*. Apparently, Todd had quickly learned from various personnel in the section, Earnest Evers Hurt had been more interested in tacking on additional computer hardware and software than in refurbishing the clumsy plumbing and cleaning systems. In fact, the rumor was that he'd cleaned out the entire Aslasi world section, native alien creatures and all, to fill it entirely with the most modern cybernetic equipment available. Exactly why, no one really knew, though rumors abounded.

A crew-cut young man tapped Todd on the shoulder. "Hey, Haversham. I'm ducking out of the game. Wanna take my place?" Todd recognized the man as one Ab Snorz.

Todd shook his head. Hard to get used to being called Haversham. "No. I'd better stick this out. Just had a block-up."

"Damn! Really? Where?" Snorz said. He was second-in-command of the section.

Remembering the recall button, Todd touched it. The screen built a color-coded schematic of the *Star Fall*. Quickly, the focus centered on the necessary section. Flowing dots of magenta, pearl and blue representing respectively Sewage, Water and Atmosphere shunted smoothly within the highly detailed representation. Todd checked the coordinates and pushed a finger toward where the blockage occurred.

"Holy cow. Again!" Snorz squinted closer.

"You often have problems in that sector?"

"Yeah. Right near the center of the ship, too. The Core. You say you had no problem clearing it up?"

"Uhmm . . . No. Once I figured out what to do." Or rather, Todd thought, once Charley Haversham's skill automatically came into play.

"You're pretty good, pal. I was stuck in the hot seat with that sector just a couple days ago, and it took me ten minutes to equalize pressure, get the chemical busters spraying, call in the right machines. And I'm no slouch at this business, believe me." Staring at the cross-section of the area, Ab Snorz shook his head. "Wish I could get some mechanics in there and fix that place up."

"Why can't you?"

"Gonna have to report this," Snorz said, leaning over the keyboard, tapping out the code for memory photostats of the condition. "Maybe *this* will convince the high mucky-mucks to let me and the crew down there."

"Off-limits?"

"Hmm? Oh, yeah. Sorry. The boss—old Earnie, you know—had the whole thing sealed up. Far as I can tell, it's just another section of computer memory storage. Damnable thing is that the pipes and valves and stuff in the older sections of the ship have got to be repaired or replaced regularly. God knows when the thing's going to spring a leak or bust, and then we'll have a real mopping-up to do, and get blamed too, most like."

With a whirring sound, two color copies of the picture on the screen slipped from a slot on the side of the machine's cabinet. Snorz ripped them off along perforated lines, separated one, and slapped it down in front of Spigot.

"Here you go. A memento of the day's activities. Frame it or something." Todd stared down, recognizing a frozen replica of the situation that had caused the emergency lights to flash.

"Uhm, thanks," he mumbled as Snorz hustled away, copy in hand. He picked up the sheet of paper and was about to chuck it into the trash when he reconsidered. A memento, Snorz had said. Not a bad idea, really. Todd folded the paper several times, then tucked it into the back pocket of his tan coveralls. Maybe Cog would be able to explain it to him. Maybe he'd actually come to understand exactly what he was doing here in front of this computer console.

The rest of the shift passed uneventfully. As Norald Marmles took his place, he said, "Hey, Haversham. Going to catch the Insertion into Underspace tonight?"

"I didn't realize that we were past Pluto yet, out of Sol's gravity well," Todd said, getting up and allowing the older man to slide into the chair.

"We're not. We've shot out of the ecliptic. New development in the Mattin Drive. Can deal with higher-gravity areas. Apparently old Hurt is hot to get under way."

"Sounds worthwhile," Todd said, noncommitally.

"See you there, then. Bring a girl. It's very romantic. Gets the hormones shuffling, don't you know."

A girl. Not likely, Todd thought, punching his exit code into the work machine. He just didn't get along with women from Earth. From anywhere. Angharad had been a fluke. She really didn't count.

Besides, she'd just been using their romance for her own purposes. To say nothing of the fact that most of it had taken place utilizing the superior male characteristics and virility of Philip Amber's MacGuffin.

Images, physical sensations, scenes flowed back through Todd, haunting him. Funny stuff, love, he thought. Joyous and carefree in its career, full of all the electricity the songs celebrate; afterward, in its absence, a hollow ache resides. Todd's innocence and naiveté had been drained away with Angharad, and he had not been sorry to see them go. But what would take their place?

Angharad. Who was probably dead now. These feelings were so lingering, so ambiguous . . .

Without much success, he tried to shrug off the melancholy as he walked to his cabin. He was back on a pleasure cruise. *Star Fall.* The fun ship. His shift of responsibility had ended for the day. He had hours to while away as he chose.

Gritting his teeth as he placed his personal magnetic key to the door, Todd determined that he'd spend the rest of the day having a bloody good time.

Waiting for him on his bed was a note from Cog.

URGENT. MEET ME AT THE STAR BAR, SECTION H, AT SHIP'S MIDNIGHT.

What was the little bastard up to now, anyway? He'd slipped back into his omnicleaner and claimed to be using that guise to explore the ship.

Todd wondered what he was looking for.

He crumpled the note, tossed it in a disposal unit.

God knew what to expect at midnight, but that was a long time away. It was only 2:15 in the afternoon.

Todd took off his coveralls. He let the molecular shower in the toilet compartment sluice away whatever grime had accumulated during the day, and let its zinging sensation buoy his spirits. With his laser shaver, he mowed his stubble away, and afterward applied bracing pheronome-full ointment. Freshly pressed pants assumed, he shrugged on a psuedo-silk white shirt and a mod set of farce-tux/tails which he'd bought in the ship's department store. Brightly polished black shoes were next. He could look down and see his reflection in their gleaming tips.

He stuck the floss-brush machine into his mouth for a full minute. He adjusted the hair-style machine to Perm and fitted it to his skull. He trimmed his nails in the appropriate device, feeling pressure, heat and curling activating over his scalp.

When all his preparations were complete, he had to admit that he didn't look bad. He felt much better now. *Much* better.

Last amenities taken care of, he examined the roster of activities available for the day by flicking on the screen of the cabin computer.

The feature program appeared to be the opening of the art display. How different the array of entertainment was on this cruise! Before, Ort Eath had merely allowed his associates to develop wide-appeal entertainment systems. This cruise, however, seemed to specialize in cultural achievements.

Instead of a showboat, the *Star Fall* had been refurbished into a culture ship, bearing not only artifacts of human and alien creativity in the arts and sciences, but actual living artists and scientists pried from their jobs by the romance of an interstellar cruise—and a healthy stipend from the coffers of Earnest Evers Hurt's plentitude.

A celebration of the Universe the journey was called. Todd had seen ads for it on the news-fax and sandwiched between Fic-Kicks shows. There had been a brief scandal concerning the recruitment, in fact. Certain wealthy individuals who wished to board the *Star Fall* for its interstellar trek were turned away while others, with every little to offer in the way of cash or credit but much in IQ or Creativity Gradient, were gifted with tickets. Mysteriously, their passports and other legal arrangements for the trips were expedited.

HURT'S EGGHEAD BOAT mastheads had trumpeted. THE HIP TRIP: NORMAL CITIZENS SCORNED, IQ DISCRIMINATION! Suits were filed. However, since the vessel was, after all, a private enterprise, legal machinations availed undesirables naught. The rule was hard and fast. A battery of tests had to be be taken before admission was acquired. Flunk the test? No *Star Fall* cruise.

Sorry.

The sleazier tabloid beamers had run a story to the effect that Hurt was recruiting not merely the intellectual and creative cream of Earth, but also the screwball pyschics, yogis, Zen masters and shamans, to say nothing of emotionally malformed espers. Investigations in this matter by the authorities proved fruitless. Besides, it was common governmental knowledge that Hurt delved into "bugga-bugga" stuff as it was dubbed by the chic skeptics. As long as he kept to himself, counting his money or whatever, buying useless planets, and keeping his political nose clean, he was considered harmless.

Besides, a cultural carnival like this one was not only to disseminate knowledge but to help firm ties between the Federation of Colonies and to keep the peace with alien worlds. Hurt was performing a humanitarian task. Right?

Right. All the same to Todd Spigot.

He'd done his share, thought Todd as he jumped into an empty tube-car and dialed his direction into the computer. He'd helped to save Earth. He wasn't sure how Cog thought he could be of further assistance. Well, whatever it was, it was better than rotting mentally back on Earth. At least he didn't feel in need of a shrink up here. He had a purpose. All he had to do now was to wait and see just what that purpose was.

The car swooshed through its tube, *thwipped* through interchanges, twisted and turned along its null-grav way, finally depositing Todd on LEVEL C, BIOSPHERE THIRTEEN. AUDITORIUM.

Prominent banners announced in bold colors that he was in the right place.

ART DISPLAY.

People milled about here and there by the entranceway, but the actual concourse did not look at all crowded. In fact, the art show seemed embarrassingly understocked with people for its grand opening.

As Todd stepped from the tube-car, a woman strode up to him extending a hand, beaming a too-wide smile.

"Welcome!" she said, grabbing Todd's hand and patting it familiarly. "You have the distinguishing quality of being our two hundredth guest for the grand opening!"

"I do?" Todd cringed. This wasn't good. Cog had suggested that though he could freely mingle with the passengers of the *Star Fall,* he should not allow himself to be too noticed. "I am? I mean, does that mean I win a prize?"

The woman laughed artificially. "No, no. Tell me, what's your name."

"Todd Spigot" leaped to his tongue tip, but he managed to quickly switch it to "Charley Haversham, miss."

"My name is Ivy Henderson, manager of this marvelous gallery. Tell me, are you a writer, an artist yourself? Or do you number yourself among the scientific portion of this star cruise?"

"I'm a janitor, ma'am." Todd said.

Ivy Henderson blinked dark eyes, brushed back slightly unruly dark hair. Her mouth dipped into a frown briefly. "A jan—" She groped for words. "One of the *technical* crew! How fortunate!" The overfriendly smile was again broad on her face, displaying bright teeth to good advantage. "As you know, this is one of the displays intended specifically for visitors shuttled up from the surfaces of colony planets. Simple working people—like yourself! My goodness, I should have thought of inviting others like yourself! We can get an immediate typical reaction of the—"

Todd smiled wryly. *"Untermensch?"*

"You *must* meet our host and benefactor." She waved blithely toward a dim form in a translucent plastic booth. Her narrow nostrils flared with excitement. "What a marvelous idea! We can have a gala . . . what was that word you used?"

"Untermensch," Todd repeated.

"Yes, an *untermensch* gala! A kind of testday for the masses. We'll invite all the crew and and see how the wonderful *energy* these art forms exude impresses them." She grabbed Todd by the hand and led him to the booth. "Mr. Hurt has been such a sweetheart to me. I've had such a *wonderful* time dealing with all these *wonderful* artists." She stopped at the door, hands fluttering at her bosom. "I feel so vibrant here amid their radiant emanations." She exhaled fervently. "Well, now—let me introduce you to Mr. Hurt."

Good grief. Cog wouldn't like this at all.

"I really shouldn't take up his time," Todd objected.

"Nonsense! I'm sure that Mr. Hurt would be more than happy to hear our idea." A delicate finger tapped a button. A door slid open. "Quickly, quickly! We mustn't let too much of Mr. Hurt's special air escape!"

Todd stepped into the rectangular room. The Art Director followed on his heels, promptly pushing another button. The door whisked shut behind them.

The man sat in a chair overlooking the aisle of the gallery concourse. Dressed in golden, shimmering robes, he casually stroked his trim, very black beard. It framed a pale-lipped mouth. Smooth, sallow skin held small pores. A delicate nose sensitively jutted from beneath eyes which, Todd noted as the man slowly swung his way, were the man's most arresting characteristic. Deep black, they were slightly flecked with silver, like coins at the bottom of a well. Their look simultaneously expressed self-confidence and sadness, control and despair. Long dark hair holding not a hint of gray cascaded delicately to his shoulders in an artistic arrangement no doubt held in place by a hair style-field emanating from a microchip button on the back of his necklace.

His voice was rich, measured, as he spoke, the accent indefinable though bearing a faint cultured British texture. "Ms. Henderson. I was thinking that perhaps I have been at fault in inadequately advertising your excellent display. Why else should there be so few attendees for such a stunning show?"

Ivy Henderson did not seem to catch the faint ironic twist to the small mouth. "Time. Time for the news to spread of all these simply fabulous artists gathered in one place, Mr. Hurt. That's all it will take. Besides, as I pointed out to you before, your intentions from the very beginning were to create a travelling museum, visiting dozens of planets, shining the light of culture on deprived citizens of the Federation." She slipped a hand around Todd's arm. "Mr. Charley Haversham has given me a simply divine idea concerning the show. You see, Mr. Haversham is with the menial staff of the ship—janitorial, am I correct Mr. Haversham?"

"Yes," Todd said, noting the faint amusement in Hurt's eloquent eyes. "It's a true pleasure to be on your terrific cruise, Mr. Hurt. I only hope I can be of adequate service. Anything I can do in the way of testing responses of Normal Joes."

"Please, Mr. Haversham," Hurt said, an expansive smile showing perfect white teeth. "I am a rich man. Ms. Henderson surely does not realize that even the crew and maintenance technicians for this jaunt of the *Star Fall* were carefully screened. I can afford quality, you see."

Ms. Henderson did not even have the grace to blush. "I merely thought that because of his role in life, his world view would be . . . I mean, he would be more similar to the regular visitors from colonies and . . . oh *my,* I hope I haven't offended you, Mr. Haversham," she said.

"Not at all. I'm just here to see the show, actually, and I'd be happy to let you know my reactions."

"You *are* a doll," she exulted, voice expressive again. "You see, Mr. Hurt. It's not such a bad idea!"

Hurt gave a pained smile. "In that case, perhaps I should take a moment or two to interview our . . . what is the term? Guinea pig, I think—before he ventures onto the floor of art treasures so exquisitely culled from Earth and arranged by yourself, Ms. Henderson. In the meantime, I notice that several of the artists have not quite completed their setting up. Perhaps you would be so good as to aid them. I will have Mr. Haversham report to you just as soon as he completes his tour."

She turned to Todd. "I shall no doubt be in the welcoming booth. I'll prepare a questionnaire for your attention."

"There's so much out there, I'm sure I'll not be able to do the whole thing today. But I'll be glad to let you know what I think of what I see."

Ms. Henderson's attention, however, was elsewhere. A flurry of activity seemed to be occurring near the show's center. Voices were raised in anger. There was the sound of fluttering paper. Todd glanced through the darkened glass. An attractive dark-haired woman seemed to be the center of the ruckus. "Oh my," the Art Director said. "I'll bet it's that Veronica March again." She clucked her tongue. "A walking disaster area, that woman. I've thrown her out of five New York shows if I've thrown her out of one. I don't even like her work."

"She is one of my favorite young artists," Hurt spoke up. "It was *I*, Ms. Henderson, who overrode your rejection of her application to contribute to this show. I trust that you will give her every polite consideration."

"Yes, of course, Mr. Hurt." Ivy Henderson replied in glacial tones. Without further ado, she spun on her heel and departed.

"Please excuse the woman," Earnest Evers Hurt said. "I find her hard to take, but she is simply the most influential organizer of these sort of things on Earth. It was only through her that I was able to obtain such a wide variety of artists of such caliber."

"I'm not offended. Better than pressing buttons on a sewer computer."

"Ah, but well pressed, I'm sure," Hurt said with a faint chuckle.

Todd found himself liking the man. Although he had an urbane, clipped manner, he seemed not merely genteel and mannerly, but honestly interested in his guest and not conceited. "Please. Sit down. Would you like some tea? I can order you something more powerful if you like, but I fear I do not imbibe alcohol or anything that might be too hard on the old brain cells, you know."

"Tea would be just fine, thank you," Todd said, settling into a comfortable chair which had popped up from the floor at the tap of a finger. The man poured steaming brown liquid into a delicate porcelain Chinese cup.

"I hope you find this satisfactory. My personal hybrid of the ancient oriental ginseng root. An honorable longevity treatment."

Todd remembered Cog's comment on Hurt's age. "You wish to live a long time?"

"You need not pretend ignorance as to my ancient state, Mr. Haversham," Hurt said mildly. "I have never claimed to be desirous of being young. I merely wish to remain old for a long time."

"You *are* well preserved," Todd observed, tasting the tea. Strong, bitter—like ground-up dirt—it nonetheless had a savory aspect.

"The best body parts that my genetic engineers can grow,"

Hurt drawled, casually running fingertips down his chest to his legs. "I'm the oldest man alive, Mr. Haversham. Did you know that? A regular modern-day Methuselah. Two hundred and twenty-one years old. And I don't feel a day over two hundred and nineteen."

Todd, disarmed by the man's manner, laughed. *This* was the person Cog was so worried about?

"How old are you, Mr. Haversham?" Hurt asked casually.

Now *there* was a question. Just how old was poor Charley? Todd took a guess. "Twenty-nine."

Hurt sipped daintily from the cup, which portrayed exquisitely painted sea gulls in flight over a blue background. The old man fitted in a young body grimaced slightly for some private reason and set the cup back in its place on a warming cabinet. "Ever have your optimum age computed stochastically? Ultimate probability, I mean, barring accidents. Bottom line. Cut-off point."

"Uhm. No. That always seemed to me to be so . . . well, morbid." Depressing, too. Among the middle class on Todd's home world of Deadrock, average life spans only just touched a hundred Terran standard years for normal citizenry; considerably less for miners.

Earnest Evers Hurt turned away with a blank gaze. "Even with the finest geriatric and longevity treatments—developed of course by my personal scientists from my personal funds"— a wry smile—"I have at best another ten years to live. My mortality weighs heavy upon my shoulders." His eyes brightened. "But please, forgive me. You are young. I've no business interrupting your enjoyment of what is, after all, a well-earned break in your prescribed duties."

"No, please," Todd said. "I find myself privileged to be able to talk with you. I never thought I'd have the opportunity."

Hurt folded his hands across his abdomen, bent in an oddly vulnerable, fetal manner. "When I was your age, Mr. Haversham, I too took long journeys, though ostensibly in search of Truth rather than to earn a living. I was happy then—or at least absorbed. I was not of this life, really. You never are when you're an innocent acolyte of the Meaning Quest, when you lose yourself in science, philosophy, religion and all the odd byways and highways that bridge them."

"What happened?" Todd straightened, terribly interested.

"Then my particular slice of reality folded upon me. My father died, you see. My father, whom I had never really known. Master of the then pioneering Hurt Associates, criminal on some worlds, practically God on others. He decayed past recall and was . . . no more. I was haunted by him. He'd literally designed me, a structural improvement over his own genetic code. As responsibility tumbled down upon me—I was his designated heir, you understand—I found myself fascinated and appalled by the man. Slowly, I found myself"—Hurt seemed to have difficulty forcing the word out—"*becoming* my father. You see, I too am a devil to some, a deity to others. I have sinned unforgivably, yet I have also done the most kind, most benevolent deeds, on a scale befitting my stature. I, Mr. Haversham, am a living testimony to the polarity of Nature. A particularly monstrous example, thanks to my power. Now, though my hunger for life continues—most selfishly, since I happen to have heirs who wait for my demise somewhat less than patiently—I can taste my mortality." He gestured expansively. "That, perhaps, is why I wished to use the *Star Fall* for these admittedly grandiose purposes. When my obituary is stamped across the news-fax screens of the human universe, perhaps fewer people will say, "Ah! Another megalomaniac—perhaps the biggest of all—has bitten the dust. Hurrah!" I should like to think that some people will say, 'Ah! That humanitarian Earnest Evers Hurt, who founded the greatest monument and museum of the human race, traveled among the worlds, a testimony to Truth and Intelligence. Founder of the Hurt Foundation!'" A finger smote the air in mock exclamation. "Benefactor of millions! He will be sorely missed!" Hurt leaned over toward Todd and spoke in a softer voice, "Will *you* miss me, Mr. Haversham?" An easy smile made Todd realize that an answer was not expected.

"You've accomplished wonders for the reputation of the ship that nearly destroyed Earth."

· "Ah yes! A phoenix risen from the ashes. Perhaps I should have renamed the vessel the *Star Spring*! Fascinating thought."

"Why are you telling all this to a stranger?"

Hurt's eyes glimmered moistly, for a brief instant young. "I should like to hear *your* thoughts on mortality, Mr. Haversham. I offer my fears and dreams to make you feel comfortable. A habit with individuals I take a liking to."

"Me?" Todd felt the familiar shiver running up his spine at the thought of such numinous matters. "You're asking to open a whole can of worms there, Mr. Hurt. You have to realize I was raised in a radically religious environment."

"How fascinating. Determinists, I take it?"

"Yes. If indeed each individual is programmed socially and culturally, then you might say I was programmed metaphysically."

"A Christian sect?"

"Hardliners. Fundamentalists. Lots of fear and anxiety."

"A natural state for rational human beings, surely? Isn't that what Kierkegaard maintained?"

"Not when your dreads are totally irrational, private niggling things that haunt your dreams."

"Please excuse my prying, but what are your religious and philosophic convictions now, Mr. Haversham?" Hurt leaned forward intently, stroking his beard.

"Mr. Hurt, I've had profound religious experiences, and therefore I count myself a religious individual in the minimalist sense of the word. I find comfort in prayer and belief, but not to a deity that has been socially and culturally drilled into me— a creation of other people's misconceptions and fears. I remain a Christian, though a Christian open to all that awaits him, interested in all thought and philosophies and yet still searching, still growing."

Hurt's eyes were wide with interest. "Tell me, Mr. Haversham, should you somehow have the opportunity to make a more literal quest—would you? A quest, perhaps to disclose as certainty the important secrets of this universe? Just how strong is your hunger?"

"No less strong than any other's, I suppose. I like to think that I would accept whatever is offered to me in the way of truth and knowledge. I accept what *is*, Mr. Hurt. The more I know, the more I realize how little I know and understand."

"A most commendable attitude, Mr. Haversham!" Todd noticed that a small blood-red light pulsed on the console to Hurt's immediate right, attracting the man's attention. "Ah, but you must excuse me. Please feel free to visit me during the journey. We can discuss these things at length. In the meantime I hope you enjoy the educational elements and entertainments at your disposal aboard the *Star Fall*. We certainly appreciate your services." The man congenially proffered his hand, which Todd shook.

"Thank you." As Todd departed, the last thing he saw was Hurt bending over a comm-unit as it slowly extended itself from the console.

"Yes?"

"None other than yours truly, reporting that Insertion will be achieved at precisely eight o'clock this evening, ship's time, with suitable ceremony."

"Can you give me the approximate time of our arrival at the optimum nexus point to commence the metapyschic attraction processes?"

"Nope. As you well know, we haven't the foggiest notion of the location or essential composition of what we're trying to attract."

"Yes. Yes of course. Arachnid. I just had an interesting discussion with none other than your friend Todd Spigot."

"Ah ha! In his masquerade as Charles Haversham!"

"Yes. He is to be plotted into one of the main scenarios."

A moment of silence. "But you promised him all to *me.*"

"They will *all* be yours eventually. He has the aptitude I need for a particular course of seeking that will create strong sympathetic pyschic harmonics to the Field. I want him plugged into the composite. Do *not* harm him."

"Arrangements will be made, brother," said the Arachnid in a sly tone.

Brother? Why had the creature called him that?

"Scenario 17, Arachnid." Earnest Evers Hurt smiled to himself. "Mr. Spigot will have his holy quest all right."

Nine

The woman stepped back a pace, her heel landing squarely on the toes of Todd Spigot's left foot.

"Ouch," Todd said.

She twirled, startled, her long brunette hair a carousel sparkling in the light from a nearby geltoid light sculpture. "Oh, my. I'm *so* sorry." She took a cigarette from her lips. Lit ash tumbled down Todd's shirtfront. "Oh dear!" the woman exclaimed again, trying to brush the stuff off, which resulted in a long carbon smear on the off-white.

Curved black lashes batted. White hands with superb nails colored green clasped in contrition. Apologetic words began to tumble from glossy lips. "Forgive me! I didn't see you!"

"That's all right," Todd said, grimacing with the pain, redistributing his weight. "I have two of them."

"But the shirt!" She swept back a curve of raven hair. "I hope I haven't ruined it. I can have it cleaned! Oh dear, just another foul-up in the day! What a botch!" A tiny foot stamped with frustration. "Dammit!"

Looking up, Todd for the first time got a full view of the woman. He had been about to utter some nothing of a dismissal, but the words stuck in his throat.

Time seemed to stop. The utterings and mutterings of the sparse crowd shuffling through the aisles, gawking at this holo-slice matte or that mozaic of charged starstone stilled in his ears as though all this were merely a movie and some dunce had snapped off the audio.

"You'd think after a dozen displays I'd have learned some grace, some élan." The woman sighed, then drew daintily at her cigarette. She released a gust of smoke with a cough. "Wretched habit. *Must* give it up. Dirty and filthy." Mascaraed eyes that held all the best of day and night fixed softly on Todd. "Oh. Would you like one?"

Though he didn't smoke, Todd said, "Okay."

Slender fingers unsnapped the mauve leather shoulder-bag folded over a rounded hip. She wore a simple ensemble of black scufflers, tight beige flyaways ridged by ivory buttons up the legs, and pale purple bandleader tails, cut to perfectly describe her body's sinuous flowings. Her white ruffled blouse dived to just above the naval, revealing fleshy hints of discreet but ample décolletage.

A wing of hair drooping fecklessly over an eye, she fumbled among odds and ends in her bag. "You like Cupid Darts?" she asked casually. "Hope so. It's all I've got. Smuggled a supply of the stuff. Toxic beyond belief. Black market, you know. Illegal. Almost as bad as Harpy's Nails."

"Okay," Todd said, all pain and inconvenience forgotten.

"Here we go!" She produced a plastic pack with elaborate art deco borders and hot pink letters constructed of hearts. "Snazzy, huh?" She tapped a cigarette out, throwing back her hair with an easy, quintessentially feminine shrug. Her eyebrows arched inquiringly. "You like modern artwork?" Her eyes darted over him: a mixture of shyness and awkwardness, delightfully fetching from someone so lovely. Absently, Todd grabbed at the cigarette, poking it into the side of his mouth, promptly forgetting to flick the tip's igniter.

"I like art," he replied. The cigarette bobbed.

Though her thin body was a study in lithe loveliness, perfectly fitting Todd's ideal of female form, its qualities were merely percussion to the concert of her features. A long curved nose was perfectly balanced by small nostrils. High cheekbones and a rounded chin were the symmetrical foundation upon which other facial aspects played to astounding effect, all mounted on a slender neck. Her smooth complexion played games with light and shadow. Her expressive mouth, in repose, was a thoughtful, vulnerable pout. In a smile, a thing of pure illumination.

But, ah, the eyes...

"You're staring at me," she said in a surprised tone.

Those eyes were curious and shy and mysterious, a certain amount of innocence in their brown embrace that no quantity of experience could kill.

Todd Spigot felt as though his brain were melting and leaking from his ears.

"I'm sorry," he said, averting his gaze. "You look . . . you look like someone I used to know."

"Oh? Back on Earth? Funny, I'm not a clone of anybody."

"It's not important," Todd said. Especially because it wasn't true. But he had to keep her talking.

Moments of intensely charged awkwardness passed.

"Here, let me light your cigarette." She took her own and touched its tip to Todd's. A glow burst. Smoke. The subtle scent of her body wafted faintly. Todd thought he would die of delight.

A glimpse of the side of a breast, and then she was back, away from him, regarding him with frank curiosity. "I'm Veronica March. I draw and paint and step on nice people's toes. You?"

"Todd Spigot." Without thinking. "Computers. I save planets." Suddenly realization flooded him, temporarily pushing back awareness of his gaffe. "Veronica March?" He spun, pointing back to the set of art displays behind him that he had just been admiring. "You did these?"

"My sins, yes."

"Very nice! The colors! The compositions!"

"Imported paints. From all over the universe. Chemical substance is as important as ambience exuded." She strode past, pointing to a picture of a woman caught in midflight between diving board and pool. "Part of the paints here are from Rigel Three mudflats. The deeper hues are from Bailey's World. Certain berries growing wild in swamps. I have degrees in physics and chemistry. My specialty is light theory and application. Reflection and refraction."

"Wait. Can't you just synthesize your paints on Earth for the right chemical composition and hue?"

A lemon twist of a smile. "But my dear, that wouldn't be—" She savored the word between dainty tongue and lips. "Exotic."

"Yes—well, you certainly know your spectrum."

"The actual composition and structure I just do off the top of my head. I just like to play with levels of light and shadow in color. Colors are quite psychoactive, you know." She glanced at the painting critically. "I like to think that my paintings can change people's moods. The brushstrokes, the molecularly measured sprays—the mathematics of emotion. What does this one remind you of, Mr. Spigot?"

"Suicide." The word leaped to his lips. "I don't know why..."

"Something like that. From the Turner-like luminosity of this corner here..." Her finger sketched an imaginary line. "To the Dutch School gloom at the bottom of the pool. Perhaps it's more depression than suicide, Mr. Spigot."

"The others just leap out at you," Todd said, fascinated, glimpsing something of the artist in the art. "And they're not holos... Are they?"

"With the methods of illusion available these days, you never really know, do you? No. I controlled the display lighting, though. Quite vital. I must admit, though, I *do* employ a spectrograph and computer in my studio. A mesh of science and craft mixed, hopefully, with a dab of talent, Mr. Spigot." She gazed back wistfully. "Certainly, feeling."

"Please. Todd or..." Todd said quickly, realizing that he wasn't supposed to be Todd on this trip. "Or Charley. Charley Haversham. Please call me that, okay?"

"Wait a moment! Todd Spigot. I recognize that name. On the news-fax last year." Her eyes grew wide. "You were on the *last* voyage of the *Star Fall.*" Her voice increased in volume, excited. "You're *that* Todd Spig—"

"Shhh!" Panicking, he stepped to her side, squashed his mouth to her mouth.

"Umph!" she said, struggling in his grasp, then abruptly not struggling. There was a moment of sublime mixture of breath and lips before Todd pulled away, saying, for the benefit of the heads that had turned their way. "Wonderful to see you again, Veronica!" Then, whispering: "Top secret. I'm supposed to be Charley Haversham on this trip."

Her eyes were wide with surprise as he drew away. "Right. Charley Haversham. But you can't keep on kissing me, *Charley.*" She placed her hand smartly to her hip. "How are you going to keep my mouth busy the *rest* of the time?" Her eyes shone playfully.

"I'll take you to dinner tonight and stuff it with food. How's that?" Todd said nervously, caught between fear and fascination.

"Very well. Where?"

"Where? Uhm. The Effervescence Lounge. We can watch

the *Star Fall's* entry into Underspace. Six o'clock?"

"I'll be there in bells." She started to walk past him, then halted, looked at him with a gleam in her eyes. "I thought, though, it was called Insertion."

Smiling, without waiting for a response, she turned and paced down the aisle. Todd watched her trip over a taped-down piece of cable, curse, shake her head, then disappear around a turn.

Although he had barely begun his tour of the show, Todd found himself drifting toward the exit. Past heart-stirring landscapes, past detailed alien float-tanks bathed in mystical color, he walked, unnoticing. By captivating collages and penetrating portraits and horrific holos, all seemingly the stuff of sorcery he traipsed, unmindful of their resplendence, heedless of their siren sounds, their luminous lure.

"Mr. Haversham!" the Art Director called at his heels.

"That *was* rapid. What are your opinions of the show?"

Partly tugged from his daze, Todd turned and said, *"Energizing,* Ms. Henderson. *Wonderful."*

Before the woman could thrust her carefully prepared questionnaire in his face, Todd let his mind float back to rejoin the clouds and stumbled to a waiting tube-car.

With a circuitry maze, relays clicked, pseudoneuronic connections formed. At the bequest of metal digits' light tap-dancing on stiff keys, power surged through microminiaturized silicon chips.

SPEC/ROBOT DESIG. CODE 9H#3BA221.

In darkness, a thing jerked, crab-scuttled, stiffened as the radioed information surged through its receptors.

SUBJECT: TODD SPIGOT. IDENTITY CRYSTAL FOR MATCH-UP FOLLOWING IMMEDIATELY.

The surface of the crystal glittered as it was lifted, showing intricate traceries of wires and chips embedded within like faults in a diamond. The metal fingers fitted it in the necessary slot with practiced ease. A soft thwup sounded as the keyed vacuum effect sucked it into the heart of the mechanism.

Toggles were touched. Verniers adjusted.

IMBED SUBJECT INTO FABRICATION PRIME, SCENARIO 17.

In the dimness: other squirmings as other units were programmed.

QUERY: INFORMATION BANKS FILLED? the biobot's fingers requested.

A blue light shone.

IN SPEC/ROBOT DESIG. CODE 9H#3BA221, tiny wings fluttered, tiny claws clutched.

Neuro-needles extended.

Rebathed, refitted in his best apparel and highly nervous, Todd Spigot arrived at the Effervescence Lounge a half hour early. He ticked off the time with sips of white wine, settled in a null-grav chair by the wiggle-bar.

The lounge resembled a bubble in a glass of champagne; a clear dome bulging from one side of the *Star Fall*'s hull. The interior was fitted in the style of the Cassiopaen pleasure domes, though with infinitely better taste, depicting refined landscapes in the glow-glob tables rather than salacious alien sexual cavortings.

A subdued resplendence sheened from every surface in shades of umber, bright turquoise and mahogony. Subaudial emanations from hidden stations cycled a controlled giddiness into the room's inhabitants similar to the effect of two glasses of fresh champagne. The substance of the room itself was the equivalent of one gigantic speaker system, rendering the light cocktail jazz tinkling from a piano, synthar and bass-perc a delightful mélage indeed; like standing in a sprinkler system of music.

Despite the valiant efforts of these mood-control devices on Todd Spigot, he felt simultaneously uneasy and ecstatic. The former because he was unsure about his conversational abilities in the crucial situation. The latter because never before had he encountered someone like Veronica March.

All the romantics of old were right about women. You just had to find the right one and there, before your eyes, was a living goddess: eyes pouring forth poetry, mouth gentle musics; all mythology in her form, all magic in her scent.

Gulping the faintly bitter golden chablis, Todd replayed the tape loop of their encounter in his mind for the hundredth time, simultaneously appreciating the humor of the situation and the almost sorcerous chemistry.

Todd straightened his mauve jacket, adjusted his tie, then yanked a handkerchief from his back pocket to attend to his nose. Bit congested today. Perhaps there had been something in the atmosphere mix in Hurt's chamber which had affected his sinuses. *Funny guy, Hurt. A gentleman certainly. Hardly seemed to be a threat to human civilization.*

Damn this nose, anyway.

He honked it twice, sniffling and cleaning his throat noisily between blows.

"Express coming through?" a voice asked behind him.

Startled, he jerked around, shocking blue cloth still affixed to his nostrils.

She stood there, a vision of pink chiffon frills arrayed provocatively about a body less than classical in its partial baring, yet precisely to Todd's taste. Classic nudes, after all, had curves that were gentler. Hers, however, were more abrupt, emphasising her boyish litheness without sacrificing a degree of femininity.

"Veronica!" he said, voice muffled in the silk. "You look— lovely."

"Thanks." She swept around the wiggle-bar. "You hiding from a wife or something?"

"Hmm?" Todd's eyes turned down to the handkerchief. "Oh. This." A perfunctory wipe, and he shoved it into the side pocket of his jacket. "My communicator." He smiled slyly. "I'm a secret agent for the Aslasi and I was just reporting in to headquarters."

A beam of light sprayed from the bar, assayed the woman's dimensions, then promptly disgorged an appropriately modeled chair into which she could snuggle her delightful posterior. "And pray tell," she breathed suggestively, half-closed eyes regarding Todd coolly. "What does"—she lifted her hands to her nose—"'Ahnk! Ahnk!' mean in Aslasi?"

Todd nonchalantly pressed plastic. A glass of wine popped up in front of Veronica. "It means, I have just met a really sexy broad."

Her long eyelashes fluttered and she coyly put a demure hand to a not-so-demure bosom. "Oh? You have another date later on?"

"Come on, Veronica! Surely you realize you're gorgeous!

Wearing her distinctive frown-pout, she said with conviction: "But Todd, truly, I don't think I am." Her eyes gently turned away and her fingers toyed with the stem of her glass.

"No really beautiful woman does," Todd said. "That's part

of their charm." Not bad, Spigot, he thought. But where are you coming up with these gems? His subconscious must be working overtime. That, or his libido was snapping the whip to his wit.

"Liar," she whispered, but she smiled. "When's Underspace time, then?"

"Eightish. I've taken the liberty to book us dinner here, in a spot giving us a terrific view. Is that okay?"

"You're asking *me?* Fine! I mean, this is a really delightful bar. What kind of food do they serve, though?"

"Delicious. I've got us a gourmet booth. We can program our own meal, right down to the thickness of the sauce or the alcoholic content of the wine." He sipped his wine. "Best place in the ship, though, is the King's Attic. You have to go there three days in advance. They take a sensory/brain reading on you then. When you arrive at the designated time three days later, they have a feast prepared exactly tailored to your taste buds."

"Take me sometime."

"My pleasure." A moment of silence as he surveyed her, his uncertainty about what to say next edged away by the sheer delight of gazing on her. He noticed that she wore a jeweled black choker around her neck, which explained the new fashion in which she wore her hair—the device could only be a force-styler. Force-styler or no, the dark hair was a delightful collection of waves and curls that tumbled and twirled, a boil of artful froth around Veronica's perfect face.

"Are you enjoying the *Star Fall?*" he asked, an easy conversational opener. He had to take his eyes away lest he stare too much.

"Oh, *yes,*" she said with childlike enthusiasm. "Just wonders wrapped in wonders, don't you think? And the notion of visiting other worlds, of having other cultures look at my work—*thrilling*. I never in my wildest dreams imagined I'd get past the solar system." Eyes wide, she looked up. Beyond the dome burned Sol, fiery bright amid the lesser lights of the planets and stars. "I feel so very . . . I don't know, *small*. Insignificant in some ways." Her voice filled with enthusiasm. "And yet so *important* in other ways."

"Relativity. Yes, I understand." He smiled kindly. "Rather like being a big fish in a swimming pool of an ocean liner.

Against the backdrop of the ship . . . you're something." Todd
gazed up at the polarized translucent glassteel which admitted
light but hindered harmful radiation. "Yet, against the hugeness
of the sea . . . you're nothing."

"All in the mind, I suppose," she murmured. "All in one's
attitude."

"No." He touched her arm lightly. "It depends entirely upon
whom you know, who's important to you, how much you give
of yourself." He laughed. "My God, but you must excuse me!
Philosophizing at a moment of celebration!" He clinked her
glass with his. "You must also forgive me for my presumption
in choosing your drink for you. Would you prefer something
else?"

"Oh! No, this is fine!" She smiled agreeably and drank some
of the wine as though to prove her satisfaction with it. "Lovely."
She shivered, wrapping her arms around herself as though
experiencing a moment's chill. "My goodness. It's quite strong.
I'm feeling a touch giddy already." Fingers to mouth. Wide
eyes. She giggled, trembling the ruffles of her dress in a manner
that almost straightened Todd's hair. She placed a hand on his
shoulder to steady herself. A kind of emotional electricity tingled through him.

"No. It's not the drink." Todd explained the effects produced
by the technogadgetry of the bar. "You won't feel woozy. Just
nice," he concluded.

"Marvelous," she pronounced, leaning over to pick up her
wineglass and promptly dumping it over. Some liquid splashed
into Todd's lap.

That won't cool me down, Todd thought.

"Oh my, I'm *such* a klutz!" She grabbed a nearby paper
napkin and tried to dry Todd off.

And that certainly won't either. Todd gently caught her
wrist, remonstrating. "You needn't worry. Watch." Even as
he spoke, colored light moved, twirling and twisting and melding within the obsidian-hued bar. The surface suffused with
glow, absorbed the splotch of wine. Similtaneously, the arms
of Todd's form-fit joined over his lap. A brief hot sensation,
then the arms resumed their normal position, with Todd dry
once more.

"The marvels of technology toward a better bar," Tod said.

even as a full glass of wine emerged from the membranous material before him.

"I'll be more careful this time," Veronica said, picking up her wine, sipping it daintily. "It was just such a shock to get high so soon. This place is *marvelous.*" The lights below them in colloidal suspension throbbed with a low gentle bass voice: "Thank, you, madam."

"I'll have another glass of wine, bartender."

"May I remark, sir, that the alcohol content of your blood is presently approaching an unstable condition."

"That's okay," Todd replied. "I don't think I'll be driving home tonight."

The Effervescence Room had filled.

Heads canted upward, waiting.

When it arrived, the Insertion was an explosion of jittering, silent colors, arcing across the surface of the *Star Fall*. It was as though someone had taken scissors, cut the vessel from the fabric of space, and dumped it into a pool of electric sparks, bubbles, and zizagging tubing that blared intricate patterns of multitextured light.

A collective expulsion of breath; a moment of silence and awe. The lights danced with cosmic intricacy, were suddenly engulfed by a starless gulf that flittered with specks of energy like the screen of a burnt-out TV picture tube.

A spontaneous burst of applause thundered in the chamber.

Slowly, the blister substance fogged, then fully opaqued. It was not healthy to stare into the raw stuff of Underspace. A force screen separated the *Star Fall* from the actual mathematically alien world, where the laws of physics were skewed.

"It's a mystery," Todd said softly after the reaction had died down to appreciative murmurs. "It's still pretty much beyond comprehension, Underspace. Physicists are still exploring its nature. All they've been able to do so far is to establish the systems and rules whereby craft protected by stasis fields can enter it, navigate their way to a spot corresponding to the place in the regular universe where they wish to go, then punch back through."

"A different universe?"

"Essentially. I must admit, I'm not much on mathematics,

but from what I understand, Underspace has something to do with our plane of existence. Black holes, gravity, psychic phenomenon."

"All the *outré* stuff?"

"Exactly. Granted, most of it—clairvoyance, telekinesis, precognition, magic, sorcery—has been hokum throughout the ages. But who is to say some of it wasn't real? Even now, the experiments with espers somehow links them with Underspace . . . which is essentially all around us, all the time. It's the literal proof of the need for a science of metaphysics, something only philosophers and theologians have dealt with previously."

"You mean, if there's really a Heaven, really a Hell . . ."

"Not precisely. I mean that this is where we get our conception, our intuitions if you will, of powers beyond ourselves. No doubt our interpretations are fairly primitive." He sighed. "Still, from what I understand, not many people are pursuing these investigations into the exact nature of Underspace. The human populace spread among the stars seems more interested in their individual concerns, thinking of Underspace totally in practical and economic terms. Just a necessary shortcut in trade routes. It changed the Morapn race, you know."

"Oh? How so?"

"Altered their goals, apparently. Made them uninterested in further territorial expansion. Somehow it physically altered their genetic makeup, turning their thoughts more toward the contemplative."

He shifted his gaze to her. "Now then, O new passenger. How about a walk through halls of wonder?"

She smiled and stood and the frilly stuff of her dress rustled like a breeze nuzzling a dryad's leaves.

"I'd love to," she said.

They hovered awhile in silence amid the Floating Gardens, regarding the shifting airscape of the flowering vines and trees of this biosphere. Around them, discreetly distant in grav-cars, mere silhouettes against the muted backdrop of light canopies and the glow-blobs nestled among the foliage, were couples serene and murmuring, seeing only each another despite the beauty that surrounded them.

Todd Spigot, however, was scared stiff.

He looked at Veronica. Chin on hands, she perched on the

edge of their car, listening attentively to the susurrations of this shifting, grav-controlled forest sculpted so exotically. He had run out of things to say. Rationally, he knew what he should do. He should *grab* her. Breathe poetry into her ear. Stroke her supple form with light fingertips and generally, as Cog might say, "emit seductive radiations."

The paralysis had entered him slowly as they had quietly toured parts of the ship. Time prohibited an extensive journey, so they had stopped at a waterworld, lingering only for an artificial sunset on a romantic beach, watching the waves play leapfrog onto sand glittering with jewels; then, briefly, in the concert hall, to take a few moments of Mozart. Throughout their walk, Veronica had become progressively more quiet, aloof, thoughtful. Uncomfortable with the silences that would often engulf them, Todd tried to fill them with talk that seemed to him more and more inane, frantic grasps at straws to save the evening.

It had started so magically! So *right!* Now it seemed to be degenerating pitifully, this delightful lady losing interest in him entirely. Where had he gone wrong? Did he have some sort of psychic curse similar to Philip Amber's—only instead of death to people, his meted out death to romance? Yet it had all started out so absolutely splendidly, he delivering witty suggestive phrases, she laughing, enjoying herself. He'd almost propositioned her then, things were going so well. But no, that would be much too forward, too aggressive. A gentle, flowing evening was what had been called for, he'd thought. Take it easy, take it slow. This was not a quick-grope lady. This was someone he wanted to know for a while, if not longer.

However, as they'd walked through the Aquarium Exotica in the water biosphere, and he had started talking humorously of his bleak and quirky youth, she had clammed up. Oh, not unpleasantly.

She uttered brief "really?'s" and "oh dears!" and she had laughed, but she seemed, to him anyway, to be withdrawing, only vaguely attentive to him, as though thinking of something entirely different. A slow panic had made his words less smooth, less humorous, more desperately confessional and awkward.

He was miserable. He knew he'd botched it. Might as well just pack it in, call it a night, shake hands with Veronica and go shed tears into his cold pillow. Clearly she'd lost whatever interest that had sparked between them.

Oh, Spigot! he thought. *You did something wrong.*

He didn't even have any Dutch courage zinging through his veins anymore. If he did, maybe he'd just make a teensy pass...

The very thought shot terror through him. She'd refuse, of course, rejecting him. Better nothing at all than rejection. He'd been rejected too many times...

Limned now by a vague rosy light, her expression was unreadable. That frown-pout again, dammit. Unnerving.

"You're very thoughtful," he observed.

She arched an eyebrow coolly. "Am I? Sorry. I must be terrible company."

"No! I'm enjoying your company." He felt uneasy, wishing the cars had portable bars or something.

"Still, it *is* late. We should go."

Todd nodded, having expected that suggestion. By voice control he ordered the car down. The plushy seated vehicle slid through a floral path, as though being slowly swallowed by a rainbow maelstrom of paint.

Quietly, they found the tube-car station.

"Well," Todd said, trying to keep the gloom from his voice. "It's been fun."

"Would you like to come up for a drink before you head back to your room?" she asked in a noncommittal voice.

"Sure," he said, expecting her to take him to some bar.

They rode the tube-car, which deposited them in a passenger section. "I have some very nice gin I smuggled aboard with the cigarettes," she explained in a small voice.

They went to her compartment. Pretty much the same as his, Todd noticed. A single, Spartan, for a luxury cruise. She increased the illumination slightly, then went to her table, upon which stood a bottle of Gordon's gin, half full. She poured two glasses. Added ice. Presented one to Todd.

They sat and sipped.

"Sometime I'd like to see you work," Todd said, trying to make conversation.

"Okay."

The ice clinked as he took another swallow, trying to drown his queasiness. "Really nice stuff."

"My favorite."

"Mine's beer, I think."

"Oh."

Deadly silence. The way she was acting, Todd had the feeling that she'd slap him even if he just kissed her goodnight. Still, there she was, breathtakingly pretty. Her prettiness cut straight through his heart. Her scent—cinnabar and tobacco— made him lightheaded.

She seemed glacial. Todd made a couple more conversation gambits, without success. Finally, he finished the last drop of gin, set the glass down on the counter beside him.

"Well, I guess I'd better go," he said, standing haltingly, smoothing his pants.

She stood as well, still holding her drink.

"Good night." He braved a step to her, a peck on her cheek. She did not respond.

"Can I see you some other time?" *Not likely,* Todd thought even as the words dropped from his mouth. He could tell she was bored stiff with him. Nervously, he looked into her eyes, which held a puzzled expression. "Certainly," she said. "But . . . but if you'd like to . . . you can stay . . ." She almost whispered the word, as though hopefully. ". . . longer."

The astonishment petrified him. He could only stand and stare, open-mouthed.

She stepped up to him, leaned her head against his chest, the scent of her hair delicious in his nostrils. Automatically he put an arm around her. She seemed small and vulnerable against him. "I'm sorry," she said. "I know that I shouldn't be this way, but I find it very hard to ask for—affection."

"But I thought—" Todd said. "You seemed so distant, I thought you'd lost all interest."

"I'm used to aggression. You're not very agressive, except in . . . quirky ways." She smiled up at him, slid slowly around so her breasts brushed the bottom of his rib cage. He could feel nipples hardening. The excitement was almost unbearable. "You haven't answered my question, Charley Haversham or Todd Spigot, or whoever you really are."

"Yes! Of course! I meant to explain all that and quite forgot . . . the bit about my identity . . ."

"You talk entirely too much." Her arms found their way around his waist. Her head tilted and her lips blended wistfully against his, lightly wet, tasting of gin and enthusiasm.

Tongue touch, shimmer of hair. Eyes, hands; a gentle dance of brightness and sensation. Her scent seemed a mysterious genie, granting wishes. Warm and electric in his arms, she moved in perfect cadence to the music that seemed to swirl through him, fleshly synethesia.

"You're a dream," he whispered in her ear. She shivered with the touch of his breath. She threw her hair back; its ends whisked teasingly up Todd's face.

"Lights," she murmured, turning, striding liquidly away.

"Camera?" Todd asked a little breathlessly, sitting on the bed's end.

"Action!" she purred. Lights dimmed to where only the shadows of romance were cast. Like some anthropomorphized feline, she strode into his arms. "Touch me between the shoulder blades," she instructed.

His hands groped, found something not cloth, not flesh. Fingered it. A feathery hiss of released energy, and the substance of her dress drifted lightly onto him as she pushed him back into the pillow. Now she was a lithe silhouette against the dim light, like some heavenly succubus, breaths low and excited. She took his hands and traced her sides with them. Ribs, waist, hips: like a human vase. An intuitive force took hold. He seemed to drift into a timeless absence of self. Totally immersed in her, he let his fingernails gently stoke the smooth skin on the inside of her thighs. She took startled inhalations.

She squirmed provocatively farther up his body, pinning his shoulders down. She leaned over him, her newly freed long hair draping into his face like a tunnel into dark intriguing pleasure. She let the perfumed hair drag over his mouth and nose, then drifted it down to the side of his head. Her lips found an earlobe, kissed it gently, then slipped her needle tongue into its groove and played it like a record. His head was propped so that he could view her perfect back sloping to her rounded rear, the vague light soft satin on downy hair diving into mystery.

Her voice was husky. "I want those clothes off. Now."

She slipped them off and curled up, eyes bright, beside him.

"Right!" Todd pushed the word through a dry mouth. He began to slip from his coat, then stopped and glanced down at the sprawl of feminine contour snuggling kittenishly into the bed. "Hey. I helped *you*."

"Sorry," she said. "I like to watch." Last word with playful humor. "What's wrong?"

"I'm *nervous,* that's what's wrong."

"Silly. Come here." She tugged him to her and kissed him so expertly that his ears seemed to ring. "Don't worry. I'll be in charge. Here, give me that coat."

Kneeling bare on the bed, she pulled. "It's caught," he said. Suddenly the sleeve slipped off, sending Veronica tumbling off the edge with a thump and a yelp.

"Dammit," she said. "I try to be sexy and something like this happens!"

She scrambled up and leaned disconsolately on the bedside, blowing back a curl of hair from her eyes.

Todd, for the first time in several minutes, was not looking at Veronica, however. He was staring aghast at the clock on the set of drawers.

11:56 blazed on its face.

"Oh my God," he said. "I didn't know it was that late!"

"Uh oh. I can hear the pumpkin line coming up—" She sat on the bedside and wrapped herself in the bedspread.

He had promised Cog that he would meet him at the Star Bar at midnight. What a wretched mistake! Here he was, making love to the most beautiful woman he'd ever met and—

"Another assignation?" she said moodily.

"I did promise someone I would meet them, yes," Todd said morosely. Then he brightened. "I told you, I'm here under cover, right? That my name is actually Todd Spigot."

"Yes. Something about saving worlds . . ."

"Doubtful this time. This is a meeting with an associate to relay information he might have dug up." Todd made sure that he sounded like he knew what he was talking about—which he didn't. "I suspect it won't take any more than a half hour."

Veronica perked up. "Oh! Well, then!" Clutching the cover close to her, she slipped to his side and smoothed a hand down his arm. "In that case, I'll be waiting for you!"

"You're a sweetheart!" he said, and he kissed her warmly. He picked up his jacket. "I'll be back soon as I can." He turned and slammed into the closed door.

Embarrassed, he fumbled for the Open switch and turned a farewell grin her way before he stumbled out in a fog.

* * *

The omnicleaner slumped over the wood bar, a frothy Mr. Clean soda in a clawlike appendage.

Todd tripped in, immediately noting why Cog had chosen the place for the meeting: the bar was practically deserted. In a dark corner squatted a group of Jent humanoids, gargling incomprehensively over some unearthly matter. A few stray, widely spaced solitary drinkers sipped pick-me-ups. Perceiving Todd's entrance, the robot bartender, wearing a tattered apron marked STAR BAR and splattered with mustard and ketchup, hummed up and placed a metal paw over the free lunch jar.

"What'll you have, buster?" the machine said in a voice that sounded like Humphrey Bogart's corpse.

"Gin!" Todd cried, exultant. "Gin! I've have some wonderful, stirring, gorgeous gin! In a glass with one ice cube."

Beaming, he sidled onto the barstool beside his otherworldly companion. A delirious glow of anticipation auraed him; a flush painted his cheeks a cute pink. This was shaping up to be the most exciting evening of his life. He could almost feel Veronica's slender fingers tracing the outlines of his face, hear her voice echoing in his subconscious.

"Cog!" he cried. "Cog, I'm so glad you brought me back on the *Star Fall*."

Optical units swung his way. "You've been drinking, Todd."

"Quick! Tell me what you've got to tell me. I've got to go."

"You're late."

"I'm here, but I won't be for long. So let's proceed with this conversation . . ." The box-shaped bartender rolled up and sluggishly set the glass before Todd.

"Put it on my tab," the omnicleaner said, dismissing the thing, which crunched away over peanut shells, unoiled limbs squeaking. When Ort Eath had created the *Star Fall*, he'd included everything possible—including shady dives. The Star Bar was one of the last remaining, mostly because its tacky atmosphere seemed to please some of the artists on the journey.

Cog—or rather, Cog's disguise—swiveled back to regard Todd. "You've found a woman, huh?"

Todd dropped a half-ounce off the gin and smiled blissfully at the machine. "Cog, a look at this lady would even get *you* excited."

"I have no sexual attributes. No gonads, no hormones circulating in my system."

"Yes, well, *I'm* in love and I'm not going to keep her waiting."

"Todd," Cog said. "I didn't bring you on this boat to intersex!"

"I don't care!" Todd grabbed a mechanical arm with fierce enthusiasm. "Cog, she's the most wonderful, luscious, delectable—"

"Hey! I'm off-duty! Don't do anything I have to clean up."

"You just *have* to meet her!"

"If we survive."

"What *are* you talking about?"

"I haven't been entirely straight with you, Todd. I've kept you in mystery." The high-pitched voice sounded sorry, somber.

"I don't care. I forgive you. Bye!" Todd drained his glass, shot off his chair, and headed enthusiastically for the door. A three-digited mechanical hand streaked, caught him by the back of his shirt, and dragged him back.

"You don't seem to understand the seriousness of the situation we face," Cog said.

"*You* don't seem to understand that the woman of my dreams is waiting for me back in her room, curled up and sighing *my* name."

"I have to show you something, Todd. I can see you won't believe me if I simply ask you to have faith in me."

"Lemme go, goddamnit! Lemme—" His mouth was suddenly stuffed with a brush. With astonishing strength, the omnicleaner hustled him from the bar. Todd cried for help, but none of the bar's inhabitants even twitched in his direction, no doubt thinking the muscling was part of the rough ambience of the pseudodive.

"It's very simple," Cog said. "I can put you out with a flick of a hypo, Todd. I'm every bit as much in control of you now as when I was the leg of the MacGuffin you rode. Or you can be cooperative and come with me. Now, which do you choose?"

"Okay!" The word came out muffled, but Cog seemed to understand. He let Todd go. Todd stood for a moment, staring down at the bossy omnicleaner. He thought about all the worth-while things for which this creature called Cog was responsible. Cog, after all, had always been right, no matter how strange his operating methods were. Who knew what planet needed saving?

Then he thought about Veronica, reclining, her dark-brown eyes skeptical and inviting.

No contest.

Spinning about, he hopped for the nearest cylinder-car.

"Todd, Todd, Todd," Cog said sadly behind him.

Something seemed to bite him on the ankle, and he belly-flopped into oblivion.

Ten

Scraping. Hollow clattering. Echoes, as though from some subterranean cavern.

Todd's eyelids fluttered open. Dimness flowed about him almost tangibly. His head felt like something had burrowed through an ear and was gnawing on his neurons.

He opened his mouth to comment on his feelings, but something quickly interposed betwixt vocal cords and open air.

"Shhh," Cog hissed. "We're in enemy territory."

He nodded. This time he kept mum.

Cog removed the brush from Todd's mouth. "Just look."

A beam flashed from the omnicleaner's side, arcing across a large chamber. At first Todd did not understand what he was seeing. They were clustered on the floor like locusts snacking on wheat. They hung from the walls like napping bats.

Thousands.

"Lord have mercy," Todd said quite sincerely.

He recognized the little wings, the antennae, the pincers at either end. He remembered the eye-stalks, the thing's gleaming body—the needlelike neuroconnectors. Metal clones of the robot Disbelief Suspender that had bloodily torn away from the back of Dr. Peters, the psychotherapist.

"But *why?*" Todd asked.

"I suspect there's one of these for every creature on board," Cog said. "But let's depart. It will be safer to talk outside."

"I'm for that," Todd remarked, feeling dread grow in the base of his spine—just the place where all that sharpness would rudely penetrate.

The omnicleaner helped Todd to his feet. A door whooshed open; Cog ushered his charge into the corridor. Only after the door reclosed did Cog pipe up in his inimical way.

"Do you remember how we enlisted aid to defeat Ort Eath?"

"Certainly. We placed you in the real-fic computer. You

communicated with all the passengers wearing Disbelief Suspenders," Todd said, exercising aching joints. Where on the ship was he, anyway?

"More than that. We manufactured a specific personality overlay. We almost *possessed* them."

"Are you saying that's what these mobile DSs are for? To hook up to passengers, take them over?"

"To connect to them, but I suspect to utilize their individualities rather than actually enslave them."

"I don't understand."

"Todd, how would you characterize my true form?"

Todd glanced, bemused, at the omnicleaner. "You're a robot leg,"

"No, no. That's my corporeal form."

"You're a Crem anchor, you said. A manifestation in this existence plane of a more elevated state where you used to live with your fellow beings in some strange combine. You're an energy being, Cog. I felt you and your siblings in that Felorian temple. A truly cosmic experience, though now I suspect much of it was illusory, just to impress me."

"Close enough for conversational purposes," Cog judged. "You realize, of course, that we Crem *used* to have carbon-based proto-plasmic bodies just like you humans. A few more arms and mouths, three sexes—or was it four? An extra sense or so, but all in all, flesh and blood."

"Right. The Galactic Council generally considers your race extinct, leaving behind all those lovely ruins like the Melphic Temple."

"We simply passed on to the next state in our particular evolutionary progression. A state similar to that which the Morapns are working toward. . . . Hence their current disinterest in territorial expansion. A state for which the *human* race has already laid the spiritual groundwork."

"You're saying that humans are destined for another plane of existence? But what does that have to do with those . . . those *machines* in there?"

"A connection exists, believe me. But let me finish. Not only are humans destined for this plane of existence, part of each and every one of you is already there."

"How could that be?"

"Collective energy emanations. Pyschic spillover, if you

will, pooling randomly in an adjacent universal flux/stasis. A different dimension, in other words. You are surely aware, Todd, that you are much more than you perceive yourself to be. Your present consciousness—your ego, if you will—is merely a filter between your perception of biologically linear space/time and your true Self. Rather like the iceberg and its tip. Over the centuries, since its development of sentience, the human minds at large have a multiple subconscious—a Collective Unconscious, residing in a vast energy aggregation beyond your immediate ken."

"Heaven? Hell?"

"Primitive notions, intuitions or precognitions of this development. Although, I must admit, there are theologians among my people who claim all this is part of some Divine Plan. Difficult to say. Beyond each Ultimate Reality there is another Ultimate Reality—*ad infinitum*. Whether there is an Ultimate Consciousness . . . well, that's not for me to say right now." Cog thumped a brush up and down contemplatively. "What occurred in the case of the Crem was simply a massive pilgrimage, choosing one state in preference to the other. However, since all planes interconnect, and the events on one echo and vibrate the other, we are naturally concerned with all events in *this* universe. Hence my participation in the *Star Fall* matter last year."

"Is that existence where an individual goes when one dies?"

"Not precisely. To digress again, your concept of yourself is not really *you*. The ego is a terrible and neurotic tyrant of the Self, a construct, an illusion. For example, Todd, would you say that your ego is the same as it was two years ago? Of course not. Your concept of yourself has changed. Thus the projection it makes on Biological Linear Time is 'dead' already. We can discuss the fine points later."

"In other words, all humans throughout the known universe are connected by this extradimensional Energy Pool?"

"Precisely. Just as all points in your universe intersect with the points of Underspace. Which, in truth, happens to be the habitation area of this extradimensional Energy Pool."

"Just an amphorus blob, floating around in mystery, huh? Sort of a cosmic acid pool into which we all eventually dissolve as the chemicals of our body dissolve into the Earth and the sky when we die in an ecological system." Todd shook his head. "That's very hard to accept, Cog."

"Bear with me, please," Cog said. "I want you to try to understand what's happening, what Earnest Evers Hurt is attempting to do."

"He seems like a rather nice fellow, actually."

"You met him?" Cog seemed alarmed.

"Yes. In the art show. We had an interesting talk."

Cog shuddered. "I would have made arrangements to immediately head back to Feloria and rejoin my race through the portal in the Temple, but for emanations I perceived in this universe plane. I lingered, I explored, I investigated. This is what I found:

"Hurt is a curious sort of megalomaniac. He not only has vast power and knowledge, he also has vast wisdom. However, his scope is limited . . . his conceptions of the universe stilted. His desire for power and personal immortality have eaten him up. They essentially control him now. He has long known of this Energy Pool I speak of. Many philosophers and even scientists have hypothesized its existence. Many mystics have perceived it through devotion and meditation into what is called the Ground State of Being or the Cloud of Unknowing. Whatever you label it, it is the dreams, the bright shadow of Reality of the human race. . . . However, unlike Hindu and Buddhist thought, there is no overriding conscious Self—at least in *this* particular psychic pool. Individually, in your biophysically supported life, you can tap into it. But generally, in such moment of 'nirvana' or 'cosmic consciousness' as the experience is called, the person involved loses sense of Self—and finds it an exhilarating experience. Sometimes, however, it is ultimately disorienting.

"Hurt is very close to death. He has studied this evolutionary energy state all his life. With the help of the Morapns, by studying their methods of penetration into the state, he is aware of how he may *objectively* penetrate this state. In other words, he wishes to explore it from without, rather than from within— and thus maintain his sense of ego, of Selfhood."

"I'm still not following the logic. Why the altered Disbelief Suspenders, then? I grasp that he thinks to penetrate this field or state or whatever using the *Star Fall* in Underspace . . ."

"By routing every Human Consciousness Center on board into a special computer-structured fabrication of Collective Unconscious—a gigantic communal real-fic, if you will—he means to create an energy field powerful enough to create a portal into the true human Collective Unconscious. The participants in this are all the humans now aboard the *Star Fall*—humans specifically chosen for their intelligence and psychological aptitude for such a use. He has collected all human knowledge in the banks of his computers on the *Star Fall* . . . By replaying every myth, symbol, magical and religious belief, all psychology and philosophy in this gigantic communal realfic, he intends to develop the process by which this mass-mind connects to ultimate human psychic collectivity, thus possibly providing himself with a fulcrum, a wedge into the Macroself of the human race. He has simulacra of all the great thinkers of mankind working for him, Todd, reliving, rethinking, re-examining the human experience for the key that will unlock control of the Human Collective Unconscious, the Macroself."

"My God!" Todd said, shaken.

"That's precisely what Earnest Evers Hurt wishes to become, Todd. He not only wants to absorb the passengers of this ship into himself—he wishes to thus seek conscious immortality by dominating and controlling the Energy Pool connected to all human minds, everywhere."

"But what can we do?" Todd said, ashen.

"Those things in there are obviously the link-ups to the artificial mass-mind, the Fabricated Reality—and also to the identity-overlay crystals which will be employed. I've discovered this access to these mobile Suspenders without Security's knowledge. Clearly, the best way to postpone Hurt's operations is to destroy them. It will give us enough time to figure out what to do."

"But how?"

"We'll blow them up."

"With what?" Todd objected.

"Leave that to me."

"Happily."

"No, I'll need your help."

Todd suddenly remembered Veronica, waiting for him back in her room. His heart sank.

"Can I have a moment to make a call?"

"Sure, but make it quick."

Todd tromped to an intercom station. Dialed Veronica's room number.

No answer. He tried again. Same result.

He moped back to the corridor corner where Cog impatiently waited. "She's not there," he sighed. "She must have given up on me." He speared Cog with a look. "All this weird stuff, Cog—Human Collective Consciousness, Hurt trying to control it—are you sure that's what's really happening?"

"That's what Hurt thinks he's doing, apparently." Cog's voice became somber. "Frankly, his chances are slim . . . unless . . ."

"Unless what?"

"Unless he ultimately attracts something . . . something I don't care to think of . . . something much less abstract. But that's neither here nor there at the moment. There's something we can do right now. Come on. We need to get some cleaning compounds in your section of duty. I'll need you to run interference. I have an idea."

"He's a nice guy. I like him." The whispery words puffed with smoke. "Don't hurt him."

"Mr. Spigot's health is not the issue here, my dear," Earnest Evers Hurt said, absently massaging her shoulders.

The Arachnid swung down from the webworking of steel cable that surrounded the control system covering most of the room's side. Crystals throbbed with particolored lights. Eerie chatter emanated from speaker grilles. Cloudy visions swirled within the screens like imprisoned ghosts. The taste of electricity filled the chamber. The biobot fitted a gemlike thing into one of the thousands of slots grouped in rows along the bottom face of the machine, then turned to address the woman. "Be assured, Miss March, I am quite concerned with Mr. Spigot's health as well." Something like laughter gurgled.

Veronica March lit another cigarette, then mashed out the stub she had lit it from. "I don't like this at all. I had no idea what you planned."

"Now, now, Veronica. We've known each other for a while," Hurt said. He leaned over and delicately kissed her cheek. "I am your patron, your friend—among other things. Trust me. Spigot and his bristly companion are misguided souls who once performed a great service for Earth."

The biobot seemed to bridle at that, but Hurt held up a silencing hand. "Now, now, Arachnid. You must admit that your consciousness then was somewhat—twisted. I have already told you, I would have done the same things they did, had I knowledge of your previous Self's activities."

"But why do you have to use people so? Without their consent?" Veronica shivered. "I knew you were carrying your experiments with you on the *Star Fall*, Earnest. But not on this scale."

"If I could have obtained volunteers of the mental caliber selected for this cruise, I most certainly would have," Hurt said, drifting over to his lowered carrier-bulb, robes whispering on the floor like a tiny chorus of worshipers. "However, I could not. Besides, my dear, I will only be using the passengers for a short period of time. When the experiment is over, it will have been like a dream to them all. Including the misguided Mr. Spigot, with whom you have my blessings to renew acquaintance with afterwards." He touched the stud on her black choker. "With or without your little device."

"I wish you'd never put that on me," she said. "I wish you'd just left me alone this afternoon, too."

"Most necessary, I assure you. Fate played into our hands."

"I don't understand," she objected. "I didn't get a chance to do anything except follow him. Anyone could have done *that*."

A smile spirited across Hurt's features as he paused before his suspended capsule. "Who said your role is through, my dear?"

"You obviously haven't gotten the full scoop," the Arachnid said, chuckling. "You see, this has all been a 'partnership' between your—uhm—*pal* and myself."

Veronica's head dipped into her hands, her hair swishing down forlornly. "What about me?"

The Arachnid examined a box of recordings from which he drew items to fill the slots. "I'm sure we've a spare personality we can stick on you."

"No!" Hurt said. "She is not for the Fabrication."

"Company, huh?" the Arachnid commented, turning its attention back to its work.

"As well as other reasons."

"Well, whatever you do, I refuse to cooperate with you anymore in whatever you're doing with Todd Spigot."

Hurt shrugged, then carefully lowered himself into his padded bulb. Automatically, neural connectors reared snakelike, then connected. A helmet lowered over his head. A gaseous purple cloud lowered over his body. "You've already provided what I wished for in Todd Spigot, who will be a welcome addition to our little universe."

"Yes." The Arachnid peered up with a chuckle. "Motivation!"

"Cog," Todd Spigot said, "this is not going to work."

"Let me be the judge of that. Coast clear?"

Todd glanced around a corner. The corridor was vacant. They had spent most of the night in the supply room of the vessel's maintenence section after Todd had changed into the appropriate outfit. Cog had adjusted the chemical mixture machine in extraordinary ways. Now, instead of cleaning compound, it produced a simple plastic explosive.

"Something feels wrong about it," Todd said. "How come you got in so easily? If those DSs are so all-fired important to Hurt's plan, why weren't they guarded?"

"Because no one knows what they are, that's why," Cog said, not attempting to mask the exasperation in his voice. "That's our one advantage, Todd. Now, hold on to the left side of this canister. It's supposed to be volatile, but I was in a hurry with the adjustments on the machine. Goodness knows what might happen if it falls over."

Todd grabbed the canister, gritted his teeth.

They reached the room. Electrical contrivances extended from the omnicleaner as it opened the door, utilizing the electromagnetic lock picks it had developed.

"With all the biospheres, all the decks, all the rooms, Cog," Todd said, "how did you manage to *find* this place? Must have been like looking for a needle in a haystack."

"Your account of the robot creature clinging to the homicidal psychologist gave me the specifics I needed. I managed to find a nice conduit of the main computer, masked myself as an operations system, and performed a discreet leech." The canister of explosive teetered precariously on Cog's back. A pair of spare nozzles jerked up to hold it in place. "Come on. We haven't any time to lose."

They proceeded into the dimness, Cog's oculars whining into night vision. "Oh, oh," he said, quivering a bit with surprise. "How—? Todd, get the canister off me. Hurry!"

Todd obliged, heaving the thing off, setting it down as easily as he could. Despite his caution, it thumped heavily to the metal floor. After a flinch, he turned his attention back to Cog, as he shrugged out of the backpack, filled with the electronic equipment. A lamp lifted from the omnicleaner's back and sprayed a cone of light, which swept the room.

Empty.

"Are you sure we have the right room?" Todd asked, a sinking feeling in his stomach.

"Of course I'm sure!" Cog declared, advancing into the empty chamber. "Look over here!" He directed the lamp to one wall, where tangles of coils hung limply. "Those were the connectors. But how were the things taken away so quickly?"

"The one I encountered was radio-operated," Todd said. "Perhaps they disconnected themselves."

Cog rolled forward to examine the shucked connectors. "Then we must be closer to the locus than I dare imag—"

A rectangular beam of energy shot from the ceiling with a fierce, strident buzzing sound, transfixing Cog to the grill-worked floor.

Instinctively Todd ducked. When he looked up, Cog was still in the same position. "Cog? Cog, answer me!" Todd said, his voice rising into a panicked scream. "Hey! You can't do this to me! You're supposed to tell me what to do! You can't just leave me alone like this!"

The flutter of wings. The swish of something knifelike singing through the air toward him. Todd hurled himself away at the last possible instant. An odd-shaped, angular creature shot past like a collection of soldered-together razors, slicing a shirt-sleeve. The flying thing arced up, flapping around for another dive.

Todd scrambled from the door, hit the closing mechanism. The robot DS was caught between door and side, clicking and scratching, its wings bent askew, oculars flashing.

Fear taking over his limbs, Todd bounced madly down the corridor for some fifty meters before he realized he hadn't the foggiest notion where he was going.

What could he do? As usual, he had just been a flunky, an assistant taking orders on this particular mission. Without Cog, he was lost. Clearly, then, the thing to do was to find a way of freeing the Cog-inhabited omnicleaner from that energy beam. But how?

Nothing to do but go back and try to find the exact nature

of the trap the Crem-ex-machina had fallen into. Luckily, he still held the lockpick device.

Cautiously, Todd sidled along the hallway, peered around the corner. The robot Disbelief Suspender hung limply in the jaws of the door. Good. Todd crept up to the door and applied the lockpick.

The inoperative robot dropped with a clatter as the door opened. Todd saw small winged things swooping around the lighted, frozen form of the omnicleaner like vultures around a dead beast. Hastily, he reclosed the door. That was no good. There must be another way.

Furiously, he thought. His maintenance duty shift was only about an hour distant. If there was anything he could do, it was through Maintenance. They were the only other people he knew. Besides, with the computer....

He found the nearest tube-car aperture, noting that people were beginning to emerge from the cabins for breakfast. Should he run screaming among them, howling warnings? What good would that do? No one would believe his crazy tale anyway. No. He had to act on his own, before the robots began to seek their victims and, vampirelike, attach to their neural systems.

Todd keyed his destination into the tube-car. The door shut and he shot into the complex transpo-system, the adrenaline of fear and frustration madly pumping through his body. Maybe he could convince the maintenance crew—they had control of or access to most of the inner workings of the *Star Fall*. If he could convince them... perhaps with the help of their computer something might be done.

The wiggling digits and letters on the control screen of the cylindrical tube-car suddenly gave a visual sputter, then stopped, signaling BIOSPHERE ZB. Deck 4. Section A. The lights in the car zipped off, blinked back on again, as though from a brief cut-off of power. Todd experienced a brief seizure of claustrophobia at the thought of being caught in a tube-car with the power cut off.

The hatch plopped open.

This was *not* the maintenance section. Wasn't even the right biosphere...

Alarmed, Todd realized that this was Veronica's section. The very touch of her name upon his mind brought forth a flood of delightful, caring memory. Recollection swiftly veered to concern as he visualized those cruel claws and needles stabbing into her back, raping her mind—

He shuddered, wondering if he had dialed up her deck and section subconsciously from his growing love. Whatever the reason, he suddenly realized he couldn't leave without retrieving her.

He squirmed from the cylinder, padded down a corridor. The lighting was noticeably dimmer, owning a strange spectral quality—like artificial twilight.

Ahead, a man leaned against the wall.

Todd, breathlessly, stopped in front of him. "Hey, mister, are you all right?" He touched the man's shoulder. The man's eyes turned up as he twisted around and collapsed to the floor. Blood spattered the back of his jump suit. Affixed on his neck, and through pierced holes in the fabric of the beige suit, was one of the mobile Disbelief Suspenders.

Terror galvanizing him, Todd ran.

Around the next corner he saw a whole cluster of the things bearing down on a group of passengers, wings flapping, needles and claws glowing with a weird light. One man whipped out a laser and managed to cut one of the things in half before another fastened to his back. With a cut-off guttural scream, the man dropped his weapon and tried to tear the thing off, but dropped onto his face before he could get a good grip.

The robots made quick work of the others and they soon lay facedown on the floor, breathing shallowly, the creatures drawing blood as the neuroconnectors performed their functions.

No spare ones to go for him. Good. Todd leaped forward, scooped up the laser pistol, its energy node still apulse, and raced off in the direction of Veronica's cabin.

Peripherally, he noted a speck of darkness detach from a wash of shadows. Spinning about, he aimed and squirted off a burst of concentrated light in a wide arc that caught the robot in its front. Reflected light sprayed for a split-second. Smoke and flame burst up; the thing dropped from the air, its wings spasming.

Todd raced on, sweat dripping down his face. He had to hopscotch over a mass of unconscious bodies lying in skewed positions in one stretch of the hallway. In another he glimpsed a flock of the batlike things flapping his way. He dropped to the floor, imitating an already hooked-up passenger among a group of bodies and let them flow jerkily past like satanic servants, eyes aglow in the twilight.

Todd rose and hastened onward.

Section Four, Cabin C, he remembered. This was definitely the way, though goodness knew how he recalled. He'd been a bit bleary with drink when Veronica had led him here, when he had retreated reluctantly. The events of the evening had quickly removed the alcohol from his system—only a slight headache throbbed now, behind his eyes.

He had almost attained his goal when something light slammed into his back. Had he not acted immediately, the mechanical creature would have had him. Near a sharp corner, he scraped it off on the edge, feeling its claws tear at cloth, scrape painfully on skin. Perch thwarted, it dropped to the ground.

Todd stepped on the thing and directed a burst of laser light across a section, effectively decapitating the portion that apparently received the radio signals.

Chest heaving from exertion, Todd raced past the other fallen passengers, finally arriving at Veronica's room. He punched the bell, which chimed inside the cabin.

"Veronica! It's Todd Spigot. No, I mean Charley Haversham! Let me in, quick!"

The door hissed open. Dark inside. Todd advanced into the gloom, hand reaching out for the light fixture. Before he could touch it, a clawed appendage chopped down on his wrist, knocking the laser from his hand.

Another mechanical hand reached down, picked it up. Lights sprang on, sparkling off the creature that had disarmed Todd as it closed and locked the door.

Dazzled by the lights, Todd stepped back, throwing up an arm to shield his eyes.

"How's tricks, Todd?" the creature asked.

Not overly large, it was nonetheless monstrous, a mechanical spiderlike thing partly made of purplish flesh, myriad eyes canted at alien angles. Its gleaming set of jaws and claws worked like an insect about to dine. With one articulated set of digits it aimed the laser gun. Without need, really; Todd was so startled and terrorized by the biobot, so dazzled by its lights, he could barely move.

"Cat got your tongue, huh?" The thing clacked sideways, clanked down into a chair. "You know, you're a lucky fellow, really. I . . . that is, Hurt has a destiny all mapped out for you."

Todd said, "But who are you?"

"Let's just say, a bit of an old friend, Todd Spigot." It chuckled: a ghastly noise. "A branch of a tree newborn from an unsuspected root."

"Ort Eath! But I saw you die—!" Then Todd recalled what Cog had said. Remembered the glitter of the scuttling orgabox through the poisonous smoke, and knew.

"A messenger, shall we say!" the biobot continued. "An angel of vengeance. An emanation. But not the creature you knew as Ort Eath. We have changed. Considerably."

"*You* killed Angharad and Amber, then! I should have guessed."

"No. They're not dead. . . . They are being used . . . for my . . . for *our* purposes. In a similar manner will you be used."

Todd remembered why he'd come here. "What have you done with Veronica?"

"Shall we say, we were cognizant of the attentions you were paying the young lady."

"You were aware of who I was all along, then?"

"Oh yes! You and your Cremian friend. Hurt has uses for you both."

"And Veronica?"

"Ah ha! Smitten! I thought as much. Let's just say that she's where you're going! A guest, Mr. Spigot. The damsel in distress. You have to find her."

Todd backed up further. "Going? Where am I going?"

One of its multitude of arms whipped around from its back. In a clenched claw wriggled a mobile Disbelief Suspender, baleful eye aspark, wings flapping.

"I believe, Todd Spigot, that this one has your name on it," the Arachnid said, advancing.

Part 2

"I" and "You" are the veil
Between heaven and
earth.

SHABISTARI

Eleven

"Everything you know is wrong!"

The voice insinuated itself among the oil-on-water shimmers, a resonant wind. Todd Spigot, floating peacefully, tasted the tenor trembles, opened his ears to the resonance in this more-than-Dream state. The current crescendoed like breakers slashing at a seashore with white-water claws. The colors of the vision quivered, then coalesced into matter . . . or something similar.

Todd found himself sprawled facedown on artificial turf, its plastic scent distinct.

Up canted his head.

Down it went again, covered by shaking hands.

"No," he moaned. "Oh, God. No." An eternity of fear passed, cool and forbidding textures on his body.

A voice, the voice, said, "Todd Spigot! Come on downnnnnnnnnn!"

Fevered clapping sounded around him: an expectant audience.

He peeped up again to see if new company had arrived. But no; the same sight assailed his vision. His universe now stretched no more than a hundred meters edge to edge, an elaborate spray-painted astroturf mandala; an island adrift in raw space. Overhead hung a magnificent canopy of stars atwinkle, planets ablaze, an occasional comet rocketing through the deep darkness in which they hung. Instead of awe at the wonderful sight, Todd felt an overwhelming sense of exposure, of agoraphobia. The sides of the mandala dropped off into nothingness. No escape. No exit.

"By Buddha's butt, you're a timid one!" the man in the purple tux said into a microphone whose cord snaked through an opening in his vest, plugging into a belly-button jack. "Don't Shiva and Shake, Todd Spigot." He chuckled, flouncing the

gilded ruffles spilling from his cuffs and below his neck. "We gonna have Veda much fun!"

Appreciative chuckles cascaded from nowhere. The thin, handsome man showed bright white teeth in a grin as he strode to Todd and helped him to his feet. He thrust the mike in front of Todd's face. "So, what's your Bhagavadgita, man?"

"Pardon me?" Todd said, realizing that he was clothed in a white robe emblazoned with the words VEDANTA YOU TOO! below an alligator insignia.

"What do you do, O pilgrim?"

"Well, I helped save Earth once."

"Cosmic, man! You must have some heavy dharma on your head."

Todd felt the top of his hair. The MC laughed. "Welcome to The Game, my friend. I'm the host of the show and resident guru, Lonnie Lingham, and if you'll just step over here to the great Cosmic Wheel, you can spin and see which game Brahma wants you to play."

"Look, I don't know what I'm doing here, but it's all a mistake! I've got to get back on the Star Fall. All humanity is going to be in a big fix if something isn't done to stop Earnest Evers Hurt!"

"Hey, cool your heels, pal! Meditate a bit on this: we're all One. I'm you. You're me. Dig it: we get squirted out in this life, forgetful of our origin, and then we gotta find our way back. Pain? Death? Fear? Just our imagination. But we're all of the same stuff, so just relax, okay, and lets have some fun!"

He snapped his fingers. A thing that looked like a carnival wheel, festooned with streamers of bright color, materialized before them.

"The joke's Om you, Todd Spigot. You're the contestant. So let's see some action."

The sound of sitars blared from somewhere, playing a curious fanfare.

Sections of the wheel were plainly marked with names, including: THIS IS YOUR KARMA! BEAT THE REAPER! and SACRED COW SURPRISE! Obediently, Todd spun the wheel, which clicked 'round and 'round, its arrow finally resting in a groove indicating MYSTERY GAME.

Another fanfare, mixed with applause.

"A favorite!" the MC cried.

The ground rocked, knocking Todd off his feet. From the side of the drifting island rose a gigantic square: a playing board partitioned into eight levels, each level holding nine garishly marked sections. Some of the levels were oddly inter-connected.

"Chutes and Ladders!" Todd said. "I played this as a kid."

The MC smiled condescendingly. "Not quite, Todd." He clicked his fingers. "Babs! The die, please!"

A breeze built, streamered into opalescent form: became a scantily clad young brunette holding a large dotted cube.

"Veronica!" Todd cried, reaching out for her. She nimbly sidestepped his lunge, grabbed hold of the MC's arm, hugging it warmly. "I want to explain what happened to me last night!"

She winked at him. "Some other time, sweetheart. Mean-time . . ." She tossed him the die.

A raucous grinding sound commenced to one side. A con-sternated expression crossed the MC's face.

With a whir that sounded like a straining, broken, air con-ditioner, a box faded into view, a red light revolving at its top. POLICE CALL BOX proclaimed the letters above a door. A door which promtly opened, disgorging a man in a frumpy Ed-wardian overcoat, trailing a long plaid scarf. His hands were stuffed in the pockets of his vest. "Leela!" he called, grinning a manic grin. "Good evening," he said to Todd. "You haven't seen a young savage lady, have you?"

The playing board suddenly blinked streamers of multicol-ored lights. Neon letters caught electric fire at its top: LEELA.

The man's wrinkle-wreathed eyes widened. "Oh dear. My Positronic Emanation Locator got the wrong one." He lifted a floppy hat from a disorganized bunch of curls. After hopping cheerfully back to his peculiar box, he checked the soles of his shoes with distaste. "Careful where you step around here. Cosmic droppings!" He shut the doors. The box noisily dis-appeared.

The MC shrugged. "Now, Todd Spigot. Please roll the die."

"I want to go home. I don't want to play."

"You must play. Play is the nature of the universe. You must strive to reach Cosmic Consciousness." He pointed up. "On the row of the Gods Themselves."

Todd rolled the die. Six.

Applause sounded. "You have entered," the MC explained,

"the Physical Plane. The plane of Maya, of illusion. Here you will be plagued by Anger, Greed, Delusion, Conceit and Lust, depending upon which box you land in. Your roll places you in the Delusion box. Babs, dear. Please take our guest to the appropriate section, where he may begin his journey."

Bemused, Todd allowed himself to be led into the box. Immediately, a door slammed shut over the section. He blinked. He was back in his mother's apartment in Deadrock, sitting in front of his three-dee set. He heard the sounds of his mother clacking pans in the kitchen.

The MC appeared in the three-dee set. "Hi, Todd."

"What the hell am I doing here?" Todd said, panicking. Any nostalgia for the place faded rapidly. The smell of beans and franks wafting from the kitchen turned his stomach—which he suddenly realized had ballooned. He was back in his old body! Fear and anxiety gripped him.

"This is the first stop, Todd Spigot. First stop of many. Such states as Uttam Gati, Dukh, Daan, and Narka-Loka await you. Right now, you're in Moha—Delusion. You *don't* see the Truth. Your mind is beclouded. You're out of harmony with the Path."

"Todd!" his mother cried in a voice that raked across his very soul. "Todd, come and set the table. Your father will be home anytime now from the mines."

"My father!" Panic seized him as he visualized his dead old man traipsing across the threshold like the corpse called back by the Monkey's Paw.

"The saying goes," said the MC, "whatever should be adopted, that is Dharma. When one does not follow the law of his own nature, he becomes mired in Delusion."

"Todd! Hurry! I think I hear the lift!"

The doorknob squeaked. Heavy boots thumped in the hall-way.

"Get me *out* of here!" Todd cried.

"Do you want what's behind the box or the curt— Oops. Wrong show. Just throw the die, Todd."

Hastily, Todd cast the die. It landed, showing three dots. Immediately, he was tugged into another section. He caught a glimpse of stars: then the section was closed off, leaving him in fragrant darkness.

"Charley? Is that you?" called a sleepy voice. "How did you get back in?" He realized he was in a cabin on the Star

Fall, *dimly lit. A figure raised itself in the bed, and all thought race from Todd's mind when he realized it was Veronica March.*

"Yes," he said. "I told you it wouldn't take me long."

"Hmmmmmmmmmm," she said sexily. "Come over here." *He could hear sheets sliding over bare skin.*

Eagerly, he hopped into the bed and into the insistent embrace of awakening femininity. At the very touch of her smoothness, he felt himself relaxing. Ah, such bliss. He held her, seemed to melt, to blend into her. Lips found lips and exchanged enthusiastic silent discussion. Tongues touched passionately. Feverish ache charged through his body as delicate fingers began to glancingly touch him in exactly the right places.

They rolled about smoothly, exchanging tingling touches. "Hmm!" *she murmured.* "Have you been off someplace practicing?"

"Only our Dress Rehearsal last time."

"This time," *she whispered,* "no dress." *She commenced parting the shirt he now wore, replacing the buttons on his chest with kisses.*

"Warning! Warning!" *a voice announced.* "Sex will screw you up!"

The MC appeared, translucent beside them. Veronica did not seem to notice his presence. She was working on Todd's belt.

"You wanna get out of here?" *Todd suggested.* "I like this section."

"You are now on the Sensual Plane."

"No kidding. I thought I heard jets throbbing somewhere."

"Kama-Loka. The Plane of Desire." *The voice sounded annoyed.* "Directly linked with Ignorance."

Todd gasped as Veronica's fingers tried to figure out the workings of his magnetic zipper. "I don't want to know anything."

The ghostly MC tapped his foot. "Please roll the die."

Todd suddenly felt the marked cube in his hand.

"Get lost!"

"Todd," *Veronica said.* "How do I—" *She raised her head suddenly. It struck Todd's hand, knocking the die onto the floor.*

It rolled, stopping on the number six.

"Damn, damn, damn," *Todd said, even as the room and Veronica dissolved.*

He found himself in another large box, open to the celestial vista. The MC stood outside, silhouetted by starlight. In one hand was the die, glowing infernally from within. In another hand was a Disbelief Suspender.

"A perfect roll, Todd Spigot." Slowly, the affable MC began to metamorphize. His trunk became squat. New arms grew. "This is precisely where we want you." Its oculars glimmered evilly. "Nark-loka. The Plane of Fantasy. But instead of a die, we have a little addition."

The biobot tossed the Disbelief Suspender into the small room.

"Have fun!"

The door slammed shut.

The walls glowed as though with phosphorescence.

The Disbelief Suspender jerked. Wings unfolded.

Terrorized, Todd backed away. Suddenly, the thing began to grow. Steel became mottled green skin. Needles became fangs. Oculars became cold serpentine eyes.

He suddenly remembered the other name for this game he used to know as Chutes and Ladders, without the metaphysics.

Snakes and Ladders.

The gigantic serpent hissed twice, then struck, swallowing Todd Spigot into Darkness.

Twelve

"I must admit," a voice said, "I was rather impressed by that fellow Kant's Categorical Imperative."

"What? You mean, 'An action is morally right if one can will that it become a universal law which all should follow; otherwise it's wrong'," another responded.

"You must admit he had a persuasive argument."

"Look. All these jokers have got fantastic arguments. They're smart. But being smart doesn't make you right. It just makes you come up with a fascinating theory that seems to fit the human condition, and then produce rigorously worked-out systems of argument to support those theories."

"Is that *your* theory?"

"Yeah. I ought to write it down for posterity or something."

Total relaxation, as though he had just come into existence for the first time. The sensations came slowly, as did awareness.

"You know, we might not be able to save humanity this time. But at least we're getting a good education."

"What? With all these famous scientists and philosophers and other luminaries bumbling around, babbling? They're just as confused as we are. At least *we* have a vague notion what's going on."

"You know, I hope we run into William James. There are a few points of Pragmatism I'd like to discuss with him. Besides, I'm sure he's counting all this as a most sensational religious experience to add to his *Varieties of . . .*"

The air that touched his nostrils had a sweet touch to it: grass; hints of flowers. Mountain, redolent of fresh glacial streams, of evergreens.

"I'm sure glad we shook off that chap St. Augustine," the deeper voice said. "Dreary guy!"

"Yes, by and large the religious philosophers are the most

puzzled by this state of being. Won't listen to my explanation
at all. They're taking this pseudoresurrection very hard."

"I thought that Descartes fellow was going to die, the shade
of purple he turned when he said, 'I think, therefore I am,'
and you said, 'Yes, but you're not who you *think* you are!' "

A sort of "hawing" sound knocked Todd from his blissful
reverie. He sighed heavily and pushed himself up on his arms.

"Well, Sleeping Beauty has been touched by Prince Charming's lips, apparently," the deeper voice—almost a growl—
said wryly. "I wonder what great mind inhabits him. Sartre?
Raspro? Sheffield?"

"Looks like it's plain old Todd Spigot to me," replied the
other voice.

Face sweeping through the high grass, Todd Spigot stared
blearily up. He was lying in a copse of conifers. Above was
blue sky inhabited by puffy cream clouds that scudded across
the heavens like an animated masterwork. Somehow, the depth,
though beautiful, was all wrong. He lifted a hand, stared at it.
It looked like a beautifully rendered two-dimensional acrylic-
covered drawing of his hand. He turned it over and the edges
blurred faintly as the palm came into view; like rotoscoping.

Startled, he looked up toward where the strange voices emanated.

Sitting by outcroppings of rock that looked almost papier-
mâché were two creatures seemingly in a pose from a sense-
surround View Master clay animation movie. The colors were
all deep-hued, rich and bright: unnaturally so.

One was a donkey with a unicorn's horn spiraling up to a
point that occasionally gave off a stylized gleam.

The other was a large lion who reminded Todd of Aslan of
C. S. Lewis' Narnia books.

They both moved like Ray Harryhausen monsters. What
was it called? Dynamation, that was it. The movements had
a faint jerkiness.

All his life Todd Spigot had been a film buff. He knew the
history of film and three-dee forward, backward and in slow
motion. He suddenly realized that he was in a strange three-
dimensional collage of animation styles.

A character in a colossal cartoon.

"Talk about karma," he muttered, getting to his feet, trying
to rub out a headache at the back of his skull.

"Welcome to the Fabrication, kiddo," the unicorn said.

"Yeah, thrills and chuckles galore." The lion stuck a paw at Todd and addressed the uni-donk. "How come *he's* not symbolic, huh? Some gangling ape or something? It's not fair."

Both voices were spookily familiar.

"Sleep well, Todd?" the uni-donk asked.

"How do you know my name?"

"He doesn't recognize us," the lion said. "Fancy that!"

The unicorn paced forward and stared Todd in the eye. "Hang on to your pants, fella. I'm Angharad Shepherd. That burly beast with the smart mouth is our pal Philip Amber."

"Fancy meeting you here," Amber drawled.

"I thought you were . . ." Todd broke out in a relieved grin. "Dead!"

"The rumors of our deaths are entirely exaggerated. Actually, right now we're just brains in nutrient baths—*private*, I hope"—she sniffed—"plugged into this Fabrication."

"Yes, Fabrication! Cog used that word. I remember now!"

"Cog?" Amber growled. "Where is he when we need him?"

"Trapped, I'm afraid. We were going to try to destroy the mobile Disbelief Suspenders before they started attaching to people."

He shook his head, astonished as he walked to a break in foliage and stared down a hill at a river that swirled, pen and pencil lines still evident. "This place is bizarre."

"Used to be a little more realistic, until the Change," Angharad said. "Apparently all the new souls added were a bit of a drain even on Hurt's mammoth computers, so various shortcuts were implemented."

"Yeah," said Amber. "I'm still looking around for Bugs Bunny. He's my favorite."

"My God, exactly *how* is he doing this? I mean, I feel, taste, see, smell . . . and yet in actual physical reality this place doesn't exist."

"Right. It's a mammoth collectively generated illusion. For all practical purposes it's real, though, Todd. If you start doubting your senses, you'll go bonkers." Angharad whisked away a fly with her tail. "As to how . . . well, Amber and I have been puzzling that out for some time."

"Yeah," Amber said, sauntering up to Todd. Around his neck he wore a collar with a pouch. "We figure that it works like a gigantic real-fic landscape, though more complex. The mega-computers feed an immense amount of information into the new brains that Hurt's acquired, sculpting a reality merely by common agreement. For example, when I do this—" Amber scooped a divot from the greensward. "The computers have to make adjustments. What's happening is that my brain in its nutrient tank is *willing* my limb to move, a cause, and has to make *effect* changes in the reality set. The computer adjusts the sensory output from its landscape appropriate to my permitted action so that *you*, wherever you are on the *Star Fall*, linked in whatever fashion, *see* what I do. If you picked up that bit of grass and dirt, it would smell earthy to you. Maybe an earthworm would fall out. We'd both see that. But our brains in the actual physical locations are merely being manipulated."

"And yet," Todd said, "our brains are actually communicating."

"Yes," Angharad said, "but only within the context of this mock-reality. I was onto Hurt's plans. That's what I was doing for Central: investigating Hurt's research center."

"And ignoring me," Todd said, hurt.

"Todd, it was important. Let me finish." She tossed her mane in exasperation. "You know about the Morapn mindfields, don't you Todd? Well, Hurt studied them, and mechanically has built a distorted and perverse mechanical version, uniting all the minds on board the *Star Fall* into an unconscious collective, overlaying the majority with Identity Crystals of famous thinkers of history."

"To puzzle out the portal to the actual Collective Unconscious Energy Field of mankind in Underspace," Todd finished. "Yes. Cog told me all that."

"Too bad the leg is trapped. We could use him," Amber said.

"But why have we kept our identities, even if you've been changed into absurd creatures?"

"Apparently this mass-mind that's been jerry-built by Hurt can't just automatically jell into perfection. It has to grope its way to wholeness and completion, even as its individual components seek the Truth in their own separate ways. When this wholeness, this Individuation occurs, then the super-mind will perceive or perhaps even create the portal into the Collective Unconsciousness field, adhering to it. All this is apparently occurring, to *our* awareness, symbolically—with the symbols coalescing merely the shadows of strange and unnameable things occurring on a much deeper level."

"And thus Hurt rides his way to immortality." Todd shivered as he gazed around. "He could be watching us, listening to us now."

"Absolutely possible. Most likely, however, he has more important things to do."

"Why did he throw us together?"

"That, I think, has less to do with Hurt than with the current incarnation of our old friend Ort Eath," Angharad said.

"You know about the biobot then?"

"No."

Todd explained.

"Curious," Angharad said thoughtfully. "That would explain a great deal. Meshed in the Core of the *Star Fall*. Not really my alien brother, but a melding of all those brains he assimilated."

"You think he threw us all together so that he could extract some kind of vengeance?"

"That's exactly what we think," the lion snarled harshly. "But God knows how."

"What can we do?" Todd said plaintively.

"Apparently you've been set down with us because you're meant to be on our particular mission."

"Mission? What mission?"

The lion tapped a paw to its collar. "Open this pouch here."

A little leery of the massive beast despite its claimed identity, Todd Spigot ventured forward and obeyed. From the pouch he picked out a folded-up piece of yellow parchment.

"You've got hands," Angharad said. "You can be our navigator. I can't tell you how hard it is to hold that thing with hooves—"

"—or paws."

Todd unfolded the paper. Archaic script flowed among representations of mountains, rivers and castles. A spot marked X was accompanied by the words THE WASTE LAND and CASTLE OF THE FISHER KING.

"We're looking for the Holy Grail?" Todd said incredulously.

"Good," Amber said to Angharad. "He knows his Arthurian literature. *We* certainly don't. Not very well, anyway."

Todd brightened, suddenly feeling one step ahead of his colleagues for once instead of paces behind. "Yes. I was always fascinated with everything about King Arthur." He rubbed his chin. "And you know, this is perfectly appropriate, too."

"Oh? Why?" the lion asked.

"The Grail Legends are very confused—"

"And *we're* very confused too, huh?"

"No. Let me finish. The Holy Grail was sometimes the cup from the Last Supper of Christ, sometimes the vessel which caught the blood from Christ's side when he was nailed to the Cross, sometimes a plate or stone. But always its symbolic nature is the achievement of a mystical oneness with the Creator."

"Which correlates with Hurt's ambition. Only he's *storming* Heaven, so to speak," Angharad said thoughtfully.

"Why are *we* assigned to seek out the Grail, if the new version of Ort Eath is masterminding some kind of revenge on us?"

"I think I can answer that," Todd said. "Of all the 'Quests' for spirituality in history and literature, the one for the Grail was always fraught with the greatest danger to the body *and* the soul. Nonetheless, its symbols have struck a sympathetic chord in mankind for ages." He looked up at the two. "Hey, but we're together again, right?" he said with a feeble smile. "We made a great team last time."

"You seem to forget, Todd, that we lack the support of a certain crucial *leg*," Angharad said through a mouthful of half-munched grass.

Todd stuck his hands in his pockets. "Well, there's nothing to do then but follow this map. Perhaps something will come up along the way. Besides, there's nothing that's *making* us search for this false Grail any—" He felt something in his pocket. "Here. What's this?" He dug out a letter, unfolded it.

HELP, it said. AM BEING HELD PRISONER IN GRAIL CASTLE. DUE TO BE FED TO DRAGON ON TUESDAY. VERONICA.

Suddenly, remembrance and accompanying love and yearning coursed through Todd with such force that he became faint, almost toppling over. He remembered the woman's soft touch, the promise in her voice, the glimmers in her eye—and was suddenly swimming again in dizzy infatuation.

"Todd? You okay?" Angharad asked, concerned.

"Oh, fine. Fine," Todd returned. "Uhm, Angharad. Mind if I ride on your back? A questing knight generally needs a steed."

Armor glinted in the sun. A sword flashed as it rang from its sheath. The white horse reared and chain mail jingled. The knight eyed them suspiciously.

"Hal Foster," Todd said. "Prince Valiant."

The knight jogged their way against the blurry watercolor background.

"Whatever are you talking about?" Amber asked, shying away from the sight of the knight's razor-sharp blade.

"Hurt and his computers must have plundered the old funny-papers of the 20th and 21st centuries. Although come to think of it, the knight here looks something more like an Arthur Rackham illustration."

"Don't look now," Amber said, whiskers twitching, "but I think you've offended him."

The knight spurred the flanks of his roan mare and commenced a wild charge toward the trio, his sword swinging mightily. The silver and dull bronze of the armor and steed, the crimson and turquoise of his helmet plume, seemed to bleed into the neutral-colored air, aswirl with the faintest hint of computer-dot animation.

Stylized dust puffed at the hooves.

Speed lines developed, trailing behind him.

"Here's a thought," Angharad said. "Suppose we get killed. We'll just get resurrected somewhere else, right? I mean, computer-generated swords can't really affect computer-generated bodies."

"Yeah," Amber said, "but it will *hurt!*"

"That's true. We'd better run." The uni-donk about-faced and raced away at surprising speed. Amber, in his lion guise, departed quickly in another direction.

Leaving Todd lagging in place.

The snorting horse and sword-bearing knight bore down upon him. "Heathen! Consorter with the Devil's creatures!" came a tinny cry. "Drink deep of Christian steel!"

Todd managed to get his foot tangled in a root and plunged facefirst into the loam.

The clop of hooves, the jingle of chain mail. The knight

dismounted noisily. Todd swung his head up in time to see the sword raise up, streaming after-images.

He wondered what animated blood would look like.

"Wait!" he cried. "I've got nothing to do with the Devil, I assure you!" Still, he heard the *woosh* as the sword sliced through air and he spun himself away. The blade sliced through a sleeve, nicking him, then buried itself in the grass and dirt.

Pain stung Todd's arm.

The blood that leaked was a theatrical bright red.

"Die, Satan spawn!" the knight said, jerking the sword up again. However, before he could drive the steel down again, a form hurled itself from off Todd's frame of vision, knocking the knight into a tumble that sounded like a catastrophe in a kitchen. The sword fell away, out of the grounded knight's reach. The lion that held Philip Amber's mind leaned on the gleaming chest.

"Now then," he purred, "what did you say?"

The incongruous animation styles made a surreal sight, like a film chroma-keyed over the wrong bit of video.

"I fear not the likes of you!" the knight declared. "My purity is holy in the sight of the Lord, and I have no need to fear either death or the hellfire from which you emerged!"

"You want to take off that helmet and tell us who you are?"

Holding his arm, Todd stood. He noticed Angharad warily returning.

The knight shed his helmet, revealing a bright-eyed, blue-haired youth. "My name is Sir Galahad, and I am on a sacred quest. No one may stand in my way!"

"And you randomly attack fancied creatures of the Devil," Angharad commented.

"This is indeed my sworn duty to God. This strange land is full of evil apparitions and illusions. Now kill me, if you must, for it is as good a route to Heaven as any for such as I."

"Modest guy," Todd said. "Mind if I steal your scarf? Your sword is quite sharp." He untied the shimmering cloth from around the knight's neck and bound his wound.

"Why don't you go and get the sword, Todd?" Amber suggested, "Before I let His Highness up. He might make a grab for it."

"Only the best knight in the world may wield that sword.

Even Gawain and Perceval could not draw it before my mother brought me to Camelot."

"Galahad is the bastard son of Lancelot and Elain," Todd explained. "According to the legend, Lancelot was bewitched into thinking Elain, who adored him, was his beloved Guinevere and bedded her. Elain immediately conceived Galahad."

"Fertile fellow!" Angharad said.

"This *is* the sword that Lancelot refused to attempt to draw from the stone, right?" Todd said, squatting by the blade.

"Yes," Galahad said. "Have you a spy at the court?"

"So tell us what happened later, Galahad."

"After the tournament, where I beat all challengers, a great feast was held. In the midst of the merriment, a great peal of earth-shaking thunder rolled. The doors burst open and the brighest of white lights steamed in, dazzling the eyes of all. All were struck dumb, even King Arthur himself, filled from within with the light of the Holy Spirit. Then, all covered in white samite, the Holy Grail ghosted in. But none could truly see it nor truly touch it. Soon after its disappearance, most of the knights of the Round Table, including myself, vowed to seek it out, that they might become one with God."

"You see what I mean?" Todd said. "The symbolism is quite significant, considering Hurt's goals."

"Who is this 'Hurt' you speak of?" Galahad asked.

"A lot like the Devil, my friend," Angharad said. "Believe us, we're on your side. You don't want Satan himself to lash his barbed tail around the Holy Grail, do you?"

Galahad shook his blue-highlighted curls vigorously.

"Well, then. We can help you," Amber said. "And you can help us."

Todd folded his hand around the leather-clad hilt of the sword. Its pommel—a huge emerald—shone green with embedded sparks as Todd picked it up. A spectrum of animated swirls twisted around the blade, then was sucked back in by the tip.

"You see," Todd said. "It likes me."

Galahad said, "You must truly be forces of Good. You may accompany me."

Amber lifted his paws from the knight. "Terrific. And you know, it just so happens that we even have a map to the place."

"The Lord be praised!" Galahad said, struggling up under the weight of his armor.

"No, I think we can thank the Devil for the map," Todd said. "Which is why it's good to have a Round Table knight along for the ride."

They traveled for the rest of the day.

With every mile of the journey, Todd noticed, things got stranger.

Apparently, as they followed the parchment map, they departed the portions of the computer landscape where the resurrected Great Minds were conferring among themselves with great vigor. Now they seemed to be delving ever deeper into a land full of shadow and symbol, mystery and magic, cosmic import and comic book heroes.

Superman whizzed overhead at one point, straight out of Max Fleisher Technicolor. The Harlequin tap-danced his way across their path at one point, then disappeared into a gloomy bower, leaving a trail of torn-up playing cards: his Twenty-First-Century trademark. Ricky Robot, Todd's childhood favorite, spun in on his rotors for a charming chat and then zoomed away.

Riding on Angharad's back, Todd caught glimpses of fabled creatures among the woods and fields. Basilisks; baby dragons cavorting in streams; elves and fairies zipping through green leaves and zigzagging tree limbs, shedding Walt Disney stardust.

The land was an amazing patchwork, shifting constantly; a collage of color dredged from the imagination of mankind.

"You see what I mean," Galahad said as the sun began to jitter slowly into something out of a Greek Orthodox stained glass window. "We are truly in Satan's province of sorcery."

The land was suddenly washed in muted pastels as the sun decided to make a quick drop below the horizon. Five-pointed stars sketched themselves brilliantly upon the blank face of the night. A full-moon rose, complete with a plaster-of-paris smile face, shedding a spectral glow over the mutating landscape.

"I thank God for my faith in Him, which keeps me steadfast and pure," Galahad said as they dismounted to make camp and dine on a bucket of fried chicken a fast-food joint had been distributing free.

"To what qualities do you prescribe this great state of yours?" asked Angharad.

"Loyalty to the Good," Galahad said. "Abstinence from strong drink, and most important, chastity."

"Chastity?" Angharad said. "What's that?" Quite sincerely.

"Ask Todd," Amber said. "He would know."

"Thanks a heap," said Todd. "Angharad, Galahad is saying that he's a virgin."

"What's that?"

"He hasn't had sex, Angharad."

She turned a horrified donkey face to the knight. "You're *kidding* me."

"Sex?" Galahad said.

"A modern word for having a woman, Galahad."

"I'd make a pass at him," Angharad said, "but frankly I'm not into bestiality." She hee-hawed.

"You jest, but you do not know the power of chastity," Galahad said. "All my attentions and affections are focused toward God, and thus I am filled with goodness, joy and completion. Can any of you sinners boast such a state?"

"You sound like St. Augustine," Amber said. "What was it he said? 'Sexuality is the yearning the human heart has toward God.'"

"St. Augustine just got jaded," said Angharad, stifling a yawn. "Now if you don't mind, I'm going to stake out a piece of fabricated reality and take a snooze. The old brain still needs to sleep and dream more normal dreams. Galahad, any dragons roaming about that we should beware of?"

"Nameless, fearsome creatures, newly crawled from the Pit itself," Galahad said, face stiff, resolute, looking more a cartoon now than illustration.

"Paper tigers too, no doubt," Amber commented, looking about for a soft bit of lawn to collapse upon. "Todd, how much further do you reckon this Holy Grail actually *is?*"

Todd rustled open the parchment and examined the map by milky moonlight. "Hard to say. Judging by the progress that you all claimed you made, I'd guess another couple days' worth of trek—if days are measured out normally here."

Todd sighed, folded the map and placed it back in the pouch.

He sat down in a clump of akimbo arms and legs, head tilted forlornly toward the ground. "It all seems so hopeless.

We're all being manipulated. Who knows what terrors the Arachnid's got programmed to strike for our jugulars, lurking among the scenery?"

Angharad strode up to Todd, nuzzled him softly with her moist nose. "Take it easy, Todd. This really is literally a battle of wills. Ours versus theirs. We have to think positively or we're defeated before we begin."

"You know," Todd said, as he watched Galahad tie his horse to a tree, "what I don't understand is, why the map? If Hurt knows exactly where this Holy Grail is, why have *us* find it?"

"It's the process, I presume, that perhaps creates the votive qualities of the so-called Grail, Todd. Hurt does *not* have full control. He's playing with powerful forces—forces which have shaped and moved mankind throughout history. It may all explode in his face—which is our hope, of course."

"Right," Amber said. "The way Angharad and I figure, if Hurt can use this Grail, then so can we. That is, if we can get our hands—or minds—on it before he does."

"The energies of the Collective Unconscious are apparently neutral," Angharad said. "If they can indeed be controlled, tapped into the manner Hurt wants—then why can't any one of us do the same thing?"

"If your definition of this Energy Pool is correct," Todd said, "then every single one of us is already plugged in. Can't we do something on *that* level?"

"'Which of you can raise your height one cubit by thinking on it,'" Angharad quoted. "It's something so deep, we really can't change it. Just as you can't mentally adjust your chromosome patterns, Todd. It has to be done from outside."

"By this artificial Macroself that you think Hurt is trying to concoct," Amber said. "And in whose very mind we presently walk. A mass-mind fuctioning as a key to this spiritual state. The landscape we travel upon now is the symbolic working-out of the Individuation of this mass-mind. Through these processes, we are slowly being assimilated into One—and one guess who intends to be in charge of that mass-mind."

Todd fell back into the cushioning grass and stared up at the twinkling, artificial stars, this time not really wanting to think about what lay beyond them.

Thirteen

The entire concave ceiling, sides and bottom of the sphere's interior were tiled with tiny screen monitors flashing multi-colored representations of the activities within the Fabrication.

Whistling softly to himself, Hurt tapped gently on one of the complex keyboards that surrounded his chair like an over-large life preserver. His chair swiveled gently as a bank of monitors was wiped clean. A composite picture replaced the separated images: the twisting energy vortices and jagged curtains that flowed through Underspace, churning out of the way as the force-field of the *Star Fall* cut through them like the prow of a submarine making its way through a particularly dark and mysterious section of ocean.

However, there was still no sign of the Energy Pool.

But then, thought Hurt, how would he know what it looked like? Would it even emit detectable radiation? He knew the complex mathematical representations cold; but the Energy Pool would not be a collection of numbers and symbols hanging amid the peculiar complexities of Underspace.

Impatiently, he stabbed a button which erased the picture. Only time would tell. The Fabrication seemed to performing its magnet function well, pulling itself ever closer to its point of attraction. Hurt had adjusted the piloting systems of the *Star Fall* to follow this compass effect, thus speeding connection of the ship with the human mind-field.

His observation/control sphere hung in an antigrav pocket, transfixed with wiring and tubing which pumped in his regulated atmosphere mix. If necessary, needles could be attached to his arms to intraveneously feed him; an evacuation tube was available to collect his eliminations; Hurt could live in the sphere indefinitely, should that need arise.

A flood of images renewed themselves upon the previously vacant screens, dancing colorful visions of myth and mystery.

What a fertile field, the human mind! Hurt thought as he lost himself in observing the parade of creatures and their inter- actions as they worked their way toward inevitable Oneness. Some unconscious part of him yearned to cast off the burden of awareness and hurl itself into the delight of integration.

But no. That natural temptation had to be ignored. Better things awaited the consciousness of Earnest Evers Hurt.

Better things indeed.

Satisfied that all operations ran properly, Hurt keyed in- structions for the sphere to lower itself from its null-grav pocket. A few more items of business demanded attention be- fore the operation's final phases were instigated.

The man lurched toward her, gnarled fingers outstretched.

Startled, she could not contain a yelp. She sidestepped him and the rumpled fellow, glaze-eyed, stumbled past her. Bits of food matted his mustache; his chin glistened with moisture from a recent drink. The Disbelief Suspender rode his back like some demonic jockey.

"The ontological argument for the existence of God states..." the man murmured, then sank into a heap in a corner alongside another man and woman. The Disbelief Suspender, its claws and neuroconnectors deeply sunk, spasmed slightly in the strip lighting of the corridor and then was still.

Veronica March felt sick to her stomach.

They were all like this. Even the children had these Old- Man-of-the-Sea devices dug into their backs. Mechanical leeches, that's what they looked like. Obscene. Two or three times a day each body would jerk itself into zombielike activity, shamble to a food station for sustenance, visit a vac-booth for elimination—then dive back into deathlike stillness.

Earnest had not even hinted of anything like the horror he was perpetrating aboard this liner. He had mentioned involving the passengers in what he called his "consciousness experi- ments." He had spoken of some crack-brained idea of con- tacting "the ultimate state of humanity." But then, Earnest had always gone on about this or that mystical or transcendental concept as they had lain pillow to pillow in the relaxation of after-sex.

He'd mixed that nonsense well, though, with words of other concerns—poetic ramblings of appreciation for her and her talents, artistic and otherwise. Immediately after she had dumped that martini on his shirt at the Space Eyes Cordial two years before, galleries and opportunities suddenly opened before her; the difficult path of success in the viciously competitive art world was suddenly free of obstacles. Everyone and their clone wanted to have their posterior's mark firmly planted in Posterity's Art Show; everyone dreamed of financial success and public adulation. With Hurt's patronage, she, Veronica March, the "odd bod" of her Commune, Kozmic Klutz of Spool School and deserted zygote of parents who'd hired a cheap spawn-tank, paid upfront, and apparently forgotten her, had gotten it all.

Earnest Evers Hurt had shown her how to combine her penchant for optics and chemistry with a certain flair for visualization into a stunning talent. Earnest Evers Hurt had made sure she was apprised of the right avenues to traverse in the tricky maze of Art. Earnest Evers Hurt had always been a gentle and amusing, if strange, lover whose amorous attentions were few, far between, and ultimately undemanding. He allowed her other lovers—in fact, occasionally supplied them when her spirit (or his ancient libido) were low. Sometimes, it turned out, her favors were lavished upon select men whom Hurt could not sway with money. All diplomatically engineered: he knew her preferences.

Still, when she did find this out, it galled her no end. However, she kept mum. Her intention had been to leave Hurt after the *Star Fall*'s year-long cruise, after her work had become known all over the galaxy and she had a measure of fame and financial independence. No longer would Hurt be able to slyly manipulate her, use her to lure unsuspecting types like Charley Haversham or whatever his name was.

Now *this*—

Earnest had *changed* after he'd bought the *Star Fall*. Subtly, but definitely, he seemed different.

Another sprawl of bodies. A shiver of dread.

She hurried the last few paces to her destination, fit the mag-key Hurt had given her, danced her fingers in the necessary code-mode. The door gave way and she found herself eye-to-photoelectric-sensor with Hurt's biobot bodyguard.

A claw caught her wrist, tugged her close to where purplish, vein-mottled flesh contracted and expanded with the thing's imitation of breathing. Its red-rimmed mouth opened, revealing stainless steel teeth.

"Ah ha. The mistress of the manor! Gliding through the dim corridors, a distressed maiden."

"Let me go, you multi-legged turd!" she said with gritted teeth. She had always abhorred the sight of Hurt's biobot. In the year since it had developed this loathsome personality, she had come to hate it furiously. The horror was that the perverse thing seemed to sense her deep revulsion and took pains to play upon it like some demented maestro of mischief. Touching her. Volunteering replacement for Hurt's amorous duties. Drooling spittle and oil.

"The master is in his study," the thing said, pointing upward at the sphere nestled in its antigrav nest, far above in the huge, cold chamber. Like a ball bearing of some invisible wheel, it gleamed amid its tapestry of wires.

Veronica tugged away from the creature. "Call him down, then. I want to talk to him."

"Mr. Hurt instructed me not to disturb him except for a matter of the greatest urgency." It scuttled back to its webbing strung across the face of the monstrous socketed computer facets. Lights cavorted beneath as he clambered up. "And you, my dear," it said with a disinterested voice, "are hardly urgent."

Veronica stepped toward the computer, stared into one of the holes that pocked the computer façade like cells of a beehive. The inside glittered, tungsten strands at its core pulsing a faerie glow.

"Why didn't *I* get treated to this one-way trip to nowhere?"

The Arachnid peeked thoughtfully at a keyboard, then cocked its head to regard the results on a screen.

"My question precisely, dear heart. I urged Mr. Hurt to include you. You would have made an excellent Joan of Arc for Scenario 34 C." The thing sighed affectedly. "But no. Mr. Hurt wants you to remain topside."

"Just who are you anyway, biobot? Just what do you plan on getting out of this . . . this *insane* real-fic charade? You've got something up your sleeve . . ."

"Sleeve? Madam, as you may or may not observe, I have no sleeves. As to my plans—well, they dovetail right into Mr. Hurt's—which is why we make such simpatico partners." The Arachnid glanced up. Light twinkled on the descending sphere.

"Well, it's your lucky day, Miss March. Your pal is checking in on Reality Prime."

Veronica stalked to the dock. Hurt was not surprised to see her. "Ah, Veronica. I've been thinking about you," he said mildly as the neuroattachments released their holds. His robes rustled as he emerged. He kissed her gently on the cheek.

"Don't touch me."

Hurt gave her a mildly consternated look. "I was just going to suggest, my dear, that you retrieve your belongings from your cabin and move into my quarters. I suspect that most of the ship must be troublesome to your sensibilities."

"It's *hellish*, that's what it is, Earnest. In the name of decency, I demand that you stop whatever you are doing *now*."

"Your chirping conscience," the Arachnid called from his wobbling perch. "How enchanting!"

"Shut up!" Hurt snapped. He turned a frown toward his mistress. "Veronica—you've never spoken like this to me before."

"You've never imprisoned a spaceliner full of humans before. Have you *seen* them, waddling about in the halls like lost souls?"

"Veronica, they must eat and attend to their bodily functions. I assure you, when this experiment is over, each individual will enjoy far better health—indeed, a superior existence. Who's to say they are noy enjoying their present state, journeying about in my Land of Dreams? You are in no position to criticize. You lack the necessary . . . perspective. Now, I'm going to take one of my chemical baths. Bring your luggage back up here, and then I would appreciate one of your excellent massages. The neurowires have become troubling of late."

"Let Mr. Legs over there massage you. I'm afraid I might try to throttle you." Fury and indignation sang in her tone. She turned away, shaking.

"Veronica—has not everything I have done turned out well for you in the course of our relationship? Do you not think I do not have wonderful plans for you, most precious female, darling of my affections?"

"What are you talking about?" she said, curiosity in her voice.

"You will be a *queen*. All humanity will worship you, my love."

"Huh? You've been cooped up in your metal marble too long, Earnest. I just thought you were a little weird before. Now I know you're off your bloody rocker!"

"Your star will shine bright in the heaven of human history, Veronica. Together we will rule wisely and well, charting the course of human evolution. Don't you see why I've selected you, my heart?" He stepped forward and stroked the fine dark slope of her hair. "We match. We are spiritually compatible. You are the yang to my yin, dear heart. You shall sit on my right hand in glory"—his words became whispers of awe— "forever."

"Queen? What are you talking about, Earnest? I don't *want* to be a queen."

"A goddess. You will see, Veronica. You will thank me. And you will worship me in my perfect wisdom, as will all mankind throughout creation!"

"So that's why you want her," the Arachnid said, clicking nimbly onto the floor. "She's to be your Balance."

"Yes. Source of my necessary Harmony. I am all too aware of the dangers of Universal Solipsism."

"You know, whatever you're talking about, it might have been nice to let me in on this earlier. Get *my* thoughts on the subject."

"Your opinions would have been irrelevant."

"That's right. I would have told you to take your whole crazy idea and shove it! I'd not have set foot on the *Star Fall*. And I would have given a good fruity Bronx cheer to your patronage." Her firm chin was thrust up in defiance.

"Consider your words carefully, my love. Everything you are you owe to me." A carefully enunciated whisper: "*Everything!*"

"I bet you think I was just some easy pushover. Well, you're wrong. I let you sleep with me because... well, because I liked you... then. I let you be my patron because I figured it was faster than going it on my own. Which I could have done, if I chose, I'll have you know. Now... now, Earnest, I feel unclean. I feel dirtied by my association with you. I can see why you make all the fuss about maintenance. Your brain cells *are* rotting, and the putrescence you exude makes me want to throw up."

"Shall I get the Joan of Arc crystal out, boss?" The Arachnid asked eagerly.

Hurt ignored the thing.

"You cannot say these things, Veronica," he said, clearly shaken. "You were made for me."

"Don't come on with that cosmic fate crap, Earnest. We just bumped into one another. Literally."

Hurt's eyes burned with intensity.

"How wrong you are, Veronica. I had hoped that your natural tendencies, your loyalty toward me, your love would have led you to support every action I take with complete trust. Alas, I was wrong, it seems."

"What are you *talking* about?" she demanded, hands on the hips of her plaid jump suit.

"I am responsible for your existence, Veronica March."

She found the words hard to push from her mouth. "You mean that figuratively, surely. Responsible for my career, my existence here and now, the air I breathe, the food I eat—" But something like understanding began to show on her face.

"You are not the only one, my dear. Be assured of that. I am a very rich man, but one whose investments are not merely monetary. You have many genetic sisters, I assure you."

A paralyzing horror swept through Veronica, biting deep into areas of feeling she did not know she owned. "Oh my God—you're my father!"

"Not precisely. A genetic variation on a potential clone, fashioned with the help of a most attractive woman I fancied at one time. I have hundreds of such sons and daughters whom I have nothing personally to do with, but nonetheless monitor. Godchildren, you might call them. And you, my love, are a godchild who somehow became just the right individual to suit my wants, my needs—" He smiled softly, stepped to her, caressed her cheek with a smooth hand. "To minister to my affections."

Anger and revulsion. Something snapped inside Veronica. The world became blank for an instant; the next, she was attacking Hurt, raking her nails across his face, drawing blood.

Hurt's health machines screeched. Red lights blazed.

The mania of her attack propelled Hurt to the floor with a bone-crunching jar. Veronica grabbed his hair and began pounding his head against the hard floor.

Metal hands wrapped hard around her body. She was ripped off him, holding bloody hanks of long black hair. The air smelled of oil and blood; the Arachnid held her steady.

"You *bastard!*" she wailed. "You perverse scummy old worm!" She strained at the biobot's arms. A slew of imprecations flew from her mouth. A sense of violation seemed to rip her inside out.

A brigade of maintenance units swarmed about their crumpled patient. Hiss of hypodermics. An emergency atmosphere tent was constructed. Plasma bottles clanked.

"Spirited young wench!" the biobot said into her ear. "You've got a lot to answer for now."

Amid the clatter and gleam of his attendants, a strong voice awakened: "Leave me. I'm all right." Earnest Evers Hurt stood, took a few breaths of his special air, then removed the flimsy plastic covering. Plastiheal marks swathed his wounds and he held his head as though it pained him.

"You have more of your mother in you than I realized," Hurt said mildly. "My misfortune. I suspect, however, you can be tamed—like she was."

She spat at him.

"Please, calm the pyrotechnics," Hurt said. "Now. You will return to your cabin. You will pack your bags. And you will return here, where we will install you in our compartments. Then we will have a reasonable discussion of the situation. Are you amenable to that?"

Veronica stopped her fierce struggling, rationality dawning again. "I haven't much choice, do I?"

"No. You haven't. Have you calmed somewhat?"

"Yes," she said, not looking at him.

"You will do as I say?"

"For now."

"Excellent." He strode to the computer banks and looked down at the screen shifting with veils of numbers. "I will see you within the hour then. Let her go, Arachnid."

The biobot released her reluctantly. It immediately assumed a position between Hurt and her to make sure that the attack was not repeated.

She heaved a shaking breath, wiped the tears from her face with the back of her hand and sniffed. "I used to dream of finding my father," she said in a haunted voice. "But never in my bed."

She turned and stalked from the chamber, her footsteps echoing eerily up into the cathedral-like spaciousness.

When the door had whispered shut behind her, the biobot ambled up to Earnest Evers Hurt.

"It seems I make a bad bodyguard. The previous personality of this mechanism would not have allowed such a show of violence. Sorry."

"I too did not expect the attack," Hurt said, eyes emotional. "They say, Arachnid, that human love is just on the other side of human hate. I truly loved the woman. But she would have killed me." His hand shook as it adjusted a vernier. "*Killed* me, when I am so close to immortality. She has flipped the coin, Arachnid. I no longer love her."

"Shall I dispatch one of the mobile Disbelief Suspenders? I believe we've a few in reserve."

"I fear there is no other choice. But deliver it personally, Arachnid. She is now a potential danger. I want to be sure that that danger is canceled. After you are through, return immediately. The destination is close. I regret having to dispose of Veronica in this manner, but nothing must come between me and my goal." A fist clenched. "Nothing."

Eagerly, the biobot scampered away on its mission.

Earnest Evers Hurt ran a cursory check of operations. All ran smoothly. He tapped up a display of the Underspace surroundings in the vu-tank. Three-dimensional swirling static, flowing past the force-field. No sign of any pattern change . . . and yet he sensed something imminent, like the psychic glimpse of a ghost in his peripheral vision.

His headache began to wane as the drugs took hold, as did lava anger from his eruption. Hatred slowly mutated to a kind of neutrality and he remembered, fondly, his moments of quiet shared joy with Veronica March, his creation and his love. Immediately, he regretted his hasty dispatching of the biobot. A quiver of horror passed through him as he realized what he had done. God! What was he becoming? Her reaction, after all, had been natural enough. Learning of her true background must have rocked her self-image. A temporary hatred of him was understandable. Her expression of her anger was, of course, intolerable; but then, so was any idea of retribution. Still, it was something he could rescind, later. Perhaps even now...

Hurt walked quickly to the nearest communication control. There was yet time. The biobot would be stopped, ordered back. Veronica could be dealt with in some other fashion.

Hurt was punching in the biobot's comm-code when the lights dimmed, then surged back on with the resupply of power. Air chutes coughed, sputtered, then continued expulsing his atmosphere mix.

What was—

A flicker in the vu-tank attracted his attention. A snapshot flash rushed, pulsed, glowed.

Wonder flooded all other thought from Hurt. Totally absorbed in the events portrayed by the vu-tank, he ceased manipulating the comm-controls and ran breathless to the edge of the large visual instrument.

A shifting, iridescent wave of prismatic color was just moving past the edge of the vu-tank. Like part of some multicolored amoeba it fluttered and streamed through the featureless static of Underspace. Overwhelmed by fascination and a sensation of numinosity, Hurt stared at the thing for minutes as it slowly grew larger.

Pseudopods streamered forth toward the ship. Then he realized it wasn't supposed to be this way.

It was as though he were staring down a microscope tube at a sample of swamp water through which some specimen of life, some one-celled creature, slowly moved in its hunt for food. The Collective Unconscious was supposed to be an amphorous mist of energy—a cosmic force—

Not *this*.

Vacuoles stared at him like pupilless eyes. Looking into the thing, whole worlds, whole stars and suns seemed to shimmer like so much stardust, circulating through what he could glimpse of its body.

This couldn't be what he had sought for so many years. Feverishly he checked the state of the Fabrication. The figures indicated that this... this *thing* was indeed what his creation was straining toward.

Observation at a discreet distance for a time was necessary. There was no reason to rush in immediately, especially considering the unforeseen nature of the—

Hurt glanced back at the vu-tank.

A psuedopod of some glittering substance slowly blotted out all other vision.

Too late.

The vu-tank seemed to explode with light, blinding Hurt. The floor beneath him tremored, then rocked violently. Shielding his eyes, he staggered toward the control panels. Suddenly all gravity seemed to go awry.

Some force picked up Earnest Evers Hurt and slammed him against a wall and into unconsciousness.

Fourteen

The thunder split Todd's dreamless sleep in twain.

He came to awareness immediately and realized that the ground was shaking violently. Above, the stars began to drop one by one from the ceiling of the heavens. One dropped just a hundred yards away, sizzling and fiery, spuming up sulfurous sprays.

Electricity jagged from one mountain to another as though they were Van der Graaf generators. Ribbons of purple slammed through the horizon, vibrated suddenly blood red, then shimmered like cracking crystal. The night itself seemed to splinter, coursing streaks of day across the sky.

"What the hell!" Amber cried.

Galahad was kneeling, eyes upward, hands folded in prayer. "It is the Day of Judgment!" he cried jubilantly.

Angharad stood uncertainly, bloodshot eyes wide in the glare, horn reflecting the weird flashes. "I don't think this is supposed to happen."

Scrambling to his feet, Todd stood swaying, finding it hard to maintain his balance. The ground he stood upon seemed to be wobbling. A gale-force wind snapped through the forest, carrying swarms of black dots that zipped through their bodies, momentarily riddling them with holes, then swept away, an agitated dance of nothingness.

"Something seems to be wrong with the computer!" Angharad cried.

And then the ground began to break apart.

A crack ripped through the grass between Todd and the rest of the party. The rift slowly widened, revealing nothingness beneath; a depthless blank. Clumps of grass and soil fell into the maw, immediately disappearing.

The ground shook again with renewed frenzy. The wind whipped the silhouettes of the trees frenetically.

All existence was suddenly leeched of color. The mono-chromatic result was a ghostly supernatural vision. Todd could feel his senses shifting, losing their foundations in his mind.

Blinded by torn-off branches that hurled into his face, Gal-ahad staggered over the precipice's edge with a wretched scream. The dark swallowed him hungrily.

Realizing his own danger, Todd turned and tried to increase his distance from the ever-widening rift. The whole mass of land upon which he stood began to crumble, tearing itself from the edge, tilting.

Todd lost his balance. He was tumbling head over heels down the soft, steep incline of grass.

"Todd!" he heard Angharad's anguished voice cry out help-lessly.

He banged into something, grabbed hold.

A bush. He'd managed to grip the base of a small bush with his left hand. He could feel his lower torso and legs dangle into nothingness. Panicking, he kicked against it as though to find some kind of foothold.

Amber's voice: "Todd! Hang on!"

However, words a decent rope do not make: the roots of the bush pulled from the soil with excruciating slowness. Flail as he might, Todd could not achieve any other purchase.

Finally, the roots ripped free, and Todd Spigot found himself hurtling downward with an awful sound which he realized, before he lost awareness, was his own scream.

"Don't touch that handle!" Charley Haversham said. "I've fallen in!"

The giant hand disregarded his objection and flushed the toilet.

The noise was thunder in his ears as the water in the bowl began to whirlpool and Charley was dragged into a tunnel of darkness.

A replay. Lots of nothingness between that and this.

This? What *was* this, anyway?

The rug was soft beneath him, but he lay in an uncomfortable position, arms akimbo as though he had been in the middle of a tumbling exercise and then conked out. He opened his eyes and the light hurt them. Squinting, he groped out and caught hold of the edge of the bed. Vague forms before him solidified.

Computer screen. Chairs. A half-naked woman.

"Oh my," Charley said. "That must have been some party!"

The woman spun around, brunette hair swirling. Automatically, her hands tugged the blouse up between her delightful breasts and Charley's vision. Her eyes were filled with surprise and horror.

"Todd! Todd, you're awake!"

"Must have fallen on my back," Charley murmured, getting to his feet. "Hurts like hell."

"Oh, *Todd*." His arms were suddenly full of her. The blouse, forgotten, fluttered to the floor as she trembled against him. "Todd, I'm sorry, so sorry. I really like you. I didn't know that this would happen."

"Must have been fun," Charley said, looking at the rumpled bed. He folded his arms around the woman, savoring her warmth. "Wish I could remember it. I don't know what I told you, but my name's Charley, not Todd."

She separated from him, arms folded over bosom, blinking. "No..." Then she smiled. "Of course. Charley. That's your *assumed* name." Quickly she shrugged into a jump suit and remagnetized its seams, which disappointed Charley Haversham no end. "Oh, Todd, I'm so ashamed of myself." Delicate hands covered a strikingly pretty face. "I had no idea what Hurt was up to. If I did—"

"Whoa there, lady! You've lost me." Charley sat on the edge of the bed. "You wouldn't have a glass of water, would you? My mouth tastes like bargain day at a slophouse."

"Of course." She got him a cup of water. He drank it, then looked up at her. She was staring at something on his back. "What's wrong? I rip them or something?"

"You've still got the Disbelief Suspender on. I don't understand. Something must have gone wrong. I felt the ship shake, the lights went out for a minute...but I didn't think—"

"Hey, lady, if any introductions were made before, I've forgotten them. *My* name is Charley Haversham. I'm a simple flunky in the maintenance division of the *Star Fall* and I've never heard of anybody named Todd or of anything called a Disbelief Suspender..." He groped behind him, felt a rod of hard metal attached to his back. "Hello! What the hell is *this?*" He tried to pull it off. Agony paraded along his back in storm trooper boots. He ceased the attempt. "Yikes! What's going *on!*"

"Oh, it's absolutely *awful,*" Veronica said, choking out a heartfelt sob. "To think that I trusted him." She collapsed into his arms and her comfortable, needful softness made him rapidly forget his own aches. "He must be *mad*. He's using everyone for his insane scheme."

"*Who's* using everyone? By the way, if I've ever met you before I've quite forgotten your name."

She drew back, looking at him with a bemused, faintly astonished expression. "Veronica. How could you forget after—"

"Listen. Please believe me. I honestly don't know what's going on. This is getting me very upset."

Her face suddenly brightened. "If *you've* awakened, maybe the others have as well." She slipped from his hold, grabbed his hand and tugged him through the open door. The corridors were surprisingly dim, a swath of mottled shadows. Heaps of bodies lay sprawled in the distance. Haversham could distinguish strips of metal on their backs, connected just below the neck and just above the buttocks.

"Holy Plumber's Helper—you're right!" Charley said. "How come then *they're* horizontal and *I'm* vertical?"

"That's what I'd like to know," Veronica said. "There must have been a computer foul-up. But you're not the same person you were before. Maybe there's been some kind of short-circuit in the overlay system and you've been plucked out of the Fabricated Reality. Goodness, this could be everyone's hope. If we could just find a way to—"

"You're talking *way* over my head, sweet face. I just signed on to make sure the sewers run smooth. I didn't expect this. The last thing I remember was getting to my cabin and seeing this—my God, that's right—I remember seeing this *leg* hopping from my omnicleaner!"

Veronica looked at him strangely. "Let's go back in my room and see if we can dig up a weapon. I'm not about to go back to Hurt's compartments now if there's something I can do elsewhere—and someone to do it with." She dragged him back. "Or maybe that's the wrong approach. Maybe I can do more upstairs. I dunno." She shook her head. "I know I've got to do *something*."

"Okay," Haversham said, suddenly feeling the emotional impact. "I take it we're in trouble." Disorientation set in.

"Not only us, Charley, but the whole human race from star to shining star." He followed her as she went back into her cabin and began to root among her luggage.

"Don't tell me. You're really a secret agent!" Charley said.

"I *wish!*" A piece of flossy lingerie was tossed into the air. It landed on Charley Haversham's head. "Where *is* that stupid thing?"

"What are you looking for?"

"Something Earnie—I mean Earnest Evers Hurt—gave me a while back, after I was attacked by a psychotronic."

"That must have been pleasant."

"It's a screamer-shock. Ah. Here we go."

Veronica produced a bulbous thing that looked like a cigarette lighter. Her fingers accidentally touched a control button. Jags of lightning jetted, accompanied by a howl worthy of a banshee. Startled, the woman dropped it. Charley, his engineering instincts engaged, advanced and managed to tap the Off button with a careful shoetip.

Breathless, hair disarranged, Veronica said, "Thanks."

Charley picked up the hot weapon gingerly, handed it back to Veronica. "You'll be more careful in the future, I trust?"

Veronica took her hand from her chest, accepted the weapon. "Perhaps we'll be able to find something better somewhere else."

"Just what are we supposed to do? Seek out and alert the authorities as to the possible presence of pyschotronics aboard the *Star Fall?*"

"No. We have to stop Earnest Evers Hurt from taking over the Human Collective Unconscious and becoming a god."

"Look, lady, I'm a fancy janitor and a simple plumber. I don't get involved in no theological matters. 'Now I lay me down to sleep' is about the extent of my devotions."

Emphatic hand on his arm, she gazed deep into his eyes. "You've got to trust me." Something deep and electric tingled through Charley Haversham, stilling his objections.

"All right. Something fishy must be going on for me to be stone cold for such a long time. And I do want to get this thing off my back. What do I do?"

"Go back with me to Hurt's control room—" she patted her

pockets. "Oh dammit! I must have left the mag-key there!"

"Stop the guy in control of the *Star Fall* with a screeching zap gun? You've got to be kidding—"

"There's also the biobot."

"Oh, *great*. Peachy keen." He stormed off to look in a closet.

"What are you doing?"

"Checking for a spare proton bazooka you might have overlooked. You know, maybe we should check my section first. There ought to be something down in the computer maintenance division that we might be able to jerry-rig into an item resembling a weapon." He resumed his futile search in silence, then turned to see that they had company.

The biobot stood a few steps into the cabin, bulging huge, mandibles clacking, optical sensors fixed on Veronica. In one claw it held a Disbelief Suspender. It did not seem to be aware of Charley Haversham's presence.

"What are *you* doing here?" Veronica said. The screamer-shock was hidden behind her.

"Hurt has changed his mind," the biobot said, moving forward. The Disbelief Suspender wiggled in its grasp. "He wants you to join the rest of the passengers for a while. Be very still, Veronica, and this won't hurt a bit."

As quietly as he could, Charley edged the two meters toward the dresser, fortunately immediately behind the biobot.

"No," Veronica said, backing away. "I don't believe you."

"Terribly sorry," the Arachnid said, "but it's true."

Two bottles stood on the dresser top. Gin. Brandy. Half full. Charley grabbed their necks, eased them up. Aimed.

Flung.

One bottle crashed into the Arachnid's head. The other smashed on its metal carapace, splashing liquid all over it.

"Veronica! The shocker!" Charley cried.

Eyes wide, Veronica pulled the weapon from behind her back.

A screech. The rush of electricity singeing the air, connecting with the Arachnid's metal armor. The alcohol ignited, roaring into a ball of flame around the thing. It fell to the floor, clicking and writhing.

"No insect spray, pal," Charley said. "That will have to do. Come on, Ronnie. Let's bug out of here!" He grabbed her hand

and together they raced from the room.

Minutes later, after weaving an erratic trail of flight through the hallways of that section of the *Star Fall*, they stopped to haul in a few deep breaths.

"You think we killed it?" Veronica asked hopefully.

"Hard to say. It's a bodyguard model. I suspect we just slowed it down some. This is our chance, though. Quick, show me where we can find Hurt! And tell me what we have to do to stop him."

"You believe me!" she said, grabbing him jubilantly, holding him tightly.

"His flunky gave you a prime testimonial. Right. We'll head up to this guy's quarters, prevent him from taking over the known universe, and then whatsay I buy you a drink to replace those bottles I smashed? I'd prefer it the other way around, but there is the time factor."

"This way," she said, grabbing his hand and pulling him along so quickly he almost lost his balance.

Fifteen

Todd Spigot woke up underneath the ground.

Static seemed to swirl about him. Matrix dots shivered and eddied around his limbs and torso in peculiar currents. In the distance, vague outlines of circuitry, solid-state and otherwise, glowed and pulsed like spectral after-images.

Striking out with his arms caused him to move in what he discerned to be an upward direction. He drifted through the thickening computer specks—like loosened atoms slowly collecting into the molecules of matter—up, up through strata of rock, clay, sand, dirt, topsoil. Finally, he broke surface, peering up at psuedo-Creation through a fringe of long grass.

Some stars were back in the sky—standing out in relief against the fuzzy black background like connect-a-dot patterns. The landscape was a shambles of unearthed trees and leveled hills; a nearby stream flowed into a yawning crevasse. All in a sketchy, vague watercolor, rather than the previous tempera-like hues.

Standing nearby, staring at the changed land of Fabricated Reality, was Angharad the donkey-unicorn, looking lost.

"What happened?" Todd asked, lifting himself past grass level, careful to control his lightness so that he didn't shoot up into the sky.

The animal turned. Obviously the disaster had affected the quality of her "animation." Stiff and jerky, like a Gumby model, she strode to Todd, eyes bulging ludicrously with surprise.

"Amber tried to grab you—he slipped into the crevasse too. I thought you were all gone for good. My God . . . look at you! You're—you're like a ghost!"

So that was why he'd been able to drift back through the ground after his fall. He examined his arm. Indeed, it did look like the arm of an apparition: milky-white, translucent. He covered his eyes with his hands; he could plainly see his companions through its outlines. He glanced down at his torso, legs and feet.

Spooksville stuff.

Also: sensory awareness, save for hearing and seeing, had dimmed somewhat. For some reason, his brain, his consciousness, was only partially active in Hurt's Fabricated Reality.

If that were so, then where was the rest of him?

"Something must have gone wrong with your connection," Angharad said, examining Todd closely, floppy ears twitching. Have you any awareness of anything else beside us and the countryside?"

Todd concentrated on that, straining to see through the bright washes of color that surrounded him to perceive the nature of the true surroundings of his *real* body, presumably still sprawled in Veronica March's cabin. He closed his eyes, recalling the details—the bed, dresser, computer console. He dredged up the painful memory of the Arachnid grabbing him, holding him down. Sympathetic trickles of agony coursed down his spine as the needles and neuroconnectors of the Disbelief Suspender again seemed to bury themselves in his flesh.

"No," he admitted finally. "Nothing."

"Damn," Angharad said. "You're obviously not all here." She glanced around. "But then, neither is much of the Fabrication. Better focused now than before. Maybe *you'll* eventually solidify as well."

"Think Hurt's machines fouled up or something?" Todd leaned over and tried to grab a clump of grass. His hand passed through the vegetation; the stalks merely swayed, as though with a breeze.

"On such a massive scale? Unlikely," Angharad said. "Hurt no doubt set up fail-safe systems on top of fail-safe systems. Something outside must have affected the Fabrication. Quite possibly the *Star Fall* has reached its destination."

"Wonderful," Todd said. "I'm a ghost for the rest of the journey."

"Could come in handy," Angharad countered. "You can levitate. Walk through walls . . . We could have used Amber, though. I hope he's okay."

Todd shivered as he gazed at his translucent arm. "Gives me the creeps."

"It's not exactly a load of fun being progressively jerkier lumps of modeled clay," Angharad said. "I can't even take a piss anymore!" With her teeth she picked up the pouch containing the map from the ground. "Fortunately you dropped this before you, Galahad and Amber took your respective tumbles."

"Are you saying that we should keep on looking for what Hurt wants us to look for, despite what's happened?"

"Call it unicorn intuition if you like, but that's the feeling I have. As far as I can tell, Hurt's purpose in constructing this mode of existence, as I said before, was not merely to attract the Energy Pool but to create some kind of portal, an entranceway into its very heart. This, apparently, is the purpose of the Grail."

Since Todd's fingers were no longer solid, they had to resort to donkey hooves once more to consult the map. This took some doing.

Certain detours, it seemed, had to be made to allow for the cracks and crevasses that had appeared in the ground. Otherwise the course was reasonably plain.

The two struck out in a renewal of their Quest.

As they traveled, they passed bewildered, lost inhabitants of the Fabrication. An occasional knight galloped by, unlike Galahad, ignoring them. Dragons wheeled in the distance; maidens pined from the parapets of castles. Before dawn, constellations similar to those seen from Earth appeared in the sky. Slowly, the watercolor gave way to strong vibrant oils.

The countryside seemed to be gradually rebuilding itself.

The land began to repopulate with creatures of imagination and symbol, performing their obtuse and arcane roles in the chants of human existence. They passed a valley filled with gigantic tarot cards, shuffling themselves, then forming a quilt of fortune telling. They skirted a plain holding murky crystal balls like boulders; they crossed a field where anthropomorphized numbers were involved in mad numerologist capers and dances. The landscape had become an Alice in Wonderland collection of painting styles crammed in upon one another; fresco here, chiaroscuro there; a forest drawn with the brushstrokes of Impressionism bordering a Rococo river complete with trumpeting angels and gigling cherubs.

One area abounded with Greek and Roman temples, among

which the creatures and gods of Mediterranean mythology cavorted, all in vivid Classical lines. Nearby was a colony of cartoon characters.

The closer they got to their destination, the odder the landscape, it seemed. The air seemed charged with electrical excitement as though something spectacular were about to occur. As he stalked along in his ghostly state, Todd idly wondered if Hurt had also programmed in some sort of Christian Second Coming scenario. The characters forged from the stuff of the Human Historical Unconscious seemed to be expectant of some sort of rapture.

Although it seemed like ages (for indeed they *were* traveling through the stuff of historical ages), only a few hours had passed since Todd's emergence from the ground when he suddenly became solid again.

Which was uncomfortable, since he was floating along several feet in the air at the time.

"Ouch!" he cried as he plummeted almost headfirst into a fortunately soft bank. He was immediately aware of the strong smell of dandelions.

Angharad turned around, astonished.

"Are you all right?"

Todd picked himself up, rubbing the back of his neck. "I wish I'd had some kind of warning."

"If there was something wrong with your Disbelief Suspender it's apparently been corrected," Amber said.

Todd's arm fell off.

"Ooops," Angharad said. "Spoke too soon."

Todd stared at the stump in horror. No bone, nor veins nor spurting blood. Just a fizzling of computer dots in the cross-section of the biceps. Todd reached down with his left hand, picked up the fallen arm and fitted it back into place.

Suddenly a dizziness came over him, like a buzz of flies and bees strafing his skull. The stuff of the landscape before him seemed to crinkle away like a matte painted on plastic wrap.

Replaced with:

An off-focus Veronica March.

Charley. Charley, are you okay?" The soft tones were like cool, comforting water lapping at his face.

He tried to reach out and hold her. A voice that was not

his emerged from his mouth. "I don't know. I feel really strange."

"We are in a pretty strange biosphere. But you just passed out for a minute, like you were back in the cabin."

"I had the strangest dream," the voice said. "I dreamed I was walking along with this ugly unicorn."

Charley Haversham! The personality overlay that Cog had given him to get aboard the *Star Fall*. It had taken over his real body!

Suddenly the beautiful face of Veronica began to fade. Todd found himself swimming in darkness which began to strobe with a light that revealed his former habitat. Angharad was looking at him, aghast.

With his mind, he stretched out, reached to touch that other individuality matrix that lived in his brain:

"Charley! Oh, Charley . . ."

—Who's that?

"The owner of this body."

—Come off it.

"No, really. I'm Todd Spigot, the real you. The part of our brain that the Disbelief Suspender is still hooked up to."

There was no immediate response. Todd vaguely discerned another conversation. An excited conversation.

Then:

—Okay. Veronica says that I'm not going crazy.

"Veronica is with you?"

Todd listened as he heard their story—and their present situation.

"Incredible." He then described the Fabrication, to Charley's bemusement and amazement.

—No shit. Looks like Ronnie's dead-on. This guy Hurt has got to be stopped!

"Hold the line. I've got to check with the companion I mentioned."

He detached himself from his interior self and allowed his sight to flow back.

Angharad stood in front of him, perplexed.

"I'm in contact with my physical body!" Todd said jubilantly.

"What?" Angharad said. "How can that be?"

"I'll explain later. But don't you see," Todd said, "we've

got a free agent now in the physical universe of the *Star Fall*. We have a chance of getting some help.

"Somehow he's got to free Cog."

God is an amoeba.

The thought throbbed through Hurt's mind, laced with pain. *The God of the human race is a gigantic mindless amoeba.*

The image of the one-celled creature, swimming through Underspace, filling the interior of the vu-tank, bilious, gelatinous energy coursing against the glittering membrane returned to him.

Kilometers wide. Two thousand, by our measurements, at least, the instruments had said. Like cilia, countless streamers of energy radiated from its skin. Each connecting with a human life? The root of humanity, planted in Underspace, its psychic branches stretching to each individual?

His eyes fluttered open and he realized that one was gummed with clotted blood. Anxiety filled him. Was he dying? What had happened?

He made to rise, but a number of tiny hands held him down.

His maintenance robots—emergency division—hovered about him like mechanical elves, repairing the damage, ministering to his needs. He let himself relax while the machines completed their duties. Apparantly he had cut himself in several places—including the head. He could feel delicate wire probes inserted through his forehead into the artificial webworking that maintained his deteriorating brain cells, performing adjustments. Managing to keep his patience despite the almost overwhelming urge to spring up and investigate the situation, he let his automated mechanisms put him back together, monitoring the progress via a computer screen extension with legs that squatted nearby for his convenience. Diagnostic computations appeared, showing that his neural-support units had been badly jogged, allowing a significant number of brain cells to die of oxygen starvation.

That much closer to senility.

At this point, however, it hardly mattered. Either he would obtain his goals or he would die. All or nothing.

When the screen revealed that the wires had been extracted, the proper chemicals injected, the permaheal stitching applied, the metal hands of the maintenance robot team removed themselves from his arms and he was allowed to stand.

He wobbled to the vu-tank, which was still on.

The holographic image no longer showed the crazy quilt of Underspace.

Something like an underwater scene showed beyond the protective force-field of the *Star Fall,* waving with fronds, streaming with bubbles. Peculiar currents swayed corruscating nodes strewn here and there through the endless depths.

God is an amoeba, and He's swallowed the Star Fall, Earnest Evers Hurt thought with wonder and a helpless fear as he stared into the protoplasmlike material of the entity. Recovering from his brief, atypical reverie, he hobbled to the interpretive channel of the computer, keyed it on and demanded harshly, "Read out compositional properties of surroundings!"

Not waiting for a response, he strode to another computer interface, where he requested: "Attempt to open communication channels with possibly intelligent creature."

Then he sped to his operation bulb to survey the Fabricated Reality which had attracted the *Star Fall* to this astonishing discovery.

Switching off the automatic neural connectors, he dialed in STATUS REPORT, then switched on the representational two-dee screens. Immediately, scenes of radical change showed, gradually resolving from absolute chaos into a fractured semblance of its previous state. Hurt's hands trembled as he ordered a complete survey. Had the Fabrication been destroyed or rattled enough that its primary purpose would be hindered? Had its internal harmony and equilibrium been thrown off-kilter? If so, then it would take days to repair. Days that Hurt and the *Star Fall* did not have.

Suddenly the status report materialized in a screen by Hurt's elbow:

PORTAL OF REQUIRED CHARACTERISTICS PRESENTLY FORMING ON QUADRANT 3, SCENARIO 17 C. RESONANCE OF WAVELENGTHS INDICATES FULFILLMENT OF EXPECTANT CIRCUMSTANCES.

Awe filled Hurt.

He had been essentially correct. Out here in the mysterious dimension of Underspace was the ultimate product of human civilization: the next step for mankind, a growing organism destined for a destiny far beyond anyone's imaginings.

How many nights had he lain awake, wondering the meaning of life, wondering how he could conquer his fear of death, continue to the very ends of human existence?

On the other side of the room, the interpretative console began to churn sheets of analysis concerning the thing in which the *Star Fall* was now embedded. Impatiently Hurt strode to the wrinkled paper. Fascinating. A jumble of old and new elements. A bizarre wedding of silicon- and carbon-based materials essentially serving as biophysical conductors of endless varieties of energy matrices: its nervous system. Yet no sign of a central nexus analogous to the brain, nor even anything similar to a spinal cord.

To his consternation, Hurt saw that the creature seemed to be feeding on the energies which constituted the *Star Fall*'s force-field. Alarmed, he directed computation inquiries. The results showed that the generators were indeed weakening from the strain. Approximately 32 hours remained before the force-fields would be neutralized.

What would happen then?

Quickly Hurt consulted the machines working on possible communications with the being. Results were negative on all radio channels: nothing even resembling a code or a language to be interpreted.

The choice was clear. Either use the *Star Fall*'s deteriorating power to ram out of the creature or continue the operation as previously planned, ignoring the dangers, hoping for immediate success.

Earnest Evers Hurt took just a moment to decide, then almost ran back to his bulb.

His head felt like it was going to explode.

Although he must have fallen for a long time, it was a dream-fall, a fantasy plunge, lacking linear dimensions. He did not lose consciousness, nor did he retain it.

Philip Amber, rather, was suddenly aware at a certain point in time later that instead of tumbling into the abyss (dammit, dammit, why had he made that stupid lunge for Spigot?) he was lying on a linoleum floor that had a bad case of yellow wax buildup. The lighting was dim, but sufficient to discern that a corridor, doors to either side, stretched endlessly away into the distances before him and behind him. The place smelled of chalk dust and mold, and had an uneasy damp quality.

Amber was no longer a lion. He wore his own frame, dressed in the robes he remembered wearing when the biobot had invaded his cell. However, as he raised his hand, there was something definitely strange about its movement—

Somebody groaned. Amber turned. Lying on the floor beside him was Galahad, chain mail and armor beginning to clank up toward movement. Something shimmied in the air above the man with his action. "God help me," the man said. "I feel so stiff. Where is my sword?" With a jerky motion, the knight's hands groped out, searching erratically before him, and slivers of light danced above his body.

Amber realized suddenly that these were strings.

Horrified, he lifted his arm. Connecting fingers, palm and forearm, an array of strong, thin threads supported the actions of his limb, which under close scrutiny was revealed to be of painted wood and ceramics. Digits and joints were segmented and could move in a vulgar parody of human patterns.

They were puppets.

Marionettes!

Amber gazed up to see where the strings led.

There was no ceiling. Instead, a soundless miniature thunderstorm seemed to be in progress, clouds swirling restlessly, grabbing at one another with lightning claws. At times they would part, revealing purple-black swaths of space, flecked with stars, diamond hard, crystal cold.

No visible hands tugged the hundreds of whisper-thin filaments from which Amber hung.

Galahad gained his feet. "What is this madness?" he cried. His mouth moved like a ventriloquist dummy's. The features on his face were colored in with strokes of lacquered paint, giving him an almost clownish aspect. Amber wondered what the effect was on his own countenance. "Who are *you?*"

"I used to be the lion."

"I recall your voice." The knight gazed about him, batting his clicking eyes: a parody of astonishment. "Where are we? I remember the Earth moving, the crack splitting across the turf. I remember falling." The eyes opened ludicrously wide. "Hell! *We have fallen to Hell!*"

The knight weaved about, stumbled. He collapsed to his knees, hands clasped in paralyzed imploration. A wisp of smoke curled from one of his ears, as though his cellulose brains were afire.

"Hey, Galahad, steady!" Amber said. "This is all just the guts of a computer! It doesn't really exist."

"Lord! Lord!" Galahad cried. "Why hast thou forsaken me?"

Suddenly the bolt of the nearest door shot open. The door slammed back against the wall. Bolts of eye-searing light shot forth, blinding Amber. He held up an arm to shield his eyes.

"Oh wimp of little faith," bellowed a pipe-organ voice. "Thinkest thou that I would forget thee, thou little snot."

Galahad rose slowly to his feet, arms outstretched. "Father, I have kept myself valiant and chaste, the greatest knight in the world, only for Thee!"

"Yeah, well, get in here before all the light gets out!"

Standing by the doorway were two angels in Old Testament robes. Amber watched as Galahad stumbled to them. They inserted strong hands under his armpits. Feathery wings unfurled, bearing the trio aloft with a pixilation effect against billowing clouds from which rose bejeweled spires. Optical enhancement bathed the shores of Heaven with kaleidoscopic rainbows.

Squinting against the brilliance, Amber stepped forward to get a closer look. The door shut abruptly, plunging the corridor back to a dimness that seemed like blackness.

"*His* Heaven, not yours," a kindly voice intoned. "But then, back in the Brotherhood, you sought *satori,* nirvana, wholeness, not some medieval Heaven paved with gold."

Standing before him, Amber gradually made out a figure dressed in a rumpled corduroy jacket. Smoke curled from a meerschaum pipe. A twisted tie dangled from around a frayed collar. Wrinkle-wreathed eyes seemed to smile wisely.

"I sought alleviation from my guilt. Penance if you will. Self-retribution. Am I still in the Fabrication?"

The man looked over the rims of half-frame glasses. "Oh, definitely."

"Well, then. This may be Hell, and you may be Satan—"

"That's possible. You *are* in a Creation of Symbols and Archetypes."

"Whatever the case, I'm not just going to sit still, strings or no strings." He ran a hand over the tight wires above him and they vibrated like a muted harp. "I might be able to throw a wrench in the works down here."

"Hmm. Perhaps I can show you a few things that might be of help," the man mused. He nodded down the corridor. "Come on."

Amber shrugged and followed.

The man opened a door. Beyond the frame, a heap of bodies tottered uncertainly, then spilled out in a sprawl of limbs, blackened faces and coagulated blood. Amber recognized some of them. Guilt choked him. He turned away and was about to run back the corridor in the direction they had come, when the man grabbed his shirtsleeve.

"Philip Amber," he said in a stern voice. "You might be of help to your friends. But that lies beyond this place."

Panic filled Amber's voice. "You . . . you expect me to climb over the bodies of . . . of the people I *murdered?*"

"There's no other way past them, Philip Amber."

"I can't." He began to walk away. Halted. Stared back. Dead eyes stared at him accusingly. Open mouths screamed silently.

"No other way, Amber," the man repeated.

Amber's mouth seemed sawdust dry. "Past them . . . I can help Spigot . . . Shepherd?"

"Past them, you can help yourself. Not all the chants, nor all the incense, nor all the penance in the universe will save you, Amber."

Amber dropped to his knees, weeping. "What *will* save me then? I'm a mass murderer."

"Find out, Amber. The answer is past this hurdle, which you've never faced before."

"I don't deserve salvation," Amber moaned.

"Very well. But think of your friends. Think of the human race, Amber. You were very near the correct state of mind when you crashed through to the Morapns. Reach a little further. Reach out to *yourself.*"

Philip Amber attempted a meditative state of mind, but found it fruitless. Wordlessly, he stepped to the pile of bodies and began to climb. A foot on the gory torso of Link Larfner of Orion Four, shot down in cold blood while vacationing with his family . . . a hand on the half-severed leg of Alfred Zetter-

son, the President of the tiny confederation of Alphus. Durt-
wood's decapitated body rolled sickeningly by him, trailing the
stench of burnt flesh.

Slippery. Sickening. At the top of the gruesome pile, a
heavy weight seemed to press down on him. He realized that
the puppet strings had forsaken him. Three Gs of force mashed
him down, into the face of a corpse. Limp blond hair trailed
down from a bloodless face. Darkened eyes opened, and he
knew who it was.

"Simone," he gasped. Simone Neel, his love...

She smiled, and her words squeaked up from the grave with
deathly seduction. "Kiss me, Philip. Make love to me."

With a hoarse scream, Amber ripped himself free of her
grasp. He tumbled frantically down the other side of the pile
of bodies, even as arms began to animate, clutch for him.

Landing hard, he scrambled up, looked behind him.

The bodies dissolved away. The man walked across the
section of floor where they had lain.

"Come," he said.

Confused, Amber followed. Somehow he felt lighter now.

The man stopped at a door. "Open this, Amber. It might
help explain things."

Wary of more bodies, Amber opened the door.

He peered into the room. Infinite walls of circuit board
stretched out in a slit-scan corridor, glittering and glowing with
channeled electricity, crystalline effulgence, layered spectra.

"The Fabrication's heart, Amber," said the man. "Call it
Heaven, call it Hell. It is what you make it, just as is Life."

"Why me?" Amber said, staring wonderingly at the shifting
sight.

"You've slipped between the cracks because of your attitude, coupled with your training at the monastery. You have
learned part of the ability to see things as they really are, even
as your brain sits in its nutrient tank, plugged into the Fabrication. Cut yourself loose, now. *See.*"

Philip Amber directed his attention once more to the corridor, trying to remember the important aspects of the meditative process. "Cut yourself loose from your *self,* and you can
see into your Self," Brother Lucius had explained countless
times. Amber concentrated on doing just that.

The wires abruptly began to wiggle. Snapshot images began to form, tearing themselves to pieces and forming bizarre collages in a kinestasis symbology.

"Ort Eath," he whispered. "The Arachnid. Hurt. They're . . ."

"Yes," said the man. "The Fabrication is a process in more ways than one."

"Is there nothing I can do?" Amber asked him.

"Nothing," the man said. "Nothing now."

Amber turned back and glumly watched the proceedings work themselves toward completion.

"Watch out for sharks," Charley Haversham said as they traipsed along the floor of the Waterless Ocean in grav-shoes, winding past pink coral and waving seaweed.

"Thanks for the warning," Veronica said dryly, eyeing a large school of bass rippling in formation nearby. "I don't know, Charley. You'd think there would be a better way."

"Hey. It's not my fault the tube-cars aren't working and we have to cut through the biospheres. Anyway, like I told you, this is a shortcut. Hurry up. I want to get to the other side before I get another message from my alter ego off in Never-Never Land."

"I'm going as fast as I can. Are you sure this is the way Todd told you to head?"

"Absolutely. We apparently have to liberate some supra-normal leg from a prison beam." Kicking up small clouds of sand below his feet, Charley blithely avoided the tentacles of a man-'o-war. "I remember that leg. I have a bone to pick with it."

"Can we stop for a shower first? This humidity is killing the body in my hair."

"Dry clothes are what we might stop for, my dear. Your hair can go hang"—he flashed her a smile—"limply."

"Are you sure there's no switch on you that will turn you back into the sweet, shy fellow you used to be?" Veronica shot him a killer look as a genetically adjusted flounder finned between them weightlessly.

"Sorry, babe, you're stuck with the best lover in the Joisy Communes." He tipped an imaginary hat. "Plumber extraordinaire! You'll be glad I'm along, eventually."

"God. I thought women strangled your type with their discarded bras centuries ago. But then cockroaches are still around too, aren't they?"

"How come *you* don't have one of these doodads riding your backbone, anyway?" Charley reached back and touched the exposed metal surface of his Disbelief Suspender. Its surface was slick with condensed moisture from the air.

"I *was* Hurt's mistress. A privileged character."

"Apparently he sent Mr. Charm to terminate the relationship. You seem to have terrific taste in men."

"I don't want to talk about Hurt, Charley. I just want to stop him from what he's doing, any way I can. He's not a sane individual. I can assure you, Charley Haversham, that if I knew then even part of what I know about Earnes Evers Hurt now, I would have had nothing whatsoever to do with him."

"Oh yeah. That business with his being your pop and all that."

Her mouth tightened. "I shouldn't have confided in you."

"Gee—sorry, lady! I mean, you know we've all got problems. How 'bout the fact that I don't really exist! Can you match that one?" He strode quickly ahead through a colony of brightly colored anenomes.

She ran to catch up with him, tripped over a bit of seaweed, knocking them both down.

"Come to apologize, huh?" He grabbed her, kissed her.

She pulled away from him and stood. "You take your apologies in big helpings, don't you, you bastard!"

Charley grinned and got up. "I take whatever I can get."

After a further march of twenty minutes through veils of warm mist, they found the transference lock that led to the level Todd had indicated to Charley as holding the imprisoned form of Cog in his omnicleaner. As the dry air hissed into the room, a voice began to chirp inside Charley's head, as though from a long distance away.

"Veronica. I do believe I hear Todd coming back on the air. I might have to space out for a while."

"Give him my love," she said sardonically.

"Right." Charley closed his eyes, opening himself to communication with the other inhabitant of his body.

"Haversham here, bucko. How's tricks in the Karmatoon?"

Images flickered. Vague pictures of riffled illustrations, accompanied by fascinating musics and evocative sensations. Charley felt as though he were immersing himself in some magical museum filled to the brim with artifacts that somehow struck home, pushed his buttons. The very fabric of his being seemed to live here, resonating in harmony with all other human beings.

—Still looking for the Grail, Charley? Todd Spigot said. You know, I can't tell you how much I appreciate your co-operation in all this. I really do apologize for the situation.

"Hey! What else can a poor engram overlay do, pal?"

—It's just damn fortunate it's happened this way, Charley. You're the wild card up our sleeves. You know, I really wonder if Cog didn't plan it all this way. Foreseeing this eventuality, maybe he placed you inside me as kind of a fail-safe measure. He certainly chose the right person.

"Actually, *I* should be thanking *you*. This lady I'm traveling with is a real fox!"

A silence ensued.

"Spigot! You stopped up or something?"

—Don't *touch* her!

"Spigot, don't be a drip. We're all liberated here. Besides, if the lady cares to get affectionate, it'll be with your body."

—Yes, but *I* won't be inside it!

"I'm not sure I entirely trust her. I told you about her and Hurt, didn't I?"

—Yes, but you also said that's she's turned on him. That the Arachnid tried to attack her. Seems to bear out her story.

"Yes, but the more I think about it, the more I figure it might just be a setup. From the story you and Shepherd and Amber gave me, this all sounds extremely convoluted, and Ms. Veronica March, pretty as she may be, I consider phylum *variable*, class *dubious*."

—Nonetheless, she may come in handy. She knows exactly where to find Hurt. Once you free Cog, she can lead you straight to him.

"Speaking of which, O Seeker of the Truth, could you go over the exact directions on how to find the aforesaid Cog, hiding out in my omnicleaner?"

Quickly, Todd again supplied the specific sector, level and

room number from which the Disbelief Suspenders had winged like bats from Hell, and in which Cog had been imprisoned.

"From the markings I made out in this airlock, we're in the correct sector, all right. We'll just have to find the fire stairs and make our way up. Like I told you, the tube-car system has been shut down. Also, I wanted to ask you: any aliens traipsing about in this Fabrication you're traveling through? I haven't seen any around here, and I'm worried."

—I noticed from the beginning that there weren't all that many on the *Star Fall*. Hurt apparently intended this to be a purely human endeavor. I suspect he's got any aliens locked up in their particularly appropriate biospheres.

"Yeah. Which is why I asked. Maybe we can enlist their services."

—If necessary. Right now we're working on a limited amount of time. *Something* has happened. We've already reached Hurt's destination. We have to move before he does.

"Right. Which means that I should sign off for now. Anyway, I can check in with you from time to time—correct?"

—That's hard to say. Concentrating like this is difficult. The ability seems to come and go. Should I not be able to speak with you again, you should know this. When I changed to another set of clothing, I put on a set of gray coveralls.

"That's what I'm wearing, all right."

—Terrific. Now, there should be, in the right back pocket, a folded-up copy of a schematic for the Core system. There had been considerable difficulty with this area. It's sort of a nerve center for the old *Star Fall* computers, and it's been sealed away from any kind of access.

"So? What's that got to do with Hurt?"

—Just possibly, a great deal. More specifically, it has to do with the Arachnid—and its source of power and personality.

"We may well have cooked its goose back in Ronnie's cabin."

—The biobot? Hardly. Its fleshly portions are regenerative. No, we two here have put our heads together and we're pretty sure that the biobot's controller is an emanation of the new form of Ort Eath.

"Wasn't he the guy that . . . I mean, the alien . . ."

—Yes. Apparently, his seeming self-immolation after our thwarting of his plans to destroy Earth was a ruse to prevent our noticing the fact that his orgobox was slinking away. Apparently, Ort Eath had somehow surgically removed his own brain and placed it in the nutrient tank of the orgabox, along with a few other brains he had stolen from here and there for his private collection.

"Nice chap."

—Yes. Apparently he had this option available to him all along. While we thought him dead, the orgabox bearing his brain escaped into the depths of the starship that split off from the *Star Fall*. Then, when that vessel was fitted back into its original place, he snuck back down to the Core of the ship's computer, embedding himself into some kind of life-support system.

"If *that* happened, why didn't Ort Eath continue with his plans to destroy Earth?"

—Our guess is that no one brain is in entire control. Perhaps a merging process is going on among the brains. That's why we say that the Arachnid is only one aspect—an emanation, a persona—of Ort Eath, or rather what Eath has become.

"Clearly this new creature is operating in tandem with Hurt. But why?"

—For its own purposes no doubt. That's why I'm calling your attention to that schematic. We may well find ourselves ultimately up against the coalesced brains of the orgabox, and there's a chance that this faulty bit of plumbing is its weak point.

"Thanks for the tip. I'll remember. Anything else before we try and get a leg up on the opposition?"

—That's all. As I said, things are coming to a head. We're on the verge of the Waste Land, which means that the Grail Castle of the Fisher King can't be far away.

The voice faded away.

"Bye!" said Charley Haversham.

He shook his head. Opened his eyes.

Veronica waited patiently for him, head in her hands.

"Ever get the feeling," he said, "that our cause is hanging from a limb?"

She groaned.

The hypothesized stairwells did not exist, so they had to resort to ladders and ventilation tubes.

Charley hauled Veronica over the lip of a shaft. She plumped to the metal flooring, breathing heavily.

"God. If I have to climb one more ladder," she said wearily.

"All rung out, eh?" Charley said, eyeing the wall for identification markings. Ah! There they were. "No trouble. We have found the right level. All that remains is to locate the right room."

As it happened, the aforesaid room was no more than a city block distant. Charley figured out how to open the door while Veronica slouched against the opposite wall, exhausted.

The door swooshed apart.

There stood the canister of plastique, the sackful of electronics. As described, a pillar of energy jammed forcefully between ceiling and floor.

However, there was no sign of an omnicleaner, nor its controlling robot leg.

"Something tells me," said Charley Haversham, "things are not exactly going our way today."

Sixteen

"You know, once upon a time I could make sense of all this," Merlin the Magician said, riffling through an arcane tome crammed with hieroglyphics, spells, alchemical formulae and symbology. With a sigh he heaved the tome over his shoulder. The book covers, as they spun, grew feathers, became wings; a sharp-beaked head sprouted. Talons ripped from a papery torso. The eagle, screeching raucously, flapped hard; then mounted the wind. Soon it was a mere speck against the clouds, like a fly caught in cotton candy.

Merlin harumphed. "Now, what do you suppose *that* means?" he asked the party, old hand tugging at his frayed vermilion robes. "I mean, it just doesn't make any sense." He tried to buttonhole Todd, but his hand went straight through ectoplasm, the substance Spigot had quickly turned back into after his initial contact with his Charley Haversham aspect. "Now, a sword in the stone makes sense. Dragons underneath the city of London make sense." He strode to Angharad, arms upraised plaintively— *"What is the world coming to?"*

He was a strange old man with stringy ropes of hair and frantic confused eyes flecked with odd colors. In one hand he held a knotted oak walking stick; in the other, a chipped and cracked crystal ball. He smelled like the week-old remains of a bacchanalia in an ancient library.

"Don't ask me," Angharad said, sidestepping the issue. "This is more your territory than ours. For instance, this patch of blighted territory we're standing on the edge of." She pointed with a hoof. "I presume that this is the Waste Land and that if we travel through it, as our map demands, we'll eventually come to the Castle of the Fisher King, or as he is sometimes called, the Maimed King."

"Yes," said Todd.

"The map calls it the Grail Castle. We have to ask the right question for the land to be healed and for the Grail to be revealed to us. The Grail has been any number of things. A cup, a dish, a stone. But the most popular Arthurian legend states it to be the cup that held Christ's blood dripped from the crucifixion. Joseph of Arimathea was supposed to have carried the cup to Britain, and it was passed down to a descendant, who misused it and was therefore wounded by the wrath of God."

"And pray tell," Merlin said, shrugging back his cowl and picking out a particularly large louse, "why are a misbegotten unicorn and a ghost seeking this thing?"

"Symbolically," Todd explained, "we're trying to contact the Ultimate—God, if you will. Actually, we know it's the only way to get out of this crazy world."

"Bah," Merlin said, and spat. "Christian gobbledegook. The Romans were bad enough, but when folks started carting crosses over the Channel, that's when things really got strange." He shook his head wearily. "Give me the old Celtic and Druidic days of eating and drinking and human sacrifice. Times were simpler then. Magic was fun. You know, I learned sorcery just to impress women. And look what it's gotten me! Look what's happened! Chaos! Absolute chaos! I just want some peace for these old bones."

"Sorcerer," the unicorn said, "we have no idea what dangers await us in the travel ahead. We're sure that the end of our quest will resolve your complaints. Perhaps you can aid us with your considerable talents."

The magician pursed cracked lips, scratched an ear, considering. "Can't say I'm doing a whole lot now. Sure. I'll take the hike with you. This Grail business could turn out to be quite educational."

"What do you see in your crystal ball concerning the future?" Todd asked, trying to peer into the murky, opaque depths of the thing.

Merlin brought the sphere up to eye level. His bushy eyebrows jerked higher as he squinted.

"I see," he said, showing rotted teeth in a frown, "I see a man, a woman—and something like a giant spider. Just for an instant." He looked up, confused. "What could they have to do with our search for this so-called Grail?"

"Quite a bit," Todd said, looking out into the land of withered grass and twisted trees. "More than I'd like to think."

They were about halfway up the side of the Nirlanian biosphere when the emotional impact began to sink in upon Charley Haversham.

He didn't exist.

The centrifugally introduced gravity of the interior of this alien world was about three-quarters Earth-norm, making the travel easy going. Conversation between him and Veronica had petered out to silence, designed to preserve breath as much as anything. Charley's mind was cut loose to wander outwards— —and inwards.

Nirlan was perhaps the mildest planet yet discovered by mankind, its climate fostering a unique sense of well-being. Although life had developed, intelligence had not. Colonists had flocked to its lakes and meadows enthusiastically; curiously enough, considering the odious history of mankind, the first dwellers upon the fourth planet in the Formalhaut system had immediately acted to preserve its natural beauty, screening those who applied to live there, carefully designing the architecture of settlements to blend with the scenery. Technology and manufacturing was curtailed to low levels; the economy was mostly geared to the agrarian and to tourism of the most genteel and select form. Thus, it was not any great surprise that Nirlan was chosen as a world to copy for one of the dozens of encapsulated environments that clustered together within the framework of the *Star Fall*.

As much as he tried to lose himself in its beauty, Charley Haversham could not shake his mental preoccupation. They were walking along in a gently rolling meadowland scattered with stands of majestic trees and flowers whose color patterns and forms were matched in loveliness only by the sweet fragrances they exuded. Herds of shy six-legged creatures grazed in the distance, peacefully. Overhead burned a mock-sun in a sky the color of serenity. The air had that fresh-textured coolness of evergreen forests, though more sublime and subtle upon the skin.

He was an aberration, Charley thought. A collection of strung-together memories and identity complexes copied and then imprinted on the mind of another man—whose true persona was now marching across an exotic landscape of make-believe toward some mystical destination. The real Charley Haversham was back on Earth, no doubt feeling used and disappointed, without the faintest idea of just how lucky he was to have been left behind to lead his dull but solid life mucking out the starport and conducting his byzantine emotional and sexual relationships in his Commune.

Dammit, though, he thought, scuffling along behind Veronica in the high grass, nearly tripping over a quartzlike rock thrusting from the ground. *I remember working the cleaning detail, my hands aching from pushing buttons, wax crusting around my shoes, the disinfected smell at dawn after a night's work as we waited for the next slew of feet and tentacles and cilia to slop their way through the terminal. I remember pushing chesspieces around in front of the blinking lights of robotic eyes. I remember bouncing on the Commune trampoline, holding Francie or Heidi in my arms, laughing. I remember the scent of Debbie's newly washed hair as we sat over our special private dinner to celebrate my selection to serve a year's term on board the* Star Fall. *I blew a wad on a real steak, blood rare.*

I remember her tears on my shoulder as I hugged her goodbye . . .

He looked up, for a moment concentrating upon the taut movement of Veronica's buttocks beneath her jump suit, the way her now dried hair bounced on her shoulders, the sleek, feminine way she moved. She was totally real, and his impression of her and his response was totally Charley Haversham's.

And yet, he was not Charley Haversham.

He was just a goddamned photocopy or something.

Feeling dizzy, he sat down on a smooth boulder and uttered a heartfelt "Shit!"

Veronica turned gracefully. Her face in repose seemed to be frowning with disapproval. "You okay?"

He spat. "Hell no."

"The connecting airlock should be only a couple kilometers distant. That should put us in a section of the ship adjacent to the complex where Hurt had his quarters. It also, incidentally, is not that far from the place that your counterpart, Todd Spigot, was telling you about. The Core, Charley. The thing you have the diagram for."

"I could give a bloody hoot, Ronnie. The *Star Fall* and its entire contents, animate and inanimate, could be shoved right up the asshole of this Collective Unconscious and I wouldn't give a good goddamn." He looked up at her mopily through the splayed fingers of his hand, in which he held his heavily burdened head. Her face shifted his way, dark rich eyes concerned, delicate hands fitted to her sides.

"What's gotten into you now, pal? Just a few hours ago when we started our trek across this delightful wilderness you were all grins and wisecracks. Getting tired I bet, huh?"

"No. The air is invigorating."

"So what's the problem?" She sat down beside him on the boulder, the scent of her sweat ripe and exciting.

The warmth of her presence, the increased awareness of his senses, the quickening of his heart and his breath which her sexuality and personality prompted, made his situation all the more poignant.

"It's just penetrating this thick skull of mine," he murmured. He lifted his arms in exclamatory excitement. "I'm the equivalent of a robot! A computer program, for heaven's sake, uneasily mortared atop the brain and body of someone else."

Veronica frowned and regarded him contemplatively.

"I don't exist. Somehow that goddamn leg managed to defeat the holistic process of this brain, imprint engram copies of a guy named Charley Haversham within Todd Spigot's neurons and axons and synapses, forming a cohesive, differentiated template of identity. Namely *me*. A kind of psuedoconsciousness, Veronica." He heaved a heartfelt sigh. "I'm just a conjurer's illusion being used as a tool in something I don't understand."

"Huh? You're a little beyond my comprehension, sweetheart. What I know is that the entirety of humanity is in jeopardy from a dangerous man whom I happen to have a score to settle with. You are a person who woke up in the body of a guy named Todd Spigot, despite that wonderful gizmo stuck on your back, who can contact Todd's mind wired into the Fabrication. You're the fellow in charge now, Charley Haversham. You're responsible for moving those legs"—she patted them gently—"lifting these arms, blinking those hazel eyes and moving those lips."

"Veronica, you don't seem to grasp the agony I'm experiencing," Charley said, shaking his head. "The real me is back on Earth, right?"

"Presumably."

"So then, if Charley Haversham is back on Earth, sweeping the floor of *my* Space Terminal, eating *my* favorite foods, making love to *my* girlfriends at the Commune, then who the hell am *I?*"

"Charley Haversham, of course. Even though you look like Todd Spigot, you certainly don't act or talk like him."

"No. We just agreed that Charley Haversham is not aboard the *Star Fall*. And yet here I am with all of Charley's memories, behavior characteristics, personality quirks—carrying on a continuity of Charley's identity to the point where a cursory brainscan reveals me to be, in fact, Charles Harrington Haversham. But that possibility is canceled out by the fact that this name, this slot in the scope of existence, is already taken up. What I'm saying is that I must really be a programmed Todd Spigot. Yet I hardly know the guy. You'd better believe I'm feeling kind of free-floating—nothing to touch down on. Alienated. Because, dammit, I *feel* as though I'm Charley Haversham, I *like* being Charley Haversham, and yet I know I'm *not* Charley Haversham!"

"Hmm," she said sympathetically. "Sounds pretty awful."

Her eyes focused on the horizon, which rolled gently upwards and around to meet itself on the other side of the artificial sun. "It's kind of like this biosphere. It matches Nirlan's characteristics—has its air, its landscaping, flora and fauna, feels like Nirlan—yet is not the original Nirlan, but a copied construct."

"Exactly. But *it* doesn't think, so *it* doesn't have an identity crisis." He spread out his arms hopelessly. "It just exists, so long as the support systems surrounding this biosphere keep on supplying water, air, whatever's needed. But the moment the *Star Fall* decides to change the atmosphere, environment, gravitation—zip, Nirlan is no more. Just like when all of this is over and Spigot takes over again. Spliff! I'll be gone. No more. Fini. As though I'm even anything now."

"But you *are* now, right?" Veronica said encouragingly.

"That's just it. I'm not who I think I am."

"But you exist."

"I *don't* exist, dammit. That's why I'm having motivational problems! That's why I don't give a shit if we succeed or not. That's why you can go ahead and do whatever you have to do, take this heavy canister off my back and begone while I'll just linger here under a shade tree by that lake yonder and laze about till kingdom come. And when Todd Spigot pipes up again inside of me, I'll just tell him to shove off! I'm enjoying life while I've got it."

"To enjoy life, though, you must admit that you *do* exist."

"Not necessarily."

"Just a moment. I can't let you do this to yourself, Charley. I took a philosophy course once. Who was it? Pascal? Anyway, someone said, 'Cogito Ergo Sum.'"

"Descartes. I think, therefore I am."

"Well, *you* think, therefore you *are*."

"That's the problem. *I'm not who I think I am.*"

"But you *am*...you *are*, I mean. The difficulty you're experiencing now is one of interpretation, not actual existence. You're not the Charley Haversham on Earth. Let's call him Charley Haversham Prime, just for the sake of argument, and you Charley Haversham Two."

"Okay, I'm Charley Two. Pretty soon I'm going to be Charley Nobody."

"Right. But for all I know, it won't be long before I'm Veronica Nobody. We'll be wedded in the bliss of Nothingness...or maybe mashed together, if Hurt is right, in a state of Nirvana, Cosmic Consciousness or somesuch slop. Maybe in Heaven, maybe in Hell, but the thing is I don't know for sure." She brushed back her hair. "I suppose what I'm saying is that neither I nor any other human being knows—whatever they may claim. We're all in the same situation as you, pal. Why do you think mankind has been knocking its head against the wall of knowledge for so long? To see if something gives. Why do you think Earnest Evers Hurt is so desperate to hook himself up to the Human Collective Unconscious? Because he's scared too. The difference is that he thinks he knows who he is—and he wants to keep it that way."

"Telling me other people's situations doesn't help me much. Besides, like I say, I'm not really a person. I'm just a construct, a copy, an embedding, an imprinting."

"Okay. You're approaching things from a dialectical materialist point of view. The universe is simply interaction of matter and energy—randomly, occasionally, forming a pattern such as humanity. Looking at it that way, though, how can you say that any human being is different from you? A collection of biochemical reactions in which Identity is just a program— a conscious interface between a being and the surrounding reality. The difference between you and the rest of us is that you've got it in your head that somehow you're different."

"Well, dammit, aren't I?" Charley fumed. He stood up and paced distractedly.

"Not under the specifications that you've just given me on what a human being is."

Charley groped for words. "I guess—I guess what I'm saying is that if I'm just a copy, I must lack a soul."

"Ah. But there you're defining yourself on a term and concept ingrained into culture. That ineffable quality—or quantity—of individuality. A religious term, soul. And yet I suppose you're right, in a way. You have to look at things from a religious point of view sometimes. Oh, maybe not with dogma and ritual—but you have to have a certain amount of faith and trust in the way things are . . . even if those things exist only to allow beings to determine and affect their own individual existence. Seems to me that as we all walk the tightrope of linear time from birth to death, we have to believe that there's a purpose for the walk, otherwise, when we stop and look around and see the precarious state we're in, we lose our gift of balance."

"Oh, all that's wonderful. Words and thoughts and blatherings about the nature of existence."

"You think I don't consider these kind of things? You think you're the only one who has examined the nature of being? How do you think I feel, learning that I was specifically manufactured by Hurt—that I've been sleeping regularly with my own father, taking his handouts—realizing that everything I am was carefully planned according to his wishes and tastes? Hmm? At least, if you are indeed a copy of someone, you're a copy of a legitimate human being. I'm a flesh and blood copy of a crazy man's idea of a woman." She stood, turned him around and stared him in the eye. "Look, Charley. Don't go staring at your own belly button too long. It doesn't suit your character. What do you think we all are, whether planned or accidents? No more or less than you. Pockets of matter and energy in a biological matrix of cooperation. You are what you are, soul or no soul . . . you just have to accept what you are in order to understand yourself. The very fact that you are having existential anxieties regarding the nature and validity of your being means that you're an individual. An individual with a purpose . . . you've got to stop a looney guy who is screwing with Mother Nature. We can talk philosophy until we're blue in the face. We can use complex terms and symbolism and point out interrelationships and feel a lot of self-satisfied pain—and it won't do shit for anyone. I must admit that I'm pretty tired myself and could use a rest, and we can't do anything here for *that*. But for God's sake, cut this feeling-sorry-for-yourself business!"

"Why should I?" he said, pouting.

"You obviously have human feelings, right?"

"Sure. I guess so."

"Okay. Then you should feel privileged. You've been created—or copied—specifically to help the human race out of a jam. Copy or not, you are a human being, and you have a chance to prove yourself. Let me ask you this. Can Charley Haversham Prime help me stop Hurt from getting what he wants—namely control of all humanity—ultimate power? No, of course not. Only Charley Haversham Two can."

Charley thought about that. He looked at the woman standing beside him in an entirely different light. She wasn't just attractive, she was damned bright. As soon as he stopped thinking about himself, his concern for her, for the welfare of humanity, rushed back. Curiously, that eased his anxiety as well. He remembered other occasions in his past—or rather, Charley Haversham's past—when selflessness had led to a similar dissolve of fear and worry. *No, strike that*, he told himself. *That was my past too*. If memories were indeed chemically stored, then his memories were just as genuine as Charley Haversham Prime's. He was a real, valid person.

He smiled sheepishly at Veronica. "Hey, kid. You're a pretty good motivator."

"You'll come along with me then?" She looked at him, her dark-brown eyes alive and moist with hope. She bit her lip, looking concerned, and something went soft inside him.

"Sure. I'll do anything I can. Not for Todd Spigot. Not for that robot leg. For humanity—maybe." He grinned. "Most of all, Veronica . . . for you."

She laughed a lively laugh and her eyes seemed to glitter with relief and something more. "You still think you don't exist?" she said with good-humored girlish bounce.

"Niggling doubts," he admitted.

"Ever hear the story about Dr. Johnson's reaction to Bishop Berkeley's theory of immaterialism?" she said, a wry expression appearing on her face.

"No. You mean Dr. Samuel Johnson? From 18th-century Earth?"

"Your memory is well stocked," she returned. "Yes. That's the one. Seems that a fellow named Bishop George Berkeley had just developed a theory of metaphysics quite new to the Western World which said that there was no such thing as a material existence. Everything was spirit—energy, if you will—or ideas. Well, one day after a church service, Dr. Johnson was walking with his friend Boswell, who was quite taken with these ideas and was expounding them at length. After Boswell finished, Johnson walked to the side of the road, harumphed, and kicked a rock, hard, with his boot. "Thus I refute thee!" he cried.

"So?" Charley said.

She leaned forward and kissed him lingeringly on the lips. "You say you don't exist? Thus I refute *thee,* Charley Haversham."

Instinctively he grabbed for her, but she slipped easily away from him. She smiled down at him, teasing.

"Hey! What the shit are you trying to do to me?"

"Identity crisis, bullshit. You were just rying to make me feel sorry for you."

"I have feelings too, you know."

"Yeah. All in your glands."

He got up, holding out his arms entreatingly, grinning. "Look, give me a break!"

"Touch me and I'll break your arm!" But her eyes had softened, amused.

"We need some rest. We've only got each other right now. I promise I'll be good."

"You rest where you are. I'll rest right here."

Charley shrugged, walked over to her and put his arms around her gently. "You know, this would be very good help for my ego—just a little cuddling, hmm?"

Reluctantly she put her arms around him. "You do *feel* like Todd. Oh God, why am I so easy?" They settled on the ground for a while, gently clutching each another.

"Charley, you're a bit of a shit, but I kinda like you," Veronica said. "Feel better now?"

"Hmm. Much better."

"Charley, you're not going to take advantage of me, are you?"

"I think right now you're taking advantage of me, Veronica."

She thought about that a moment, then smiled at him. "You know, I do believe you're right."

Seventeen

A sun that was not real shouldered its way through nonexistent mountains to spread a filmy pink wash of false light over the Fabricated Land.

Unable to partake of the illusion of sleep in his spectral state, Todd Spigot sat watch over the snoozing company of strange bedfellows. Odd that bodies strictly immaterial should need food and rest—but the illusions propagated by the Fabrication Computer adhered at least partially to the normal cycles of real life.

Half in this pseudoreality, half out, Todd Spigot's emotions were in a quandary. He had tried to contact his alter ego, Charley Haversham. His attempts at communication had failed dismally.

Mists roiling in the cracks and crevasses of this stark Waste Land curled up, drifted forth tentacles of vapor as though to slap back the sunlight, faded away in the effort. A morning breeze pregnant with death and rot rattled the sketetal, leafless branches of a nearby tree. Chill moisture, no doubt designed to inspire dread, swept through Todd Spigot's ectoplasm.

All that was prearranged data, electric bursts shuffling through steel dendrites, plasti-neurons, squirming through transistors and resistors and semicolloidal microchip harnesses in a vast, mad computer that funneled the sight, sound, smells and tastes of imagination through radio beams into his befuddled brain, then somehow monitored his responses, instantly feeding them into the structured consensus reality the machine policed. This linked all the passengers attached to Disbelief Suspenders into a temporary mass-mind which set up sympathetic harmonies with the true Human Mass-Mind, trying to physically attract and link with it. That was what Angharad said, anyway, and Angharad had been the one who had spent weeks in Hurt's Consciousness Center, uncovering his plans.

This crazy patchwork of strangeness seemed so real, though, so substantial. Now *there* was an interesting philosophical question. If all the present inhabitants of the Fabrication perceived this existence as real, was it in fact real? After all, wasn't that the way Reality worked? Who could tell, after all? The only way mankind perceived existence was through the senses, filtered through self-awareness. Maybe there was a macroscopic counterpart to this system, a true cosmos giggling mindlessly as it deluded the inhabitants of Earth, Deadrock, and the whole human empire into thinking that the things they perceived were physical fact.

A game. Some multiuniversal game.

And he was a pawn, swept along in gales of laughter among the stars. Todd Spigot felt ill.

Idly, he wondered if he should throw up; would the vomit be ectoplasmic? He chuckled humorlessly at the thought.

And he thought he had problems when he had entered that shrink's office.

He lay down on the hard ground and put his arms over his head as though in protection.

Okay, God, he thought. *I've been a bad boy. Stick your head out of the curtain for a moment and tell me it's okay. I'll say my prayers, I'll find a church and marry a nice Christian girl and raise cherubic children. This is too much for me.*

No response. As though he'd expected one.

Right. I give up. I surrender. I don't know who You are, but I sure don't know who I am either. What should I do? Hello? You up there? Todd calling God, Todd calling God. Come in.

"Todd, are you all right?"

Todd jumped literally ten feet into the air, then slowly floated down, staring in astonishment. Below him was Angharad, gazing up with limpid equine eyes. Todd altered his drifting course downward so that he would not inadvertently impale himself on her horn. "As well as can be expected, I suppose."

"What were you doing?"

"Praying."

"Praying?" She gave him that skeptical Angharad look

which shone even through the donkey face. "You've got to be kidding."

"No, Angharad. I'm not kidding. I figure we need all the friends we can get, so I'm praying to God to get us out of this mess."

"This affair has affected your mind, Todd. Maybe we better have a little heart-to-heart." She regarded him quizzically.

"Our affair certainly affected my mind. It screwed me up properly," Todd said, finding an odd kind of comfort in his anger. "Everybody has done their level best to mess me up... starting with my parents onward. Most of all, though, I screwed myself. About the only one that's innocent, it seems to me, is God Himself, if He exists, so I figure I'd better get to be better friends with Him if I want to get a handle on my own sanity."

"Hmm. I suppose it won't hurt, Todd," she said somewhat condescendingly. She glanced over to the sleeping form beside the tree. "I'd better wake up Merlin. We've got a job to do."

Exasperated, Todd said, "This really hasn't affected you, has it. Your ego is much too strong. As long as you've got a job to obsess yourself with, you're just fine, and you use anything in your path to get what you want. Like you used me, regardless of the feelings you triggered."

"Hmm? Oh. The old knee-jerk midbrain mammalian stuff, huh? Love, commitment, family. Any violins about? We've got everything else in this garbage pit of the imagination. Maybe they should strike up and play a sad song or so. Hey, fella. You had fun, I had fun... and our teamwork helped save Earth. That's good enough for me. Now we've got another job to do, an important job, so stop whining and groveling before some fancied God of yours. You think I like stomping about looking like an ass with a pointed skull? You know, your problem, Todd Spigot, is that you're just so incredibly self-absorbed, so mopy and sorry for yourself, you can't see how much you've achieved and how lucky you are to be in the position you're in."

"What? *Lucky?* I don't know what's going on here. My body is again being operated by someone else, while I'm floating about without corporeal form in a land that doesn't really exist, looking for the bloody Holy Grail so that some guy won't get a shot at being head honcho of humanity. Well, maybe I don't believe that. Old Hurt is clearly around the bend. Given, he's accomplished this . . . this weird existence that we're parading around in. But all the rest is just hearsay from you. Anyway, how do you know that we're just not playing into the guy's hands? He wants us to look for the Holy Grail . . . or whatever it is. Why?"

"I told you. He's developed some method he thinks will enable him to become Lord of the Human race. Now, Todd, I don't know if it's possible, but I do know that I don't like the idea of a man like Earnest Evers Hurt directing the course of human destiny. He's not a fun boss. I used to work for him, remember? He might be all off in his crazy calculations, but there's more than a chance he's not. We're damned special people, Spigot. We've been given another chance to thwart something awful."

"I don't know, Angharad. I just can't work up any enthusiasm this time."

The unicorn eyed him thoughtfully. "Well, that's not terribly surprising, considering your rather insubstantial state presently. You know, Todd, there's another factor that we haven't been discussing much. Something that bothers me."

"What's that?"

"From what we've been able to piece together, we know that Ort Eath is still around. Who knows what role *he* plays in all of this? Mystery layered upon mystery, Todd, and the only way we can deal with it is to keep forging ahead, find what's waiting for us. Now, if you want to sit here while we go on and *pray,* well, that's up to you. But you're an important part of the group, Todd. You're our only contact with the *Star Fall.* You're our link to the people who may well be the key to true success in this business. So how about it? All for one and one for all?"

"Shit."

"Now is that any way for a ghost to talk?" Angharad gave a donkey laugh.

"I feel like Titania in Shakespeare's *Midsummer Night's Dream.*"

"Oh? How so?"

"Charmed by an ass."

"I'm not sure if I should take that as a compliment or not. C'mon. Let's wake up our wizard, eh?"

Still, Todd figured that prayer wouldn't hurt much at all, considering their circumstances.

Merlin the Magician turned out to be of great help in guiding them across the stretches of blasted wilderness. Several wild beasts that charged them were promptly zapped by bolts of power and cindered into stinking gobs of smoking flesh. The sorcerer manufactured a bridge across an abyss it would have taken quite a while to skirt.

In the distance, tongues of lightning tasted the horizon from low-slung black clouds. They walked along a field of rocks that vibrated with thunder.

A flash of ball lightning tore across the distant hills, illuminating the contorted configurations of the landscape. Black fungus and moss were the only kin to live vegetation over the expanse of the landscape. The stones themselves seemed to have an unnatural color, like the sallow flesh of the dead.

"You know," Angharad said, glancing at Todd, "you look quite at home here."

"Thanks. Glad to know it."

"Any news from the Other Side?"

"Absolutely zilch," Todd returned. He scooted over beside Merlin. "I can't make heads nor tails of the map. Apparently the recent cataclysm changed the landmarks. How far do you think we are from the Grail Castle?"

The wizened old man turned a bloodshot eye toward Todd, pursing his cracked lips. He hazarded a look into his crystal ball, muttered a curse. "Damned if I know. I'm a sorcerer, not a navigator," he grumbled. "But some sort of intuition—heed it if you like, I don't give a damn—tells me that the castle borders that lake yonder, in that valley."

"That would make sense," Angharad said. "From what you say, the owner is generally called the Fisher King. He'd need someplace to fish, wouldn't he?"

The general decision was to follow Merlin's intuition, so they struck out toward the lake, which was a good three-hour march away. As they traveled through the bleached and blackened field, the sorcerer continued with his lecture on Arthurian stories and their importance in understanding the myth, the universe, and the mind of medieval man.

"Talk about screwed up! These folks take the cake! It's natural that twisted and absurd stories like those of King Arthur and his Round Table should crop up from their warped brains," the wizard concluded. "I'm totally disgusted to be a part of the milieu. It turns my stomach, I tell you. Turns my stomach! Tristran and Isolde, ptooie! Barf on Lancelot and Guinevere. And finally, piss on this stupid Grail, the most absurd of the lot. That's one of the things I could never deal with in medieval Christianity. Too blasted complicated, too damned *hard*. Now druidism, paganism! You had a sense of immediacy there! Of belonging to the land, to the cosmos."

"Isn't that the importance of the Grail?" Todd said. "Or of any other symbolism in Christianity? The reaching out to something beyond appearances, beyond the general misery and degradation experienced by most people. That's why I'm sure that the Grail Quest has turned out to be the channel which is succeeding in Hurt's plot. Because it's something tangible, something physical, which the minds combined within this Fabrication can grasp, imagine, focus upon. Despite the diversity of faiths, philosophies and beliefs, the Holy Grail somehow is a mystical crossroads for them all."

"Hey," Angharad said. "Those prayers of yours have hit paydirt, fellow. That certainly makes sense."

"It's not surprising, really," Todd continued, pleased with himself. "I recall reading that the Grail legend, indeed the whole Arthurian cycle, has its roots deep in history, perhaps even all the way back to India, cutting its way across Hinduism, Buddhism, Islam and Christianity, filtering of course through all kinds of paganism on the way. It's a locus for philosophy, symbolism and religion. I suppose it's totally reasonable that the point of contact between this amalgamation of symbols and historical and mythological personalities and Hurt's hypothesized human mind energy-fields should take the form of the Holy Grail.

"So if it already exists, maybe Hurt is already using it. The purpose of this Quest has already been achieved, and our use has vanished."

"If that were so, we'd be back in our real time states, wouldn't we?" Angharad said. "That, or something else significant would have changed in this crazy scheme of things.

We certainly wouldn't be slouching toward Bethlehem, that's for certain." She turned a curious eye toward Merlin, who tromped along beside them, tattered robes stirring in the foul gusts of breeze. "Which brings up a certain question, Merlin. According to legend, the Grail could only be obtained by the perfectly chaste and pure in heart. In legend, it was Galahad who achieved that goal. As we mentioned, in the cataclysm a while back, Galahad checked out, shall we say, of this particular game. None of us are particularly worthy of the Grail—and certainly Hurt isn't. Do you think the man has cooked up an impossible route to the Ultimate?"

"Bah," Merlin snarled, wiping his nose. "No man or woman is chaste or pure in heart. Bloody Christians are right there. Bunch of brawling, selfish animals, mankind. If you let them have their individual ways. But no. In my experience, to take a pot of gold, a man, good or bad, has but to reach out. The difference is perceiving that the pot is indeed of gold. Bad men tend to be stupid and ignorant. They'll grab for the gold all right, but what would they make of a holy relic? Its merits would be apparent only to those whose concerns lie outside their selfish motives."

"But the antagonist in this case," Angharad said, "is a decided baddie. From what we can discern, his means have been odious and his motives arise entirely from self-interest. Merlin, you're just a constructed pawn in his plan as well, as self-assured as you seem. He wants to plant himself firmly in the central point of humanity out here in Underspace. If he succeeds, at the slightest whim he could make monarchs dance widdershins, send armies and starships roaring into oceans like lemmings. He could hurl human beings through the universe like stones, spreading like a disease with him as root, to consume whole planets and cultures. I certainly don't even begin to understand the implications of what he's up to, but I've learned about Hurt, seen enough of what he has done to know that he's not what you might call a good man. Yet he obviously knows the value of this hypothetical Grail—and means to put it to definitely selfish use."

The legendary druid's eyes grew distant and thoughtful, glittering their subtle color-flecks. He scratched his crusty nose. Flakes of skin fell off onto his salt-and-pepper mustache and beard. "What you claim to be the truth of our presence in this most strange land may be as illusory as everything else I have encountered. And yet, I know of the ways of the universe, of some of the forces that shift and shamble behind the curtains of existence. I know enough to realize that what you have told me of our situation rings with truth. Perhaps there is indeed a man named Hurt who has created all this expressly to discover a portal that will give him access and mastery of an Overreality. From what you have said, his means have been ruthless, and yet you have only guesses as to his true ends. From what you have related, I would hazard that most of his more ruthless acts arise more out of desperation than inherent evil. He clearly feels he has some kind of deadline in which to accomplish his goals.

"He is intelligent and wealthy enough to believe he can find a way to stop himself from dying—or at least continue his existence in some form. How very curious. How like the follies of mankind. In talking with the various philosophers and wise men who roam this land, I have heard of the thought processes called deterministic, a thought pattern which arises from nihilism. You would think that after all of this study to peer into the very nature of existence, he would have achieved more of that simple yet marvelous commodity, wisdom. That which allows an old man to bear his death as a baby bears its birth."

"I suppose it has something to do with power. Hurt has power and he doesn't wish to lose it. In fact, he wants more," Angharad said. "Motivation enough, I guess. They say that power corrupts. If absolute power corrupts absolutely, then if Hurt gets what he wants, he's going to be one corrupt fellow!"

"He seemed nice enough to me," Todd said, "when I spoke to him. Of course, everything that's happened since then has put things in a much different light."

"Yet you can still only guess at his motives and ultimate goals," Merlin said. "And you are approaching it all from an entirely negative point of view. Can negativity but produce negativity? That's hardly the way to deal with the situation. Mustn't one face up to one's destiny?"

"Anyway," Todd offered, "it's not exactly as though we can escape. I'm the only one among us whose real time body is mobile. The rest of you are pretty much physically fixed in place. Your minds are doing the roaming."

"So, it's to the Grail Castle then, eh?" Merlin said, satisfaction in his voice.

"Sounds like you're the only one who's sure that's where
you want to go," Todd said.

"I like," the old man retorted, "to be where the action is."

The door was shut.

Veronica leaned against the wall and slowly slid down into
a heap in the shadows. "That's the chamber. Wish I hadn't left
my mag-key there. Anyway, that's where we should find the
Wizard of Oz."

Charley Haversham knocked hard and loud. He waited. No
answer. He examined the opening mechanism. Combination
double mag-lock. Clearly old Hurt did not relish the idea of
possible interruption in his private procedures. This room
would take a bit of work to get into.

"Hey? You still alive down there?" he asked, peering down
at the pretty mass of mussed hair and sprawled limbs.

"Oh, sure. Just still tired."

"Look at it this way. You've motivated me."

"How delightfully romantic you are, Charley."

"No, really. I'm already feeling markedly superior to Charley Haversham Prime, despite the fact he's the real McCoy.
I'm already feverishly jealous of Todd Spigot and hope he
decides to do a Peter Pan in Never-Never Land."

"Todd's a sweetheart. A lot nicer than you."

"Maybe sometime you'll give me a chance to prove I've my
own qualities with women. Let me show you how much I really
care about you, Veronica."

"You lay down more lines that a cocaine addict, Charley."

"Well, princess"—he stroked her head affectionately—"I
hope you're ready for a bang right now."

She scooted away from him. "Charley!"

"Don't get excited." He grinned mischievously, then continued. "There's no way in hell we're going to be able to get
through these locks by just picking them." He unslung the
canister and backpack. "I'm afraid we're going to have to make
use of some of that glop we found back at the scene of Cog's
temporary prison." He picked out the compound, wire and
plunger, then gazed dolefully down to his companion. "Uhm,

Veronica, you wouldn't happen to be an explosives expert, would you?"

Merlin the Magician lay facedown on the blighted ground in a rapidly expanding pool of blood.

He groaned. "You know, for not being real, this certainly hurts a great deal."

"Psychosomatic, I'm sure," Todd said. "Our nerves are wired into the Fabrication. Don't know what effect it has on your real body. I don't suppose you can summon another of those fireballs, can you? Your first put a real dent in the thing."

The smoking creature wheeled about and slashed a razor set of claws at Angharad. She dodged, capered back, then tilted her head, feinting a charge, her strategy merely to keep the beast occupied.

As monsters went, the Questing Beast was not terribly large. But it was a nasty bastard.

"You think Ort Eath's intended revenge has got something to do with this?" Todd had asked when the thing had snarled and hissed its way up from a crevasse before them, its single gigantic eye glaring balefully. "He lets us almost reach our goal and then rends us to bits?"

"You haven't got much to rend to bits, Todd," Angharad had said. "You go try to reason with the thing before it gets any violent ideas into its ugly head."

"You needn't bother," Merlin explained. "That's the Questing Beast." A serpentine tail flicked over the cliff edge, winding around a convenient boulder. It tugged its woolly body up and over the precipice.

"You mean *it's* after the Grail too?" asked Angharad.

"No. It quests for the flesh of questers for the Grail."

"That's not quite the way *I* heard the legend," Todd said.

"Looks like that's the way it is now," Angharad remarked.

That was when the beast had sprung forward with incredible speed. While the others scattered, Merlin had stayed put and tried to zap off a firebolt. Before the blazing mass had ballooned fully from his fingertips, however, the beast had landed a blow. The blast knocked the thing back, singed and seething, dealing it a wound from which pus and burned blood oozed now between blackened scales and fur.

Now Merlin strained to heave off another fireball as the

beast rallied itself for another whirlwind, snarling attack. The
magician groaned as he attempted to lift his limp fingers. Feeble
pulses of reddish energy bloomed like dying flowers from his
hand, only to wilt away into hissing nothingness. The magician's eyes dropped. His arms sagged. The creature advanced
toward Angharad, who seemed to be having second thoughts
about charging it, preferring to gallop back and forth beside
it, confusing and maddening it.

"Hey, Todd. You there, chum? We really need you."

Charley Haversham's voice.

"Charley!" Todd cried out. The interior piping had caught
him just as he was about to hurl his vaporous self at the Questing
Beast, futile as that might be.

—You wouldn't happen to know how to detonate a pile of
plastic explosive, short of using a sledgehammer, would you?

"I can't talk to you now, Charley. We've got a bit more
pressing problem at the moment. A particularly nasty beast has
taken a dislike to us and—"

—What's the problem? It doesn't really exist, does it? Not
in any kind of physical reality. So it can't really harm you.
Now, you see, I've got these wire ends and I'm not quite sure
what I stick where and—

Slathering foam dripped from lips and fangs. A heart-
wrenching roar erupted from a throat no doubt yearning to be
crammed with fabricated flesh. Claws flashed in sunlight.

"Wait a second. What did you say, Charley?"

—It's just an illusion, right?

"Sure, but an illusion that is directly grafted in with sensory
perception. Capable of dealing pain and the impression of
death."

Angharad charged and dealt the creature a quick stab, then
managed to dodge a blow from its tail.

—Yes, but if you are all directly connected into this projected reality, this computational matrix, then isn't there some
kind of feedback control available? I mean, if it's a dreamscape,
then it's a matter of will. You many not be able to wake up
from where you are—but you ought to be able to affect the
things you are dreaming. I've been thinking about that. If you
folks are indeed part of a collective mind, then surely you have
some say in the events that occur in that mind. The trouble is

you've been treating it all as though it were a confused, distorted reality. But it's not reality.

"It's worth a try," Todd said, and he stared at the beast and concentrated. Something small...Suppose, as it made its snarling way toward Angharad, it lost its balance just ever so slightly, so that one of its limbs hit that boulder and—

The Questing Beast stumbled, then recovered quickly.

Surely a coincidence. All the same—

He tried again, this time harder, wishing he had more help. Todd imagined the beast's front legs crumping beneath it, sprawling the thing onto the ground—he attempted to reach out and change the nature of the picture, bold and real before him.

A blur. A smudge of color. Binary dots, bleached of color, turned a blinking black and white.

The legs he had focused on shifted as though some invisible eraser had rubbed them out and a soft pencil had drawn in new, awkward ones.

With a surprised squeak, the thing looked down at its changing legs, then fell directly on its nose.

Angharad shot a surprised look at Todd, then speedily galloped back. "Hey. What happened?"

The Questing Beast roared as it tried to regain its feet; they were as unsteady as rubber beneath it. The result was the same as before: it got a mouthful of dirt.

"We really should have realized this before," Todd said quickly. "Since our minds are embedded in this reality—in fact, constitute the substance of the reality, gulled by whatever psuedosensory perceptions that are fed into them—merely by altering the nature of that flow, we can change it. The Fabrication Computer feeds us data which our senses tell us is real but isn't, despite appearances, despite the pain or pleasure involved. We can't halt the flow of the data—but by concentration...together...we can alter its nature and its effect. Since this is in part our creation, we can control part of it."

Angharad said, "I suggest in that case that we start putting our heads together again. Our vicious friend seems to be on its way once more."

Todd glanced up. Sure enough, the Questing Beast had regained the use of its front limbs and was now making its way to reengage its attack, with increased rancor.

"So what do we think," continued Angharad. "That it's dead?"

"No. Too difficult. Why don't we will its attitude to alter. Let's change its *mind*. As one . . . concentrate!"

Todd directed his sight and his willpower toward the manic monster approaching. He visualized it halting, developing a big Cheshire cat grin through which its ragged, forked tongue would dangle like a panting dog's. He imagined soft amiable sounds issuing from the thing's snout in place of harsh growls. Finally, he mentally directed the beast's hurt hide to heal, so that it would have cause for all this good feeling.

The Questing Beast stopped in its tracks. A puzzled expression drooped its features comically. Like a swarm of silent bees, conputer composition dots seemed to reassemble on its smoking side and the wounds magically healed, pus drying, blood disappearing, no scars, no scabs. The beast examined this change, then, eyes ablink, directed its attention back to the individuals it had once desired to dine upon with a light in its eye that had nothing to do with aggression.

It yawned once, stretched its scaly limbs, then curled into a tight, domesticated ball and dropped into a snoring sleep.

"Voilà!" Todd announced happily, trying to rub his hands together briskly. They blended into one another. "Now, if we keep this frame of mind, the creature will remain harmless as a lamb." He became thoughtful. "You know, why can't we just will this all to be over?"

"I'm beginning to understand that," Angharad said. "Clearly the suggestion was given that we not try any recourse other than what would appear feasible in our world views and according to the situation. Clearly, that beast attacked because we expected it to. All of which adheres to the dictum that one generally creates one's own destiny. I suppose if we wanted to, we could make it rain. Or cause a few flowers to bloom in this parched land. Simply because it's all a part of us—and we're a part of it. Rather like our real existences when you come to look at it philosophically."

"You think we can heal Merlin with philosophy?"

"Goodness, I'd forgotten all about him," Angharad said, clopping over beside the magician. "Is he still alive, do you think?"

"Barely," the magician groaned.

"Think we can put him back together with willpower?" Todd asked.

"A tiny bit of your horn will do, I think," Merlin announced in a weak voice.

"Of course," Angharad said. "The unicorn's horn is supposed to have healing powers." She whispered in Todd's ear. "As long as he thinks it does, that's the important thing." In a louder voice: "I'd better find a way to chip off some of this bony protuberance. We don't want old Merlin to fade away, now do we?"

"And I'd better see if I can't tune back in on old Charley," Todd remarked. "He said he needed a bit of important advice."

Eighteen

The Sleeper stirred from its rest, as it had done some hours before when the Projection had been cut off abruptly and violently. A part of its factioned mind was eager to renew that Projection. There was also the New One, dreaming troubled, painful dreams.

"The biobot has been renewed, regenerated," explained the part closest to consciousness to mollify the uneasy rest.

Awakened, the Sleeper knew pain. Confused fragments of vision assailed its inner eyes. Tastes. Feelings. Smells.

Memories, jumping, clamoring in confused display:

The gigantic grav-suspensions bridging the mammoth peaks thrust from the crusty soil of Altair Six. Engineering derring-do unheard of in the history of mankind. The numbers, the symbols paraded like nimble dancers, pirouetting and leaping one another, slowly forging into alloys, beams and wires cemented by forec-fields like breaths of a sun. Flickers of conversations, hissing a half-heard name, submerged by a sea of time.

Bertrand . . . Bertrand Melthusius.

Recollections of the invitation to meet secretly with a Morapn. A majestic project, the communication claimed. An engineering monument to his genius. The most luxurious spaceliner of the universe! The journey to the neutral world, feelings of trepidation yet curiosity tingling him. He had brood sons, his preciously bought clones to carry on his genius and accomplishments throughout history . . . but this was an undreamed of opportunity for technological sorcery within his own lifetime. Stamped with the brand of his own personality, not copies. The tickling of his ego.

The meeting with Ort Eath. The testing.

The darkness . . .

Though the memories whispered Bertrand Melthusisus, somehow that name blended into another name, the memories with other memories.

Wolfgang Reither. The sweep of thundered scores of majestic sound. Wagner trumpeted through the universe on wings of the techniques of space-art. The ardent interest of the creature known as Ort Eath. The interview. The commission to work upon the Morapn world on the entertainment section of the *Star Fall*... meeting the designer of the biospheres...

... *Vanderbilt Morgenstern.*

... The blending, becoming Morgenstern.... The strange murkiness. Shambling about on metal legs, glimpses through a faceted, multigraphed window... the coming of others... the shadow presence...

The final addition, merging them all into another mass, another world view, another name... the name that held on to its identity. The name that, briefly awakening in wholeness...

(My name is Russell Dennison. Russell Dennison!)

... had shot forth vision of imagination, jarring the Dark One from its tunnel vision, kaleidoscoping black and white into endless spectrums of possibilty... distracting it from its intentions for just long enough to prevent it from pressing...

Then, the confusion. The mixing, the terrorized flight, the feeling of programmed actions. The Merging Selves, even the Dark One, hooking their umbilicals into the Deep Womb of the Core, being pressed into a disjointed, troubled sleep that lasted for centuries until the arrival of the Intruder.

Then the Odd Things had happened... the unexplainable things the Sleeper had done in moments of consciousness, as though controlled by some greater power... Things had happened aboard the *Star Fall,* important things which the Sleeper only vaguely remembered... yet knew he played a vital part in...

In what?

The Sleeper allowed the Projection to renew itself and power the biobot again, which he could feel immediately hopping to its legs to be about its business.

The Sleeper attempted to submerge itself again in unconsciousness, that blessed release from the agonies of awareness, but found it warring among its selves.

"Stay awake!" cried an insistent voice. "Stay conscious! There are things to be done."

But consciousness was torture, and the Sleeper finally dragged all its selves to slumber.

It dreamed it was a spaceship, suspended in the bowels of God.

Veronica March stoppered ears with fingers.

Charley Haversham pressed the plunger.

Nothing happened.

A quick peek around the corner later, Charley sighed.

"Are you sure that Todd gave you the right information?" Veronica asked, annoyance plain in her voice.

Charley checked again. A mound of plastic explosives hung on each of the mag-locks, pierced by bright copper wire that snaked back along the corridor some ten meters to the small canister in Charley's hands, which blinked its lights slowly and solemnly.

"Maybe I've got the leads on wrong," he said, unscrewing them with the small whining sonic screwdriver that had been in the bag. He took the lead wires out, switched them and—

"Charley, the plunger—" Veronica said.

—connected them.

The explosions merged fire, smoke, and sound into one gigantic messy concussion that caught them both and whacked them off their feet.

"—the plunger is in," Veronica finished in the wake of ear-ringing silence after the boom.

"Did the job, though," Charley said, gathering up the bag of equipment. "Now let's go and have an interview with our Mr. Hurt."

The floor of the corridor was splattered with debris. An acrid stench hung in the air, like the morning after Fourth of July. They picked their way through the mess and reached the doorway, braced now by two blasted-out holes.

"Interesting version of doorbells," Charley said, examining the twisted, newly exposed wires, trying to figure out how to open the still-closed door. "Let's try this." He touched two wires together. With a burst of air, the door slid open. The chamber that stretched before them was dark save for the pulse of eerie white lights here and there.

"I suggest we be careful," Veronica said. "Our method of

entrance was not exactly friendly. Here. Wait a moment." She stuck her head into the dimness and called out, "Earnest! We have to talk to you, Earnest. Are you there? It's Veronica."

Only silence and the murmur of machinery answered her.

She turned to Charley, shrugging her shoulders. "I dunno. This is where I left him. This is where he should be, it's his center of operations." She fumbled for the light switch, found it. Soft flows of color brought the illumination to an acceptable level.

Machines upon machines. Levels of blank screens, inanimate computer consoles. There was no sign of activity.

"Funny," Veronica said, gazing about quizzically. "Last time I was here, it was a regular beehive." Footsteps echoing, she walked to the slanted face of a wall, riddled with holes. "This is the Artificial Personality Storage Bank. Each hole has an Identity Crystal."

"Any way of identifying who is hooked up to what?" Charley asked, studying the huge thing, above which hung a web-working of cable.

"There's a code under each slot, but I don't know it." Uneasily, she turned around, eyes sweeping the chamber. "This *is* peculiar. This is his center of operations. It's where the Fabrication is controlled. I thought, anyway. But where is Earnest? I thought that we might be able to talk with him, reason . . ."

"Vu-tank. Controls . . ." Charley said, touching this button, that toggle. Nothing seemed to respond. "They don't work. Nothing is working. But I just spoke with Todd, and he's still in the Fabrication . . . it still exists." He tapped his back. "This thing is still fitted firmly in place, as well. I don't understand."

He noticed that Veronica was looking up.

A bulb was suspended from the ceiling on gossamer cables, around which wound a multitude of insulated wires that sprawled out to their connection points on the upper surface of the ovoid. The room's lights gleamed on the shiny curved surface. On one side was the outline of a door. From the bottom of this dribbled liquid, which collected at the bottom of the egg-shaped thing, then dripped down, forming a puddle on the floor below.

A red puddle.

Charley went to the spreading puddle, dipped a finger, sniffed.

"Either my judgment is addled or this is definitely blood," he said, lifting it up to show Veronica.

"Oh my God! Earnest! The Arachnid must—"

"Still a little soft on him, huh? There's no guarantee that this is Hurt's blood." Pursing his lips, he looked up at the bulb. "Now, how do we go about getting that thing lowered?"

"Earnest always operated it from within—" She put a finger to her chin. "Except once, I saw him . . . Just a moment." She sped over to a panel full of buttons and switches, hit a few.

Nothing happened.

Charley joined her. "Eenie meanie meinie moe," he said, then selected a random control and punched.

With a angel's whisper, the bulb lowered to within half a meter of the floor.

Charley slipped his hand down alongside the doorway until he felt a protuberance, which he twisted.

The door slowly opened. Purplish mist began to flow out, like the tendrils of an evaporating spirit. A limp foot fell out, its patent leather shoe clacking on the floor.

Veronica grabbed Charley's arm, gasped, then turned away.

Slouched in the cushioned center of the bulb was Earnest Evers Hurt. His face was barely recognizable, split raggedly in two from crown through temple through jaw. The entirety of his chest and abdomen was torn open, raw and bloody.

A glint of metal . . .

"Come to think of it," Charley Haversham managed to choke out, "maybe that Arachnid *did* have something to do with this. But why?"

Suddenly a leg dropped from the shadows of the ceiling, landing squarely on the corpse's belly, splashing a gout of blood onto the couple.

Charley Haversham gaped.

Veronica screamed.

In one of the creature's metal hands was a bloody scalpel. Cog held the other out defensively. "I realize this looks *very* bad."

"I was waiting for the other shoe to drop," Charley said. "But this is ridiculous."

They found their destination tucked away in a rocky valley in the middle of nowhere.

A small thing in terms of castles, the building was a ram-shackle affair, covered with moss, lichens and ivy. Tattered pennants hung from crumbling towers. Rusted metal barred the windows. It smelled of age and rot and stale whiskey.

The cracked sign that hung over the broken gateway announced in Old English lettering: FISHER'S BAR AND GRAIL

Merlin said, "You know, somehow I believe that in the Collective Unconscious you speak of, the concept of the Holy Grail has changed somewhat."

"This *can't* be the place," Angharad said, shaking her recently chipped horn back and forth. "I mean, I was expecting at least a general halo around the place, and trumpeting angels."

She sniffed around and discovered no bestial smell to indicate dangerous guardians. "Well, shall we venture inside? This may be just a delusion, a sidetrack. Then again, this may be the best the human mind can do in constructing a transcendental portal to total communion with the species Collective Unconscious."

Merlin uttered a few protective spells under his breath, then suggested they walk through the door instead of yapping. Despite the magician's sarcasm, it was clear that his estimation and opinion of his companions had risen since they had dealt with the Questing Beast so well and restored him to health. One swallow of unicorn horn powder had immediately stanched his bleeding. Within minutes, healing had begun. Merlin had immediately expressed his gratitude to be retaining his particular form, Fabricated or not. He had come to like it, he claimed.

Finding the Grail Castle (if indeed that was what it was) took only another hour of travel through the ever-bleaker landscape. No other beasties had barred their way, to their general relief. The strange sun had dipped toward evening, and strips of ominous cloud had flowed over the horizon where they now huddled, moaning thunder, touching ground tentatively with fingers of lightning. The air tasted of storm and danger. It was difficult to realize that it was all just a gigantic supersensory real-fic plugged into thousands of souls.

Angharad was first. She paused to knock on the door with a hoof. The door promptly toppled from its hinges, pluming up a large cloud of dust. Angharad jumped back, startled, then warily addressed herself to the slow exploration of the shadowy interior foot by foot—or, rather, hoof by hoof.

Her swishing tail disappeared into the gloom. "Coast clear!" she called eventually.

One by one they passed through a small corridor which deposited them in a courtyard, choked with weeds and overgrown with bushes. They picked their way across the brambled pathway, careful of the briars and thorns that hung down.

"You'd think we were trying to wake up Sleeping Beauty," Todd commented. Angharad cursed as a drooping branch of thorns caught in her side. Merlin advanced and gingerly tugged it out.

"That looks like our destination," the magician said, flopping along on sandled feet, indicating a candle glowing in a stained glass window. "The door must be on the other side of that hedge."

They navigated the obstacle, not without a few prickings, then found themselves facing a large closed door of oak, etched with runes.

"Can you decipher these, Merlin?" Todd asked.

Merlin approached, squinted and said, "Yes, I believe so. It reads, 'Abandon sobriety, all ye who enter here.' To the point, I'd say. Well, come to think of it, this does correspond interestingly with Celtic custom and legends."

"Oh? How so?" Todd asked as he examined the doorknob for any kind of trap.

"The Celts, of course, were notorious drinkers and they often brewed their version of beer—made of bracken often as not—in vats or caldrons. These were served at feasts and celebrations, and no doubt the legendary ideal of horns of plenty extended to caldrons of plenty. The story goes that in some otherworld of the gods there existed a caldron of beer that had no bottom. Endless alcohol. According to the *Mabinogion*, a Welsh book of legends which precedes all the English and French books, Arthur and his men stole it. When the Christians got ahold of it, they naturally changed it to more etherially spiritual themes. Thus the caldron became variously the cup that held the Last Supper's wine, or more distastefully, a vessel that had caught the flowing blood from Christ's side when He was crucified. Slowly the tales were woven of seeking the Grail as a way to achieve final spiritual perfection."

"You're saying that one of the most exalted and symbol-laden myths of Christianity started with a bunch of drunken barbarians telling tall tales between belches?" Angharad asked.

Todd remembered suddenly that her father had been a Christian missionary to Raxes Three.

Merlin raised his eyebrows. "This is the origin, I'm afraid, of many myths, to say nothing of religions."

"But Druidism is the One True," she said tartly.

"Of course," Merlin returned with a superior air, comical beside his general emanation of confusion and dishevelment.

Angharad added, "Come to think of it, I've heard a number of planetary anthems that had their starts as drinking songs."

The magician tried the doorknob after Todd had determined nothing was amiss. The door was locked.

"Didn't notice that," Todd said. "I think I'll have a quick look inside to make sure everything is all right before we attempt anything rash."

Todd slipped his head easily through the door. Inside was a warm, brightly lit antechamber connected with a corridor leading deeper into the castle. Todd separated his ectoplasmic self from the solid oak. "Perhaps we should try knocking?" he suggested thoughtfully.

"Just for chuckles, I think we should do the mind trick," Angharad proposed.

"Why not? This time we even have Merlin to help us. At least we won't have to kick the door in or use one of those fireballs."

As one, they turned their willpower on the door, imagining it to be open; no lock.

Merlin tried it again. It swung open easily, revealing the room that Todd had told them of. The corridor in turn led directly into a large room with tables, a leather-upholstered bar, slowly revolving fans, and a mirror behind it all, complete with bar paraphernalia from all over the universe, no doubt dredged from the minds of passengers. The air felt cool; a genial dimness held sway. Somehow, the room seemed to hold the best possible atmosphere for a drinking place: relaxed and detached from the rest of the universe, a place to sit and put beer or cocktails between oneself and any kind of unpleasant reality. Background music piped over invisible speakers—music that changed merely upon the desire of the hearer.

"Hello?" Angharad called. "Anyone at home?"

No response.

"I rather like the chamber music they're playing," Todd remarked.

"Funny," Merlin said. "I hear chants. *My* favorites."

They discovered that although they agreed upon how the lounge looked, certain elements, such as the music, were different to individuals. Essentially, the ambience of the place . . . the feelings each got, depended on individual taste. Merlin's version naturally differed most from the other two. He claimed to experience a moderate-sized, well-appointed drinking hall that would have done King Arthur himself proud.

Merlin was elected bartender by default, as neither Todd nor Angharad could do the job. Graciously, the magician complied, moving behind the polished wood, tapping a beer for Angharad in a bowl so she could lap it easily. Todd looked dismally at the stuff, wishing he could partake. However, his ghostly state prevented him. He sighed. "Well, there was no guarantee that our particular format was the right one. Probably it was just a ploy to keep us busy, keep us from finding the right portal and doing something to prevent Hurt from using his gateway to immortality and mastery."

"Yes, but why use *us?* Apparently we've had some important role in the proceedings," Angharad pointed out. "Was it Ort Eath's revenge simply to involve us in all this? I mean, if he had power over our separated brains, he could have placed us in a truly hellish scenario."

"This hasn't exactly been teacups and roses," Todd said, watching with fascination as Merlin mixed some kind of bubbling, smoking potion, then sipped it with obvious delight.

"So what do we do?" Angharad said impatiently. "Sit around and drink, waiting to see what's going to happen?"

"It occurs to me," Todd said, "that if we concentrated very hard—"

At the end of the bar, a door opened.

All heads turned its way as a creature strode out.

Angharad choked on her beer. Merlin dropped his glass and it smashed to pieces on the floor. Todd simply stared.

A bright crimson robe covered the body, which bulged here and there with the characteristic protuberances. The vaguely humanoid head stared at them with large eyes that registered no decipherable emotion.

A Morapn, no question.

But could it be—

Even as the thought entered his head, Todd saw the tubular device undulating from the base of the alien spine.

The beaded curtain parted and something on the other end of the connecting line hobbled out.

"Ort Eath!" Angharad cried, hackles rising on the back of her neck.

However, instead of an orgabox shadowing the Morapn, the puppetmaster was the Arachnid, wheezing with laughter, a grin on its parody of a mouth.

"Just call me Mr. K. Fisher if you like," he announced gaily. "You may well be wondering why I've summoned you here today. I believe you have at least one question to ask before we get down to brass tacks."

Nineteen

The leg hopped to the vu-tank, leaving a trail of bloody footprints. Hastily, its extended digits danced over buttons and verniers. When only a tankful of static erupted under his ministrations, Cog impatiently leveled his tiny energy cannon, blew a small hole into the console and commenced some hot-wiring.

Charley Haversham looked over Veronica March's shoulder. She clutched him now, shaken from what she had seen. "All right, Cog, or whatever your moniker is. I think you owe somebody an explanation, and as long as we're the only somebodies around, you might as well start with us."

The leg's screwdriver buzzed and squeaked within the guts of the vu-tank. "Save your tears, Ms. March. Earnest Hurt isn't dead."

A spark snapped. Cog leaped back to the controls, tapped a toggle or two with a whoop of glee, then hopped over to other control consoles, where its frenzied fingers flew.

"Not dead?" Veronica glanced quickly back at the mess that was Hurt's body, and grimaced. "He looks very dead to me. What do you mean?"

Information in words and numbers began to spew on a multitude of screens. "Holy moly!" Cog screeched. "I suspected as much, but I never really thought..." Its oculars began to swivel about excitedly. "This explains *everything.*" With a hop and a skip, it was back at the lip of the vu-tank, where a blurry image had begun to form.

"Do you want to answer the lady?" Charley demanded angrily.

"Take another look at the deceased. That's what I was examining when the door closed on me and lifted me up. And *that* after hours of work getting out of that force beam. By the way, thanks for letting me down," the leg said distractedly.

Containing his nausea, Charley examined the limp body again and saw what Cog was talking about.

"His brain," Veronica said. "It's all metal and wires— *what* . . . ?"

"When I found him here, he was stone dead. I did a quick autopsy. The psuedobrain is quite similar to the one used in Blicia Ginterton during the *Star Fall's* first voyage, possibly programmed to match Hurt's identity spectrum all the way from subconscious to ego, with certain remarkable and unique other properties . . . or it was operated from a distance, most likely by Hurt's true brain, safely tucked away somewhere abroad the *Star Fall*. And I'll wager anything that in either case the real Hurt was not in control of himself. He was just another manifestation . . . a stepping-stone."

"What are you talking about," Veronica asked, hands placed on hips.

Cog did not respond. His attention was fixed on the image in the vu-tank. In vivid colors, the view seemed to represent the inside of some gigantic brain in the midst of Underspace, vortices of bright energy coursing through strands of nerve ways, through axons, neurons—cosmic synapses.

"I wonder if this machine has a memory. Then I'll know for sure . . ." Already Cog's eyes were searching. Its arms struck out, fiddling with a knob.

Instantly the image was replaced from an interior to an exterior view. To Charley Haversham, it looked like a radiant combination of a paramecium and an amoeba, streaming through the raw stuff of Underspace. Some kind of humungous one-celled animal—

"That's the Human Collective Unconscious?" Charley said incredulously. "It looks like something you might find in a bit of swamp water!"

"No. I thought that the human mind-fields might be too nebulous at this point. Nothing like the sophisticated concentration the Morapns have developed." Quickly, he examined compositional readouts. "Not that there aren't human radiations swirling in cosmic broth, *in vitrio* as it were. In fact, that's what the gigantic thing that's swallowed the *Star Fall* is tapped into."

"Huh? You've lost me," Veronica said, gazing in wonder as the image in the vu-tank returned to a view of the Underspace creature's interior.

"We Crem have a word for it, which roughly translates into

Terran as *Thought-Egg*. Something from an entirely different universe. A Jakror, Mr. Haversham, Ms. March. We call it a Jakror."

"What does that mean to *us*, though?"

"A great deal, actually. Jakror are fascinating creatures, vital to the multiuniversal ecology. What you say of it is quite true. It's a one-celled creature, an egg laid by goodness knows who, or by what cosmic process. At any rate, it drifts through energy-dimensions—such as this plane you call Underspace—until it finds what it needs to begin its growth process. Life-energy fields. *Life* fields, if you will. Call it the Collective Unconscious if you like—but this Jakror is firmly nestled in the human fields, a harmless parasite. It forms its identity by recording what it finds, allowing itself essentially to be seeded. When the seed is firmly in place, it will detach itself, journey back to suitable territory, where it will begin to grow into whatever Jakrors become—even the Crem aren't sure of what. Jakrors are wonderful, mysterious creatures when grown, somehow beyond the boundaries of time and space."

"This thing isn't God, then?" Veronica said, dazzled.

"No. Even my mind is much too tiny to even begin to encompass the idea of God."

"So there's no threat, then. Hurt can't take over the Human Collective Unconscious, wherever he is now."

"I didn't say that. In fact," said Cog somberly, "this solid-ifies my worst fears."

"What are you talking about?"

Absorbed in thought, Cog studied the pulses zapping across the Jakror. Information continued to run excitedly across the screens. Finally a blinking red light caught his attention. He examined the figures below it and said, "Oh, oh. There's less time than I thought."

"Stop being so damned oblique!" Veronica said.

"Jakrors," Cog said, "live off ingested materials. The only thing that's keeping the *Star Fall* from cosmic digestive juices are our force-fields—which are apparently being sapped at a faster rate than previously plotted."

"Can't we contact this thing, tell it to spit us out?" Veronica suggested desperately.

"Contact *what?*" Cog said. "This thing isn't intelligent yet. That's what it develops from parasitic attachment to intelligent energy-fields. A mind. We've got only about two hours before its energies break through our force-fields and we're all broken down to our component enzymes and become cosmic protoplasm. If only I knew where the true central controls are . . . this isn't it, that much is for sure. If only I knew where Hurt's brain is . . . where Ort Eath's orgabox is nestled. We might be able to do something then."

"Charley!" Veronica said. "The schematic in your pocket! The thing that Todd told you about!"

Charley pulled out the folded paper, gave it to Cog, who opened it up. "Of course," said the leg. "I should have known. The Core. They're hooked up to the Core!"

"What is the meaning of life?" Todd asked dejectedly.

"Sorry, no cigar," Ort Eath said. Even as he spoke, the Arachnid at the other end of the connecting cable was busy hauling something that glimmered gold into the roon. It plopped the huge chalice onto the surface of the bar, then began dumping all matter of alcoholic beverages inside. Mist seeped up, glittering with rainbows. "Rather, you should ask me to spare your puny, insignificant lives. Or maybe you should inquire as to the manner in which I wish you to bow down before me."

"Not likely!" Angharad said. Horn tilted down, she charged. Casually, Ort Eath raised a hand. A multicolored energy beam streamed out, catching the uni-donk and slamming her abruptly to the ground.

"Please do not attempt what you perceive as violence upon my person," Ort Eath said. "You see, at long last I am coherent again, whole. My fragments are cemented together and I am fully in control again. It is *my* consciousness that is dominant now, after a year of struggle. In my mastery, I operate fully the ins and outs of the Fabrication. Observe, O sister!"

Suddenly Angharad metamorphosed into a giant bat. A soda machine with eyes and a mouth. Then, most surprisingly, she became herself again, her true self. Angharad blinked with vexation, then looked down with great surprise at her body.

"You as well, friend Merlin."

A halo of brightness grew above the magician's head. It widened to a hoop which slowly descended. As the lines passed over the wizened body, it transformed itself into the smoothness of youth . . .

. . . became the image of the man Todd Spigot knew as Earnest Evers Hurt.

"What—" Hurt said. "What am I doing here? What's going on?" Hurt gazed around, baffled. "I've been having the craziest dream. The *Star Fall*. Something about the *Star Fall*."

"A puppet," Angharad said, eyes bright with realization. "All along, Hurt was just your puppet, wasn't he, Ort Eath?"

She turned to Hurt. "What is the last thing you remember, Mr. Hurt?"

"The *Star Fall*. The ship that I'd bought out . . . a starliner. I'd started plans to change it. I was also hoping to accomplish some experiments in Underspace, utilizing the ship's real-fic computer processes. Wait a moment. I was exploring the ship's computer systems . . . the Core . . . That's the last thing I remember clearly. The Core talked to me . . . yes . . . and then my own bodyguard, my biobot *turned* on me, came at me—"

"And then, the strange dreams . . ." Hurt blinked, a disoriented cast filming his eyes as he stared back into dim memory. "I was me, and I wasn't me. Two places at once, doing things, thinking things . . ." He gazed at Ort Eath, his eyes hardening. "I was used, then. Somehow my hopes, my dreams, my fears . . . they were *used*."

"I should have suspected this all along," Angharad said, sitting down woefully on a stool. "Mr. Hurt . . . I'm afraid that despite appearances, right now you're being used as well. You're just a brain, floating in a nutrient tank, connected with wires. Just like me."

"I don't understand at all," Hurt said, looking around in wonder. "The Fabrication . . . it's been constructed? My God, if it were in the wrong hands." A look of horror flitted over his features simultaneously with realization. "Oh God. What have I done?"

"You seem to be in a jolly, expansive mood, brother mine," Angharad said sardonically. "Care to gift us with a thorough explanation?"

"Gladly," came the familiar monotone. "Although do not expect the plottings of a brilliant mind, nor the ravings of a mad one. I have changed. My obsessions have subsided somewhat."

"You *did* escape then, brain intact inside the orgabox," Todd said.

"Hardly intact, Mr. Spigot. I was defeated and fractured. I lay jumbled in a mass of other identities, drowning there, unable to assert my will, *owning* no will. The orgabox sought refuge, as programmed. It burrowed into the *Star Fall*'s Core as prearranged by myself, allowing for what I considered highly improbable: my defeat. For a long time, I was dead; slowly mixing with the other brains and identities in the combine. And then, something woke me—an intruder in the Core! It woke us all, but it was *I* who struggled from the sea of unconsciousness, clutched for support, for a being to infest myself with, to possess."

"Hurt's biobot!" Angharad exclaimed. "You became the Arachnid!"

"Partially. I also seized Hurt. The Core had been fitted with the necessary surgical and storage equipment. I removed Mr. Hurt's brain, effectively absorbing it into myself. Through it I programmed a cyborg analog mind into his body, which I monitored directly through my cortex link with Hurt, thus literally assuming his identity, contouring it to fit my own needs. This was an almost instinctive process, for I was still trapped in the Others, and inevitably dragged back into almost total unconsciousness. I was awake long enough, however, to program both the Arachnid and the psuedo-Hurt with a Prime Directive: *free me!* From time to time, I awoke sufficiently to concoct and implement plans. Confused, disjointed plans, certainly, but *my* plans. Plans which have come to fruition."

"I don't understand," Todd said. "It was Hurt who wanted to tap into the Collective Unconscious, who wanted to live beyond his normal lifespan."

"As I utilized Hurt's mind as a connector to the cyborg mechanism, a feedback developed, mixing some of Hurt's obsessions into *my* obsession. Hurt had already discovered something curious about Underspace. Hurt was frightened of death. In my incarnation as Hurt, his means merely became more ruthless, his ends . . . broadened in scope, shall we say.

"But you must understand, I was not exactly *I* then. Only at certain times was I able to surface, alter programming. Hurt's will and mine were curiously intertwined. Only slowly was I able to separate myself fully from the minds in the orgabox, using Hurt's ego as a lever. Gradually I retreated into my own natural brain, pushed the intruders out.

"Until recently I was fragmented, disjointed. Transforming Hurt's ideas and obsessions into reality played handily into my need for regrouping, for unity of Self—Individuation, if you will."

"I only meant to experiment," Hurt muttered. "It was to be part of my research program . . . " Unable to slough off his guilt with words, Hurt cast his eyes downward.

"No, Hurt. You sought the prize that *I* will have. For the *Star Fall* has truly reached its destination. Soon I will have a new body."

"You used the Fabrication to re-establish your identity?" Angharad asked.

"Exactly. And I know exactly what that identity wants," Ort Eath said. "Power. Continuation. Rulership. More than I ever imagined! Once the Portal opens, I shall control the minds of the human race! Even now the means are being effected in the *Star Fall*. We work now, here, only with the metaphorical, the symbolic, representing shifts and changes in the mechanisms that will line me through the Fabrication to this strange new creature. I will become the controlling consciousness of *it, you* . . . and perhaps even the entire human race. Imagine! Whole planets—not just the Earth—that I can destroy at whim!"

"You wouldn't!" Angharad said.

An uncharacteristic trace of humor in the monotone: "Of course not. I've reformed, as I mentioned. I don't want to harm anyone. I just want to be in charge." Its features contorted. "And just maybe I might use the position to wreak my vengeance upon the race that spurned me. My *beloved* Morapns."

"Why did you bring us here?" Todd demanded. "What have you done with Amber?"

"Allow me to guess," Angharad said. "At first, reflexively, your desire was to kill us. Then you changed your mind. You decided to use us. Just our presence fired up your hatred for us, which in turn gave your ego, your identity, something to grasp hold of. Your delight at our dilemma, your torturing of us, was one of the key things that allowed you to individuate. But what, may I ask, are we doing here now? And where *is* Amber?"

"Oh, wandering somewhere within the Fabrication, out of harm's way, performing his function in the Quest formula," replied Ort Eath.

"Oh my God," Todd said. "I see. The Holy Grail we've been seeking . . . It's not so holy is it? It represents the coming together of your personality, your renewal as a separate entity, as well as the means by which your new individuality—meshed into the Fabrication—opens up the portal to the Collective Unconscious."

"Something like that, yes," Ort Eath said. "And you ask why you are here now? Need you really? Before, you witnessed my defeat, my betrayal and my agony. Now you shall witness a far greater victory than what I sought before. You will become me . . . and thus I will have my revenge upon you all."

The Arachnid dumped one final bottle of liquid into the chalice.

"Our final communion," Ort Eath said. "Drinks on the house!"

"Are you sure this is the right way?" Veronica asked as they ran down the shadowed corridor. Ahead of them hopped Cog, who in his excitement occasionally lifted clear of the ground in bursts of tiny rocket fire.

"I have an eidetic memory," Cog squeaked. "Having previous access to a detailed map of the *Star Fall,* I find no problem navigating its byways. The schematic supplied by Charley fills in the necessary blank and—"

They turned a corner, directly into a cul-de-sac.

Cog stopped in his tracks. Tiny limbs twitched, fretting.

"You were saying?" Charley said, adjusting the straps of his backpack.

"Ah ha! I should have taken that left back there," Cog said, executing a flaming about-face. "Hurry! There's no time to waste. Several things can happen in the next hour, and most of them are unthinkable."

"What I'd like to know," Charley said, breathing hard, keeping pace with the manic robot leg, "is why you let it go this far."

"What? You think I'm a god or something?" Cog said. "I do my best, I assure you! I had no idea that it wasn't truly Hurt behind this, but Ort Eath. It threw me entirely off, I assure you!" Cog found the turn, executed it, trailing puffs of smoke. "It all fits into place now! I understand."

"Understand *what?*" Veronica said, annoyed.

"Part of what threw me off was the erratic nature of Hurt's methods. Like groping in the dark. It was vaguely threatening, but mostly confusing. Now that I know Hurt really wasn't Hurt, but a tool of a disjointed being struggling to re-form its mind and its identity... Bad enough *that* should happen... Bad enough that Ort Eath should plan to try to muck with the Human Energy-Fields... But if he should get control of the Jakror.... Well, that would put some heavy tremors through the cosmic fabric!"

"It's possible then?"

"Absolutely. And Ort Eath is bright enough to figure out exactly how to. I don't like to contemplate the results... I don't think even Ort Eath realized what he's playing around with. I'm not even aware of the full scope of possibilities."

"How 'bout a guess. Motivation for the troops, you know," Charley Haversham said.

"You've heard about Satan, haven't you?" Cog said.

"Sure," Veronica said. "Christian myth."

"Well, if it's a myth—myth would become reality, should Ort Eath mesh himself with that Jakror. Goodness knows what powers he would accumulate... He'd cause a great deal of mischief, certainly." Cog stopped, gazed about. Numerous antennae suddenly pricked up. "Hmm. Sensors indicate that our destination is just a little ways ahead."

Veronica shuddered. "We'll have to go through that crowd of passengers on the floor up there," she said. "So watch where you step."

Carefully, they picked their way through sprawled heads and limbs.

"You know," Charley said, "I wonder if Ort Eath has safeguards, protection against possible trespassers."

"Why would he?" Cog said. "He thinks I'm trapped. He probably thinks you're wandering about. Lost and..."

Veronica screamed.

"You know, Cog, you're full of shit," Charley said as he gazed in horror.

The unconscious passengers, Disbelief Suspenders stitched into their backs, were rising up, like the walking dead.

It started as a spark.

The spark became a flame, a flare, a fiery hole punched in the air. A glimpse of the very stuff of strangeness glimmered through.

"No long," Ort Eath said. "The focusing power of my mental

energy grows even as I speak. I have harnessed, through the Fabrication, the latent psychic abilities of the elect of Earth. They have guided me here, and now, through the lens of my willpower, a hole burns straight into the heart of the creature. The creature that will be mine as well, soon."

Ort Eath had forced them to drink from the chalice his Arachnid had prepared. Save for Todd, of course, who could not. The potion apparently served the purpose of numbing the party sufficiently for Ort Eath to utilize their latent psychic abilities.

Twinkles and dazzles of sun-heart resplendence twisted and curved through the kaleidoscope corridor that was being revealed by the widening hole. Fused star-stuff ganglia glittered like crushed jewelry; sparkled diamond-white, carbuncle-azure, shot through with the rich red of arterial blood.

Todd averted his gaze from the hypnotic scene represented; turned it toward where the Arachnid twiddled its limbs with delight, and Ort Eath stood surveying the corruscations that sprayed his body and face like an insane blend of Heaven and Hell.

"Beautiful, isn't it, Mr. Spigot? I almost feel as if it's been calling to me all my life, and I misinterpreted that call."

Todd's only weapons against the creature were words, and, feeling helpless, he slung them as they popped into his mind: "All that time, it wasn't Hurt's obsession that fueled this; it was your insanity. Why? Ort Eath, *why* do you persist? You know the difference between right and wrong . . . surely by now you do. Angharad has told me your story. You've got bits of other personalities composing you now. Why continue?"

"Right? Wrong?" The light made his face appear almost human. "Relative things, surely. All my existence has been a battle—a fight with unnameable forces toward something intangible." Something like poignancy crept into his voice. "My life has been a struggle toward knowing who I am, toward an identity. I have discovered that identity now, an identity I choose, an identity that is not layered on me, infused by culture or society. I am no longer Morapn or human; my destiny is much greater than that. My godhood beckons. I finally will become who I truly am, and my struggles, my agony, my doubt and despair, will cease."

"You think you're unique in these things, Ort Eath? You don't think that other intelligent beings have despair about identity? It's like Chinese handcuffs, Ort Eath. The more you struggle, the more trapped you are—but if you relax, turn inward and contemplate, you are released."

"Nonsense words!" Ort Eath said.

"No, truly! This is what I've realized in the past few days of self-doubt. Becoming yourself is not clinging to what you think you want—be it possessions or a stranglehold on billions of lives. It's letting go, being yourself. The struggle to be godlike is what makes one demonic, Ort Eath. There is nothing of the release and contentment you seek in control of this creature, whether it is the Human Collective Unconscious or not."

"Only *I* can define what I wish to become! My *will* shall conquer, for it is all that I truly have!" Ort Eath said.

"That's been my problem too," Todd said. "The eye is meant to perceive other things, not itself. So it is with the *I*, which is the other cutting edge to the sword of consciousness. In striking out at fancied oppressions in nature, we are actually striking inward and wounding ourselves."

Ort Eath laughed. "The constructed Philosophers of the Fabrication have surely curdled your reasoning abilities, Todd Spigot. Truly I should not wish revenge upon the retarded!"

"I have been a fool in many ways, but now it's *you* that's the fool. The more you reach out for control, the more you belittle your true Self."

"Silence your ravings!" Ort Eath commanded, turning his attention back to the widening portal. "I must concentrate in order for the portal to transcend the symbolic and take material form that my physical self may enter it."

Ah ha, thought Todd as he looked over the drugged eyes of his companions. A chink in the armor. He could be a gadfly, an annoyance.

"Once you've achieved your godhood, your power, your revenge, Ort Eath . . . once you've absorbed as many souls into yourself as you care to, once you have more power than you've ever before dreamed of . . . what then, Ort Eath? What then?"

"Silence, I said," Ort Eath flung a hand, and a wave of force knocked Todd back a bit—but because of his only partial presence in the Fabrication, he was not stilled.

"It will be only *you* then, Ort Eath. Only *you*, floating amongst the galaxies and stardust and nebulae. All alone, Eath.

Torturing yourself forever. Sounds like an awful destiny to *me*."

Only mildly troubled, Ort Eath turned his attention away from the spectral form of Todd Spigot and fixed it fully on the aperture—half a meter wide now.

With a glee that transcended his usual monotone, Ort Eath said,

"It's entering the plane of my—

"—physical reality."

Here, too, it began as a spark. A spark that grew like a firefly in the gloom of the dank Core, flowing fitful light upon the newly cleaved machinery, upon the recently exposed orgabox, upon the form of the Arachnid. Cut wires dangled from the dark ceiling, swaying softly with the tangible force of energy that began to fly from the portal, which singed open the very air, marked with jagged electric borders.

The lid of the orgabox was now open, exposing its contents—four lumps of gray matter. One emplacement was empty. To the left were three tanks filled with greenish, bubbling fluid, each containing brains and spinal cords and riddled with wires. Atop the Arachnid was a new hump, transfixed with wires linking it to the organic section of the biobot.

This was the brain of Ort Eath—released now, independent of its former nesting place and nest companions. Several connections served to plug him into the Fabrication, allowing him to focus, affect and control thousands of minds and thus pierce into the creature. With one part of his mind, Ort Eath stood in that Fabrication, visualizing himself before his hated enemies—and with the other he was nestled firmly behind the oculars and sensory nodes of the Arachnid.

Finally! Finally, he had cut himself free of those other wretched minds. They slept still, in the orgabox. Soon he would have his vengeance upon them as well!

It had been like an endless swim from the depths of an ocean, but finally he had surfaced. Finally he was in control.

He was changed, certainly, but still he was himself again, and before him grew his entryway into power, into immortality. The discovery of the creature attached to the energies of the human energy-fields had not surprised him; he suspected the existence of such, and this was why he had directed the *Star Fall* to seek out the cosmic Underspace creature. His machines had ascertained that yes, the organic aspects of the nexus point of the creature's "nervous system" was suitable, as though it were an empty brainpan just waiting for him to plop in.

An empty throne, awaiting its king!

He had merely to enter it, protected by his force-bubble, and connect.

So simple.

Only a short wait now and the aperture would be wide enough.

Ort Eath directed a portion of his attention to the business of the intruders. Sensors had revealed them to be three, including that damned robotic leg! And Todd Spigot's body, which for some reason was beyond his power to control fully despite the Disbelief Suspender it wore. There was no time to correct that techincal problem. But there had been time to call his "guards" into service.

Just a few more minutes, he thought. *If they can be detained just a few dozen seconds more, victory will be mine—*

He adjusted the calibrations of his inner eyes—

— saw, through multiple viewpoints, a struggle—

—switched off, to avoid the pain.

Good. The intruders would be detained just long enough. Even if they were able to make it through to the Core, it would be too late, and Ort Eath would hold total power over them all. Total and immutable power!

... still, troublesome doubts remained—hints and memories, echoes of the mesh that he had formed with the other individualities of the Sleeper...

... he had not been so sad then... he had not been alone... there had been peace, and rest and...

But no. There was still the *burning*, the demanding *urge*, the *desire*, the *wanting* that framed his identity, drove him onward. That was what had caused him to engineer all of this... plant the artificial mind in the body of Earnest Evers Hurt... and again use the *Star Fall* as the vessel to bring himself to fancied completion.

The steady widening of the hole in the air suddenly stopped.

Quickly, he diverted himself back to the symbolic, allowing himself to return fully to the Fabrication...

Floating, waving wonder. A panorama of marching images that danced awe down his spine. Snowflakes of energy cas-

cading into vistas of the most beautiful music he had ever
heard . . .

. . . home . . . perfection . . . tranquility . . . love . . . ease
. . . comfort . . .

Abruptly, Todd was yanked away from the opening through
which he had stuck his head.

"Get away from there!" Ort Eath cried angrily. "It is *mine.*"

"Just looking," Todd said, as he was gradually thrust away
from the aperture by a wave of Ort Eath's hand. "Doesn't look
like your sort of place, Ort Eath. Entirely too nice for the
likes—"

Suddenly things changed.

For an instant, he shifted to solidity with the Fabrication.
Panic swept him. In this state Ort Eath could do what he pleased
with him. He controlled the Fabrication after all, and . . .

PLINK

Another shift. Blurs of motion shot passed him. Dim lights.
He felt himself falling. His spine felt like a fuse someone had
lit. He tried to roll over.

Arms reached out to grab him. Zombielike eyes turned his
way. Metal gleamed as it bounded up and down.

"Cog?" he said.

And then the fuse licked all the way up to the TNT charge
in his head, and everything exploded in an avalanche of thunder
and pain.

He woke up entirely too soon for his taste after a nice cool
swim in oblivion.

"Charley? Charley," came a female voice. "Oh my God,
I think he's dead! Charley, don't die . . . oh jeez, there's blood
all over his back. They ripped out the Suspender part way."

Slowly, his vision faded back in, and he saw a beautiful
woman bending over him. The message had been right. Veronica *had* been at Grail castle. He'd *found* her!

Then came the leg. He wasn't so sure about the leg. It
canted over him, oculars gazing quizzically down. A sense of
déjà vu flooded him.

"He's opened his eyes. Charley! Say you're okay, Charley."

"I'm okay," he said, "but I'm *not* Charley."

Veronica blinked. Something like grief invaded her eyes.
She turned away.

The pain that bloomed in Todd at her reaction was worse
than his backache. He swallowed it down, drew in a deep

breath and turned to Cog...

"What's happening? We've got to hurry! The aperture—"

"Yes, yes, I know. Can you get up?"

Unsteadily, Todd managed to get to his feet. Around him, he saw fallen bodies.

"Just used stun beams on them," Cog explained. "They're not harmed. Certainly gave us a tussle. But hurry. According to the schematic, we might be able to get in through this entryway."

Cog hurried ahead.

"Do you need help, Todd?" murmured Veronica in a voice and with a look that said nothing.

"Uhmm... yeah. I'm quite dizzy." He leaned against her and they followed Cog.

The agitated leg stopped at the doorway. "This would normally be the entrance. But look. It's sealed. It will take forever for me to drill through."

Todd pulled off his blood-stained pack, and the awful pain renewed itself. "There's another way," he said.

Angharad Shepherd's blurry vision swam before her. She felt detached, disoriented; pregnant with a dead child of defeat.

Her victory before: an illusion. And now, her despised half-brother was on the verge of something unthinkable... and there was nothing she could do. She felt drugged, helpless. Listless.

The act of simply focusing was a mamoth struggle. She hoisted herself, weary, from her lethargy—and the sight of the simulacrum of Ort Eath, hovering expectantly before the doorway, which shivered like a circle of flame, energized her.

Sitting beside her, head drooping, was the Fabrication's representation of Earnest Evers Hurt. Todd Spigot's translucent image had disappeared. Who the hell knew *where* Amber was?

Just brains, thought Angharad. Brains floating in tanks somewhere aboard the *Star Fall*. Brains raped by wires. Streams of thought running into a common electrochemical river, dammed and channeled now by her enemy... A single stream, a solitary current could not rebel... but perhaps more *could*. Just as two minds tamed the Questing Beast...

"Hurt!" she whispered harshly. Neither Ort Eath nor his attachment seemed to take notice of this nonthreatening act.

"Wha—"

"You think you can concentrate on something, Hurt? You think you can use your imagination?" Even as she spoke, she used her own: *He is awake. Aware,* she thought. *He has a grasp of everything that's happened, and of his own role.*

Hurt gasped. "God!" Clear-eyed, he looked at Angharad, and his expression was that of an age-hardened, experienced man. "I'm sorry." A haunted look was in those eyes...

"Yes, well you can give me a hand to try to restore the balance. The Fabrication is composed of many minds, right?" Angharad said. "Many minds presently being used to form that portal. And we're attached to those minds, just as Ort Eath's Overmind is... we're in potential communication. What would happen if we somehow could wake up those minds dreaming directed dreams?"

"Possibly the portal would close," Hurt replied thoughtfully.

"And somewhere in the web is Philip Amber—who has the most powerful pyschic ability of us all! It was *his* mind that broke through mentally and emotionally to the Morapns."

"I shall do what I can," Hurt said solemnly.

"Hurry! Concentrate!"

In tandem with Hurt, Angharad pulled her thoughts in, imagining the thousands of human minds plugged into the Fabrication... one mind in particular. If they could but contact them, wake them for a moment... that well might be enough. A mental quest... And suddenly she could feel the surge, the companionship of Hurt...

(*...and Amber?...there was* something *else...*)

...as they directed their thoughts toward similar ends.

Synergistic spirals soon eclipsed any sensory awareness that the Fabrication was feeding her. She felt images raining down upon her, translated thought patterns of a multitude of altered minds, all funneled into the maelstrom of mental force that was not only tearing a hole in space and Underspace but changing the organic and energistic matrix of the creature surrounding the *Star Fall*. Ort Eath was using the psychic powers of the passengers to transform part of the creature's interior to biologically accept the implantation of his brain, his mind, his will.

As he had served his unholy communion, Ort Eath had explained the true nature of the thing that they had contacted, that had enveloped them... and Angharad's mind had reeled with the immensity of the thing.

A living being, strands of pyschic energy tapping every single human alive. Ort Eath's plan was all too possible, now that she understood that spiderweb strangeness and glistening beauty.

You can't allow this! her mind screamed at the other minds. *Wake up! Awake and stop this horror—*

With a jolt, she was abruptly returned to the interior of the Bar and Grail. The eyes of Ort Eath burned into hers like lasers.

"Not this time!" he cried. "No, not this time. You have seen enough. You attempt to meddle. The power is all *mine*, here. All mine."

The Arachnid behind him chuckled maniacally as Hurt tottered back to awareness as well. Ort Eath motioned with a hand. Suddenly Hurt began to decompose, screaming as dripping flesh fell from his bones and eyes dropped from sockets.

"You see," Ort Eath said. "I control this Reality. You are helpless. You can do nothing."

Angharad Shepherd watched in terror as her hands began to drip blood.

"Wake up! Wake up! Stop this horror!"

The voice was tiny but insistent, echoing in the foggy corridors of his consciousness.

The Sleeper stirred.

Different . . . something was *different*. The Dark One . . .

Gone, yet somehow still there . . . Stronger now, separated . . . dominating.

The inclination of the Sleeper was simply to pull the mental covers back over its mind . . . *not complete yet . . . not One . . .*

But it could not. Somehow, the pain was gone . . . gone with the Dark One.

Outside, the Sleeper sensed . . . *Another*.

Like the flex of long-unused muscles, the Sleeper stretched its mind out through the avenues of the computers, and its body, the ship . . . and felt the Other surrounding it, pressing in upon the force-fields that kept out the destructive madness of Underspace.

The Sleeper reached out further, thoughts borne upon wings of radio-waves, searching, questing—

"You must rouse yourself," the voice said. "For all our sakes."

And suddenly the Sleeper awoke, knowing why it had been called.

The alien air streaming through the portal caressed Ort Eath's nostrils. Sweet, promising, it beckoned like the Perfume Trees on the Morapa escarpments, swaying in the breeze...

Beyond, he could see the stuff of the Jakror's interior changing, molecularly mutating to his mental specifications. He could see a chute forming, the path to his fulfillment; a latticework of silicon crystals, icy effulgence leading to a glittering throb of warmth.

A shame his enemies in the Fabrication had attempted to stop him; he wished they were conscious to view this culmination of his Selfhood, his Godhood, the spanning of the chasm between Mortality and Eternity.

Through the optical equipment of the Arachnid, Ort Eath watched patiently as the width of the portal grew centimeter by centimeter. Very soon now, very soon indeed, it would be wide enough for these spindly metal legs to transport him and his temporary body into the beckoning chamber.

The explosion shocked him from his reverie.

He swiveled about, employing all eight legs. Metallic debris rained down on him. Murky light streamed down from a hole blasted through the wall. Smoke poured in, then dissipated.

Ort Eath recovered his composure, then laughed a quiet laugh to himself.

So, the others were still active. But it was much too late, and the hole that they had managed to blow into the Core room was much, much—

"—Too small!" Todd cried. "We can't fit through." He coughed and waved away the smoke. He peered in. "Geez. There he is, right down there. The Arachnid, with something riding his back like a mechanical jockey.... And there's this flaming hole... we'll have to try another blast."

"No time," Cog said. "You two can't fit through. But *I* can. Here. Give me a hand."

Quickly, Veronica and Todd hoisted the leg up. Cog immediately retracted all excess paraphernalia. It was a difficult fit, and Todd managed to burn his hands on the hot metal from the plastique blast, but Cog squeaked through.

—and fell, clattering, to the floor of the Core—

A thrill of pain, a wave of nausea from the effort crested over Todd. He curled up against the wall, breathing carefully, trying to push the dreadful sensations away from him.

Veronica peered into the gloom. "Cog! What—"

Todd managed to hitch himself up the wall. "What's happening?"

"I don't know. Look for yourself," she said, and Todd took her place.

Flashes of light. Stumbles and thumps sounded through the crypt-dark chamber. In the scattered illumination he could see at first vaguely, then more clearly, clawed hands catching hold of the leg...the glow of a personal force-field, preventing Cog's energy-cannon burst from affecting the Arachnid or its terrible rider.

"Damn!" Todd exclaimed. Then a desperate thought occurred to him.

He crammed his hand into his coverall pockets, dragged out the tattered schematic of the Core, studied it feverishly, forcing back his pain. Yes...there it was, conveniently circled for him by the maintenance computer.

"Veronica? Have you got any weapons? *Anything?*"

"Just a screamer-shock."

"Jeez. I dunno.... That will have to do." He looked up. "Just what does it *do,* anyway?"

"Emits a burst of electricity. But it only reaches a few yards...it won't be any help at all."

"Give it here."

She pulled the thing from her carry-bag, pressed it into his palm. It was simple-looking. Trigger. Nozzle.

"Oh yes. It also makes an *awful* screeching sound."

"Great. We'll scare old Ort Eath to death." He looked through the hole again, saw the outlines of the pipes, tried to—

Yes. There it was. Even in the dim lighting, he could see how one section of the plumbing had twisted under the stress. No wonder there were problems. If he could just alter the gravitation suction field for a moment—

He poked the weapon through the hole. He extended his arm as far as he could in the general direction of the faulty area.

Pressed the trigger.

Electricity ripped through the damp air, fixed lightning talons upon the metal. The scream that accompanied the trigger-pull was indeed ear-piercing, but Todd managed to keep his finger on the trigger, despite the additional source of pain.

A ripping . . . like the grinding of gears.

A groan, a wrenching throbbed through the hole in the wall. A blast of force suddenly pushed through the hole in the wall, smashing Todd back against the opposite wall of the corridor.

Stars streaked his vision, but he clung to awareness. With Veronica's help, he quickly regained his feet, staggered back to the hole.

The three separate pipes bulged incredibly, then tore—

Water, sewage and gravitational pneumatic fluid roared from the openings, coursing under tremendous pressure directly at the struggling duo below. The stream caught them both, hurling them into the opening maw. Both the Arachnid and Cog were swallowed completely.

Todd felt faint. "Oh *no!* I just wanted to knock . . ."

The room below began to fill with fluid, which spilled into the aperture . . .

. . . which slowly began to close.

"What happened? What happened?" Veronica demanded, hysterically shaking him.

The automatic seals in the plumbing tubes turned on with a squeal, and the pulsing liquid stopped.

Todd pushed himself away from the hole.

"I'm not very sure," he said. "But I think we lost."

He fell into Veronica's arms and ragged darkness speared through his head.

Twenty

"Todd?"

A demanding feminine voice pierced the darkness.

All Todd wanted was to burrow deeper, shut out everything.
He felt as though he had been shoved into a garbage compactor,
crushed into fertilizer. This was a condition he could get used
to if only the racking pain would cease its prancing throbs, if
he could dive back into a dreamless sleep.

"Or are you Charley now?"

Charley? No, he wasn't Charley. He was *Todd. Todd Spigot!*
He got up and told her so.

"You're a very confusing man," Veronica said. Despite her
disheveled, dirtied state, with makeup smeared and clothing
torn, Todd still found her remarkable attractive. Then it occurred to him that there were more important things to do than
moon over Veronica March's beauty.

"I thought you should know that the sealed door is open.
Also, it's glowing."

An empty feeling invaded Todd. "Whatever it is, whatever's
going on, we'd better face up to it."

Soberly and silently Veronica helped Todd to his feet. As
he rose, the Disbelief Suspender, somehow entirely freed, fell
to the floor. Up ahead in the corridor, he noticed the previously
stunned group of passengers stirring and groaning.

Their Disbelief Suspenders had disengaged as well.

Ahead, the doorway was open, as Veronica had indicated.

The glow emanating from the Core's interior was greenish.
An emerald luminosity, it shimmered, waved, sparkled.

Awed, Todd cautiously approached the door, noting that
the reinforced welding of the seal had simply sagged away.

They descended a ladder immediately below the door, discovering the floor, previously aslosh, astonishingly dry. All
about them stood a complicated array of machinery. Layer
upon level of tubes and pipes and jewel-like facets, centered

about something embedded into the metal, hooked up by wires and crystalline attachments.

"What's *that?*" Veronica asked, pointing.

"Ort Eath's orgabox." The lid, he saw, was closed. "That's where the fellow kept his brain, along with a few others for company."

"That's *awful.*"

Todd sighed. "You think *that's* bad." He pointed to three separated plasteel boxes, plainly revealing their contents: lumps of gray matter. "I do believe that one of those used to fit inside the body you found upstairs."

"Earnest? No kidding!"

"That's right. I daresay it's the one directely connected to the orgabox, thus integrated into Ort Eath's power."

"What about those other two?"

"Strong chance those belong to my two friends, Amber and Shepherd, dug from their skulls on Earth, then shipped here by the Arachnid...one of Ort Eath's 'fragments' or 'manifestations.'" Todd flung his arms wide. "And all this is the real central point of operations for the Fabrication—which explains the importance of Amber and Shepherd in the formation of the connecting portal. All the time, the Holy Grail was in their *heads...*"

"What does all this mean?" Veronica asked. "Is it over?"

"I don't know, Veronica," Todd said wearily, leaning against a bulkhead. "I just don't know. Apparently, both Cog and Ort Eath were washed into the Jakror." He shook his head. "Me and my dumb ideas. Blow a sewage line. Really!"

"You did your best, Todd," Veronica said. "I doubt if even that schmuck Charley could have done better." She pronounced the name sardonically but affectionately.

"Correct, Todd," a rich, echo-enhanced voice boomed above them. "Cog was in pretty bad shape. You gave him another chance."

Todd jerked erect. "Who's that?" he demanded.

"Todd! That box! It's lighting up!"

Sure enough, the orgabox looked like a miniature department store on Christmas Eve. "What happened?" Todd asked.

"A cosmic event of the first water," the voice said with good humor. Not Ort Eath's voice, not Cog's, nor the Arachnid's...but still it *was* familiar...

"Who *are* you?"

"I used to be a guy you met, Todd Spigot. Russell Dennison. Remember? I was a chief programmer for the real-fics on the *Star Fall.*"

"Don't tell me! I'm going to wake up and discover that all this was just a put-on manufactured by *you.*"

"No, no. I'm one of the brains Ort Eath dumped in his orgabox. We're a conglomerate now. Me, a few others . . . since we're rid of Ort Eath, things are a bit easier. Earnest Evers Hurt is partially connected now, but he's a tiny bit comatose. I wish I could smoke. I could use a cigarette."

Todd had a sudden thought. "You're connected to all the *Star Fall*'s systems, right? What's the status on the force-fields protecting us from being ingested by the Jakror?"

"Shot. Absolutely run down, ten, maybe fifteen minutes ago."

"But we're still *alive!*" Veronica said. "That space thing was going to eat us! I saw . . ."

"Not to worry, not to worry!" Dennison's voice interrupted. "You just had the wrong slant on the situation. You were thinking in terms of Earthbound biology. Dog eat dog. Your heads were in monster-movie land. We're in a different dimension. That creature, the Jakror . . . it's slipped into us, integrated its molecules with ours after the force-field fizzled. It's a part of the *Star Fall* now. We're a part of *it*. We're now multidimensional, partially in normal space, partially in Underspace. That's the source of the glow. The powers the Jakror gives us . . . well, we still haven't delved into them. No wonder Ort Eath wanted control of the thing."

"He didn't get it then!" Todd said jubilantly.

"But what happened to Cog?" Veronica asked, mystified. "If the Jakror is a part of us now, where does that put him and Ort Eath?"

"I'm sure he'll make his appearance eventually," said a new voice.

"Angharad! Are you all right?" Todd asked.

"Oh, I suppose. You're really missing something, Todd. We're connected into the whole ship. A real sense of power. Still, I'll be glad to get a retread on the old genetic mix and slip into a new body. It'll be nice to get back to reality."

"And Amber?"

"Slumbering in his tank. Registering strong mental activity, certainly alive, but . . . somewhere else. Goodness knows what he's been through. Can't wake him."

"And Cog? Is he in control of the Jakror?"

"Something like that." A pause. "Wait a minute. I do believe he's asking for a portal. Good. I've got a few questions for him."

With a cracking of energy and a smell of ozone, a hole was rent in the air.

The mechanical leg scooted out precariously, crash-landed on the floor and skated directly into a wall with a loud crash. Wobbling, it got up and footed over to ogle Todd and Veronica with distinctly bent oculars. Todd's nostrils cringed. Cog smelled terrible.

"Hey," Cog said, noting the reaction. "What do you expect from a guy after that sewage bath that you gave me? Still and all, I can't complain. That biobot Eath was hooked onto more than I bargained for!"

"Where is he?"

"Uhm, I don't know. Drifting in Underspace somewhere, hopefully."

"You don't know? What happened?"

"I'm not really sure. I only remember grabbing onto something inside the compartment that Eath had created inside the Jakror. The Arachnid and Eath just kind of drifted away into the nether parts."

"But you made contact . . . you're in control now?" Veronica asked.

"Let's just call it an uneasy alliance. Turns out the Jakror had developed more than I gave it credit for. I'm connected mentally, and for all intents and purposes, in charge. Which was the way it was supposed to be all along."

"I don't understand," Todd said.

"Just a moment. Apparently I'm going to be hanging around this universe for the time being, and it's getting damned annoying being just a leg. Let's see what the Jakror can cook up for me." The leg made a few squeaking noises. Moments later, something moist and gooey slid into the room from the portal, like a glob of scintillating particolored jelly.

"Hmm," Cog said. "Ah!"

He leaned over and stuck himself into the blob of protoplasmic gunk.

Immediately, lights began to whirl about it, purple, red,

yellow, like a rainbow lathe, cutting form into the mass, length-
ening it, giving it a head, legs, arms. A cocoon of dazzling
brilliance spun about the body, then burst, dashing effulgence
into every corner of the Core.

Lying on the floor below them was a man, dressed in 18th
century Earth finery. Ruffles and lace burst from his maroon
jacket and vest like frozen foam. Pantaloons extended to below
the knees. The rest of the way to delicate leather shoes was
covered by snow-white stockings. On the other end, a powdered
wig covered the head, whose face, while male, was effeminate
and finely cut in the angles of nose, chin and cheekbones.

The petite nose twitched.

The man stood on his head, then opened his eyes.

"Oh dear," he said with Cog's familiar nasal twang, softened
somewhat by human vocal cords. "What a botch!"

"Try it the other way," Todd suggested.

With gymnastic grace, the newly formed body pushed up
with its arms and landed on strong legs.

Eyes blinked. "Oh, yes, that's *much* better. You're rightside
up now." He dusted off the jacket's arms, straightened cuffs
and lapels. Smiling at Todd and Veronica, he leaned over and
rapped his right leg smartly. The responding sound was purely
metallic. "For all practical purposes, I'm still down here, but
since I'll be traveling amongst you humans for a while to come,
I might as well assume the proper costuming."

"Among us for a time?" Todd asked suspiciously. "Exactly
what does *that* mean?"

"It means this universe plane has been assigned to be my
detail by my fellow Cremians. No longer can they partially
ignore the events that occur in this level. Apparently the en-
tropic forces afoot on this plane have spread cracks throughout
the multilayers of the cosmos. Why do you think I remained
after the business last year?" He turned to admire his new looks
in a partially reflective screen. "Now that a working symbiotic
relationship between myself, the Jakror, the *Star Fall*—and,
I might add, the Human Collective Unconscious—exists, I am
in a perfect situation to maintain homeostatic conditions in this
foundational existence plane." He wiggled fingers beside his
ears like quotation marks. *"Cogito Ergo Sum—Defender of the
Starways*. Catchy ring to it, eh?"

Todd could not contain a grin. "I think it's a *crock*, myself.

I'm just grateful all this is over. I'll just pack up my angst and find some place nice to settle, thank you. You can let me off at the nearest port."

The resonant voice from the orgabox voice piped up: "Well, you know, Todd. Uhm . . . things didn't work out exactly all *that* well, and—gee, I don't know how to tell him."

A pained look appeared on Cog's new face. "Yes. A minor, *wee* little thing, Todd. Otherwise triumph is ours in trumps, and goodness will abound because—"

"Okay. I can take it straight. What happened, Cog?"

"Well, this Jakror I'm meshed with now is a very mysterious and quite fickle beastie, I'm afraid. And the—uhm, neither the docking procedures nor the absorption of the *Star Fall* occurred under the ideal circumstances. Apparently the process caused a tiny little disruption in a fragile aspect of the Underspace Time/Space Continuum. A slight carophony in the very precise stasis harmonic, cutting loose vital strands of the spatial mechanics webbing—"

"You mean we're lost?" Veronica said.

"You could say that. That's not the problem." Cog looked sheepishly away. "We're lost about four hundred years away from our starting point. Apparently, the disruption caused a timeslip and—well, to be honest we won't be able to go back."

"The passengers aren't going to like this much," Veronica said in a small voice. *"I* certainly don't."

"Where's your sense of adventure?" Cog ased. "Just think! All of us are now bound on a grand adventure."

"With your friend the Crem guiding us, I trust," Todd said.

Cog cringed a bit. "I fear I've temporarily—just temporarily, mind you—lost contact with my dear fellow Crem."

"Well then, the Jakror . . . surely utilizing whatever its powers are, you can—"

"Todd! Todd, please, I'm only a finite creature. To be perfectly honest, I—er—I am not in total control, nor do I have complete communication with the creature, which seems to have priorities of its own. But I'm sure that soon—very soon!—all difficulties will be mended completely and we'll know exactly what is going on."

"When?" Todd demanded.

Cog shrugged, then brightened. "I say, though. You know, being in a human body, I *have* developed something of an appetite. White we're waiting around for an answer, I think we should have supper."

"Hey!" Angharad said. "What about me? We've got to do something about Amber too!"

Cog said, "A little more complicated, that. I do believe, though, we can work something out with the Jakror once we know exactly what's afoot!"

"You think you could hazard a guess?" Todd asked.

"Truth to tell, I haven't the faintest," Cog said cheerfully, experimenting with his new body by trying out a limber softshoe dance step.

"Whatever it is," the Russell Dennison voice trilled from the speakers, "it will be *cosmic*. Truly cosmic!"

"That," Todd said, "is exactly what I'm afraid of."

Philip Amber watched as the last projected traces of individuals faded from the Fabrication. However, the resonant field remained, shadowy and uncertain, like a colored-in carbon copy.

Leaning against the doorframe with fatigue, he turned to his companion, still standing sentinel behind him.

"Was I of any help?"

"You touched their minds," the man said. "You added your psychic support. You helped more than you know, Philip Amber."

Amber sighed and stared back into the room, whose depth of field was slowly telescoping back into the two dimensions it had started with. He remembered the shuffling visions that had assailed his eyes, strobing images of the truth of the identities of the Arachnid and Hurt; Ort Eath's struggle for renewed unity and control; the true nature of the creature they had melded with. He had witnessed all that had occurred, even the final conflict between Ort Eath, mounted atop the biobot, and Cog. The resonances and colors of that battle within the strangeness that was the Jakror still remained in his mind, a burned-in series of after-images.

"All the others have been released," Amber said. "Yet I remain here in this strange netherworld. Why is that?"

The man was thoughtfully silent for a moment, draped in the dimness of the hallway. "Let us say simply that you are not finished here. There are many more inner vistas for you to traverse, Philip Amber. With the advent of the Jakror, there are a multitude of realties that only you can perceive, touch and influence."

"What do you mean?"

"The song ceases to be a song if a single note is held too long," the man said, putting away his pipe. "We must keep moving."

"You seem to have a vague answer for everything," Amber said. Absently, he noticed that he seemed to be flesh and blood again. The sound of blood pulsing through his ear was a welcome rhythm, and he quietly rejoiced in his renewed corporeality . . . at the very least it was a comforting illusion. "Can you at least give me a vague answer to who you are?"

"Does it really matter, Philip Amber? Has it occurred to you that existence by its very nature is but a sequence of questions, flimsily connected by vague answers?" The man spoke in an amused, compassionate voice.

"I want to know," Amber insisted.

"Very well." The man reached up to the side of his face. As glittering lights softly streaked around him from the open room, his fingers found a hold. With a sucking, tearing sound, the man's skin began to pull off. Cheeks, lips, nose, mouth: all were slowly separated. The mask hung limply in the man's hand, then was tossed into the room of lights and colors.

Amber stood, stunned, as the man remained still, allowing the wash of illumination to fully light his features.

The man smiled softly, then shut the door, plunging the corridor into darkness. "Come. We have much to experience. Much to do," emerged the voice, which metamorphasized even as it spoke into the sound to match the wide-spaced eyes, the long nose, the small mouth.

One by one, down the length of the corridor, doors began to open, spilling opalescence and strange musics.

The Voice was in his head now, and he recognized it as something that had been there all along. "Come. We are one now."

Amber reached out, grasped his own hand firmly and resolutely, and allowed himself to be led into bright mystery.

Epilogue

"Cosmic," Todd Spigot muttered to his glass of beer.

The beer effervesced.

He drank deeply, then repeated "Cosmic" unenthusiastically. A low sweep of background music swept his musings with sympathetic strings. "Suppose each little bubble inside you is a universe. Slowly it rises up, roundly symetrical, to finally burst and wink at the surface. Maybe we're all just bubbles in God's glass of beer." He drained the stuff, then tapped out an order for another. It appeared presently, frosted and cheery.

Everything was back to normal. That was, only semicrazy.

Cog had disappeared back into his Commune with the creature called the Jakror. The bio-labs were busy cloning a new body for Angharad Shepherd—as well as one for Amber, whenever he decided to wake up from his fugue. Hurt and the orgabox aggregate had elected to remain in their present form and survey the *Star Fall*'s operations, eager to be of use in this new mission . . . whatever that mission was, Todd thought wryly.

So far, the passengers weren't exactly sure what had happened, and still stumbled around with dazed looks. Telling them they'd never see home again would be a real kick.

Oh well. The *Star Fall* wasn't a bad place to be stranded on . . .

If anyone complained, they could always bring back the Fabrication. The Disbelief Suspenders were still hanging around, ready for use.

And what had become of Ort Eath? Cosmic dust, presumably. Absorbed back into the All, the Cosmic Circle, or whatever the hell you wanted to call it. Life was a game all right. Even the winners lost, though.

"Cosmic," Todd murmured to himself and drank his beer,

feeling burnt out, jaded, wasted away. Low-level anxiety rumbled in the pit of his soul.

"Howdy, pal," came a voice from behind him. Veronica swooped cheerfully around to face him, then flounced into the chair beside him. "Mind if I join you? I was just down in the Core, straightening things out with Earnest. He *is* my father, after all . . . in a sense. Fancy that! He's really wretched about his whole affair, and pledges to use whatever mortal life is left to his little gray cells in the service of mankind. How about some champagne, Todd. To celebrate."

He smiled at her. He found her charming, even though she no longer wore the device meant to attract him. In fact, her presence lent a wonderful buoying effect to his spirits.

"Sure," he said.

He tapped out the code for champagne. Two long, fluted glasses popped up alongside the bottle. Todd poured.

Veronica swept back her hair and sipped.

She leaned over and put a hand on his arm. "How are you doing, pal?"

"I'll survive." God, it was starting all over again: the quickening of the pulse as he looked at her, as the scent of her perfume jump-kicked desire under his nostrils. Worse, even with the alcohol, his nerves seemed frayed.

"I know what you mean. Who would have believed all this could have happened? Well, we're still alive. That's what counts, isn't it?" She tapped fingertips on the table's surface musingly. "Todd. You mad at me? I wouldn't blame you if you were, I really wouldn't. But you have to understand how I am . . . or rather was. Maybe we can talk about it, huh?"

"Sure. Sometime. Not now."

"Okay. Whatever you say." She sipped champagne quietly for a while, then looked away.

Todd didn't know what to say.

—Asshole. A voice growled inside his head.

Todd barely contained a gasp.

—Wimp, came the voice again.

"Charley?" he said out loud.

"I guess that's whom I wanted to talk about, Todd," Veronica said. "I'm very confused about Charley, Todd. Can you understand that?"

"You liked him, didn't you?"

"Sort of, the chump. I kind of miss him, and I'm very confused about who *you* are now." She eyed him hopefully, as though looking for compassion.

—Tell her you understand, dope.

"I understand, Veronica."

—Well, what *do* you know! The pretty klutz misses me. Hmm. Well, can't really blame her. Tell her that I was you in most ways, disguised. C'mon, spit it out.

"Veronica, you have to realize that it wasn't just Charley, it was me too, all along."

"I know, Todd. You'll just have to give me some time to adjust."

—Bull*shit*, Todd. Don't give her *any* time. Grab while the grabbing's good.

Charley? You're still there. What happened?

—I guess I switch on from time to time. Let's just say to help you out. Keep you company. I kinda like the job.

Did you and Veronica . . . ? I mean she . . . misses you.

—Naw. She's not my type. Still, she could be interesting to share.

"Todd? Are you all right?"

"Hmmm? Oh yes. Just the champagne, I think."

What do you mean *share?* Todd demanded. I can have you *erased* if I wanted.

—Murder, Todd? Naw. We'll make good buddies. And like I said, I'll only be around once in a while. So go ahead. You won't be sorry, I promise you.

What'll I say, though?

—Tell her you forgive her. Tell her you understand. Tell her she's still the most wonderful woman you ever met in your life. Ask her if she wants to see your etchings. Cripes, fellow, just move your mouth!

Todd took a hasty gulp if champagne. "Veronica, it doesn't really matter, whatever has happened in the past. I still find you a really terrific person and—

—And you wanna ravish her.

"And I'd like to stay good friends with you."

—Turkey. Wimp.

"Oh, Todd. Really." She blinked back tears. "God knows, this is a very hard time for me. And for you too."

—Okay. Just scoot around and put your arm around her.

Todd obeyed, and found himself holding Veronica warmly.

—Fingertips across the back of the neck, Charley suggested. I'll bet she really likes that!

Todd let his fingertips drift accordingly. Veronica sighed and melted into him. Her hair draped into his face.

Suddenly his anxieties evaporated. Holding her, he felt relaxed, alive and yet . . . and yet able to just let go of himself.

Warmth and cinnabar. Softness and life.

—Things aren't so bad after all, are they, Todd?

No, Todd thought. *I guess they're not.*

—Cosmic, said Charley Haversham, and Todd's interior reverberated with a laugh. —Really *cosmic.*"